Stephen Aryan

THE SORROW OF THE SEA

THE NIGHTINGALE AND THE FALCON BOOK 3

ANGRY
ROBOT

ANGRY ROBOT
An imprint of Watkins Media Ltd

Unit 11, Shepperton House
89 Shepperton Road
London N1 3DF
UK

angryrobotbooks.com
twitter.com/angryrobotbooks
Waters dark and green

An Angry Robot paperback original, 2025

Cover by Sarah O'Flaherty
Edited by Eleanor Teasdale and Andrew Hook
Map by Nicola Howell Hawley
Set in Meridien

ISBN 978 1 91599 873 6
Ebook ISBN 978 1 91599 882 8

Printed and bound in the United Kingdom by CPI Group (UK) Ltd, Croydon CR0 4YY.

The manufacturer's authorised representative in the EU for product safety is eu-comply OÜ - Pärnu mnt 139b-14, 11317 Tallinn, Estonia, hello@eucompliancepartner.com; www.eucompliancepartner.com

9 8 7 6 5 4 3 2 1

MIX
Paper | Supporting
responsible forestry
FSC® C171272

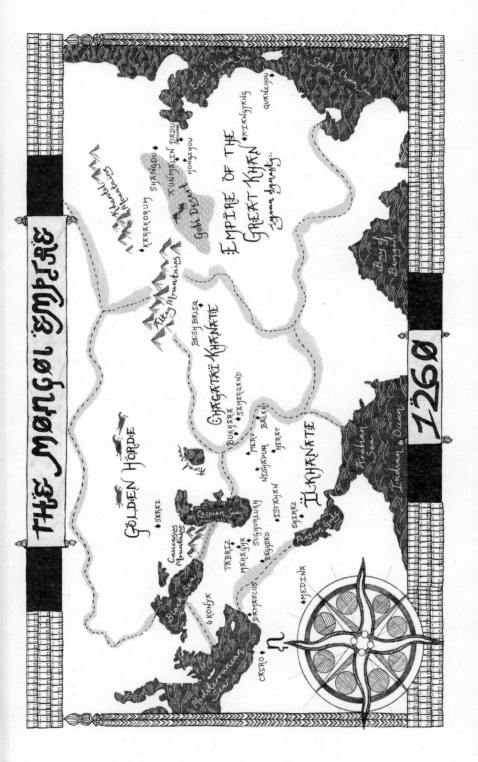

THE STORY SO FAR...

Behrouz, a mysterious Kozan who serves Hulagu Khan, makes a deal with the Vatican, offering them a chance to reclaim the Holy Land. The Ilkhanate has been betrayed by the Golden Horde and cannot fight two enemies at once. A deal is struck between Behrouz and the Church, although it chafes both parties to become allies.

As a member of the House of Grace, Kokochin is working to disrupt the Mongol Empire from within. But after being captured by Empress Guyuk, she is forced to hunt down Temujin, or else she and Layla will be killed. Realising that her task is impossible, and that she has to give Guyuk something of value to save their lives, Kokochin betrays Ariana who is hunted down and killed in front of her eyes.

Kaivon hates Hulagu but he must help the Khan win his war against Berke Khan and the Golden Horde. A new Persian rebellion is growing, but it needs time to build its strength and train new warriors. Kaivon and Esme must convince the rebels and the House of Grace to support Hulagu in the short term.

Temujin begins his training in earnest as a Kozan under the guidance of Katarina, Eraj and Teague. He also learns about the war between the two opposing factions of Kozan who support Order and Chaos. For thousands of years the Kozan have altered the course of major world events, but even they are not without enemies. The Servants of Time lurk in the shadows, waiting for the right moment to strike. Temujin realises that destroying his father will result in the death of many innocents, but he accepts the price in the service of Order.

Behrouz proves his loyalty to Hulagu by rooting out traitors and burning them to ash with his powers. After Behrouz declares Prince Thoros a traitor, Kaivon gathers allies against the Khan as they realise any of them could be accused.

Kokochin realises Guyuk will never let her and Layla go, so she orchestrates an escape from the palace. They seek refuge with Two, from the House of Grace, but cannot stay in the city. Several of the regional governors of Persia are siding with the Mongols over their own people. Kokochin and Layla are dispatched to persuade them, through any means, to become more patriotic.

Temujin works with the other Kozan to raise the status of Timur, a Warlord who has the potential to defeat Hulagu. Spreading stories of his victories swells Timur's ranks as warriors are keen to get a share of the wealth. In order to for Timur's army to maintain its momentum, Temujin kills several scouts, committing himself to the cause.

In Tehran, Kokochin manipulates Governor Darius to support Persia instead of the Mongols. She makes some unpleasant choices and justifies them with the outcome, but in doing so, she's becoming someone else.

Outside the city of Derbent, the army of Hulagu Khan is ambushed by the Golden Horde. With no other choice, Hulagu orders his army to attack and thousands die in the ensuing battle. Kaivon is knocked off his horse and nearly drowns in the river but fights his way to freedom and is rescued.

While The Twelve dislike using their resources to help Hulagu, they understand the long-term benefits for Persia. As such, they root out spies and find one sent by the Vatican to spy on the Ilkhanate. While the latest Crusade rages on, the Church and its allies have not forgotten the Mongols. Persia remains surrounded by enemies.

When a town is attacked by Timur's forces, but the Kozan take the time to rescue one woman for a political alliance, Temujin expresses his doubts. However, Katarina and the others have been waging this war for centuries, and he is persuaded to trust that they know what they're doing.

After Kaivon recovers from his injuries he returns to serving Hulagu, only to be accused of being a spy by Behrouz. The Kozan has no evidence, suggesting that the spies he'd previously identified were actually innocent. Kaivon expects Hulagu to support him but is gravely disappointed. Behrouz seizes Kaivon with his magic and he is seemingly burnt to ash.

Temujin bears witness as more towns and cities are sacked by Timur. The toll in lives is immense and his belief in the cause starts to waver. Temujin is approached by Melchior, the oldest and most powerful Kozan in the world.

In the city of Qom, Kokochin and Layla meet up with Souri, an ally in the House of Grace. The governor is being controlled by several powerful families and a different approach is required to manipulate him. When Souri is killed, Kokochin kidnaps a child from one family and places her in the hands of an opposing family. Using the child's life as leverage, Kokochin rescues Souri's daughter and gets what she wants.

When Esme hears the news about Kaivon, she and his brother, Karveh, hunt down a possible spy in the rebellion. She turns out to be Maryam, a Kozan working with Behrouz and Melchior.

While the city of Delhi is decimated, Melchior tells Temujin the truth. He has been lied to and manipulated since his first meeting with Katarina. She and the others serve Chaos. Feeling utterly betrayed Temujin flees, leaving all of the Kozan, and their eternal war, behind for good.

Maryam reveals she, Melchior and Behrouz are allies and agents of Order, who are working against Hulagu Khan and the Mongol Empire from within. She suggest Kaivon is still alive and that Esme and Karveh should try to find him.

After what Kokochin did in Qom, Layla doesn't recognise her anymore and doesn't want to be with her. Kokochin has become like Empress Guyuk, someone willing to do whatever is necessary to win, regardless of the cost. Layla leaves her for a job in the north and Kokochin doesn't know if they'll ever see each other again.

Esme and Karveh make a difficult journey to a secret training camp in a remote part of Persia. There they find Kaivon, alive and well, training Persian warriors to fight the Mongols. Their reunion is joyous but the war isn't over and Timur is growing in strength.

Betrayed by the Kozan, and still angry at his father, Temujin embraces the worst parts of himself, becoming someone utterly ruthless. After slaying all of his siblings, and a palace full of guards with his powers, he cripples his father and takes his rightful place as Temujin Khan, ruler of the Ilkhanate.

PART ONE
Year of the Water Mouse (1263)

"SOME SAY THE WORLD WILL END IN FIRE,
SOME SAY IN ICE.
FROM WHAT I'VE TASTED OF DESIRE
I HOLD WITH THOSE WHO FAVOUR FIRE."
– ROBERT FROST

CHAPTER 1
David

In Tbilisi, the capital city of Georgia, King David was in his private chapel when Temujin stepped out of thin air.

The altar to Jesus was modest, and the king knelt directly on the tiled floor. Dressed in plain clothes, and bearing no mark of his status, the king could have been anyone, but the former prince had found him without difficulty. It appeared as if Temujin's powers allowed him to go anywhere. Walls and locked doors no longer mattered.

David saw him glance around the sparsely decorated room, then Temujin became perfectly still. He seemed willing to wait, so David finished his prayer, using the time to slow the frantic beating of his heart.

It had been four months since the Ilkhanate had suddenly found itself with a new ruler. There were many stories flying around about how Temujin had cut a bloody swathe through the palace. In some ways, it paralleled that tale of how the Kozan, Behrouz, had come to serve Hulagu Khan. Only this time, all versions ended with the death of Hulagu at the hands of his youngest son.

David hoped that Temujin would assume the sweat on his brow was from the summer heat. Trying to maintain an air of calm when someone had appeared out of nowhere was difficult. Despite the fact that David had been expecting a visit for almost two weeks, it had still caught him off balance.

When he felt more composed, David made the sign of the cross on his chest and stood to face his guest. This gave David his first proper look at the former prince. It was difficult for him to unite the two disparate versions of Temujin in his mind. For years, Temujin had been a slightly bumbling, insecure young man, searching for his place in the world. Living in the shadow of Hulagu Khan was never going to be easy, but Temujin had struggled more than his siblings.

The man standing before David was radically different from the person he remembered. This version of Temujin had the bearing of a Khan, and the inner stillness of a monk. Before, he had been uncertain of himself, and almost boyish. As Temujin stared at him now, David felt concern for his life. Temujin's father had possessed the same unpredictable quality. Most of the time, Hulagu's moods could be anticipated, but sometimes he would develop a dangerous gleam in his eyes. There had been no way of knowing if it was a precedent to a violent outburst or not. Temujin now had the same look.

Even when Temujin had destroyed the walls of Aleppo with his unholy fire, there had been some doubt in his bearing. A whisper of who he had been. All of that was gone. The shaven head and sand-coloured robes might fool some into thinking Temujin was nothing more than a servant. David knew that Temujin had remade himself into someone completely new.

"I was expecting a messenger to come from Tabriz. I did not think you would visit in person," said David, lying to cover up how much he knew.

"I thought it important we talk face to face, so that there were no misunderstandings," said Temujin. Even his voice had changed. It had a new intensity that matched his unwavering stare. Some might find it unsettling, perhaps thinking Temujin could see into their soul, but David had no such fear. Only God could judge his worth.

"Why have you come?" asked the king.

"To remind you of your obligation, to serve the Mongol Empire." Temujin remained perfectly still. He seemed happy to have such an important political discussion standing in the chapel.

"Come, let us sit and take some tea," said David, delaying his response. It made him uncomfortable to discuss such material things in a sacred space. Normally, in this room, the only thing he contemplated was his ability to faithfully serve God.

David led the way through the corridors of the palace, turning his back on Temujin. He didn't believe the new khan had come all this way only to kill him. When David saw a servant approaching down the hallway, he waved the man away. If this meeting should end badly, he did not want to put anyone else's life at risk. Word spread ahead of them, and for the remainder of the walk, they were alone.

When David stepped into the library, his usual place to meet with guests, he was pleased to see that someone had raced ahead and laid out refreshments. The bookshelves stretched from floor to ceiling along two walls. There was no fireplace, but large windows brought in a lot of light and warmth. To his surprise, Temujin paused to peruse the shelves.

"Have you read all of these?" he asked, a sense of wonder creeping into his voice. Temujin ran his hand down the spine of a few books, tracing the titles with a finger.

"No, but perhaps one day I will," said David, checking on the tea. Being freshly made, he left it to steep. Taking his current book from the chair, he put it aside and sat down facing the windows. Golden sunlight dazzled across his face until it moved behind a thin cloud.

A moment later, Temujin joined him. His sombre, almost lifeless expression had returned.

"I believe you're a different sort of man to your father," said David. This earned a slight nod, so he continued. "Then let us speak plainly, in a way that he and I never could."

"I would like that," said Temujin. His voice carried so little emotion, David didn't know if he was being honest or not. But if these were to be his final moments, the king had no intention of meeting God with a falsehood on his tongue.

"The Ilkhanate is not the same as it once was. You can no longer count on support from the other khanates. Your father's army was decimated at Derbent, by the Golden Horde, and now you are surrounded by enemies. You cannot survive without help from others."

The latest news he'd received from the east indicated that the civil war between Kublai Khan, and his brother Ariq, was nearly over. Despite the speed at which messengers could travel within the Empire, the news had already been weeks old by the time it reached Georgia. Any day now, David expected to hear that the Great Khan's forces had crushed the uprising.

"All of what you've said is true. However, we both know that once the Great Khan has dealt with his brother, he will be able to send reinforcements. Any strength that was lost at Derbent will be restored."

"But it will take months for them to arrive," said David, pouring half a glass of tea. Finding it a good colour, he poured the rest and filled a second glass for Temujin. "In the meantime, you need to make preparations, and come up with a strategy to defeat your enemies."

"As you said, I am not my father," said Temujin accepting the tea. "I am not someone prone to violent outbursts. We both know that I could kill you now, but that would accomplish nothing. I am also not a strategist, or a leader of men. I need your warriors, but more than that, I need your knowledge and expertise of war, to defeat my enemies. I have already made the same appeal to the other kings and princes, asking for their support."

Temujin sipped his tea, picked a succulent date and chewed it thoughtfully before spitting out the stone. David took a moment to consider his response. The threat on his life had not been idle. Temujin's ability to appear anywhere at any time was evidence enough that nowhere was safe. The new khan had been startling people for weeks with sudden appearances.

"If I were to support you, what would be the benefit for my country?" said David, choosing his words with care.

"Independence," said Temujin. "True independence. If we survive, then you and I can quibble about the details, trade agreements and so on, but Georgia would be its own nation, not beholden to anyone as a vassal state."

"If I were to agree to help," said David, "what you're proposing could still take years, and it would cost a lot of lives. Many of my warriors would die fighting for your cause."

"I am aware," said Temujin, "but without allies, Georgia will be overrun by the Golden Horde. I also doubt that Berke Khan would be as accommodating as I am willing to be. You know his views on religion. It was one of the reasons he turned on my father."

The murder of the Caliph in Baghdad had been the spark that had led to civil war between the Golden Horde and the Ilkhanate. If Georgia became a vassal state of the Golden Horde, every one of his people would be expected to convert to Islam. Failure to comply would result in death or enslavement.

David was also aware that Temujin was trying to manipulate him.

"It seems as if you have left me with no real choice," said David, setting his glass aside. He stood, and Temujin followed suit, moving with fluid grace he'd not possessed in the past. Bathed in sunlight, David offered his hand to Temujin who shook it readily.

"I am ready to serve, my Khan," said David, inclining his head.

"Thank you," said Temujin with a smile, but then his grip tightened, and all good humour trickled away. "But make no mistake, if you turn on me, or your warriors abandon my army like they did to my father at Derbent, you will not live to see another sunrise."

"I understand," said David, struggling to keep his voice level.

Temujin finally released him, paused to glance at the bookshelves on his way out, then disappeared. One moment he was walking towards the open doorway, and the next he had simply vanished. David counted to one hundred in his head before he finally relaxed.

"He's gone," he said to the empty room.

There was an audible click, and one of the bookshelves slowly swung outwards into the room. Two figures stepped out of the alcove, then joined David by the window. Despite the sun beating against his skin, David felt cold, all the way down to his bones.

"You heard?" he asked.

"Every word," said Hethum, shaking his head. Beside him was his younger brother, prince Thoros. Until recently, they had thought Thoros was dead and had been burnt to ash. It seemed as if the Kozan, Behrouz, had been playing his own game while in service of Hulagu.

"Temujin is a viper who will turn on you," said Thoros. "Even though I was spared by Behrouz, I do not trust the man. These Kozan, with their ungodly powers, are all the same. Who can know what they truly want?" he asked.

"My brother is right," said Hethum. "Each of them is playing their own game. They serve themselves, or another master that is unknown to us. Either way, we are the ones who will suffer."

"Then we are in agreement," said David. "For now, we will all agree to follow this new version of Temujin. We will serve the Ilkhanate, and in doing so, serve our countries. But when the opportunity arises, we must be ready to kill him."

"That will not be easy. He tore through more than a dozen Kheshig with his bare hands," said Hethum.

Temujin spoke of real independence, but David did not believe him, not even for a moment. There would always be another reason, another excuse to extend Georgia's service to the Mongol Empire. He, and his nation, would forever be slaves.

"We will have time to find a way, but when the moment presents itself, all of us must be ready to strike without hesitation," said David. The others gave their agreement.

David stared out of the window at his city. Much hung in the balance, far more than his family, or even his country. Staring at the two men beside him, David knew that they fully understood what was as stake. Now that Temujin was the last of his line, when he died, this part of the world would be changed forever. If it all went according to plan, never again would any of them be under Mongol rule.

CHAPTER 2
Temujin

Temujin Skimmed away from the palace in Georgia. He covered a hundred miles in a few seconds, then stopped to rest in a remote canyon. He scanned the surrounding area, but there were no people in sight, not even a wild goat. After sitting down on a large rock, Temujin let go of the Eternal Fire, allowing himself to feel everything.

Emotions he'd been suppressing rushed to the surface. For a while, he was utterly overwhelmed. Tears ran from his eyes, and he lost all sense of time. Sobs wracked his body. Temujin hugged himself with both arms, trying to do nothing more than breathe. His thoughts wandered, focusing on his recent actions and what lay ahead.

Slowly, the emotional storm passed. When he came back to the present, Temujin found he was curled up in a ball on the ground. He dusted off his clothes, wiped his face and then battled to find a version of inner peace. A chill ran through his body. It was the tail end of winter, and the drying sweat on his skin was icy cold. Doing his best to ignore it, Temujin sat down on the rock again, closed his eyes and waited.

The familiarity of meditation brought structure to his thoughts. It took much longer than normal, but eventually the mediocre and the mundane drifted away, leaving him with a sense of calm. But he was not at peace. Part of him wondered if he would ever be able to relax. Since deposing his father, he was constantly on edge, always watching others for any sign of betrayal. Even when asleep in his bedroom, behind a locked door deep inside the palace in Tabriz, he didn't feel safe. Every night, before getting into bed, he pushed a chair up against the door. It wasn't much, but it would give him a few extra seconds. Hopefully, it would be just enough to stop a mortal attack. It wouldn't prevent a Kozan from appearing inside his rooms, but so far, the others had left him alone. Temujin didn't expect it to last. He was an unknown, and despite his limited abilities in comparison to theirs, it created an imbalance between the two sides of Order and Chaos.

The calm he projected around others was merely an illusion. They only saw what he wanted them to see. He kept the turmoil and the doubt locked deep inside. Even if they stared into his eyes, none of his doubts would be visible.

The ruthless mask he wore all day, every day, allowed him to do what was necessary. It also meant he could live with himself, especially after what he'd done to his siblings. It had been the most difficult decision he'd ever made, but Temujin knew there had been no other choice. In their own way, all of his brothers and sisters, with the exception of Jumghur, had excelled. If even one of them had lived, there would have been questions about his worth as ruler. Factions would have formed, and soon there would have been another rift within the Empire. This way, the Ilkhanate could focus its strength on defeating existing enemies, not creating new ones.

Now that he was khan, and ruler of the Ilkhanate, Temujin found it increasingly difficult to find any time to be alone. Only then could he be himself. The real Temujin. The one he seemed to remember, but no one else knew.

With each passing day, it became a little bit harder to take off the mask.

Sinking deeper into the calm that surrounded him, Temujin surrendered completely to the Eternal Fire. Nodes of energy filled his vision, stretching out to the horizon in all directions. There were thousands, perhaps millions of glowing balls. It seemed unbelievable that something so vast and complex remained hidden from almost everyone in the world. It made Temujin wonder, what other mysteries were still obscured from his primitive senses?

Slowly and methodically, Temujin built his own Rigour. He created a tight bubble around the perimeter of his body. The world outside it blurred, becoming a vague representation of reality. Noises were distorted, and soon, the only thing that sounded normal was his breathing.

Moving inside the Rigour, Temujin travelled a vast distance on foot, heading south and east until the roads became familiar. He'd previously attempted a similar journey on horseback, but the end result had been messy. His Rigour had been unstable, and his horse had been ravaged by the flow of time. Parts of its body had dramatically aged, but not others. To end its suffering, Temujin had been forced to put the beast down. This way, he only had his own needs to worry about. It was still an enormous struggle to maintain, and he felt as if it could collapse at any moment. So, the fewer distractions there were, the better.

Landmarks stood out on the periphery of Temujin's vision, telling him he was getting closer to home. It was difficult to judge time, but in what he guessed was the final hour of his journey, he noticed two Servants keeping pace outside his protective bubble. Their eyes were swirling pits of darkness, and each rode a massive huffing beast. Even in his present mind-set, removed from his emotions by the Eternal Fire, Temujin could feel their burning hatred. They desperately wanted him to lose control, just for a moment, so they could swarm over him. He'd seen what one of them had done to Katarina with a brief touch, and she had centuries more experience than him. They were patient, and never wavered in their vigilance. Temujin tried to stay calm, but he continuously checked the stability of his Rigour and made repairs.

With a final lurch of distance, the road into Tabriz came into view. The Servants peeled away, leaving him to walk the last mile alone. As instructed, a clear path had been left to a private courtyard on the outskirts of the city. As a precaution, a pair of Kheshig stood guard at the entrance to the house. Temujin had no idea what would happen if he walked through someone, or reappeared back into the normal flow of time in the same space as another person. Without a teacher, he'd been left to fend for himself and come up with practical solutions.

When he finally released the Rigour, it was such a relief that he dropped to his knees. Temujin hadn't realised the level of strain until he let go. He was left breathless, dripping with sweat and light-headed. After stumbling into a bedroom, Temujin collapsed and slept through the rest of the day.

He woke at dawn the next morning. After drinking lots of water, scrubbing his skin and changing into fresh clothes, he felt more human. He ate a generous meal at a local tea room before walking back towards the palace. On his way there, the Kheshig informed Temujin that he'd been gone from Tabriz for four days. It was difficult to keep track of time when moving inside the Rigour.

It started the moment he set foot in the throne room. Guyuk, the former Empress and now merely an advisor to the throne, sidled up to him with a warm smile. Temujin wasn't fooled. Her arrogance and vicious nature weren't gone. They were merely buried, beneath a layer of fear and a thin veneer of charm. At times, he could still see her true emotions behind her veiled eyes.

Temujin's greatest frustration about being a Kozan was that he had no one to show him how to use his powers. The best part was, no one knew really what was possible, so they always assumed the worst. Some had speculated that he could read minds, or sense when someone was lying. Neither was true, but Temujin had done nothing to dispel the rumours. It kept everyone on their toes. They weren't always honest around him, but lies were easier to spot when someone was nervous.

There were already over a dozen people in the room. Word of his arrival brought others at a run, scrambling ahead of each other to be seen first. They all wanted something. In theory, they were there to serve him, but most often it seemed as if the opposite were true.

"Could I ask you for a small favour, my Khan?" asked Guyuk. It was always the same with her. She only wanted one thing. Temujin took his time getting settled on the throne. He arranged his clothes, and adjusted the cushions before addressing her directly.

"No, you may not. Send for my Trade Advisor," he said. His face gave nothing away, but a range of emotions swept across hers. He saw a flash of anger, regret and even hate. "Something you wish to say?" said Temujin, raising an eyebrow.

Guyuk bowed low and backed away. "No, my Khan," she muttered.

It wasn't every day that you found out your adopted mother had hired someone to kill you. He'd been even more surprised to find out that it had been Kokochin, one of his father's many wives. He should have had Guyuk killed, but she still had her uses. The other wives had fled, in fear of their lives. There were now a lot of empty rooms in the palace, which suited him fine.

"Lord Khan?" said Rashid, taking a step forward. Temujin had not forgotten how Rashid had treated him. The vizier had urged him to murder the defenceless spice merchant in the torture chamber beneath the palace. Cold and ruthless barely seemed adequate terms to describe the vizier. Temujin knew he was as dangerous, if not more so, than Guyuk.

Killing Rashid would have been a pleasure, but again, he was too valuable to waste. Despite keeping meticulous records, his father's vizier had a lot of contacts that Temujin needed.

Replacing him with someone else would cause a delay that Temujin could not afford. However, Rashid understood he was standing on thin ice. That was why there were four young men directly behind him. They followed the vizier from the moment he woke up in the morning to when he went to sleep at night. In time, one or more of them would replace him. It was only a matter of when.

"Report," said Temujin, staring down at the shrewd little man. In the back of his mind, Temujin realised he was echoing how his father had dealt with his attendants. He squashed the worrying thought and focused on what his vizier was saying.

"As you ordered, training exercises continue. We are also still gathering men from the west of the Ilkhanate."

With too much free time on their hands, bored warriors got into trouble. Temujin needed them ready for war. A series of mock pitched battles and complex exercises were keeping his army sharp. Once King David and the others arrived, they would take over the training.

The ground his father had gained in Iraq and beyond was lost to them. The men that had been under his brother's command in Baghdad were now back in Tabriz. They would need every single warrior for the battles yet to come against Timur. More than anyone, Temujin knew exactly who they were up against.

"And the Masons Guild?" asked Temujin.

"At first, they grumbled, but now they appreciate the free labour."

Drills would not be enough to tire some men out. Temujin needed them exhausted to minimise potential damage. The hard work would keep them physically fit, and build stamina. There was always rebuilding and construction work to be done in the city. Although he hoped it wouldn't come to it, he'd given orders that the city's defences were to be shored up. It was better to be prepared than wish for something when it was too late.

"Recruits?"

"They have been mixed in with more experienced units." Having spent time in his father's army, Temujin understood that there was much that veterans could teach, but only in practice. Working together through hardships created strong bonds between the men. Friends would fight even harder to save one another. In the grand scale of the coming conflict, it was the smallest of margins, but they needed every advantage, no matter how small. "Good. What news from Europe, Lord Mansour?" asked Temujin, turning to the bearded Jordanian. The shrewd merchant had a healthy business, which gave him access to a lot of people and, more importantly, information. Most pertinent to Temujin were those involved with the latest European Crusade.

"My Khan," said Mansour, sketching a bow. "As you expected, fighting slowed during winter, but now that spring approaches, Europe will send more soldiers. The Mamluks are also readying themselves as well."

"Are you guessing, or have you been told this?" asked Temujin.

Mansour began to squirm, but there was no one to come to his aid. "I have not received word, but I am confident it will happen."

Temujin stared at the man. He was probably right, but he could not operate on rumours and hearsay.

"The Pope is sending another ten thousand men," said a new voice, cutting through the tension. Temujin recognised the speaker as that of his newly appointed Trade Minister. He wanted to smile, but repressed it. As the Khan, he could not be seen to have favourites. It was a weakness that someone, friend or spy, would seek to use against him. Also, it would put the Minister, and anyone connected to them, at greater risk.

The Trade Minister strode into the throne room, drawing the eyes of everyone. While Lord Mansour's trade business was reasonably successful, it was dwarfed in size several times by the Minister's interests. In truth, the various businesses were owned by her fat, lazy husband, but Temujin was not under any illusions. Kimya Rouhani was the brains behind the sprawling business empire. It was rumoured that her network of contacts rivalled that of Guyuk. In addition, because she was Persian, the Minister had access to more people across the Ilkhanate than anyone else. Strangers were a lot more willing to talk to her than the former Empress. Due to friendships built up over many years, Kimya's reach extended all the way into Europe. She had contacts across the Ilkhanate, which he intended to use to the full.

"Apologies, my Khan," said Minister Rouhani, bowing deeply before she approached the throne. "I was only just informed that you had returned."

Temujin noticed her face was slightly flushed. She must have dropped whatever she'd been doing and hurried to the palace. A few strands of her dark hair had come loose from her headscarf, and her cheeks were red. He almost smiled and told her to catch her breath.

"Ten thousand warriors. Are you sure?" he asked instead.

"Yes, my Khan. A trusted contact in Rome sent word. I believe the Church is planning to send more, but that has not been confirmed."

If Egypt and Europe continued fighting one another for their Holy Land, it was one less problem to worry about. One out of a thousand he had to deal with. Temujin felt a laugh bubbling up and tried to repress it. At the last second, he managed to twist his face into a grim smile.

"Good. Let them grind each other into a bloody paste. Each death is one less enemy for me to deal with."

The Minister bobbed her head but didn't reply. From his eye corner, Temujin could see Guyuk was staring at Kimya with open hatred. No one liked being replaced and superseded.

"Tell me about the food shipments," said Temujin. An army marched on its stomach, and his army was large and hungry.

He was only half listening, enough to nod along in all the right places. She had everything under control, and he was already thinking about his next meeting.

He didn't have to do it, but he wanted to. Why was that? Was it arrogance? Pride? Temujin had expected to feel happier. After all, he'd won. Hadn't he?

Coming back to the present, he realised Kimya had stopped speaking. The whole room was waiting for his reaction, while he stared. In truth, he was looking past her, but all they saw was his hard gaze lingering on the Trade Minister. The air crackled with tension. They were used to dealing with his father. They were anticipating that he would also have similar violent outbursts.

"You have done well," said Temujin, breaking the hush. "I'm impressed."

"Thank you, my Khan," said Kimya.

"I'm sure you have much to do. If I need you again, I will send for you. Otherwise, go about your duties as normal," he said, dismissing her. She was far more useful to him elsewhere, and probably safer too. It wasn't much, but right now it was all he could do to offer her a little protection.

The Minister bowed again and backed away, while Guyuk stared daggers.

"I'm going to see my father," said Temujin, getting up from the throne. Guyuk's already pale face lost all remaining colour. Her stained lips stood out against the white of her skin. Temujin ignored her and the others in the room. Any other business would have to wait.

Four Kheshig escorted him through the hallways, two clearing the way ahead, and two others behind, keeping anyone from following too closely.

In the palace, in the heart of the khanate, the bodyguards had previously been nothing more than ceremonial. It was only on the streets that there had been the possibility of trouble. Now, Temujin expected attempts on his life at any time and anywhere. From friends, and even rivals of his father. From spies in Europe, or the Golden Horde. Even from other extended members of his family who were also descendants of his great-grandfather, Genghis Khan.

There were some who had always disputed the notion that only those from the line Tolui, his grandfather, were worthy to become khans in the Empire. The feud between branches of the family had started with his grandfather, and naturally it had been perpetrated by his father and siblings. It was part of the reason his uncle Kublai had been chosen as the Great Khan.

There were those descended from Ogedei and Jochi, brothers to his grandfather, who wanted to rule. Each man had their own brood of children, and now grandchildren, hungry for positions of power within the Empire. As the last of his father's line, Temujin made a tempting target for many killers. Killing them would be easy in comparison to his siblings, and when it happened, he would not hesitate.

The temperature dropped as he descended the stairs into the corridors beneath the palace. He passed through the torture chamber, trying not to stare at the various implements and wicked-shaped blades. He'd seen them often enough that the terror should have faded. In spite of all his power, he was still terrified of being held down and taken apart, piece by piece.

When he'd stormed the palace, Temujin had not enjoyed killing the Kheshig. They were in his way, and it had simply been necessary. However, he'd taken great pleasure in tearing Elbuz apart. He was willing to use some people that had previously served his father, but not the torturer. He'd gone to an unmarked grave, and no one had mourned his passing.

All of the other prisoners in the dungeon had been taken elsewhere. He'd told Rashid he didn't care where they went, only that his father was completely isolated. Temujin had personally chosen the prison guards with great care, and so far, there had been no issues.

The two local men were brothers, big and burly from time spent in the *zurkhaneh*, but with cherubic smiles. They weren't simple, merely happy to be given such an important task. Both hated Hulagu for what he'd done to Persia. Temujin suspected they would have done the job for free.

One of the brothers was asleep in an antechamber while the other sat alone, reading a book. He glanced up as they approached and stood, looming over everyone in the room.

"Any trouble?" said Temujin, speaking slowly and carefully.

Cyrus and his brother, Ahrash, were completely deaf, but they could read lips. They hadn't always been deaf, so although they were capable of speech, they usually spoke to one another with their hands.

"No trouble," said Cyrus, shaking his head. His words were slurred and slightly uneven, but still understandable. "Talks a lot, mostly to himself. I think he's bored and lonely."

"Good," said Temujin with a smile, which the big man mirrored.

Isolation and boredom were forms of torture for some people. His father loved an audience, and with no one to talk with, or more accurately talk at, Hulagu only had his own thoughts for company. It was as close as Temujin could get to forcing his father to meditate on the past, and the decisions that had led him to this moment.

Despite the lack of exercise and regular meals, Hulagu had lost weight. His skin was pale from being without sunlight, and he lay on the straw mattress staring at the ceiling. Temujin dragged a stool to the middle of the corridor and sat down, facing the cell.

For a while, his father continued to stare at nothing, blinking slowly. Temujin had learned patience from meditation. He was perfectly happy to sit and watch the rise and fall of Hulagu's chest. Time passed, and although Temujin's eyes were open, he travelled inwards, running through plans in his mind. There was still a lot of work to do.

"Now, you're beginning to understand," said Hulagu, interrupting his thoughts.

"Understand what?"

"What it means to be khan. What it takes to win." Hulagu swung his feet to the floor and sat up. They faced one another across the open space. Their view of each other was only partially obscured by the bars of the cell. "I can see it in your eyes."

Temujin smiled and raised an eyebrow. "See what?"

"The fear."

"I'm not afraid of you."

"Oh, I know that." Hulagu chuckled, a wet unhealthy sound in the back of his throat. Temujin wanted him to suffer, but he didn't want him dead. Not yet, at least. He would have to arrange for his father to be let outside, for fresh air and exercise. It would have to be under heavy guard, of course. "You're afraid of what you must become in order to win."

Temujin said nothing. Winning was a tiny speck on the horizon, at the end of a long and twisting path. There were many obstacles on the road ahead that he had to overcome before he'd even let his mind drift that far.

"Have you won over the northern vassal states yet?" asked Hulagu.

Temujin had told him nothing about his plans, and he knew the prison guards had not spoken. His father must have been working through various plans in his mind. Temujin found it slightly disconcerting that his strategy aligned with that of his father.

"Or, have you gone straight to my cousin, Berke Khan?"

"I sent several letters, but have received no reply." At least the messengers had not been murdered, like some his father had sent in the past. Two of Temujin's messengers had made the difficult journey during winter, traversing dangerous roads to Sarai. Each time, upon arrival, they had been treated amiably and sent home without a message from Berke.

"Unlike you, I am patient."

"You are wasting time. He cannot be reasoned with. There is no bargain to be struck." Hulagu clenched his fists, but didn't raise his voice. His calm attitude was at odds with his usual demeanour, and a little eerie. "He is a traitor and a liar."

"Let me guess, your advice is violence?" said Temujin.

"He is not a diplomat, and you will not win this battle with words. He is a warrior, who is fast becoming a zealot. Berke made his choice when he betrayed his own kind. He must face the consequences of those actions."

"If I kill him, I would be no different from you, and as you can see, we are not the same," said Temujin, cocking his head to one side.

"No, we are very different," said Hulagu, but then he smiled in a way that reminded Temujin of a wolf. There were far too many teeth and the rage his father was holding in check danced behind his eyes. "But you will have to do great and terrible things if you want to win this war."

"I promise you that will never happen," said Temujin.

Hulagu grunted, lay back on his bed and resumed staring at the ceiling. "Then you have already lost, and the Ilkhanate will be destroyed."

Although his expression was calm, strong emotions roiled through Temujin. He barely saw the others as he walked back along the hallway, then up the stairs into the light. There had to be another way. He was determined not to repeat the mistakes of the past and follow in his father's footsteps. Otherwise, what was the point? He could simply have left Hulagu in charge, and nothing would have changed.

Alone in his rooms, Temujin meditated for hours, trying to find a solution. When dawn came, he was sandy-eyed, stiff and without answers.

Just then, there was a knock at the door. "Enter," he said.

"Humble apologies, my Khan," grovelled the servant,

bowing so low his forehead almost touched the ground. "You have an unannounced visitor. He said you would want to meet with him."

"What's his name?" asked Temujin.

"It's General Kaivon," was the reply.

CHAPTER 3
Kokochin

On a busy street, in the ancient city of Lahore, Kokochin paused at a fruit stall to check if she was being followed.

Over the last few months, it had become part of her daily routine. Nevertheless, she was patient and methodical in her search, because out here, she had no protection. No one was going to come and save her. Every single day, she had to take care of herself.

The city sat in a no-man's land between the Ilkhanate to the west and territory claimed by Timur to the north and east. Just over twenty years ago, the city had been sacked by the army of Genghis Khan. A large number of its inhabitants had been slaughtered or enslaved, and many buildings damaged. Rebuilding had begun, but it was slow, and the city still bore heavy scars.

On his way to Delhi, Timur had bypassed various towns and cities. However, as the self-styled Sword of Islam consolidated his power and expanded the new Chagatai khanate, Lahore would be one of the first places to fall. The city authorities knew what was coming and were prepared to surrender, rather than suffer Timur's wrath. However, there was no guarantee of a peaceful outcome.

He might take offence and still decide to slaughter everyone and burn the city to the ground. It was one of the most dangerous places in the world, which was why Kokochin was there.

It was only mid-morning, but already the heat was more than she was used to. Despite the headscarf that kept the worst of the sun off her head, sweat ran down Kokochin's face.

As she scanned the crowded market, Kokochin caught sight of a woman with glossy black hair cut in a familiar style. But when they turned around, it wasn't Layla. It was never her. She was somewhere far to the north, in the Golden Horde, but that didn't stop Kokochin's heart from lurching. It still hurt, just as badly as when it had happened. It served as another reminder that she was alone.

Today, the market was busier than normal as there was an abundance of fresh lamb for sale. Merchants were keen to shift the meat. Many of them called out in loud voices, fighting for dominance amongst the general din. Rumours of a disease among a neighbouring town's flocks were rippling through the crowd, along with fears that it might spread. Kokochin suspected it was a story someone had concocted in order to lower the price, but she couldn't prove it. There had been a large cull in the last two days, and now prices were falling even further. No one wanted to be left with rotting meat.

Kokochin bought a bag of apples, checked the crowd around her for any familiar faces, and then moved on. Like many others in the city, she crawled through the stalls at a lazy pace. She gave the appearance of being just another person with time on their hands, and money to spend.

The person she meant to observe hadn't appeared, but they were a creature of habit. She just had to be patient.

She bought half a dozen smoked fish, some fresh olives, flat bread and soft white cheese. She visited several stalls quite often, and because she was known to the owners, they gave her a discount. Kokochin made sure they didn't give her anything stale, which they usually reserved for anyone who wasn't local.

On her way home, Kokochin stopped off at a leather stall and pretended to inspect the belts. In truth, three scholars were standing not far behind her, and she wanted to eavesdrop on their conversation. Every day, they took a break for a walk and some fresh air.

The stall owner smiled and waited to see if Kokochin needed any assistance, but otherwise he left her alone. He'd glanced at her clothing, and judged her not to be a serious customer. Instead, he fawned over a rich merchant, whose fingers were dripping with gold rings. How times had changed.

"I saw the woman's body," hissed one of the three men. He was the youngest, with a slim build and black hair. The other two men were shorter, rounded and had grey hair. Their faces were weather-beaten, and they had indulgent smiles. Risking a glance over her shoulder, Kokochin saw each man had a stylised hand embroidered onto their clothing. It was the Hand of Miriam, indicating they were all healers. "The wounds were vicious. Someone had tortured her for information."

"It was an accident," said one of the others. "The result of a nasty fall. Nothing more than that."

The youngest was about to speak again when the other man grabbed him firmly by the elbow. "It was unfortunate. Do you understand?"

The young healer closed his mouth, nodded grimly, then all three men shuffled away. Kokochin waited a short time before heading home, in the opposite direction. She had been following the young healer for two weeks, and had gradually pieced together his schedule. He and the other two worked at the public hospital, dealing with bodies that were brought in from the streets. Unlike the other two, he wasn't jaded and was still passionate, which in this case meant he was outspoken. They often spoke freely in the market, believing the noise of the crowd would swallow their words.

Kokochin didn't know who the victim was, but it was clear the woman had been murdered, and the others were keen to cover it up. It could have been nothing, a random death as a result of thieves, but she thought it was worth investigating.

The House of Grace had a few contacts in the Chagatai khanate, but they didn't have a network in Lahore. Working alone, that made it impossible for her to piece together a picture of what was happening in the city. Using her initiative, she'd improvised a solution.

Back at the tea shop, Kokochin entered via the back door, locked it behind her and passed on the fresh goods to the cook. Glancing at the shop from behind the counter, Kokochin saw that less than a third of the tables were occupied. It was a slow day. The two serving girls were capable of managing without her.

She climbed the narrow stairs up to her office, checked that nothing had been moved, and then took a journal from the drawer. The afternoon passed slowly while she went over the ledger, but eventually it was time to close up. She helped the girls tidy up and prepare everything for the next day. Together they cleaned the kitchen, then she paid them their wages for the week.

Kokochin left the shop in darkness, but lit a pair of candles in her office upstairs. People expected her to follow certain routines. As such, she did her best to go unnoticed, never doing anything that others might think was peculiar and noteworthy. That was how rumours started, and that could lead to questions. If there was one thing she'd learned from the House of Grace, it was patience. Slow and careful was always the way.

Barely an hour later, there was a faint tapping at the back door. Kokochin admitted a woman, checking the alley both ways, before closing the door.

Mehr was twice Kokochin's age, solid, reliable and unflappable. So it came as quite a surprise to see her nervous and pacing.

"What's happened?" said Kokochin, trying to stay calm. Her first instinct was to snap at Mehr and tell her to sit down. Instead, Kokochin dug her fingernails into the palms of her hands and took a deep breath.

Mehr went to bite her fingernails, then realised what she was doing. "I haven't chewed my nails since I was your age. Worrying about a boy or something."

"What happened to him?" asked Kokochin, mostly to keep her talking. It would also help her relax by speaking about a safe topic.

"I thought we were in love, but he was only getting close to me because he wanted to court my best friend. It broke my heart."

"Did they marry?"

Mehr squinted and thought about it. "No, she married someone else. He was trampled to death by a horse."

"So your husband isn't your first love."

Mehr snorted and shook her head. Delicate gold earrings inlaid with blue stones swung back and forth in her wavy dark hair. "No, he came later. I made him chase me."

There was no fresh tea, but Kokochin poured some cold water for both of them and offered Mehr a glass. Her hands only shook a little as she raised it to her lips.

"I understand if you want to stop," said Kokochin. After only doing this for a few months, Kokochin respected the Twelve a lot more than before. Their slow and steady work was conducted over years, even decades. Kokochin didn't think she'd have the patience for such a long road.

She was also finding it difficult to walk the line between manipulating people and genuinely trying to help them. It would have been so easy to remind Mehr what the Mongols had done to her city, and her people. How much damage they had caused, and that she should be angry about it. But that led to revenge, and then Kokochin would still be that other version of herself. The one she hated. The one that had done horrible things, never worrying about the consequences. The one that had driven Layla away.

"No, it's not that. I want to keep going," said Mehr. "I just never thought it would work." As Mehr met her gaze for the first time, Kokochin saw her anxiety was masking something else. Excitement. "I haven't felt this alive in years."

"Tell me what happened," said Kokochin, pulling out a seat and getting comfortable.

Her only orders from the House of Grace had been to build a new life in Lahore and gather information on Timur. When his army approached the city, she was to withdraw to the relative safety of the Ilkhanate and continue working from a safer location.

The wealth Timur had taken from Delhi would help a great deal, but since that time, his conquest had not stopped. More towns and cities had fallen, and his army was still growing. A conflict between the Ilkhanate and the Chagatai khanate was inevitable. When was important, but not as significant as how and where.

"Abban's business runs on his reputation," said Mehr, warming to the subject. "His customers could go elsewhere for their clothing, but he's beyond reproach and well respected. If they found out he had a mistress, and had fathered two children with her, his life would be over."

Kokochin had asked Mehr to target Abban because of his standing in the community. He had no official connection to city authorities, but he had extensive access to them. Ruining his life was nothing less than he deserved, but Kokochin had repressed her first impulse in favour of a long-term solution that would help the local people.

"What did you say?" asked Kokochin.

"What we discussed. He offered me money to keep his secret, but I refused. Now I have access to his diary."

Abban's customers were some of the wealthiest in the city. They could be in his shop for two or three hours, choosing fabrics, as well as being fitted for new clothes. And all the while they talked, confident of his discretion and absolute privacy. Several of them were wealthy Mongols, or people who worked closely with them as part of the Chagatai khanate.

"That's good," said Kokochin. The urge towards anger and violence was still there, so she dug her fingernails deeper into her palms.

"In return for keeping his secret, Abban is going to share information about what he overhears."

There was no way for Kokochin to get access to the upper echelons of power without being noticed, but this way, she didn't have to. Mehr would pass along anything she found out, and together they would find a way to put it to good use.

The local population hated the Mongols for what they had done to their city twenty years ago. However, many people still remembered local heroes that had stood up to the army of Genghis Khan. The fort commander at the time, known as the White Falcon, had fought bravely, despite the overwhelming odds. His courage had inspired ordinary people to take up arms against the invaders. Ultimately, the local forces were beaten, but he was still celebrated as a martyr. Kokochin had even heard rumours of a group calling themselves the Sons of the White Falcon. So far, her attempts to find anyone connected to them had failed, but she continued to try.

It was this rebellious and unbreakable spirit that she was trying to rekindle in the people. Only this time, the battles would not be fought in the open with opposing armies. It would be the subtle knife. The slow and careful erosion from within, until true control rested with the local population once more.

The people of Lahore were tired of war, and tired of having their city attacked by Mongol warlords. It had not been difficult for Kokochin to find people who wanted freedom and independence. However, it had been a laborious and painstaking process to find those who would act on those feelings, rather than just talk about it.

"Be careful, and make sure you have a back-up plan," Kokochin reminded her. "Make sure Abban understands that if anything unpleasant were to happen to you, his secret would still be revealed. He will not be willing to take the risk. It would destroy his business and his entire life."

"I will be careful," said Mehr, smiling for the first time since she arrived. "Once I have something useful, how often should I visit?"

"Don't set a schedule, or fall into a routine. During the day, just come in for tea when you have something. When I see you, I'll know to expect a visit from you that night."

"And you'll pass on the information to your superior?"

"I will," said Kokochin, smiling at the irony of her situation. She was mirroring what Two had done, pretending to be nothing more than another subordinate in the network. No one in Kokochin's group of contacts knew she was actually in charge, or that she was alone in Lahore. They all believed she reported to another person in the city. She sent information back to Tabriz once a month, via a trusted merchant, but so far, she had not received any messages in return.

"We're going to make them suffer," said Mehr, startling Kokochin with her ferocity. "For everything they've done to my people."

"We will," said Kokochin, treading carefully. "But if your plan is murder, I will not help you."

"You've killed before," said Mehr. It had been necessary for Kokochin to reveal who she was in order to gain the trust of new contacts. Kokochin had also shared some of what she'd done to gain freedom for Persia.

"Yes, but only as a last resort, and I still regret it." The nightmares came and went. Kokochin wondered if they would ever completely fade. "We both know the Mongols will soon invade Lahore again, and if you kill one of them, they will just be replaced. Then more of your people will suffer. We need to prepare for their arrival, then slowly remove their support.

Once that's done, it will be easier to drive all of them out. I know it's frustrating and slow, but murder is not the answer. It will change you, and I don't want that for you, Mehr."

Something in Kokochin's voice penetrated Mehr's rage. The heat drained from her cheeks. "As you say, we'll drive them from the city. Then we will be free."

"We will," said Kokochin, forcing a smile.

"I must get back. I told my husband I was visiting a sick friend. Thank you." Mehr clasped her hand, then dashed out the back door.

And so it went. Four more contacts from Kokochin's network visited her that night, and five more the following evening. All of them from different walks of life. All of them ordinary citizens, who hated what had happened, and could see what was on the horizon. And, if it came to it, all of them were willing to sacrifice their own life for the greater good.

One contact mentioned knowing someone who had met with the Sons of the White Falcon. Kokochin urged him to be extremely careful. If the group existed, they were almost as well hidden as the House of Grace. They would not take well to people prying into their business, especially an outsider like her.

The last contact to visit her was a young woman who worked as a nurse in the public hospital. Smart, practical and dedicated, Olma was willing to do anything to keep her city free of the Mongols.

"She was definitely tortured," said Olma, getting straight to the point. "They had me clean the woman's body for the family."

The healers had been determined to convince their young colleague of their version of events. The question was, why?

"Same as before?" asked Kokochin.

"Yes, heavy bruising of the torso, broken ribs and fingers. Someone had also ripped out her fingernails." Olma spoke calmly and without any emotion. It wasn't that she didn't feel, or even care. It was just after years of dealing with the dead, she could separate her emotions. Kokochin knew that when Olma was alone, she would rage and grieve.

"Who was the victim?" asked Kokochin.

"No one you know, but," said Olma as Kokochin started to relax, "she was a newcomer to the city. She'd been here less than a year."

It was as Kokochin had feared. She was being hunted. Or if not her, then people like her in Lahore. The questions then became, who was the hunter, and what were they trying to find out?

Kokochin suspected someone knew who she was, and that she was in the city. It was possible they were coming after her because of her growing network, but that seemed unlikely.

Kokochin had been extremely careful with her contacts. None of them knew anything about the others, and she met with each person separately. They might have suspicions about a network, but Kokochin never answered any of their questions. It kept them safe, and unable to share any information if they were ever questioned. The only name they could give to a potential torturer was hers, and she was capable of taking care of herself.

Kokochin had been extremely careful since her arrival, doing her utmost to blend in and not ruffle any feathers. Even her business was owned by her fictional brother. He was the only contact she had in the city from the House of Grace and was only there to be called on in an emergency.

This was the fifth torture victim in a month. The bodies were never found in the same place, but all of them were new arrivals. Before coming here, she had been assured there was no local equivalent of the House of Grace. However, her stalker could be a local spy, a Mongol hunter sent by Guyuk, or even a hired killer. She had created a lot of enemies in Persia, and many of them wanted revenge. In particular, she was thinking of Yasmin. After all, Kokochin had kidnapped her daughter. She had the money, and the motivation, to fund such an extensive operation.

"Do you know who is doing this?" asked Olma.

"No, but I intend to find out."

"How?"

Finally, here was someone upon whom she could release all of her pent-up anger. Someone who was truly deserving of a brutal ending.

Kokochin's smile was feral. "I'm going to hunt down whoever is doing this, and revisit every injury they inflicted on their victims."

"And then?" said Olma.

"I'm going to find whoever hired the killer, and make them suffer in kind."

CHAPTER 4
Kaivon

High in the Hindu Kush mountains, the city of Kabul sat just within the borders of the Chagatai khanate. This made it the perfect place for Kaivon to launch attacks against Timur.

Time was their greatest enemy. The Ilkhanate was not ready to face Timur's forces in open conflict. After wrestling control of the khanate from his father, Temujin was in the process of rebuilding its strength, but it wouldn't be enough. Even if he succeeded in convincing old allies and vassal states to rejoin and bolster his army, the Ilkhanate would still be at a disadvantage. Timur's army was vast and growing every day. Temujin needed to recruit more warriors, and for that he needed time.

It had been a risk for Kaivon to visit Tabriz and reveal that he was still alive, but there had been no other choice. The rebellion in Persia could not continue to operate in secret. Their numbers were growing, and while concealing the training camps had worked until now, the drain on resources and money was considerable. With so much activity, in so many different locations, it had only been a matter of when Temujin would find out.

He could have killed Kaivon on sight, but in the grand scale, it would have changed little. The new khan had been surprised to see him, but he'd also listened with interest as Kaivon told him about his secret army.

A temporary alliance had been struck, with Temujin supplying whatever money and resources he could, and in return Kaivon would try to buy the new khan some time. The new Persian warriors were young and hungry, but they were untested in battle. Training and learning drills weren't enough. The danger was never real. The warriors needed to have actual combat, and experience the fear of death. Only then would they find a way to master their emotions. It was better that Kaivon found out which of them were reliable now than when they were on the battlefield.

Today's hit and run attack was designed to be another brutal and bloody affair. It was meant to shock and appal, as well as scare those intentionally left alive, to spread the story.

A short time later, Esme returned from scouting the streets around the mosque. Kaivon stepped out of the alley and walked beside her. Neither of them spoke until they were alone on a quiet road. Although he was slowly getting used to the high altitude, even the short walk made Kaivon more aware of his breathing.

"Nothing has changed," said Esme, loosening her head scarf. They had been planning the latest mission for a week.

"Bodyguards?" asked Kaivon.

Esme shook her head. "Nothing."

There was an invisible border between the Ilkhanate and the Chagatai khanate. It was not patrolled or manned, so moving warriors from one territory to the next had proven to be surprisingly easy. Each day, they trickled a handful of men into the city. This kind of warfare required speed, more than a large number of warriors. Kabul was a thriving city, with several marketplaces selling local produce that was transported both east and west. There were always people coming and going.

Esme checked that they weren't being followed, and once she was satisfied, they went to the meeting point. Twenty Persian warriors were waiting for them in a warehouse. All but three of them were new recruits. The others were two veterans and a junior Persian officer that Kaivon had fought beside under Hulagu Khan. Today, it would be twenty-one men against ten. The odds were heavily in their favour. Surprise was also on their side. It should be simple, and yet, Kaivon was still nervous. Plans could, and often did, go wrong.

"It will be fine," murmured Esme, squeezing his hand. He forced a smile and gathered the men together.

Kaivon noticed the young men were staring at him with something approaching reverence. He'd tried to explain the truth to them. They'd listened but hadn't really heard a single word he said. They all believed he was a risen martyr. Everyone knew the story of when he had been burnt to ash in front of the whole army. To see him whole, and in command again, was inspiring. Esme had told him to stop trying, and to use the adoration to make sure they followed orders. If they truly believed he was holy, then they might do as they were told. It still made him extremely uncomfortable, but for now, he left it alone.

"You all know what we have to do. We've rehearsed this." Kaivon stared at each man in turn, trying to impart some of his confidence. They weren't boys anymore, but they all still looked so young to him. Kaivon was reminded of the time he and his brother had led rebels against the census office. Everything had fallen apart. Almost everyone had died, and soon after, the southern rebellion had dissolved. The memory left a lump in his throat that wouldn't go away.

"Hit them hard, and if something should go wrong, run. Don't follow them. Don't get caught up in a prolonged fight. Try not to seriously injure anyone else. If someone gets in your way, or tries to restrain you, do just enough to get away."

"Get back here as fast as you can," said Esme. "If it's not safe, I will mark the door with red paint. If that happens, fall back to the old carpet shop. If that's not safe, leave the city immediately. We meet two miles due west. You all know the place. After that, you'll be returning to the training camp to await further orders."

Kaivon wanted to say something more. Some final words of wisdom, but looking at their eager faces he knew it would fall on deaf ears. They were desperate to prove themselves, to him and to the world. Most of them were young men who thought they were immortal. In their minds, victory had already happened. This was just a formality. None of them were thinking about what it would feel like to kill someone. To see the fear and pain in the eyes of their victim. To feel the warm splash, and accidentally taste the blood of a dying man.

"Be safe," said Esme, giving his hand a final squeeze. Kaivon didn't need to say it. She knew exactly what he was feeling.

"Let's go," said Kaivon.

The group left the warehouse in pairs. Each of them took a slightly different route to the mosque to make it less conspicuous. A short time after noon, they were all in place, scattered throughout the streets. From his position in the shadows beside a carpet shop, Kaivon could see some of the others, but not all. He had to trust they were there and had not run into any problems along the way.

Kaivon had always found waiting to be a challenge. In the moments before a battle, his stomach would clench, his heart would race, and his mind would run through different scenarios. Today was so different from a coordinated battle that it made him even more anxious. There were so many unknown factors and small things that could go wrong. As ever, all he could do was trust in the plan, and if the worst should happen, try to adapt and still get the job done. Bas, the young man beside him, was wide-eyed and anxious. The reality of what they were about to do was hitting him.

"Just breathe," said Kaivon. "Deep and even."

Bas nodded and swallowed hard. His breathing trembled, but at least he didn't run.

There was a faint rumble, and then the double doors to the mosque flew open. A crowd of men emerged, all of them talking and not really paying attention to their surroundings.

Kaivon immediately moved towards the flow of bodies, merged with the group, and walked against the tide. Some from the crowd had stopped a short distance from the doors to talk. Others hurried away, presumably heading back to their home or business. He was vaguely aware of Bas on his right, but Kaivon didn't have time to check on the others that were positioned throughout the crowd.

Finally, he spotted the targets. The intelligence they'd been given had proven reliable. There were many who did not like Timur. Not only what he had done, but how he had done it. A man such as him had many enemies, and many knives waiting in the shadows.

Their targets were ten men dressed in disparate armour. None of them were carrying weapons, but all of them had a red strip of cloth tied around their right arm. There was a crude symbol stitched into the material, but Kaivon didn't have time to identify it. He didn't need to study it to know that they served Timur.

Although all men were supposed to be equal, the other supplicants gave the warriors a wide berth. Everyone knew exactly who they were and, more importantly, who they served. That was far better protection than any armour or weapon. Or so they thought.

The ten men were oblivious, talking and laughing amongst themselves. Kaivon reached behind his back, slipped out the long knife and held it flat against his forearm. He sensed the others drawing near, and saw flickers of movement on either side.

The converging of twenty men was drawing attention from others in the crowd. This was the riskiest part of the plan. A stranger might realise what was about to happen and shout a warning, alerting the targets. There were a few grumbles and complaints in the crowd, but Timur's warriors remained unaware.

Kaivon moved to stand beside one of the targets, risked a glance and saw that all of the others were ready. He heard someone inhale in alarm, but didn't wait for it to become a scream.

With a downward stabbing motion, he sank the point of the blade deep into the man's shoulder. All around Kaivon, the screaming began. Knives rose and fell, blood gushed into the air, and the crowd dissolved as everyone ran for their lives. Bas slashed their target across the back, once, twice and then he stopped. The others were still going, making sure their victims would die. All Kaivon could hear was the squelch of steel biting into flesh. His nose filled with the stink of blood. The whimpers of the dying rang in his ears.

Kaivon left his weapon buried in his victim's shoulder. The pain from his wounds made the warrior drop to his knees, giving Kaivon a view of the other targets. Nine men were on the ground, gurgling their final breaths, wheezing, dead eyes staring.

"Move. Now!" said Kaivon. "Go."

He didn't wait. He simply turned and ran, crying out in alarm, pretending to be another person fleeing for their life. He ran down an alley, around a corner and then sprinted to the end of another lane before he skidded to a halt. Kaivon checked his clothing and found that they were spattered with blood, but it hadn't soaked through his coat to the shirt beneath. Even so, there was still too much to hide. Kaivon pulled off his coat and tossed it onto a low roof.

Pounding footsteps made him reach for his other dagger. Kaivon relaxed when he saw that it was Bas, sprinting around the corner. The young man's face was pale. Their target was supposed to live, and judging by the superficial wounds they'd given him, with luck, he would survive. Even so, Bas had seen what the others had done to their targets, and it had left an indelible mark. There were a few spots of blood on his face, but he was otherwise physically unmarked by the ordeal. Kaivon wiped it off his chin, checked the young man's hands and, finding them clean, propelled him forward.

"Walk, slowly. Just as we planned."

Every muscle of Kaivon's body urged him to run. To get as far away from the danger as fast as he could. He could feel Bas's body trembling beside him and knew that the young warrior was suffering from the same internal struggle. Following the route that had been set out, they took a winding path back to the warehouse, but stopped a short distance away down the street.

"My legs are shaking," said Bas. He was still in shock and sweating profusely. He reeked of fear, just like their victims had in the moment before they'd died.

"Wait here. I'll check the street," said Kaivon.

Trying to act as casually as possible, he walked down the road. Kaivon even managed to pause at a shop window, pretending to be interested in the leather goods inside. Although his eyes were staring straight ahead at the glass, he was actually scanning the area behind him for any signs of trouble. Finding nothing amiss, he carried on, but then walked past the door of the warehouse. He circled around the street and came up behind Bas, nearly scaring him to death.

"It's clear," said Kaivon. "Remember, slow and steady."

Bas was trying hard not to look scared, but all Kaivon could see was the boy he must have been a few years ago. Although Bas now had a full beard, which hid part of his face, such a thing did not make him a man. The walk down the street seemed to take forever, but they made it to the warehouse without drawing any undue attention.

They were the first to return, which was slightly worrying, but Kaivon didn't say anything as Bas had enough to deal with. Inside the building the air was cool, and Kaivon heard Bas's teeth rattling together. He found an old blanket and wrapped it about the boy's shoulders, waiting for the shock to pass.

They sat together in silence for what felt like a very long time. When the door finally opened, it was Esme who was first through. Bas managed to shrug out of the blanket when the hinges squeaked again, as some of the other warriors were returning. One or two were smiling, pretending they were fine, but in general there was a visible shift in their attitude. When someone made a joke, Bas chuckled along with the rest, but the laughter sounded forced. Kaivon was pleased to see all twenty men had returned.

The work was vital, but it was also brutal. Taking a life was never easy, but it had been necessary. Kaivon hoped the young warriors would learn the right lessons from today. This had been nothing more than another training exercise for them, but it had also served as a useful distraction from the real mission.

The men they had killed were the enemy, but they were nothing more than pawns. Junior officers and a few hirelings on a supply run. In the grand scheme, it would make little difference in the upcoming war against Timur. But on the other hand, even a large beast could be felled if it were stung enough times. Kaivon tried to be optimistic about its long-term impact, but he had doubts. News of this attack would probably not even reach Timur and would be dealt with by someone else. That meant they just had to work even harder.

"You know what to do," said Kaivon, gesturing for one of the veterans to take over. He led all of the men away, leaving Kaivon alone with Esme. They sat together in silence for a while, listening to the creaking timbers.

"How did it go?" asked Kaivon.

"It was a little rushed, but we managed it," said Esme. "All of the supplies have been tainted. It won't be obvious, and the effects shouldn't be noticed straight away. Once ingested, it will take a few days."

As a healer, she knew how to repair the body, but also how, with a few minor adjustments, to inflict crippling pain and even death. While they had launched their attack at the mosque, Esme and four of her contacts from the House of Grace had carried out their mission. The supplies Timur's men had been sent to collect had been poisoned. Disease, plague,

and even a bad belly could cripple an army. Kaivon had seen
it happen before, and it was never pleasant. Mongol armies
were renowned for their speed, but if a warrior couldn't ride,
it didn't matter. Poisoning the horses would have been easier,
but they could be replaced more easily than warriors.

Once the survivor from the mosque attack had recovered,
he'd carry on with his supply run. He'd not only spread word of
what had happened, but would also take the tainted food back
to Timur's army. It was another small delay, hopefully the first
of many, to buy Temujin enough time to rebuild the Ilkhanate.
Thinking too far ahead worried Kaivon, as the future was still
bleak. Instead, all he tried to do was focus on the next mission,
and hope that their efforts would be enough.

CHAPTER 5
The Twelve

One had always been careful in arranging meetings for the House, but now that she was under increased scrutiny, she was meticulous. As the owner of several businesses, it was perfectly normal that, from time to time, she would meet with those in charge.

Today, she was sitting down with the men who ran one of the caravansaries in the city. She was there to check their accounts and to inspect the facilities, looking for any improvements or repairs that were needed.

On her way there, One noticed a familiar face in the crowded street. It was someone that she had recently seen on two separate occasions. Guyuk was desperate to find something untoward that she could report back to the new khan, in a vain hope that it would mean a return to power.

Like his father before him, Temujin had a host of people waiting on him in the throne room. Advisors, minor nobles, sons of important people wanting to learn or just observe a seat of power. The room was always overflowing with a crowd of different faces, curios from overseas and sycophants. The Empress had been reduced to one of the mob. Just another voice, fighting to be noticed, begging for a scrap of the khan's attention. Her power had been significantly diminished, but not her ambition or ruthlessness. One knew it would be a mistake to underestimate Guyuk, even in her current position.

After an hour of exploring every room of the caravansary, One sat down to study the ledgers. She had several people who normally did this kind of work for her, but from time to time, it was good to shake things up. It kept everyone on their toes, and while she didn't mind a little skimming, she wanted to make sure they were not fleecing her.

When the two men left her alone in their office to go back to work, they looked a little worried. Her inspection had not prevented visitors from coming in and out of the building. There was a lot to be done, and she was perfectly happy to be left alone for a couple of hours. A cursory glance at the books showed that everything was in order, but she kept perusing until the first of the Inner Circle arrived.

Some were there on official business. Other members had slipped in with other visitors to the caravansary, but all of them had taken extra precautions. One felt the absence of her sister, but she respected Esme's choice, and was immensely proud of her. Two other women were absent, Three and Six, making the group feel even more incomplete than normal.

"Four, Eight, what news from Europe?" asked One.

"Little that is new," said Four. "The Church is fully committed to this new Crusade. They are not relenting, and are pouring a lot of money and holy warriors into the assault. With the khanates caught up in civil wars, they believe they can defeat the Mamluks and finally reclaim the Holy Land."

This was not the first Crusade, but it seemed as if the Pope was determined to make it the last. In the past, the Church had gained territory only to be driven out by those they called infidels. The land was soaked in so much blood, One was surprised anything grew there anymore.

"An appeal has been made to the King of France for aid, but

he's reluctant," said Eight, picking up the story. "Even so, the conflict is not going to stop any time soon. Neither side will relent, and any kind of negotiation is impossible."

"How is the mood in the Golden Horde?" asked One, turning towards Five, who blew out her cheeks.

"Jumbled. There are some in Sarai that fully support Berke Khan and his bid to wage war on the Ilkhanate. Others think that while Europe and Egypt are tied up in a war, he should make peace with Temujin, then they could work together to expand the Empire. Some want to focus on spreading Islam through peaceful means, while others would prefer to use the sword."

"What is our noble khan doing about it?" asked Two, curling her lip.

None of them were happy that she was working for Temujin, but they understood she had not been given a choice about becoming his Trade Minister. Also, the role gave her direct access to a lot of useful information about how the Ilkhanate was being run. At the moment, One had done nothing out of the ordinary. She'd continued to run operations like the Empress before her, but when the time was right, the knowledge she had access to would be extremely beneficial for the cause.

"Temujin sent letters to Berke, but has received no response. The messengers were not harmed, which was surprising." One knew Temujin had been talking with his father, but she hadn't been able to discover what had been said. Even she couldn't get someone into the cells without them being noticed. "Temujin will have to deal with the Golden Horde soon. He cannot focus on the threat of Timur with an enemy at his back."

"*He will have to visit in person,*" signed Twelve. One thought she looked tired. She suspected her old friend had been working too hard, but she would not slow down. "*Berke will see diplomacy and negotiation as weakness. Mongols are conquerors, not diplomats. He may follow Islam, but Berke is still a warrior at heart.*"

"She's right," said Two. She had her walking cane with her today, and was leaning against a table to ease her bad hip. "He will not respond to threats. Berke will see them as promises from a weak man. A show of force is needed, but Temujin doesn't yet have the numbers."

"He has other powers at his disposal," said One. Several of the women grimaced, and a couple made the sign of the cross on their chests.

"What of the others?" asked Twelve, leaning forward in her chair. *"Maryam and Behrouz."*

"There has been no sign of them. Everyone at the palace says Temujin is on edge, and I think he fears their return." Servants frequently gossiped among themselves. A few new hires at the palace shared what they learned with One, via an intermediary.

"A problem for another day," said Ten, keeping them on track. "We can only do so much."

"We still need to know how to kill these Kozan," said Eleven.

It galled all of them to be indirectly working for Temujin, using their network of contacts to help him rebuild the Ilkhanate. But every member of the Inner Circle understood that, at the moment, he was not the biggest threat to Persia. However, when the time was right, the new khan needed to be removed.

"They can be injured, and therefore can be killed," said Twelve. *"They bleed like us, but they can also heal themselves. A knife through the heart, or cutting off their head would work. No one can recover from that. They are still human."* The others waited for Twelve to explain how she knew such things, but her hands remained at her side.

"Then when the time comes, we shoot Temujin with a dozen arrows," said Eleven, hungry for blood.

"Or send the Widow after him," said Four. The others were too busy grimacing with distaste, but One saw the thirst in the eyes of Four. Most days, she walked the path of a Christian, but there were times when she was as hungry for vengeance as the rest of them.

"Has there been any news from your sister?" asked Two.

"Only one letter," said One, smiling at the memory of her sister's handwriting. "Kaivon's gamble seems to have worked. Temujin is giving them what they need, and in return, they are carrying out strategic attacks in the Chagatai khanate. They also have someone within Timur's camp, but obviously she didn't say who it was."

It was dangerous work, but One also knew her sister's mind. Like Twelve, she would not relent until the work was done, or she was dead.

"I'm sure she's being careful," said Ten with a sympathetic smile.

"You've been unusually quiet," said One, turning towards Seven. In fact, she had not said a single word since arriving. One would have said she was distracted, but Seven had been closely following their conversation. "Do you wish to add anything?"

"I will say it, since no one else seems willing," said Seven. "Why is the House now helping our enemies? Why are we using our precious resources to support Temujin? This is madness."

"You know why," said One, not having the patience for one of Seven's dramatic outbursts. She should have been an actress. It was a job that would have suited her.

"Temujin will have a strategy of his own," said Seven. "One that he hasn't shared with anyone. How can we possibly beat him if we don't know what he's planning?"

"The same way we always have," said Two, "with patience, subtlety and care."

"Slow and steady," sneered Seven.

"I know all of you are frustrated," said One, raising her voice to stall any more interruptions. "I feel the same way, but for all of his powers and his position, Temujin is just one man. The House of Grace has existed for hundreds of years, and it will be around for a long time after he is dust."

"We will decide the fate of our nation, not him," rasped Twelve. Her grating voice startled many in the room. They had never heard her speak out loud before. Twelve's hands twitched as she fought the urge to sign. "Remember that we are the knife, subtle and quiet," she said, repeating the mantra often quoted to new members.

A loud knock at the door startled everyone, making them jump. "Madam, a messenger has arrived from the palace. The khan requests your presence."

She knew it wasn't really a request but an order. If Temujin had sent a messenger, then it was urgent.

"I'll be there shortly," said One. She listened to the footsteps withdraw before she relaxed. With no other pressing news to discuss, they ended the meeting. The Inner Circle dispersed around the building, and a short time later, One left the room via the main door. As she walked out of the caravansary, One spotted Two arguing with a merchant over the price of a shipment of rice.

"How much?" said Two in a loud voice, drawing the focus of many. "Do you want me living on the streets, begging for food?"

The merchant paled as her tirade continued, making One smile. The price was only a little steep, but the argument served as an excellent distraction for some of the others to slip away unnoticed.

Seven's words rang in her ears all the way to the palace. It wasn't as if One had forgotten who Temujin was, and what he represented. So far, he had been respectful and had showed One as much leniency as he could without favouritism, but she wasn't fooled. He was not her friend or ally. He was still a Mongol. An invader and occupier of her home. He was also a Kozan, which added a new layer of danger. But Twelve was right. Temujin might sit on the throne today, but so many dangers surrounded him, One did not think he would last very long. To survive in such a hazardous environment, he would need to be more ruthless than his enemies, and she didn't think it was in him.

By the time Kimya stepped into the throne room, she was surprised to see the crowd of onlookers was considerably larger than usual. As she approached the throne, most of them stood aside out of respect. A few people hurried into the room after her, red-faced and dishevelled. At least she wasn't the last to arrive. Everyone had been summoned in haste, which meant it was an important meeting.

Four Kheshig strode into the room ahead of Temujin. He still resembled a monk more than a khan. His grey robe was plain and unadorned. He wore no armour and carried no weapons. His face was bare and his skull freshly shaven. If he had been barefoot and chanting, it would have fit better with his image. But when Kimya looked into his eyes, all thoughts of him being a holy man evaporated. Most of the time, his emotions were held firmly in check. Today, a terrible cold fury radiated from behind his eyes. She had the impression that he'd also been summoned, or at least manoeuvred into having this meeting.

The doors were thrown open by guards and a stranger entered. He was a young handsome Latin, with dark curling hair and a tidy beard. The most striking feature was his blue eyes, which sparkled and danced with mischief. A smile tugged at the corners of his mouth, but it vanished as he approached the throne, bowing low.

"Greetings Lord Khan," said the stranger in a loud voice. "My name is Marco Polo. I bring gifts and warm tiding from your uncle, the Great Khan."

Four servants shuffled into the throne room carrying two heavy chests between them. They lugged them to the front of the room, then scurried away. Marco opened one chest and then the other with a flourish, like a performer on stage. Dipping his hand into one, he came out with a small green glass vial which he held aloft.

"The finest, most expensive and delicate perfume from the east," said Marco, tipping the bottle slightly to one side. "This one bottle took six years to make, gathering nectar from rare autumnal flowers that grow high in the mountains."

It seemed an odd gift to Kimya. She guessed that it had been intended for Hulagu's wife and Empress, but the Venetian didn't mention that. He produced more presents for women from the first chest, including delicate silks, a platinum choker and a pair of rings with huge emeralds. The other chest was full of gifts designed for a warrior. An armoured shirt. A curved dagger encrusted with gemstones, and a peculiar pair of what resembled miniature scythes connected to a thin metal chain.

Temujin's face had shifted into the familiar mask, giving little away about his true feelings. There was no way to know if he was pleased with the gifts or not. Undeterred, Marco pressed on, speaking mostly to the crowd who made appreciative noises.

The gifts were nothing more than trinkets. Objects being shared between conquerors from lands they had decimated and stripped of wealth. The real reason for Marco's visit, and his actual gift, had yet to be revealed.

"What news from the east?" said Temujin before Marco could pick up another item.

Here, the merchant paused. From inside his clothing, Marco produced the golden paiza. The three-foot golden tablet was inscribed with script that essentially made him untouchable within the Mongol Empire. Anyone who failed to show the bearer the proper respect would face the wrath of the khan, and in this case, the Great Khan. Tucked into the leather pouch with the paiza was a bundle of letters which Marco passed to Rashid, the khan's vizier.

The old man licked his lips, clearly wanting to read the letters, but instead he handed them directly to Temujin. Gone were the days when Rashid would read all of the khan's letters first, then deal with those he deemed to be low priorities. Now, everything went directly to Temujin. Guyuk was not the only one whose power had been greatly reduced.

A silence settled on the room as Temujin stared at the letters. Marco said nothing and waited, showing no signs of impatience or discomfort. After being in Kublai's court, he was probably used to the peculiar whims and moods of his own khan.

"Did my uncle send you with a message?" said Temujin eventually.

"He did, Lord Khan," said Marco. "I am to inform you that the unholy war that was started by his brother, Ariq, is now at an end. Ariq's forces have been defeated, and he has been imprisoned. Despite all that he has done, the Great Khan loves his brother and would see that no harm comes to him. Mongols do not kill Mongols."

It was a saying that had not been true for some time. Although it wouldn't happen immediately, Kimya suspected that once he had been forgotten, Ariq would suffer an unfortunate accident. One day, he would simply be found dead in his cell. It would not be difficult to make it look like suicide.

Marco's words had the sound of a prepared speech, or at least something that had been rehearsed. He'd probably been working on it during his long journey to the Ilkhanate. Even she had heard of the Venetian, who was famed for his way of describing the world. So much so that it had captured the imagination of Kublai Khan, who had kept Marco in his court and his service for years.

"The Great Khan has now turned his attention to the Song Dynasty, which he will crush with ease," said the merchant. While Temujin buried his emotions behind a blank mask, Marco's shield was a confident smile. Kimya had no idea if he believed what he was saying, but he looked convinced.

She didn't think Kublai's conquest would be that simple, and from the raised eyebrows around her, others thought the same. Marco sounded confident, but then again, he'd had time to prepare. His life, and the livelihood of his merchant family, rested firmly on his ability to convey sincerity. On certain occasions, Kimya could see beneath the mask that Temujin wore, giving her a glimpse of his real emotions. There were no cracks in the Venetian's visage. He'd been wearing it for a lot longer, and was a master at concealing his thoughts.

"Is there more?" asked Temujin.

"Yes, Lord Khan. In addition to the gifts I have delivered, your uncle is sending warriors to aid you with the expansion of the Ilkhanate. In fact, they are already on their way. I was sent ahead, but I expect they will arrive within six weeks, if not less."

This was the real reason for Marco's visit. Many times in the past, Hulagu had called for support from Kublai, and finally here it was.

"How many warriors is he sending?" asked Temujin, leaning forward on the throne.

"Twenty thousand veterans," said Marco.

"That is most generous," said the young khan.

Marco winced as if uncomfortable. Kimya didn't know if this was part of his performance or genuine unease. "Lord Khan, I was told there is a new enemy in the south."

"Yes, what of it?"

"There was a second part to the message, but I believe it was intended for your ears only."

Marco was still smiling, but Kimya noticed a little perspiration trickling down the sides of his face. He wasn't as infallible as she thought. Then again, when Marco had departed Karakorum, he'd been expecting to deal with Hulagu. So far, he'd done well to cope with the changes. He'd not mentioned the absence of Hulagu. Marco had no way of knowing what this khan would do, and if the stories about his inhuman powers were true.

Temujin took a moment to consider his response. Eventually he gestured for Marco to continue. "What was the rest of the message?" he asked.

"The Great Khan wanted me to stress that his warriors are to be used against this new enemy in the south." Marco swallowed hard and licked his lips before continuing. It was not his place to tell Temujin how to wage war. He might be favoured by Kublai, but he was nothing more than a curiosity. If Temujin killed Marco for being insubordinate, there would be no repercussions. The Great Khan would just find someone else with a silver tongue to keep him amused.

"He also wanted me to convey his wishes, that you resolve the disagreement with the Golden Horde, as soon as possible."

The atmosphere in the room had already been tense, but now it became strained. Even though he had done his best to dance around the subject, Marco had delivered a veiled ultimatum. A visible ripple of shock and fear passed through the crowd of onlookers. Hulagu would have raged and possibly killed the messenger. There was no way to know what Temujin would do with the news.

"And if I don't resolve it quickly?" he said in a harsh whisper.

"His warriors will return home," said Marco.

"Tell my uncle that the Golden Horde will fall in line. Tell him that I gave you my personal assurance."

"I will immediately send him word. Thank you, Lord Khan," said Marco bowing low. He straightened up and was balanced on the balls of his feet, hoping to be dismissed and escape with his life. Instead, Temujin said nothing for a time and merely stared at the merchant.

"Are you not returning to Karakorum?" he said eventually.

"The Great Khan graciously said that once my business here was concluded, I might return to Venice." Even though it didn't show on his face, Kimya heard a faint tremor in Marco's voice. She wondered how long he had been a guest of the Great Khan, unable to return home.

"It must have been a long and tiring journey," said Temujin.

"You will rest here awhile, and be my guest in the palace. I look forward to hearing stories of your journey, told in your famous, colourful style."

"It would be my honour, Lord Khan," said Marco, although Kimya doubted that was true. He would be a prisoner and remain beholden to Temujin's whims until such time as the khan released him, or tired of his latest toy.

Kimya, along with the rest, kept a rigid smile on her face until Temujin had left the throne room. When the door closed behind him, there was an audible sigh of relief and a flurry of conversation. Marco had not moved from the centre of the room. He had been completely forgotten. Kimya saw him deflate and finally wipe the sweat from his brow. A shudder passed through Marco's body, she guessed from exhaustion, fear or both. It was clear he knew just how close he'd come to being burnt to ash.

All of them were nothing more than toys for the khans. Distractions and oddities that they collected. As if people were just possessions to own. Their rule had to end.

Kimya hoped Twelve was right and that Temujin, as a Kozan, could die like any other man. As khan, he was marginally better than his father, but Temujin was still a danger to them all. When the time was right, she intended to make sure he died and didn't come back.

CHAPTER 6
Melchior

In the north of Persia, on the coast of the Caspian Sea, sat a small fishing village. Every morning before the sun rose, local men went out on their boats hoping to fill their nets. It was hard work, but they did it because it was necessary to earn a living and feed their families. It had been this way for a long, long time, ever since Melchior was a boy.

Other places surrounding the village had expanded over time. Tiny, no-named gatherings had become towns and even cities, but this village had barely changed. There were more houses and more people, but they all held to their simple way of life. Families were fed, children grew up and moved away, but some of them chose to stay and fish like their ancestors.

Melchior waited on a small wooden bridge overlooking a lagoon. It was an unusually warm day. Celebrations for the first day of spring were a month in the past. Below him, tiny wooden rowing boats drifted around in the reeds, where children dangled poles in the water. A few coots grumbled, but otherwise it was quiet and peaceful.

One or two people glanced at Melchior, but otherwise they ignored him. He resembled everyone around him enough that they took him for a local. An old man walking by took one look at his face and raised an eyebrow.

"Woman?" he asked.

"No. Family," said Melchior.

The old man grunted. "Even worse. Good luck, boy," he said before shuffling off.

Melchior smiled, thinking of the significant difference in age between them. It had been a long time since anyone had referred to him as a boy.

As a shadow fell over him, Melchior's smile faded. "I'm here. What do you want?" said a familiar voice.

"Do you remember the home you grew up in?" he said, turning to face Katarina. Dark rings circled her eyes, and her cheeks were more gaunt than the last time they had met. Her hair was tied back in an untidy plait that touched her shoulders, and her clothing was worn and dusty.

Katarina shook her head angrily. "I didn't come here for this. We're not going to reconnect over shared memories, then cry and forgive each other for past sins. We are far beyond that and there is no going back. Talk, and I will listen. That is all I agreed to with this meeting."

"No matter what you say, or how much you hate me, you are still my daughter."

"I haven't been that little girl for a long time." Katarina stared out at the water. As the sunlight danced across her skin, he was reminded of her mother. Melchior watched the muscles twitch down the side of Katarina's face. "But in your eyes, that's all I am to you."

"Why do you say that?" he asked.

"Because even now, you still treat me like a child. Instinctively, you always think that I am wrong and you are right. You think I've been deceived, bullied or corrupted into believing Chaos is the right way forward." Katarina laughed and shook her head. "Everything changes over the years, except you. We've had this argument countless times, and I will not go through it again. So, for the final time I will ask, what do you want, Melchior?"

Her usage of his name hurt worse than any insult. She did not see him as her father, a mentor, or even a friend. Truly, they were strangers, and yet he could not treat her the same as the others who stood in opposition. Even though that was what she wanted, more than anything, she was still his flesh and blood. If the opportunity arose to kill the Cynic or the Nordic King, he would not hesitate, but with her, Melchior knew his hand would waver.

"Your warlord, Timur. Will you abandon him?" he asked.

"Why would I? His army grows stronger every day. Soon, he will be powerful enough to crush the Ilkhanate, and then the rest of the Mongols. He may achieve the dream of Genghis Khan, and unite the world under one banner, but I doubt it. In time, another will rise to challenge him, or it will all fall apart. But that is how it should be for true progress to occur. New growth always comes from the ashes of the old."

Staring into her eyes, Melchior was disappointed to see only quiet confidence in her decision. It would have been easier if she had the fervent gleam of a zealot. Or the haunted eyes of someone who had been forced into their position. She had chosen this, by herself, without coercion.

So be it. He would find a way to treat her exactly like the others.

"We will oppose your plans. No matter the cost," said Melchior. A small colourful bird flew past on his left. He caught sight of a blue head and orange chest.

"Will you take direct action?" asked Katarina. She tensed up, in case he tried to attack her, which further saddened him. She really thought he was capable of anything.

"No. As long as your people refrain as well."

"They do not want a war between the Kozan either, but what of Temujin?"

"What about him?" said Melchior. "His plans for the Ilkhanate are his own. He acts as the khan, not one of us. We have not interfered or directed him. He stands alone, like a human."

"I see," said Katarina. "Then, will you get involved if we move against him?"

Staring down at the lagoon, Melchior saw something moving beneath the water. The kingfisher had spotted it too. Moving with blinding speed it skimmed across the surface, dipped its head into the water, and emerged with a fish in its beak.

"We will, because unknowingly, he stands for Order. He will remain unaware of our assistance. It's better if he believes his victories are won on his own merit, just as with your champion."

"This cannot continue indefinitely," said Katarina.

"What are you saying?" said Melchior, turning to give his full attention.

"This ongoing stalemate across the centuries. This relentless back and forth, where we push and pull against each other. First one side gaining an advantage, and then the other. Are you not exhausted?" The question seemed to catch Katarina by surprise. It was as if she had not intended to say it out loud. Melchior thought she was far more tired than even she realised.

"If not Temujin, then the day will come when another will tip the balance, and all of this will be over. For us, at least," he said, gesturing at the world around them. "There are those who believe we have outstayed our welcome, and that our deaths are long overdue."

Katarina shuddered in revulsion as her thoughts inevitably turned to the Servants of Time. It was the only thing any Kozan truly feared. Her hand involuntarily brushed her thigh where one of them had touched her. If not for his interference, it would have killed her.

Despite his many centuries of walking the Earth, Melchior had found no clues about their origin. Several attempts at communicating with the Servants, in the hope of finding some common ground, had come to naught. He did not think they were mindless creatures. There was cunning and ruthlessness in their demeanour. They were also relentless, and acted with a purpose of their own. What that was, or who had tasked them with it, he still didn't know. There were few mysteries left for him to unravel, but this was one that frustrated him.

"Do you want all of this to end?" asked Melchior, noting her melancholy.

"My life? No. This endless war? Yes." Katarina spoke in a whisper, as if afraid of being overheard.

Moving slowly, so as not to draw attention to what he was doing, Melchior scanned the surrounding area for observers. It took a while, and they were a great distance away, but eventually he found one. They were well concealed, but Eraj had never paid much attention to nature, nor his impact upon it. Animals had always shied away from him. It was as if they could instinctively sense a predator, and someone of malicious intent. A clutch of songbirds were cawing at the interloper in their midst. Melchior saw a flash of red in response amongst the reeds.

"Is it spider poison?" said Melchior, while rubbing his beard. It was unlikely Eraj could read lips from so far away, but just in case. Katarina turned to face him, putting her back towards her ally.

"What are you talking about?"

"I know Eraj is behind you, pointing a crossbow at my chest. I'm assuming the bolt is poisoned?"

Katarina shrugged. "It was insurance, in case you tried anything. He won't fire unless I get into trouble."

A small part of Melchior was tempted to end it now. He could snap Katarina's neck, then Skim to where Eraj was hiding. By the time he realised what was happening, Melchior could be standing over him, and then cut the Cynic in two. Then again, he'd always been sly and mercenary. The moment he moved against Katarina, Eraj would turn and run. He would not cry out in shock, or make an attempt at vengeance for the loss of his friend.

In all the years they'd been on opposite sides, Eraj had never once attempted a direct attack against Melchior. It was always through intermediaries, and only when the odds seemed to be in his favour. Even then he'd failed, but unlike many, Eraj learned from his mistakes.

"We will continue as before," said Melchior, addressing Katarina in a formal tone. "We will not directly interfere with your human champion, as long as you do the same with Temujin. Let them make their own choices, up to a point, at least."

Melchior thought the war to come would be a horrific waste of lives, but there was no avoiding it. A final conflict to decide the fate of the Mongol Empire was inevitable. All he and the other Kozan could do was try to minimise the damage and its impact upon the world. Although it seemed as if the Mongol Empire had either consumed or was battling with every nation in the world, there were still some countries that had never heard of them. It was far better for them to remain ignorant for as long as possible.

"This war will change the world for the better," said Katarina with a smile. She was truly pleased by what was to come. "You'll see."

Melchior had nothing more to say. He knew that anything else would be wasted breath. No matter what he said, she would not listen. When he didn't respond, she shrugged, as if it didn't matter, but her mouth was tight.

She left him standing on the bridge looking out across the water to where Eraj was hiding. A short time later, the reeds moved and the Cynic withdrew. When another shadow fell across him on the bridge, Melchior forced a smile, even though his heart was heavy with regret. There were many things in his long life that he wished he could change. Many mistakes he would correct, if only it were possible to go back in time. But for all of their powers, the past was unreachable and resolute. What had happened with Katarina was chief among the stones that weighed on his soul.

"Was it just the Cynic?" he asked.

"Yes, Teacher," said Behrouz. "You should have let me kill him. Then the three of us could have hunted down Teague and ended this, once and for all."

"She wants it to be over," said Melchior. Much to his surprise, he realised his eyes were wet. He let the tears run into his beard, amazed that even after all this time, his heart could still ache. It was not the only thing, but sentiment, and the hope that a familial connection still existed, were partly responsible. How much pain could have been spared if he had let go of her sooner?

"Then, is this the final battle?" asked Behrouz.

"Yes," said Melchior. "It must be."

Rise or fall. After all, letting humanity decide its own fate was what they believed. If there was no opposing force preventing Chaos from making it worse, then he and the others would finally be able to rest. There was much of the world Melchior had yet to see. Secrets to unravel, and mysteries to try and explain in a rational manner. The notion of becoming an explorer was immensely appealing. Or perhaps he would find a tiny remote island and live in isolation for the rest of his life.

"If the moment comes, and you have a chance to end it, do not hesitate," he said. "I will tell Maryam the same when I see her."

"Are you certain?" asked Behrouz.

Melchior knew what he was asking him. There had been opportunities in the past. "Don't hold back," he said. "All of the other Kozan must die."

"As you say, Teacher," said Behrouz with a sad knowing smile. A long time ago, he'd also had a family, but seeing them age and die, over and over again, had been too much. Since that time, Behrouz had not fathered any more children. His bloodline ended with him.

They embraced, and then Behrouz Skimmed away south and east, back towards Timur and his army.

Melchior wondered if Katarina was right. Was he truly incapable of change? If there was no war to fight, what would he do?

CHAPTER 7
Temujin

Pain is a great teacher. It was the sort of thing Temujin would expect his father to say. A half-remembered phrase, taken out of context, and twisted around to serve his own purpose.

For Temujin, pain was a warning. It told him to stop. To run. To escape whatever was causing it. But sometimes, pain had to be endured. Not for the sake of penance, but to fully realise his limits. And sometimes, to try and understand the nature of that which was mysterious and unknown.

The Servant of Time glared at Temujin, its face mere inches from his own.

He was temporarily safe within a Rigour of his own making, but each passing second was a new study in enduring agony. The pain never diminished, and he never got used to it. There was no muscle to strengthen. His whole body throbbed, as if his skin had been set on fire. His nerves burned, and there was a deep ache in his bones.

The burning heat inside Temujin was like a candle in comparison to the waves of hatred rolling off the creature. He could see more clearly now that it was not a man, and never had been. Its limbs were too long. Its neck was crooked, and it had swirling pits of darkness instead of eyes. No mouth, no ears, just smooth unblemished skin on a hairless skull. The rest of its body was obscured by the haze, but he had a vague impression it was wearing some kind of robe. One hand loosely held the reins of its massive beast, which wheezed and huffed, shifting about even while stationary. The other hand rested on the edge of his Rigour, probing and testing for cracks.

It had no mouth, and yet Temujin knew it was speaking. Its raw emotions told him everything. Temujin did not belong, and the Servant's purpose was to remove that which was unnatural.

A fresh lance of agony ran up the nerve from Temujin's ankle to the top of his skull. He stumbled, closed his eyes to blot out the spectre, and carefully released the Rigour, moving back into the normal flow of time.

The stone floor beneath him was cold and damp. Bright-green moss had gathered in corners, and he could smell mould. The faint scamper of tiny feet told him there were vermin, but none were brave enough to approach. Not yet, anyway.

His eyes were heavy, and his body throbbed in time with his pulse. Drenched in sweat, Temujin was desperate to sleep, but he didn't want to wake up and find he was being nibbled by rats.

It took a long time, but he eventually managed to drag himself upright. The pack he was carrying felt as if it had been filled with rocks. Leaning heavily against the wall, he shuffled down the alley. This part of Sarai was poor, and some of the buildings were falling apart and had been abandoned. Temujin shuffled into one empty shell through the stone doorway. It had been stripped of anything useful, and with no doors or windows, the only things gathered inside were dirt and dust. With heavy feet, he made it upstairs, fell into one of the rooms and was unconscious before he hit the ground.

Temujin was so exhausted, he'd expected to sleep without dreaming. Instead, he found himself aimlessly wandering around the abandoned building, while his body lay on the floor.

Hours later, with sunlight dancing across his face, Temujin came awake. Nothing had nibbled on him while he slept, but perched on the windowsill was a scrawny grey cat. It had a chunk missing out of one ear. Its fur was matted and balding in places, and it had only one green eye. On the floor in front of it were three dead rats.

"My thanks," said Temujin. Instead of running away, the cat merely cleaned some of the blood from its mouth, then it waited to see what he did next. As Temujin licked his lips, he tasted blood. The pressure of maintaining the Rigour had caused something to rupture and a nose bleed. Mirroring the cat, he washed his face with water from his pack and the hem of his robe.

The food he was carrying was enough for a full day, but Temujin ate all of it. He offered the cat a piece of meat for watching over him, but it was more interested in its rat buffet. They ate and washed together, Temujin scrubbing his skin clean before dressing in fresh clothes.

It was mid-morning when he arrived at the palace in Sarai, and he felt a little better. Somehow, he was still hungry, and there was a strange lingering ache in his legs. Temujin did his best to ignore all of it. Outwardly he appeared calm and in control, while inside, his stomach churned.

The guards took one look at his impassive face and didn't even try to bar his entry. They must have been warned about him and what he could do, as the fear in their eyes was apparent. Several ran ahead through the hallways, so that by the time he arrived at the throne room, the khan's vizier was waiting.

"Lord Khan," said Gurban, bowing deeply. "My Lord is currently at prayer, but he asked me to make you welcome and that you forgive the slight delay."

They both knew he hadn't been told to make Temujin welcome, but he didn't say anything. He was shown to a richly appointed room and made to wait for Berke to return. Temujin picked at some of the fresh fruit that had been laid out, but otherwise he was too anxious to eat.

Closing his eyes, Temujin meditated, sinking deep into a trance-like state until he became only vaguely aware of his surroundings. The image of the Eternal Fire sprang into his mind. By surrendering to it, the fire washed away his fears, and even the primitive wants of his hungry body.

"My Lord Khan is ready to see you now," said Gurban.

When he opened his eyes, Temujin had no idea how much time had passed. Judging by the angle of the sun on the windows, he guessed it had been at least a couple of hours. The vizier walked ahead of him through the hallways while a pair of guards followed behind at a distance. Both of them were desperate to draw their weapons, but they'd also heard the stories. Temujin knew they were terrified of him. He didn't need special intuition to tell him that.

As he'd expected, there was a significant audience in the throne room. Minor nobles, Mongol warriors, warlords and senior officers from across the Golden Horde. Four of Berke's sons and his First Wife were also in attendance. Ambassadors, religious figures, along with several curios from across the world, which all khans seemed to collect over time. An English knight. An aristocrat with a drooping moustache, dressed in a lace shirt with long cuffs. A black-skinned tribesman from an African nation. There were also faces from across the Mongol Empire. All of them were loyal, or at least in alignment with the Golden Horde and its current ruler.

This was to be a spectacle.

"Lord Khan," said Temujin, giving a short bow. Technically, they were equals, but he showed deference, given that he was in the capital city of the Golden Horde.

Berke stared down at Temujin from atop his throne. "Welcome to Sarai," he rumbled. He spoke as if Temujin was just another visitor that had come to his court. Some random diplomat, begging a favour.

"I have come to offer compensation to you, Lord Khan, for the siege of Baghdad."

Berke didn't react to Temujin's proclamation, but Gurban's eyes lit up at the mention of money. A few in the crowd stirred but remained silent. They were here only at the khan's invitation to act as witnesses. No doubt their true purpose was to spread rumours about the Ilkhanate, and how badly it had treated its neighbour and former ally.

"My father wronged you and I would see that you, and your warriors, are suitably rewarded," said Temujin.

"That's very generous, although a little late," said Berke. His forehead was knotted in concentration. Someone must have schooled him before this meeting about staying in control. Losing his temper would send the wrong signal. Especially to all of the observers he'd invited to witness this political theatre. Berke's knuckles were white on the arms of his throne from the strain.

Temujin shrugged. "As the sole survivor of my family, only recently was I eligible to become ruler of the Ilkhanate. Before that, I had little power to make significant changes." One of Berke's eyebrows crept up his forehead. There were many rumours swirling about what had happened to the rest of Temujin's family. He wanted there to be no doubt as to who was responsible, or the legitimacy of his position as ruler of the Ilkhanate.

"You speak of significant changes. Do you have more planned?" asked Berke.

Temujin could easily predict where this was going, but he wasn't ready to discuss that just yet. "Of course. But first, I would like to heal the wound between our khanates. Now that the Great Khan has defeated his traitorous brother, ours is the only outstanding disagreement across the Mongol Empire."

Berke bristled at his choice of words, despite the fact that Temujin was downplaying the khan's role in causing the rift. After all, Berke had caused it. In a way, Hulagu's reaction had been utterly predictable. What followed had been a pointless battle at Derbent, where thousands of warriors on both sides had died for no reason. Nothing had been gained and no territory taken.

"Indeed," said Berke, though it clearly pained him.

"If we are to fulfil the dream of my great-grandfather, the khanates should be united as one. Then, we can expand the Mongol Empire, fighting side by side. After all, Mongols do not kill Mongols," said Temujin, playing to the audience. They didn't know the full ins and outs of what had happened, only the outcome. Different territories at odds and widespread civil war across the Empire.

Berke thought all of the observers were on his side, but Temujin could see the glee on the faces of some. They did their best to hide it, but it was there in their eyes, and in the subtle lean in their posture. The smartest among them could feel the underlying tension. The idea of an ongoing civil war in the Mongol Empire meant some of their nations would not be at risk of invasion.

"I agree. We should unite the khanates," said Berke. A sly smile crept across his face. "And what better way is there than for all of us to be brothers and sisters?"

"We are already family," said Temujin. "Our blood is the same."

"Our earthly bodies may be connected," agreed Berke, "but not our eternal souls. We should all serve the one true God. If the people of the Ilkhanate were to convert to Islam, I would be happy to put aside our disagreement. Then there would be peace between us."

Berke grinned, thinking himself clever and that he had trapped Temujin. A few in the crowd murmured in agreement. Whether they actually supported Berke or not was irrelevant. He controlled their fate and their lives. It was in their best interest to stay on his good side.

"Are all men equal in the eyes of your god?" asked Temujin.

"None are superior," agreed Berke, happy to speak about his faith. "We are all the children of Adam."

"Then, are you turning your back on your Mongol heritage?" asked Temujin. "Do you put your god before your own people and the Empire? Is that what you want me to tell the Great Khan?"

As Berke started to lose his temper, Gurban smoothly stepped in front of the throne. "My Lord Khan would never put anything ahead of the Empire," said the vizier.

"That's right," said Berke, through gritted teeth.

"Interesting," said Temujin, pursing his lips. "Then why did you side with your Muslim brothers in Egypt over your own people? Why did you sell slaves to them, bolstering their army?"

"That's a lie," said Berke, shaking his head.

"Why did your warriors raid towns and cities along the northern border of the Ilkhanate? Why did you kill your own people? Why did you betray my father?" said Temujin, running his eyes over the crowd. There was a faint rumble of conversation, and a few whispers. People began to look between Berke, barely holding on to his temper, and then at Temujin.

"Those are just foul rumours," said Gurban smoothly. "There is no truth to the stories."

"Isn't lying a sin for a Christian? Don't you fear for your immortal soul?" asked Temujin, putting the vizier on the spot. "I know you have been in regular contact with your counterpart in Cairo. And I know you have been sending slaves to Egypt for years."

Temujin stared at Gurban, waiting for the little man to deny it. To call him a liar to his face. As a khan and ruler, Temujin could kill him with little fear. After all, Gurban was merely a servant. It would inconvenience Berke, but no more than that. Under his glare, the vizier wilted and turned his face away, knowing that if he spoke again it would mean his death.

"Words. Talk. You are weak," spat Berke, finally letting his anger off its leash.

"Do not make this situation worse than it has already become," warned Temujin. "My father killed three of your sons for your betrayal, and for turning your back on your people."

Gurban tried to soothe the khan, but he shook off the little man and stood, trying to assert dominance. "Your father killed a holy man. Hulagu deserved everything that happened to him. As for my sons, they were loyal and brave, whereas your brother begged before he died," said Berke, his voice dripping with scorn. "I wonder if you will do the same."

Berke seemed to have forgotten about the crowd he'd assembled in the throne room. If more than a handful had shared the khan's religious beliefs and his fervour, then perhaps they would have stood with him. Instead, all but one or two looked appalled, chief among them his Mongol officers. It was one thing to wonder if the rumours were true, but another for their khan to boldly admit to betraying the Empire.

"I am a Mongol warrior. It is my destiny to rule. I do not know what you are, boy. You look like some kind of monk to me," sneered Berke, pacing back and forth. "Your words are meaningless and will change nothing. Say what you will about your father, but at least he was a warrior. We met on the battlefield of Derbent, and it was glorious. I wonder, will you do the same?"

"You would have me fight you, and waste more Mongol lives in a pointless battle?" asked Temujin. "We should be fighting against our common enemies, not each other."

Berke knew he had made a mistake. He'd shown everyone where his true allegiance lay. But he was too angry, proud and stubborn to try and fix it before it became irreparable.

"I do not know what you are," said Berke again. "But you are not a Mongol."

"And you are not fit to lead the Golden Horde," said Temujin.

"Get out of my sight, before I have you killed!" shouted Berke. His face was flushed with anger, but also embarrassment. He didn't call for the guards to escort Temujin out, nor did he give the order to kill him. Perhaps he knew that it would be pointless. Stories of what Temujin had done to the walls of Aleppo had spread. In addition, there were rumours about him slaying a hundred Kheshig with his bare hands.

"I will return," said Temujin, "and when I do, I hope that you will see reason and join forces with the Ilkhanate."

Berke slumped into his throne, breathing hard. He had been embarrassed, shamed and exposed in his own palace. Temujin walked away, leaving him to stew over what had happened.

As he walked through the streets of Sarai, Temujin received a few curious glances, but without guards or insignia to announce his title, most people assumed he was a monk. He passed a couple of men who were similarly dressed in simple robes with shaven heads. The mood in the city was relaxed. They were a long way from any fighting or the battle of Derbent. Ordinary people in the street didn't care who was khan, as long as they were free to live their lives.

As he passed down a wide street, Temujin paused before the remains of a scorched building. Once, it had been a tall and elegant structure. He could see the remains of a spire. It was charred and broken, but a few windows with coloured glass had survived. The roof had collapsed, and clouds of ash were swirling around as men crawled over the wreckage.

A crowd had gathered. Temujin merged with them, listening to their conversations. The general mood was outrage and a deep sadness.

"What has happened, grandmother?" asked Temujin, asking a woman beside him. She had a deeply lined face, silver-grey hair and a bent back. Her eyes were kind and her cheeks marred with tears.

"It was a beautiful church," said the woman. "Some young men thought it was a blight on the city. They burnt it to the ground."

"Fools," said someone else.

Temujin felt a faint stirring in the air and glanced around. No one else had noticed the breeze, suggesting it was unnatural in origin. It was only because he was searching for the source that he saw the woman step out of thin air.

She'd appeared in the shadowy mouth of an alleyway. Even if someone had spotted her, they would have thought it a trick of the light.

He didn't need to see her different coloured eyes to know that she was a Kozan. With dusky skin and a light-blue headscarf wrapped about her head, she easily blended in with the crowd. From across the street, she locked eyes with Temujin and waited.

He immediately separated himself from the crowd and walked towards her. Unlike most people, it was difficult to read much from her body language, but he thought she was relaxed. She idly glanced at people passing in the street, but her eyes always returned to him. When they were standing face to face, Temujin was surprised to realise she was much shorter than he had thought, barely coming up to his shoulder.

"Shall we take a walk?" she asked.

"I know who you are, but I don't know your name," said Temujin. He had met Melchior and knew of Behrouz, so this had to be the third Kozan on the side of Order.

"You can call me Maryam."

"Lead the way," said Temujin.

Maryam looped her arm through his as if they were family. He tried not to recoil, but she felt his muscles stiffen in surprise. "I'm not going to hurt you," she said, although her smile was feral.

Temujin knew she was someone who, like Eraj, had killed and if necessary, would do so again. She might not be as ruthless as the Cynic, but he sensed she possessed the same level of determination. Anyone that stood in her way would be wise to move aside or risk being run over. The rest was concealed from his heightened intuition, as if hidden behind a layer of fogged glass.

"You sought me out for a reason. So if you're not here to kill me, what do you want?" asked Temujin.

Maryam guided him down the street towards a different part of the city. They merged with the sea of bodies, squeezing through the tide that was filling every available space. If anyone had been following him, they would soon lose his trail.

Temujin heard cymbals and drums, together with dozens of voices chanting something. It was a parade of some kind, but once they were free of the crush, Maryam steered them away towards a park. It was a peaceful oasis with a winding path around a small pond. A few spring bulbs had already flowered, but otherwise the beds held only empty soil. Small birds flitted from branch to branch in the bare trees above their heads. It was a soothing place, but Temujin could not relax in Maryam's company.

"I am here to give you two warnings," she said.

"I am under no illusions about my abilities," he said. "I know that any of the other Kozan could kill me."

"That's true. You have the potential, but you are not a Kozan," said Maryam. "As such, we have all agreed to treat you like a human. Even so, the others may still break the accord and try to kill you."

"Then why haven't they tried yet?" asked Temujin.

Maryam shrugged. "Maybe they don't see you as a credible threat. But if you continually interfere in their plans, they may change their minds."

"I see," said Temujin. "And will you try to stop them?"

"We will, but there's no guarantee we'll be successful." He understood exactly what she was saying. Essentially, he was on his own. Even with all of their abilities, they could not be everywhere all of the time.

"Thank you for the warning." Events were moving faster than Temujin had anticipated. "And what was the second warning?"

"It's about Berke Khan. You will not change his mind with words. You need to try a different approach."

"I've already been given this lecture by my father," said Temujin.

"Then you would be wise to listen to him," said Maryam.

"Do not lecture me on Mongols," said Temujin. "I know exactly what kind of a man Berke is and how to deal with him."

"I hope so, because there's a lot more at stake than your life. He has a lot of influence, and the Golden Horde is powerful." Maryam paused at the edge of the pond, and for a moment, Temujin thought she meant to drown him. Instead she picked up a pebble and tossed it into the water. Ripples spread out in all directions from the point of impact.

"Are you going to lecture me on cause and effect?" asked Temujin, gesturing at the water.

Maryam snorted. "No, I didn't want the fish getting eaten by that hawk." Hovering not far above their heads was a small bird of prey. With an irritated screech at being denied a meal, it wheeled away to another part of the city. "Not everything is about you."

Instead of embarrassing himself any further, Temujin said nothing. A few silver and red shapes darted about under the water. A stone bridge crossed a section of the pond. Standing atop it was a little girl and her mother, both of whom were staring into the water.

"I take it you have a plan for Berke?" asked Maryam.

"I do," said Temujin, hoping she didn't ask him to go into detail. He was still working out some parts, and his ideas kept evolving. If he tried to explain it rationally, Temujin knew it would sound ridiculous.

"Good. Then I will leave you in peace. Be on your guard."

"Thank you," said Temujin as she turned to go.

"What for?"

"Being honest." Katarina and the others had deceived from the start, never telling him the whole story.

Maryam gave him a long thoughtful look. "You should have joined us, but your fate is now your own. If you survive what is to come, I hope you will reconsider."

This time he saw the air ripple in front of where Maryam was standing. Temujin felt a cold prickle against his skin that made the hairs stand on end. Maryam took two steps away from him, then vanished into thin air. Just before the distortion faded, he thought he saw the black swirling eyes of a Servant of Time. The moment he blinked, the image vanished, leading Temujin to believe he'd imagined it. He certainly hoped so, because it seemed as if the Servant had been staring at him.

CHAPTER 8
Kokochin

It had taken weeks of slow and painstaking work, but Kokochin finally had access to the governor of Lahore.

Thanks to Mehr blackmailing Abban, the tailor, one of Kokochin's people now worked for the governor. After Mehr had been told that a personal aide would soon be leaving, Kokochin made arrangements for an unbeatable replacement.

Abban had enthusiastically recommended one of his many cousins for the vacant position. Of course, he had not actually known this person until a week ago. The governor's senior advisor was a long-time customer, which had given Abban some leeway. He had slightly overstepped the bounds of their relationship by taking part in a personal conversation in his shop. In truth, the senior advisor had been moaning about finding someone who was suitable for the role. So, on this occasion, he'd let it pass without comment, and had been willing to listen.

Now, Nabil followed the governor around for most of the day and was practically invisible. No one paid the aides any attention or spoke directly to them. Most people in the governor's social circles barely noticed they were even there.

The young man had no guile but was exceptionally clever and organised, which appealed enormously to the governor.

It had also made it a lot easier for Nabil to pass the screening process. All of his answers had been direct, to the point of brutal honesty. Although Nabil was a little quirky, his obsessive focus on detail had turned out to be a boon. Finding someone to suit the particular tastes of the governor had proven to be extremely difficult. Kokochin could not have done it without her growing network of locals.

Now, the governor was happy, his senior advisor was delighted, and Abban got to keep his job and his secrets.

"And then he met with the local fort commander," said Nabil, happily regaling Kokochin with every item from the previous week. Since she had arranged it, he saw it as a fair trade to tell her about his job. "After that, he spoke to a group of merchants who were pushing for–"

"What did the fort commander say?" asked Kokochin, cutting in.

Nabil thought on it for a moment. "He rambled on a lot. Mostly about insufficient numbers to defend the city against a Mongol horde. The governor wasn't happy, but eventually they came to an agreement on what they would do when Lahore was invaded."

She noticed Nabil had said when, not if, without realising. He was merely parroting back what he had heard without fully comprehending the nuance.

"And what did they decide?" asked Kokochin, trying not to sound eager.

"That when Timur's forces arrive, they will offer no opposition and an unconditional surrender of the city."

It was what she had expected would happen, but it was good to receive confirmation. Offering no resistance gave the city the best chance of survival and its ability to continue operating before Timur's forces took over. There was also the possibility that the existing governor would get to keep his head, and his job. However, it really depended on who was in charge of the army and the general's mood on the day.

"Has there been any news on when they expect the enemy to arrive?" asked Kokochin.

"Scouts have reported seeing a significant increase in the number of warriors on the road, but none had been heading this way. The commander believes they are warriors returning to the army, now that winter has passed. The rest are fresh recruits who want to join Timur. I wish I had precise numbers," said Nabil, tugging at the sleeve of his robe. It was already frayed from previous occasions when he couldn't find exact details. Not knowing made him fret, and that could lead to an episode.

Nabil's story tallied with what Kokochin had heard from several merchants in the city. A lot of food was being transported east. Enough to feed a large army on the move.

"They will be arriving soon," said Kokochin, thinking out loud.

"Based on everything I've heard in the governor's company, I estimate within seven to ten days' time," said Nabil. "If not sooner."

"Thank you, Nabil, you've been very helpful."

"But I haven't finished telling you everything," he said, tugging on his sleeve again. Another thread came loose in his fingers and drifted to the floor.

"Go ahead," said Kokochin, getting comfortable. An hour later, he had finished talking. In that time, she'd learned a few things that were of interest, but not actionable. Nevertheless, she'd avoided Nabil getting upset, so he left the tea room with a smile.

A short time later, Olma sat down. The tea in the pot had gone cold, but Kokochin gestured towards it.

"No, thank you," said Olma. "I won't stay long."

Kokochin shared the news about the imminent arrival of Timur's forces. Olma reacted in a manner Kokochin had come to expect of the nurse. She merely grunted and rolled her eyes in annoyance.

"With luck, little will change on a day-to-day basis," said Kokochin.

"Luck, and how drunk the general was the night before. Hopefully he won't be in a bad mood when he arrives." As ever, Olma was practical about these things. Kokochin knew it galled both of them that their lives, and countless others in the city, would come down to the whims of one individual and his state of inebriation.

"There's little we can do." Kokochin didn't like it, but she had to accept it.

"Then I take it you will be leaving soon?" said Olma.

"Why would I leave?"

Olma's smile was a rare thing, as it seemed to cause her pain. It slid onto her face but didn't hang around. "I know what you are, even if I don't know who you serve."

"I've underestimated you," said Kokochin, feeling foolish. She had told Mehr her real identity, but not everyone. Thankfully, she knew that Olma wouldn't betray her secret. She was a patriot. As long as their goals aligned, she didn't care who Kokochin worked for.

Olma shrugged. "It happens. But, you would be wise to leave and go back to your home."

"I'm not going anywhere," said Kokochin. The House of Grace wanted her to withdraw, but from the beginning that had never been her intention. There was still a lot of work to be done, and she could best serve the people by remaining in Lahore. "Besides, I don't have a home anymore, except for this one."

She gestured at the meagre shop around them. It was a long way from a suite of rooms in the palace of Tabriz. There were no heated baths here, or servants to attend to her every need. She had no bodyguards, and no weekly stipend to spend on whatever she wanted. It had been a prison, but a very comfortable one.

"I thought you might say that. You're stubborn," said Olma, risking another brief smile. "It's one of the things I like about you."

It had been a long time since Kokochin had laughed. "Thank you, it's nice to be appreciated."

"Everyone needs friends that are honest," said Olma with a shrug. "So, what's next?"

"It's better if you don't know. Did you have something new about the murder victims?" The nurse didn't visit the tea room at night, unless she had new information.

Olma fidgeted in her chair and struggled to make eye contact. "No, I just thought you might want to talk."

"To talk," said Kokochin, drawing out the words.

"Yes, talk. And eat a meal some time. With me. At night."

Kokochin startled Olma by touching one of her hands. "That's very thoughtful, but—"

"You're not interested. Of course. I understand," said Olma. She tried to get up to leave, but Kokochin held her in place by the wrist.

"It's not that. There's someone else." Well, there had been, and it still hurt. Right now, Kokochin wasn't ready for anything new. It would be another distraction, and she needed to focus on the work. "I'd still like us to be friends."

Olma's brief smile was pained for a different reason. "Of course. You have a strong grip," she muttered as Kokochin finally let go. She rubbed her wrist, bobbed her head and went out the door before Kokochin could ask her to stay.

Kokochin pulled on her best cloak, wrapped a colourful scarf around her head and stepped out the back door. The night was still warm and humid, but she knew the temperature would soon drop. Hopefully, her next appointment wouldn't take too long, but if it did, she'd be glad of the cloak.

The Gilded Lily was not the first brothel Kokochin had visited, but it was certainly the most luxurious. The front room had a lot of silk curtains hiding shadowy alcoves where beautiful women waited at ease. Brightly coloured carpets covered the floor, and all of the furniture had been polished to a shine. The air smelled of jasmine and rose, but there was also a faint citrus smell. None of it was overpowering, but the blend was certainly intriguing.

During one of her night-time excursions, her curiosity had led her through some of the pleasure houses in Tabriz. At the time, the volume and the variety of women had astonished her. Here, the owners understood the tastes of the local men, as every woman in the reception area certainly fit a particular style. Curvy with dark hair, demurely dressed, but with clothing that hinted at plenty. Most surprising was that none of the women were particularly tall. A few glanced at Kokochin with curiosity, but none of them approached her. They lounged together in small groups on comfy chairs. All of them had flawless make-up and were dressed in brightly coloured clothing.

"Deliveries and messengers use the back door," said the madam, bustling up to her. A stocky woman with greying hair, the madam barely came up to Kokochin's shoulder. Her clothing was functional, not designed to entice, and her make-up was scant.

"I'm not here for that."

The madam looked Kokochin up and down. "I'm not sure you'd get much work. You'd need fattening up first," she said, pinching Kokochin on the waist. "My clients like curvy women. You're pretty enough, though."

"That's very kind of you," said Kokochin, "but I'm not here for that, either."

The madam stepped closer, searching Kokochin's face for something. A woman in her line of work excelled at reading people. Their intentions, their desires, and their darkest wants. It was probably what had kept her alive and in business for so long.

"Business?" she asked, a curious inflection on the word.

Kokochin wasn't exactly sure what that meant, but she nodded.

"Come back in an hour. Use the back door," said the woman.

An hour later, Kokochin went around to the rear of the building. Set into the door at eye level was a metal grill, which opened the moment she knocked. A man with a thick neck peered out before closing the grill and opening the door. The thug was so large, that as he stepped out to meet her, his bald head brushed the top of the doorframe.

"Arms up," he said in a surprisingly light voice. The madam lurked in the doorway as her eunuch searched Kokochin for weapons. He was thorough but professional, never lingering unnecessarily. "Clean," he muttered.

"Come in, milady," said the madam, treating Kokochin with a little deference.

The rear of the brothel was far less luxurious than the front. The furniture was functional, scarred in places, and the walls were bare stone. Kokochin followed the madam through a storage room, then down a short corridor to an office. The madam sat down behind the desk and Kokochin took the seat opposite. The eunuch closed the door and leaned against it on the inside, effectively blocking the way out.

"Don't mind Carim, he can be trusted," said the madam. "Do you want to give me your name?"

"You don't need to know it," said Kokochin.

"You're new," said the madam, tapping her painted lips with one fingernail. "You're not with one of the gangs, or any of the usual customers."

"Usual customers?" said Kokochin, not sure where the madam was going.

"The ones with dozens of servants. More money than sense."

"No, I represent a particular organisation that's new in the city," which was true, from a certain point of view.

"Go on," said the madam, leaning back in her chair.

"Do you know who Timur is?"

The madam blanched. "Yes. Do you work for him?"

"No, but in a few days, a part of his forces will arrive to take the city. Assuming they're in a good mood, little will change. However, the commanders and senior officers will seek out entertainment for a few days. Maybe a week," said Kokochin, thinking back to when Hulagu's men had returned from a campaign. The first two weeks often passed in a drunken, sex-fuelled haze where they endlessly indulged until they were sated, or until they passed out exhausted or drunk.

"They'll be coming here," said Kokochin, not intending it as a threat, yet it still sounded like one. There were other expensive brothels in the city, but none as famous as the Gilded Lily. If they had enough time, the Mongol officers would sample all of them, but they would start with the best.

On the one hand, it would mean a lot of money flowing through the doors. On the other, the invaders would do whatever they wanted to whoever they wanted. They would take their passions and desires to the extreme, and not even Carim could stop them. If he did interfere, they would kill him, and probably everyone in the building, before burning it to the ground out of spite.

The madam fully understood the ramifications of what Kokochin was telling her. A range of troubled emotions ran across her face. Finally, a grim smile settled.

"When?" was all she asked.

"Soon. Days," said Kokochin.

"So, why are you here?" said the madam.

"I need information. Men talk when they're at ease," said Kokochin. She didn't need to elaborate. The madam knew that very well, and probably had a lucrative side business using that knowledge.

"For someone so important, there are others who will want the same access."

Kokochin didn't know if the madam was trying to raise the price or was simply being honest.

"I'm not here to get into a bidding war. I want to stop them from burning the city to the ground," said Kokochin.

The madam's eyebrows lifted. "You're with a rebel group?"

"Yes. More than that is dangerous for you to know."

Kokochin heard Carim shift behind her. The wooden door creaked under his weight. The madam shook her head slightly, and the big man resettled. Without looking over her shoulder, Kokochin wondered how close she'd come to being stabbed in the back. She had taken a small risk appealing to the madam's patriotism, but thankfully it seemed to have paid off. If the madam had known who she was, greed may have won out. Kokochin could have found herself locked in the store room waiting to be shipped back to Tabriz.

"I have a space where you can listen," said the madam.

"I'm only interested in the general of Timur's forces. The others don't matter to me."

They haggled a bit over the price, but eventually they settled on a fair deal.

"I'll be in touch," said the madam. Kokochin turned to leave and was pleased when Carim stepped aside, letting her out of the office. Fighting him would have been extremely challenging, especially in such a confined space. Looking at the thickness of his neck, she didn't think it was a fight she could win.

Outside, the temperature had fallen, but it wasn't so cold that Kokochin had to rush home. She took her time, watching for followers as usual, but given the hour, she stuck to busy areas. She needed time to think, not only about next steps, but also Olma's interest and why she had turned it down. Kokochin was lonely, and she knew spending too much time alone wasn't healthy. A small part of her hoped she would see Layla again, but in reality, she knew it was unlikely. Kokochin had become someone the jeweller no longer recognised, and in hindsight, someone she no longer knew either. Finding her way forward, to become the kind of person she wanted to be, was complicated enough without entanglement. Perhaps in a few months' time, once she was more settled, Kokochin could think about a romantic life. Of course, that was assuming she survived that long.

A wry smile twisted her mouth as she unlocked the back door of the tea room.

The moment she stepped inside, Kokochin knew she wasn't alone. There was a peculiar stillness in the air. It was as if the room had inhaled and was holding its breath.

"Who's there?" she asked.

Kokochin heard a click, and then someone lit a covered lantern. A faint yellow glow peeled back the darkness inside the shop. She could see the outline of furniture in the room, but little else. A man stepped out of the deeper shadows on her right side. The top half of his face was covered with a grey cloth mask. A thick black beard covered his chin and she saw his teeth flash.

"What do you want?" she asked.

"I hear you've been looking for us," said the man in a gravelly voice.

"Who are you?" said Kokochin, a second before she asked. "What do you mean 'us'?"

A second masked man stepped out of the doorway on her left. "We're the Sons of the White Falcon," he said. "Who are you?"

CHAPTER 9
Kaivon

Kaivon was pacing the room when Esme walked in. He threw his arms around her and tried not to sigh too loudly. She'd been gone far longer than they'd planned.

"I thought something had gone wrong."

"I'm fine," said Esme, talking into his shoulder as she hugged him back. "I'm all right."

For a time, the world disappeared as he kissed her, their tears of joy and relief mixing together. She smelled of dust from the road, but also smoke, as if she'd been standing too close to a fire.

"How about the others?" asked Kaivon, wiping his face.

It was Esme's turn to sigh. "We lost three, but none of them were captured alive."

Ever since the attack on Timur's men outside the mosque, they had been carrying out a series of raids across the Chagatai khanate. Esme and five warriors had gone deeper than ever before, travelling all the way to Islamabad. Timur's army was so large that he had men stationed all across his territory. He was slowly gathering his forces for a major assault against the Ilkhanate, but that took time, and an enormous amount of planning. Esme's target had been the fort in Islamabad. Timur had stationed a large number of men there, but more importantly, a sizeable cache of food. An army could not fight unless it was well provisioned.

"My sister's contact was right. It was mostly dry goods in the fort," said Esme. "It was well-protected, and there were a lot of checkpoints to get inside."

"Since we started our attacks, they've become a lot more cautious," said Kaivon. His most recent mission had been difficult. Although all of his men had escaped, two had later died from their injuries.

"Once we lit the fire, it took a long time to get back out without it looking suspicious." Esme shook her head sadly. "We were almost at the main gate when the guards raised the alarm. Three young men bought our freedom with their lives. Two took on the guards, and the other set fire to the stables. I don't know if many horses were injured, but in the smoke and chaos, we managed to escape."

"Were you followed?"

"I think so," said Esme. "That's why it took us so long to get back. Kaivon, I don't even know their names. Why didn't I ask?"

Kaivon felt Esme's body trembling against him, but she didn't cry. He told himself they were patriots and martyrs who had died to defend their nation. He believed sending young people into dangerous situations was justifiable, but it still wasn't easy.

"Our contact wants to meet with us. He said it was important."

Up to now, their contact had been reliable, but that didn't mean Kaivon trusted him. In fact, he had every reason not to, but these were desperate times and they needed all the help they could get.

"When?" said Esme.

"Today. I was getting ready to leave."

"I'll come with you. I just need to get into something clean."

Esme stripped out of her clothes and ran a comb through her long, dark hair to untangle the knots. Kaivon noticed fresh cuts and bruises on her neck and shoulders. Her escape had been a much closer thing than she'd let on. He knew she could take care of herself against an individual opponent, but right now they were always outnumbered, and that made everyone vulnerable.

"I'll be all right," she said without turning around. Somehow, she'd known he was staring and had noticed her injuries. Esme had more bruises across her ribs and a nasty lump on one hip, which explained why she'd been limping.

"We're meeting him at the pits."

Esme grimaced. "All right, let's go."

Vast amounts of goods flowed back and forth across the Mongol Empire, and this included people. Slave pits existed in every major city across the Mongol Empire, and Kaivon did his best to stay away from them. But today, it couldn't be avoided. Kaivon found slavery abhorrent. In all but name, he'd been a slave, but Esme had actually been captured and sold to Hulagu for her medical skills.

As a defector from Timur's army, their contact Amir-Hossein was justifiably paranoid about being recognised. He always chose incredibly busy places to meet. It made it easy for him to hide in a crowd and for their conversations to go unnoticed. He jumped at loud noises, and twice in the past, Amir-Hossein had run when he thought someone had recognised him.

It was the smell that hit Kaivon first. Streets away from the pits, his nose was assaulted by the awful stench of unclean bodies. The area was always packed with buyers, merchants, moneylenders and slavers and their hired muscle. The city authorities had also stationed pairs of guards around the perimeter to help maintain the peace. Dozens of conversations overlapped in countless languages from across the world. Some he recognised, and he could follow the basics back and forth, but others were not even vaguely familiar. It spoke to the size of the Empire and the number of countries it had conquered.

In the pits, there were several raised platforms where semi-clad men and women were paraded around. Cages holding more slaves, yet to go on display, ringed the space. Tall and short, light-skinned, dark as pitch, and every skin tone in between. At first glance, many were different, but all of them had the same bleak look in their eyes. They had given up and were ready to die. This was the last stop on a long road.

There were other more refined places to buy slaves in the city. Servants for the rich. Those with skills and knowledge, such as the pits where Esme had found herself years ago. This slave pit, however, held the dregs. The unruly. The sick and infirm. The dying and the desperate. One of Esme's hands crept into Kaivon's, and he held it tight.

Due to the press of bodies, their progress through the crowd was slow. Several times they were forced to detour around people haggling over slaves.

"He won't last six months," laughed one man, pinching a slave's arm. "There's nothing to him."

"Nonsense. He's strong," said the slaver. "Show them!" he said, jabbing the slave with a wooden baton. The man grunted, but otherwise didn't react. His eyes remained on the ground, his shoulders hunched. There were already dozens of bruises on his body from previous beatings.

On their left, a naked woman with pale skin had just been bought by an extremely fat man. When he grabbed her by the arm, she broke free of his fingers and ran. She dove off the platform into the crowd while he squawked and waddled after her. Rather than do anything to help, people in the crowd merely watched and laughed at the chase.

The poor woman vainly searched for a way out while the fat man tried to catch his property. When she reached one of the exits, she was turned around by the guards, sending her back towards her new owner. Whenever he came close to catching her, she sprinted away towards another street, only to find it blocked as well. The terror in the woman's eyes was horrific.

Never in her life had she expected to end up here, corralled and sold as an object while onlookers laughed and made bets. It was misery as entertainment. To most of the people here, she wasn't a real person.

Esme tightened her grip on Kaivon's fingers until it became painful. He was just as desperate to intervene, but they had to remain inconspicuous. Swallowing the lump in his throat, Kaivon turned his back on the awful scene and pressed on, pulling Esme along in his wake. There was a final cheer from the crowd. The laughter tailed off, suggesting the chase had finally come to an end. Either the woman had been caught, or she'd been killed. Given her desperate attempt to escape, Kaivon wasn't sure which would be a worse fate.

"Good fun, yes?" said Amir-Hossein, sidling up to them in the crowd. He was short and skinny with a twitchy disposition, as if constantly in withdrawal from a drug addiction. But Amir-Hossein didn't take drugs or drink, and he barely ate out of fear of being poisoned. As usual, there was a distinctive smell of lemon and ginger clinging to his skin. He drank tea all day, claiming it cleansed the blood and prevented illness.

Today, Amir-Hossein was wearing a battered set of clothes dotted with singe marks. He wore a thick apron and a wide belt, all trademarks of someone from a forge. His disguises were always worn and ill-fitting, suggesting he bought or stole them from other people.

When neither of them responded, he just shrugged, leading them to the edge of the slave pits, where it was less crowded. Kaivon counted at least three ways out if Amir-Hossein had to run. As ever, their contact had planned ahead, leaving nothing to chance.

It was cooler here in the shade of two buildings, and Kaivon was glad to get out of the heat. Not far away, he spotted a dozen women chained together sitting on the ground. A bored-looking guard kept an eye on them. His job was easy, as all of the women were broken. None dared even raise their head.

Amir-Hossein pretended to be perusing them, walking slowly down the line, checking their teeth and muscles.

"Why are we here?" said Esme.

Her sharp tone made Amir-Hossein glance at her before he went back to the slaves. "Do you have my money?" he asked.

Apart from being a defector, this was the main reason Kaivon didn't trust Amir-Hossein. Greed was what moved him. He was like a magpie, easily distracted by shiny objects, constantly searching for something brighter and more colourful. Amir-Hossein claimed to have left Timur's army of his own free will, but Kaivon's instincts told him it was something else. He suspected Amir-Hossein had stolen from Timur, and now there was a bounty on his head. Why else would Amir-Hossein be so paranoid?

Kaivon also had a niggling fear that one day, someone from Timur's army would offer Amir-Hossein more money. Then he'd immediately betray them.

Kaivon passed over a pouch of money and Amir-Hossein carefully counted the coins. With a grunt, he tucked it away and moved down to the line to the next slave.

"Virgin?" he said, nudging a grey-haired woman with his boot. The guard laughed, and Amir-Hossein offered him a toothy grin.

"Talk," said Kaivon, not trusting himself to say anything else. He knew Esme really wanted to stab Amir-Hossein in the face. If they didn't need him so badly, Kaivon would have held him down while she did it. For all of his cunning, Amir-Hossein didn't realise he was living on borrowed time with them. At some point, he would outlive his usefulness, and then he'd become a liability. He already knew much of their attacks against Timur.

Amir-Hossein shuffled closer to them and spoke in a harsh whisper. "You wanted his attention. Well, it worked." There was a quiver in his voice, and Kaivon could smell him sweating with fear.

"Do you mean—"

"Don't say his name. Never say it," said Amir-Hossein. "Yes, him. All of your little bee stings have added up, and now he knows there's a problem. Someone even burnt a food store in Islamabad. It was an important cache for his army. Was that you? No, don't tell me." Amir-Hossein waved the question away before they had a chance to answer.

Kaivon and Esme exchanged a look and he shrugged. Maybe this would be their last meeting with Amir-Hossein after all.

"He's sending someone here, to find the problem and fix it." Amir-Hossein swallowed and shifted from one foot to the other.

"Does this mean you're leaving?" asked Esme.

"I should, but I'm a little short on money at the moment," he said, which didn't come as a surprise. Amir-Hossein seemed to spend money as if it was burning a hole in his pocket. He ate rich food, frequented expensive brothels, and had bought several pieces of jewellery. Later, he'd been forced to sell them when the money had run out. It seemed as if Amir-Hossein was trying to cram a lifetime of luxury into a few months.

"Do you know who it will be?" asked Esme.

"It could be one of half a dozen men." Amir-Hossein's teeth started to chatter together. "I need sun," he said suddenly.

Kaivon was thankful when Amir-Hossein led them away from the slave pits and down one of the side streets. They stopped at a crossroads, where he leaned his head against the wall, basking in the sunlight like a cat.

"You may think you're tough," said Amir-Hossein, squinting at them, "but these hunters solve problems, and they never fail, do you understand? They cannot go back to him in defeat. There are no second chances. They do not make mistakes."

Kaivon might have suspected Amir-Hossein had been such a hunter, if not for his cowardly demeanour. It would explain his inability to go home, and why he was not happy to betray his former khan. There was a lot more he wasn't telling them about why he had run and turned traitor.

"Who are you?" asked Esme. "Don't try to tell us you were one of his officers. This is personal. You hate him, don't you?"

"What are you talking about?" said Amir-Hossein, but Kaivon could see that she had gotten under his skin. He was squirming and his eyes were roaming around for a way out. Kaivon pinned Amir-Hossein to the wall with one arm, holding him in place by the shoulder.

Esme moved up to stand on the other side, effectively trapping him. With nowhere to go, Amir-Hossein started to fidget. He tried to move Kaivon's arm away, but he pushed harder, grinding Amir-Hossein's shoulder into the stone. Faced with two grim stares, unable to escape, the defector deflated.

"I'm his brother-in-law," he whispered. "He married my sister. Just another wife for his collection. He wanted our name and the connections made by our father. He took our money for his war. My money."

That explained Amir-Hossein's obsession with money. He was used to luxury, being waited on hand and foot by servants, and had probably never gone without a meal in his life. He'd made one mistake, and suddenly had found himself ousted by his family. Kaivon didn't know what Amir-Hossein had done, but he suspected it hadn't actually mattered. Timur had just needed an excuse to get rid of him.

"He'll kill you, won't he?" said Esme, digging for the source of his discomfort. "Even if you turned us in, it wouldn't be enough."

"I was a prince, in all but name, and now I'm a pauper. Forced to live in the gutters with the filth." Amir-Hossein's anger was a short-lived thing, and he soon went back to squirming. He was hardly destitute, and with the money they'd been giving him, he could have lived quite comfortably. Instead he'd spent it all because he was used to having an inexhaustible supply.

"We should sell you back to him for a reward," said Esme. Amir-Hossein thought she was joking until he saw her face.

"Don't," he gasped.

"Who will he send?" said Kaivon. "Don't lie to us."

"The barbarian," said Amir-Hossein. "He'll send the barbarian. Don't you understand? He cannot be stopped. You should run."

Amir-Hossein was no stranger to fear, but the terror in his eyes was something else.

"No. We'll continue, the same as normal, and you're going to help us."

"Don't you want revenge?" asked Esme. "Don't you want your old life back?" The promise of money sparked his interest more than getting back at his brother-in-law. Kaivon knew a return would be impossible, but Amir-Hossein's greed had its uses.

"There's a large and very slow merchant train on its way west. It's been on the move for some time."

"Weapons?" said Kaivon.

Amir-Hossein grinned. "Of a sort. Siege engines. I also heard a rumour about black powder from the east."

All of the preparations confirmed that Timur was getting ready for an extended war against the Ilkhanate. Of course Timur could rebuild, but if his siege engines were destroyed, it would put him at a significant disadvantage against a fortified city. The weapons would be heavily guarded, and overseen by engineers to make sure they were not damaged. The speed at which they would move would also be incredibly slow.

It would require a large investment of men on Kaivon's part, not to mention an abundance of luck. No matter the outcome, a lot of warriors would die on the mission. Their timing would also have to be impeccable, hitting the merchant train at precisely the right moment.

Maybe destroying them was the wrong approach. Kaivon remembered something Esme had told him once about the differences between the House of Strength and the House of Grace. A subtle approach was needed.

"Where and when?" said Esme.

CHAPTER 10
Hulagu

It felt good to be outside and see the sky again. Until he had been locked in a cell for a few weeks, Hulagu hadn't realised how much he missed it.

Today, there was a faint breeze. Tilting his head back, Hulagu inhaled and picked up the aromas of smoked fish, garlic and wood smoke. There were many things he missed, many comforts, but being deprived of them had focused his mind like never before.

Normally, he could have anything he wanted at any time. There was no one and nothing that could have stopped him. He had taken much for granted, and never once considered the origin or the cost. His wives, daughters and vizier had taken care of the tedious details. They were better at it than him. Hulagu had not been born to count beans and horses. But now, from time to time, he thought about where it all came from.

As a prisoner, he had been stripped down to the barest necessities. Any luxuries he received came at a high price. His clothes were worn and in need of a wash. His skin was itchy from dried sweat, and his body was getting soft from lack of regular movement. The food was much the same, although with little motivation, he didn't have much of an appetite and ate sparingly. He had also not drunk anything besides tea or water in weeks. Hulagu could not recall a time in his life when he had been sober for this long.

The two guards kept pace as he walked, matching their strides to his long legs. He needed to stretch, to feel the muscles pull from being worked. It would mean more sweating, but he'd grown used to the smell, if not the itching.

It galled Hulagu that he was in a walled paddock, walking in circles like a pony being trained, but he tried not to show it. If he complained, it would be taken away. He suffered the indignity because it was temporary, and those around him were still afraid. Hulagu was diminished, but in their minds he was still dangerous and unpredictable. They treated him carefully, almost bordering on deference, just in case the balance of power shifted again and he ended up back on top. Hulagu knew it was only a matter of when, not if it would happen.

Guyuk appeared at the doorway to the paddock. It was peculiar to see her in such an environment. Hulagu could not recall if she liked riding horses. He hadn't seen her on a horse in years. Both guards moved to intercept her, but Hulagu left them to it. As before, they would haggle and charge an extortionate price for so little, but the end result would be the same. They would be allowed to spend a short amount of time together.

Turning his face to the sky, Hulagu wondered what fate the gods intended for him. He did not think this was it, but if so, he found it a poor ending.

A price was reached, money changed hands, and Guyuk took the place of the two guards. No amount of money would get them to release Hulagu, or let her pass him a weapon, but it made no difference to them who accompanied him on his daily walk.

"I think it's going to rain," he said, staring at the drifting clouds overhead.

"What are you talking about?" asked Guyuk. She looked tired, and there were shadows under her eyes. "Is your mind so addled that you only care about the weather?"

With fewer distractions, he was more focused, not less, but Hulagu knew there wasn't time to explain. The guards would bend the rules, but not break them.

"What news from the city?" he asked instead.

"Kublai's warriors have arrived."

"How many?" asked Hulagu.

"Twenty thousand. Temujin is giving them a little time to rest, but then they'll be marching south." It was good news, and yet Guyuk's mouth twisted as if she'd tasted something bitter.

"What's wrong?"

"Nothing," she said, so he waited in silence, counting the steps before she gave in and answered. With days alone with nothing to do but think, Hulagu had learned that silence was as effective at extracting answers as peppering someone with questions.

"The new Trade Minister has made adequate provisions. The warriors will be well treated before they leave."

No one liked being replaced. It was even more galling when they did as good a job or better than their predecessor. No one was irreplaceable. However, from birth, some were destined for greatness, and others merely stole it.

"Is there going to be a banquet for Kublai's men?" It was what he would have done to welcome the senior officers who would soon be under his command. It made the transition easier, but also sent a clear message. Their loyalty was now to him and the Ilkhanate, and they would be wise to follow his orders.

"No, Temujin is busy elsewhere. I have made the offer, and will attempt to win over the generals. Doquz is assisting." Guyuk could be very persuasive when she wanted to be, but she was also good at finding out what people desired. If she could uncover what moved the generals, they might be persuaded to help with his release and reinstatement as ruler.

"What is Temujin doing?"

"He's dealing with the Golden Horde, and making other preparations for Timur. Warriors from across Persia are also gathering."

It had previously come as quite the surprise to learn that General Kaivon, and several others who Hulagu thought had been killed, were still alive. It turned out that since the moment of his arrival, Behrouz had been playing his own game. Even with so much time on his hands, Hulagu had still not figured it out. He didn't know who Behrouz served, or what his endgame was.

"Tell me about my son," said Hulagu. His rage over what Temujin had done to his other children had faded, but not the grief. It often caught Hulagu unawares, bringing tears to his eyes and fresh misery to his heart. He had not spared a thought for Jumghur, but the others were savage wounds upon his soul.

Hulagu had not seen much of Temujin in the last two weeks. There were times when Hulagu thought Temujin watched him while he lay sleeping, but whenever he woke up there was no one outside the cell. Hulagu knew that it was nothing more than a fantasy created by his mind because it lacked adequate stimulation.

"He trusts no one. Sometimes Temujin is gone for days, and when he is here, he barely sleeps. He also travels long distances, on foot." Guyuk grimaced and kicked a loose stone, sending it skidding away from them.

"What of the other Kozan?" Hulagu had heard rumours of two factions and at least half a dozen people, but he had no names beyond Behrouz. If Temujin knew more about them, he'd not shared it with anyone.

"Nothing. It's like Behrouz has vanished." She sounded pleased, but Hulagu didn't think he was truly gone. The Kozan had interfered in events for a reason, and he was probably continuing to do so elsewhere. And if there was a faction opposed to Behrouz, perhaps they could be persuaded to side with Hulagu this time.

He'd walked half a dozen steps before he noticed Guyuk had stopped. Hulagu turned and walked back to stand beside his first wife.

"What is it?"

"There's a growing darkness in Temujin," said Guyuk. Her eyes were distant and scared. "He's changed, and it's not just his strange abilities. He worries me."

In different circumstances, Hulagu would have been proud of his son. He had seized power and eliminated potential rivals. He also seemed to be doing a reasonable job at maintaining order while also preparing for the future. He had become unflinching in what was required to be a khan. It was unfortunate that Hulagu would have to kill his only remaining son. But the good news was, he could always have more children. After all, he had plenty of wives and concubines.

"Once you have won over Kublai's generals, we can take back control of Tabriz," said Hulagu, refocusing her on the task ahead. He could not afford for her to break down under the pressure. He was relying on Guyuk and Doquz to free him.

When he was back on the throne as ruler of the Ilkhanate, everyone would fall into line again. Temujin had done some of the hard work for him, but he did not have experience for what was to come. He had not commanded armies or led a war council. Plans were always made ahead of time, but all of them changed in the moment. It was the outcome of those decisions that could win or lose a battle. Temujin, and the Ilkhanate, did not have the time for him to learn these lessons.

Hulagu glanced over Guyuk's head to where the guards were chatting. They were too far away to hear each other's conversations. Hulagu knew exactly who he could trust and who would be culled when he returned to power. A little kindness towards him now did not exonerate them for betraying him earlier. He had been far too lenient.

Hulagu was still not sure if he believed in the gods, or one god, but he knew there was such a thing as fate. He was not destined to die forgotten in a cell, a prisoner of his lacklustre son. Hulagu's deeds would leave a mark on the world that would be remembered for a thousand years. He would decimate the pretender, Timur, an outsider who fashioned himself as a khan. Timur had come from nothing and would return to being nothing.

Soon enough, the world would know Hulagu's name once more. His day of ascendance was approaching.

CHAPTER 11
Temujin

It had been another long and difficult day – two days, in fact. Temujin was losing track of time. He never seemed to have enough of it. A Kozan that was out of time. It would have been funny if it wasn't so tragic. A laugh bubbled up, but he shoved it back down.

It was too risky for him to show any real emotions. Everyone was watching and waiting for him to fail. Many were hungry for his position and the power that came with ruling over the Ilkhanate. There were other descendants of Genghis Khan who thought they were more worthy. Even his uncle, Kublai Khan, would prefer to see Temujin stumble so that his brother could be reappointed. Then there were his enemies, such as the Kozan, Berke Khan, the Sultan of Egypt and his Mamluks. There were even powers in Europe, and the Christian Church, that were keen for him to suddenly, and unexpectedly, die. Temujin knew they thought of him as a savage and uneducated barbarian. Of course, at the top of the list of enemies was his father.

Temujin wasn't deluded. He was young, and there was still much he had to learn. But at the same time, that didn't mean he couldn't teach others a few lessons.

Today had been months in the making, and nothing would get in his way. The cost had been high, and very soon

STEPHEN ARYAN   111

it would become significantly worse, but Temujin knew that
it was necessary.

Alliances and promises had been met, and now warriors from
Georgia, Cilician Armenia, and even some from Antioch, were
arriving in the Ilkhanate. The warriors sent by his uncle would
soon be leaving Tabriz, but there was still much to be done.

Sinking to his knees, Temujin sought inner calm as he
navigated his way towards the Eternal Fire. He was alone in an
abandoned building on the edge of Tabriz. There was nothing to
steal here, so few would bother to venture inside. Those living in
the neighbourhood also knew that he often came here, so they
gave it a wide berth. Word of his unholy powers had spread. Fear
was a powerful tool, and he did nothing to repress the stories.
Just in case that wasn't enough and greed overcame thoughts of
self-preservation, there were two Kheshig on duty outside.

The only sound in the empty building was the echo of
his slow and steady breathing. As Temujin surrendered, the
Eternal Fire spread throughout his body, opening his mind
and expanding his senses. Even now, months after he'd first
achieved it, the effect was startling and revelatory. Until that
moment, it felt as if he had been living his entire life with
blinkers covering his eyes. But it was not just heightened
intuition. All of his five senses were more acute.

He knew one of the Kheshig had eaten a lot of garlic the
night before. He was sweating in the heat, and Temujin could
smell it emanating from his pores. The other had a sore left hip
and kept leaning to the right. His feet constantly shifted about as
he tried to find a comfortable position. There was more, much
more, but he tried to block it out and turn his senses within.

A scream broke into his thoughts. Temujin smelled the spray
of fresh blood as one of the Kheshig was cut down. As Temujin
rose to his feet, he heard the clash of steel, men grunting and
cursing, and the twang of a bowstring. A second later, there
was a squawk of pain. He heard a scrape of metal against skin,
and then the release of a final breath.

Five armed men, with blood dripping from their weapons, filtered into the room. A sixth man lingered in the doorway, a crossbow resting on his shoulder. Temujin thought he looked vaguely familiar.

"Are we related?" asked Temujin as the five warriors spread out around the room.

"I think we're distant cousins. I'm a descendent of Genghis Khan," said the leader. Temujin didn't feel that now was the time to point out that his great-grandfather was rumoured to have fathered hundreds of children. Such a claim was not nearly as powerful, or special, as some people thought.

"You want to be khan?" asked Temujin, studying the men around him.

All of them were similar in age and build. Young, arrogant, and determined to be the one that struck the killing blow. Maybe they had been offered extra money if they managed it. Only one man was having second thoughts about murdering him. Temujin knew that two of them had killed before. He could see it. There was a lingering shadow in their eyes. For all five young men, this was just an unpleasant and necessary task that needed to be done. After this, there would be glory and riches. Murdering an unarmed man, five against one, didn't seem to bother them.

"Why not me?" said his distant relative. "You don't deserve to lead. You're not worthy."

The man on Temujin's left was nervous, but he still had a dagger held ready. He was the closest and would strike first. A fatal jab to Temujin's kidneys. Two of the warriors had swords, and the others carried short curved daggers. It was safer for close work when there were so many bodies. If you weren't careful, swinging a sword could be lethal for the man standing beside you. Temujin grinned, which alarmed a couple of the warriors, but not enough for them to run.

As he embraced the Eternal Fire, the endless web stretched far away in all directions. Temujin focused on one of the globes immediately behind the man on his left, and then he waited. With a scream, the man ran forward. A second later, the rest followed his lead.

Temujin Skimmed through the knife-man until he was standing behind him, then gave him a shove. He'd already been running forward, and now he went flying. The warrior's dagger jabbed into the stomach of the man opposite. Staring at the hilt, and the blood seeping from the wound, the warrior dropped to his knees.

Skimming to his left, Temujin grabbed the wrist of the next man, who was wielding a sword. With a firm shove, he made the warrior's swing even wider, then Skimmed away. The blade sliced into the arm of another man, severing it just above the elbow. The tang of fresh blood filled Temujin's nose.

Temujin Skimmed behind another man, plucked the dagger from his hand, then stabbed the warrior in the neck. Before the pain had registered, Temujin had moved on again.

Criss-crossing the room, he nudged and shoved the warriors, making them inflict savage and lethal wounds on each other. In only a few seconds, two of them were dying from wounds to their neck, one was on his knees holding his stomach, and the other two had lost arms.

"No, no, no," one man was saying, staring at his severed limb across the room. The shock was so severe, he couldn't understand why it wasn't still attached. Dark, rich blood pumped from the wound. Temujin knew that he would be dead in seconds.

Spattered with blood, with more streaked across his face, Temujin turned towards the leader.

"So, tell me again, dear cousin, do you think I'm worthy?"

The warrior frantically tried to reload his crossbow. He'd been so confident that his friends would succeed, he hadn't bothered. Taking his time, Temujin stalked towards his enemy. As his fingers gripped the warrior by the throat, Temujin's calm evaporated, and the Eternal Fire disappeared. Rage carried him forward, and with a roar of fury, Temujin drove the man's head into the wall. Grabbing him by the forehead, Temujin smashed it into the stone, over and over again, until he heard something break. The wall was spattered red, and the warrior had become a dead weight in his arms. The moment he let go, the man dropped to the ground. Unconscious or dead, it didn't really matter. His distant cousin could not be allowed to live. None of them could. A message needed to be sent to anyone else that thought he was an easy target.

Picking up one of the daggers, Temujin went along the line, slicing open the throat of every man. Dripping with blood, with adrenaline surging through his system, it was impossible for him to find inner calm.

Sinking to his knees amidst the carnage, Temujin closed his eyes and meditated. He told himself the sights, sounds and smells no longer mattered. They were distant and forgotten. It took him a long time before he felt capable of summoning the Eternal Fire.

A day later than he'd planned, Temujin approached the front doors of the palace of Sarai. As before, the guards immediately gave way, then followed behind at what they believed was a safe distance. The khan's vizier escorted him to a room, and this time, Temujin only had to wait a little while before being led to the throne room.

The audience was smaller than before, and Temujin thought Berke had been more careful with his selection. There were a few of the outsiders and curios Berke had collected, but the majority were warriors, senior officers and members of his extended family. All of them were Mongols, and all of them glared at Temujin from the moment he approached the throne. As an equal, he didn't need to bow, and this time he didn't even acknowledge Berke's seniority. He merely stood there, waiting. That earned him more frowns and grumbling, which he promptly ignored.

For a while, the two of them just stared at one another. Wrapped in the calm of the Eternal Fire, Temujin focused his senses on Berke. The khan was concerned by Temujin, but not afraid. He was also confident that, regardless of what he said today, all of the people in the throne room would support him. Some of them had been here the last time Temujin had visited, but the rest would have been told what had transpired. If any of them had concerns about Berke's past behaviour, it was obvious he was determined to put them to rest. He needed their support to continue his war against the Ilkhanate, as well as his alliance with Egypt.

"Are you ready?" asked Temujin, breaking the silence.

"For what?" asked Berke, shifting on his throne. The guards around the room tensed, as if expecting an attack. Berke wasn't carrying a sword, but as usual, he was dressed in armour.

"To face judgment for your crimes," said Temujin. "For making an alliance with an enemy of the Mongol Empire. For conspiring with them to attack my father, and for doing nothing while your own people fight amongst themselves."

Berke's frown deepened. He had probably expected nearly all of what Temujin had said, but not the last. "What are you talking about?"

"When last I was in Sarai, I saw that a church had been burned to the ground. Here, in your own capital city." Temujin shook his head in dismay. "There is unrest and a growing division between people within the Golden Horde. How can anyone trust you to expand the Empire if you cannot even protect your own people?"

When Gurban stepped forward to cover for his khan's hesitation, Temujin pointed a finger at the vizier.

"One word out of you, worm, and I will burn you to ash."

The vizier swallowed hard and closed his mouth.

The crowd that had previously been behind their khan was now divided. Those who belonged to other faiths looked concerned. The strength of the Empire was built on the backs of the nations it had conquered. It exploited their resources, but also their skills and knowledge. The best way to placate the conquered and keep them calm was to allow a version of their previous lives to continue. There were always changes, but law and order and freedom of worship were two of the most important pillars to keep the peace.

This was something Temujin had indirectly learned from his father. Hulagu had appeared generous as he gave with one hand, but he always took twice as much with the other. He bestowed gifts and favours on his senior officers, but in return, hundreds and thousands of their warriors died for the Empire.

"More words," sneered Berke, falling back on old habits. "If you were truly a Mongol, you would challenge me." He stood up and gestured towards one of the guards. The man approached the throne and Temujin saw that he was carrying a sword. Berke strapped the belt around his waist and settled the blade on his left hip.

"Prove that I am unworthy. Draw your blade and show everyone here that you are the better choice to be khan." Berke pointed towards Temujin and raised his hands. "But, where is your armour? Where is your blade, mighty khan?" he said, playing to the audience. A few of the crowd chuckled, and cynical laughter echoed off the walls.

"I do not carry a blade. I no longer have need of one." Berke meant to embarrass him, but Temujin felt no shame in who and what he had become. He was nothing like Berke or his father, and that filled him with pride.

"Then how will you challenge me?" said Berke.

"As the ruler of the Ilkhanate, I have enough duties of my own. It was never my intention to rule the Golden Horde."

"Then why are you here, boy?" said Berke, walking forward until he was almost nose to nose with Temujin.

"To show everyone who you really are, in the hope that someone else will step forward and issue a challenge."

A heavy silence filled the room. Berke glanced at the others expectantly, and when no one moved, he turned back to Temujin with a grin. Just as he opened his mouth to gloat, there was a scrape of steel.

"You are not worthy to be khan," said a voice.

"What madness is this?" said Berke, staring at his younger brother, Tokhtamysh.

"You have been blinded by your faith, and have forgotten much," said Tokhtamysh, pushing his way to the front of the crowd. The others gave way because he was a respected warrior in his own right, but also because his words had merit. "I have been at your side since the beginning. I have always supported you, but in the last few years, you have changed. I made many requests, but you have refused to listen to reason."

"You would side with him against me?" said Berke, jabbing an accusing finger towards Temujin.

"No, I serve the people of the Golden Horde and the Mongol Empire. Who do you serve, brother?" asked Tokhtamysh. "Your God, or your people?"

Family had constantly sought to undermine Temujin, and now it had proven to be Berke's undoing as well. Over the years, as they rose to power, Kublai and Hulagu had made many enemies. Rivals from other tribes. Relatives and even siblings, in the case of Ariq. Temujin didn't know if Kublai had cheated his brother, or if it had all been a misunderstanding. Given all that he had witnessed, the cynic in Temujin, or perhaps it was the realist, told him it had been carefully orchestrated. The answer to all of his problems with the Golden Horde had been staring him in the face. Mongols do not kill Mongols, except when they did.

"You would truly do this, brother?" said Berke.

Tokhtamysh sighed. "You brought us to this moment."

With a snarl, Berke drew his sword. Tokhtamysh raised his blade and waited for his brother to attack. The onlookers scattered to the edges of the room, trying to get as far away from the fight as possible. Temujin had been forgotten. No one tried to stop him as he walked out of the throne room. The sound of clashing weapons followed him down the hallway as the leadership of the Golden Horde was settled in the most primitive of ways.

Walking without any direction in mind, Temujin found his way to a small walled garden. Someone had planted herbs and colourful flowers, and there was a pond that was large enough to sustain a few frogs. Sunlight pooled in the garden, creating a warm oasis. Temujin sat on the bench and meditated, but in the distance he could still hear faint cries from the fight. He stayed wrapped in a cocoon, removed from his emotions by the calming effect of the Eternal Fire. There was nothing he could do to tip the scales. The outcome had to be settled between them. Any interference, no matter how slight, might come back to haunt him in the future. It was another reason he had removed himself from the room. That way, there would be no doubt as to who was the victor and why.

Eventually, the fight ended, and silence returned to the palace. Soon after, a shadow fell across Temujin, blotting out the sun. Tokhtamysh's armour was splattered with blood, and he was bleeding from a wound on his arm. At least he wasn't carrying the sword that he'd used to kill his brother. Despite being the victor, his face was grim. This had been a last resort. Had it not been for Temujin's support, he would never have contemplated this course of action.

"It's done," said Tokhtamysh. Even though Temujin was sitting down, and had to look up at the warrior, he could see Tokhtamysh's hesitancy. Theirs was not a partnership of equals, and it never would be. It was good that the warrior understood the situation.

"Do I need to remind you of our deal?" asked Temujin.

"No, but I will need some time. To calm the rebels, to sever ties with Egypt, and restore order in the Golden Horde. Then there are Berke's wives and children to deal with."

The latter was something Temujin didn't want to think about. He knew what had to happen, but it didn't make it any easier. Tokhtamysh would marry all of his brother's wives, and take on some, or all, of the concubines. It wasn't their fate that preyed on Temujin's mind. It was that of Berke's children. None of them could be allowed to live.

"How long?" said Temujin, knowing he was asking an impossible question.

"A few weeks," said Tokhtamysh with a shrug.

"Do it quickly, and get Gurban to draw up proclamations in the meantime. Everyone must understand the war between the khanates is over. A greater threat looms, and the Golden Horde will be needed for what is to come."

Tokhtamysh smelled of sweat, blood and fear. He didn't understand all of what Temujin could do, but he knew enough to be afraid. Temujin suspected he was trying to find the right words for a question he didn't know if he should even be asking.

"Say it," said Temujin.

"If this Timur is truly so dangerous, could you not remove him by yourself?"

"No. There are forces more powerful than me that protect him."

Tokhtamysh paled at the thought of what that meant. Temujin released the Eternal Fire so that his raw emotions were on show.

"The war between us is over, but we must unite if we are to stand a chance against him." Temujin gripped Tokhtamysh by the wrist, pulling him down onto the bench. "Do I need to worry about you?"

Tokhtamysh tried to pull away, but Temujin tightened his grip until the warrior hissed in pain. "What are you talking about? We made a deal."

"There is far more at stake than you realise, and I have many things on my mind." Temujin let his frustration and anger bubble to the surface. "If you think, even for a moment about betraying me, I want you to remember what I did to my own family."

"I would never betray you," said Tokhtamysh.

"I will make your suffering last for days," promised Temujin. "But before you die, I will rid the world of your family. I will rip it up by the roots. Every child, every brother and sister, aunt, uncle and distant relative. It will be as if your line had never existed."

Fear of death was common, but it was also an unavoidable obstacle that could not be overcome by any means. Not even the Kozan could outrun it forever. Fear of being forgotten by history, of being erased, that was something that terrified ambitious men even more. Tokhtamysh was passionate, driven, and had dreams for the future of the Golden Horde. Temujin suspected the thought of losing that opportunity scared Tokhtamysh more than the promise to murder his entire family.

"I won't betray you. I won't," he babbled, desperately trying to get away, but Temujin still held him firmly by the wrist. Finally, he let go. Temujin was surprised not to see scorch marks on Tokhtamysh's bare skin. Without the calming effect of Eternal Fire, it felt as if Temujin's rage could burn down the palace and everyone inside.

"When I return, I expect to see progress," said Temujin. "He will be coming. Get your army ready."

Tokhtamysh didn't actually bow, but he came close, bending forward at the waist. Taking a deep breath, Temujin forced his anger away. He preferred the serenity he gained from the Eternal Fire to the churning turmoil of so many emotions.

He managed to Skim away from the palace, heading north for a few miles, before his concentration wavered. Temujin stumbled to his knees beside a shallow stream and vomited his last meal into the mud. Waves of exhaustion ran through his body. His skin tingled, as if he'd been sitting too close to a fire.

Moving back on his haunches, Temujin realised his face was wet. As he wiped a hand across his nose and mouth, he was surprised to see blood on his fingers.

Part of him wanted to just lie down and sleep. A few days, maybe a week, then he'd have enough energy, but there were still miles to go and much to be done.

He was alone. It had been his decision. Now he had to face the consequences of that choice. No one was coming to help. It was all up to him. Groaning like an old man, Temujin pushed himself upright and stumbled away.

CHAPTER 12
Kokochin

Both masked men were unarmed, but Kokochin still wasn't confident about the odds. They were not thugs, and they held themselves with the relaxed stance of someone with training. They also maintained their distance, and were equally spaced out on her right and left.

She had to turn her head to look directly at one, effectively putting the other in her blind spot. Even if she'd been carrying a bow, it would have been impossible to attack both of them at once. The Sons of the White Falcon knew their business.

"You were looking for us," said the man on her left. He was clean shaven and slightly taller than the other. "Who are you?"

As Kokochin turned to answer, he rushed towards her, aiming a casual punch at her face. She instinctively stepped back, just in time for the second man to grab her around the waist from behind. Using *Squirrel Climbs* she slipped out of his grip, spun him around and pressed gently on his right ankle. With a squawk of surprise, he tumbled to the floor. She could have countered with something more vicious, but Kokochin didn't want to cause serious injury until she knew the reason for their surprise visit.

The other man was more cautious and kept her at arm's length. They traded blows, ducking and weaving, grappled a little, and every time she tried to pull him off balance, he countered. He was more than twice her weight, and he used it effectively, leaning back or widening his stance. His style wasn't anything she'd seen before, but the principles were a little familiar. At one point, he managed to toss her over one hip, but Kokochin kept her grip on his belt. Using her full bodyweight as a lever, she pulled him to the ground beside her. They rolled away from each other, then made it to their feet at the same time.

This time, when the other man grabbed her, Kokochin didn't hesitate. She slipped around his back, pulled him tight against her chest, and put the edge of her dagger against his throat.

"Stop, or I'll kill him," she said.

Strangely, the bearded man in her grip was relaxed. He wasn't breathing hard and hadn't tried to escape. Even more peculiar was that he kept both hands down at his sides.

"You can break my body, kill me and bury me in the ground, but from the seeds of the old, new life will grow," he said, speaking calmly. The words had a peculiar rhythm, as if they were a mantra he'd repeated many times. "Another will take my place, and then another. We cannot be stopped."

Kokochin shoved him away from her, but kept the dagger in one hand.

The other man grunted. "You have good balance, and a strong core, but your flexibility needs work."

"You're not just the owner of a tea room," said the bearded man, dusting off his clothes. Neither of them were out of breath and both were smiling.

"This was a test?" said Kokochin.

"Of a sort. I'm Usman," said the clean-shaven man. "This is my brother, Bilal."

Given the differences in their build and skin tone, Kokochin didn't think they were related by blood. Perhaps all Sons of the White Falcon regarded each other as brothers.

"Why are you looking for us?"

Kokochin hesitated before she answered. She had only one contact from the House to call on, but he knew little about her activities. It kept everyone safe, but it was also very isolating. Apart from him, she was completely alone and without any real friends. Olma was the closest thing Kokochin had, and the nurse didn't know everything about her. If Usman and Bilal made her disappear, no one would ever know what had happened.

Bilal folded his arms in annoyance. "Now is the time to speak."

"Patience, brother," said Usman. "We are not here to harm you."

Kokochin had little choice but to take a risk. The alternative was to tell them nothing, and try to carry on in the city without their help. "My name is Princess Kokochin. I was married to Hulagu Khan."

Usman's eyes widened. "I was not expecting you to say that," he admitted, running a hand over his chin. Kokochin heard the rasp of stubble against his fingertips. "You're with a rebel group, yes?"

"Yes, and I'm here because Timur is coming. In fact, part of his army could arrive any day now and occupy the city."

"We know," said Usman, leaning against the wall. "We've made what preparations we can, but we do not have the numbers to repel an army."

"Our work is carried out in the shadows," said Bilal.

"We operate in a similar fashion," said Kokochin, being careful not to say who she worked with, or how many there were in the city.

"What are you suggesting?" asked Usman.

"That once the city is occupied, we pool our resources," she said. "I have contacts and connections to people in power."

"We don't need your help," said Bilal. "We've been here a long time."

STEPHEN ARYAN   125

"All of those who serve freedom are brothers in the cause," said Usman, putting his right hand over his heart. Bilal copied the gesture and nodded. "Or sisters," added Usman with a smile.

"I'm sorry," said Bilal, forcing the words out. "I'm not used to working with foreigners."

As the first outsider in the House of Grace, that was something Kokochin knew very well. "I understand," she said. "It's difficult for me too."

"Let's take it slow," suggested Usman. "A few streets away, close to the market, is a carpet shop with a blue sign. The man who runs it is a friend of ours. He can get word to me. If you want to share information, or you need our help, speak to him."

"That's fair," said Kokochin. "You know where I'll be if you want to talk," she said, gesturing at the tea room.

"True enough," said Usman with a smile. Bilal went out the door, but Usman paused on the threshold. "You need to be more careful. It wasn't difficult for us to find you. There are others out there who are less friendly. Keep your blade close, and work on your flexibility."

He closed the door and Kokochin locked it behind him. She'd been so busy of late, she'd been skipping her stretching exercises. Kokochin had barely made it to the top of the stairs when there was a frantic knocking at the back door. Keeping her blade ready in one hand, she unlocked the door and opened it carefully.

"They're coming," said Nabil. He was red-faced and out of breath, probably from running. It wasn't something he did very often.

"Come inside and sit down," said Kokochin.

"Can't. Need to get back to the governor," he panted. "Scouts reported back. Timur's men are nearly here. He guessed twenty thousand men, but it could be more."

"When?" said Kokochin.

"Tomorrow. Maybe the day after."

It suggested Timur was gathering his army in preparation for an invasion of the Ilkhanate. It had been inevitable, but it was happening much sooner than Kokochin had expected. She thought about trying to send another message to Tabriz, but knew it would be pointless. By the time they sent her a reply, it would be too late, Timur would be on his way to invade Persia.

Two days later, Kokochin watched from a rooftop as rank after rank of warriors marched into Lahore. Many were Mongols, but there were also thousands of warriors from other conquered nations that formed the Chagatai khanate. Most were on foot, with officers on horseback, but at the front of the group were ten men riding sturdy beasts. Eight of the ten were warriors, while the remaining two were without armour or weapons. Kokochin guessed they were important servants, viziers or those who would deal with the city's authorities.

In front of hundreds of citizens, who'd come to observe the transfer of power, the governor surrendered to the warrior on horseback. Kokochin was too far away to hear what was said, but the general, a hawkish Mongol, stared down at the cowering governor from his saddle. Kokochin feared the worst because he sat perfectly still and said nothing. Perhaps he was disappointed, or hungover, or the governor's grovelling had been insufficient to satisfy his ego. The governor finished his speech with a deep bow, and those around him bowed as well. Soon, fifty or sixty men and women were bent at the waist with their hands on knees and faces directed towards the ground.

Finally, the general got down from his horse, approached the governor and made him stand upright. The city held its breath, waiting to see what happened. There were stories about what Timur had done in other cities. Slaughtered sections of the civilian population and formed towers from severed heads to drive out any thoughts of rebellion.

Kokochin sighed in relief as the general embraced the governor, then gripped him by the shoulder as if they were old friends. The governor played along, forcing a smile, but even from where she was standing, Kokochin could see that he was terrified. It was only when the rest of the army began to disperse that she relaxed. There would be no pillaging or looting, no rape camps, and no sacking of the city.

Hours later, Kokochin approached the Gilded Lily, which was awash with noise from inside. She could hear several men singing in a drunken, off-key fashion, and many overlapping conversations from a large crowd.

There were two Mongol guards on duty at the front door, and half a dozen more nearby keeping warm beside a fire pit. It was an odd thing to have dug on the street, but no one complained and they kept their distance. The guards must have realised they would be staying for a while, so they wanted to be comfortable.

As before, Kokochin went the long way around to the rear of the Lily, keeping several streets between her and the guards. When she arrived at the back door, she wasn't surprised to see two more Mongol guards on duty. The madam had given Kokochin specific instructions, and she walked straight up to them.

"What do you want?" asked one of them.

"Maybe she's supposed to be working inside," said the other guard, leering at Kokochin.

"I'm here to look after the girls," said Kokochin, holding up her bag. She wore a nurse's smock, which she'd borrowed from Olma, over the top of her normal clothes. The back door opened and Carim emerged from within. One of the guards reached for his sword before remembering where he was.

"There you are, come in," said Carim, gesturing for Kokochin to get inside. "The girls need you."

"I bet they do. All worn out," said one of the guards, and his friend laughed. When Carim didn't join in, they dismissed him and Kokochin. She squeezed past them, but was still close enough to hear them muttering. "I thought he'd lost his balls, not his sense of humour."

If he'd heard them, Carim ignored the guards and locked the door. He led Kokochin to the madam's office, where they found her dozing on a small cot. Even with her eyes closed, there was an anxious expression on the woman's face. Carim put a finger to his lips and leant close.

"I'll bring tea. Let her rest."

Moving quietly, Kokochin sat down, but the older woman must have heard as her eyelids fluttered open.

"No need to be quiet, girl, I'm awake." With a grunt, she stood up and settled behind her desk. A short time later, Carim returned with a pot of tea.

"You should be resting," he said, setting down the tray.

"You're not my mother," said the madam, but then her expression softened. "Thank you, old friend," she said, resting a hand on Carim's for a moment. With a smile, he left the room. Although the two women were silent, sounds from other parts of the building invaded the space. Kokochin heard several women moaning, men crying out on the verge, and the tinkle of gentle music.

"His name is Miran Shah," said the madam, inspecting the tea. She poked it with a spoon and then sat back. "So far, he's been well-behaved."

"But?" said Kokochin, sensing there was more.

"I think he's been given orders. If it were up to him, things would be different." That meant Timur, or someone else, was keeping him on a tight leash.

"And the rest?" As the best brothel in the city, Miran Shah would be treating his senior officers and closest friends to the delights found at the Gilded Lily. With so many, the party could last for days. It depended on their endurance, their mood, how satisfied they were and how long they intended to remain in the city. It explained why the madam had been sleeping in her office and the guards outside were set up for a long haul. She didn't risk leaving the premises, just in case something happened and she was needed.

"A few bruises and swollen lips. Nothing that won't fade in time." The madam shrugged, because it was apparently commonplace and expected. Kokochin bit the inside of her mouth, but said nothing.

"The general?" she asked, as the madam finally poured the tea.

"Still drinking, but he's already got a couple of favourites that he's requested again. They're bathing, so we have some time."

After drinking tea and making small talk, mostly to try and blot out the sounds around them, someone rapped three times on the door in quick succession, but didn't come in.

"Follow me," said the madam.

She led Kokochin down a short corridor to a storage area beside the kitchen. Behind a heavy barrel was a small doorway that Kokochin would have to crawl through. The madam unlocked it, then bent over to point inside the dark space.

"You can't get lost. It goes straight, then just around the corner is the bottom of a ladder. At the top is a small ledge, where you can sit and listen. The walls are thin, so be careful. This door will be closed, but it won't be locked."

"Is there any light?"

"No, nothing. You may have a while to wait before he starts talking," said the madam with a frown. "The general is young and enthusiastic."

"Is there something you're not telling me?" Kokochin thought she sounded hesitant.

"No, it's fine."

Sensing she wouldn't get anything more if she pushed, Kokochin let it go. Getting down on hands and knees, she crawled along the dirt floor. The dark became absolute when the door closed behind her. She was thankful when she didn't hear the key turn in the lock. Feeling ahead with one hand,

Kokochin found the first of the metal rungs hammered into the stone wall. Scaling twenty two rungs in the dark brought her to a small oval alcove. If she bent her legs, it was big enough for her to lie down on her side, or she could sit upright with her feet dangling over the edge.

On the far side of the wall, she heard two or three women talking. A deep voice announced the general's arrival in the bedroom. The women fell silent as the bedroom door banged closed. Kokochin lay down in the alcove, and despite not being particularly comfortable, found herself falling asleep. She was exhausted from long waking hours, and when she normally slept, it wasn't very restful. Back in Tabriz, she had no problem being alone with her thoughts, but now she found it difficult. Inevitably, her mind turned back to what had happened with Layla, and the reasons why.

As rhythmic banging and moaning sounds filtered through the wall, Kokochin blocked the noises from her mind. As ever, she thought about the path not taken. About what might have happened if she had not followed so closely in the footsteps of Guyuk. She and Layla could have been living elsewhere together, far away from the Empire, or so she liked to pretend.

Since arriving in Lahore, there had been several occasions where Kokochin had been forced to restrain herself. Too often, her first solution to a problem was a violent one, or worse, one that was cruel. It was the main reason she'd decided to run her own group of contacts. That way, there was always someone else between her and the person being manipulated. She would never be tempted to take it one step further because she felt personally slighted or affronted by their behaviour. Kokochin had unknowingly stumbled down a dark road and had ended up becoming someone she barely recognised. It was someone Layla couldn't be with and, with hindsight, Kokochin didn't blame her. It was going to take a long time for Kokochin to navigate back to who she used to be. Some days, she wondered if that was even possible.

One of the women in bed was so loud, her dramatic moans broke into Kokochin's thoughts. Either the young general was the most skilled lover she'd ever encountered, or she was a talented actress. The wails reached a crescendo in parallel with the general's moans, and then silence filled the room. At first, she thought something had gone wrong, but leaning closer to the wall she heard the faint murmur of voices.

"It will soon be your turn," said the general, to which a second woman giggled.

"Are you really a general?" said the first woman.

"Yes. I command fifteen thousand men." Nabil had almost been right about the numbers. The next time she spoke to him, Kokochin would give him the exact number, which would make him happy.

"That's a lot," said the first woman, who sounded genuinely impressed.

"It's nothing compared to my father. His army is vast." Kokochin was desperate to catch every word. She risked leaning closer, almost putting her ear against the wall. A heavy, pregnant silence filled the bedroom. She waited patiently for one of the women to ask.

"Who is your father?" someone asked.

"The greatest military genius who has ever lived, and soon, he'll be your khan."

A chill ran down Kokochin's spine. A few people had commented that the general was young, but she hadn't thought to ask why. She wondered if this was what the madam had not told her. Perhaps it wasn't public knowledge, but the madam had sensed something unusual about the young general. He was Timur's son.

There was a loud bang and everyone in the bedroom gasped.

"We didn't order any food," said one of the women. "Go away."

"I'm not a servant," said a new voice. She sounded older, and Kokochin heard a faint accent.

"Then what do you want?" asked one of the women.

"I'm here for him," said the newcomer.

"We don't need your help. Get out!"

Kokochin heard a squeak and a thump as something heavy landed on the floor. "Are you crazy?" said one of the women. Miran Shah just laughed at whatever was unfolding.

"What is wrong with you?" asked the second woman.

"Oh, I like you," said the general. "You can stay, but first, tussle with the other girl some more."

There was another squawk, and then the door slammed shut. Kokochin heard someone banging on the door, but it quickly stopped.

"You are something," purred the general. "And now, you have me all to yourself."

"Yes, I do."

Something was horribly wrong. He thought this was a seduction by a dominant woman, but a cold prickle of dread was creeping down Kokochin's spine.

She wanted to see inside the room, but there were no holes in the wall. Kokochin slipped onto the top rung of the ladder, and prepared to descend.

"And what are you going to do with me?" asked Miran Shah, oblivious to the danger.

As soon as he'd said it, Kokochin knew it was the wrong question. "Did you know I used to be married?" said the woman.

"Why would I care about that? Come here," said the general.

"But one day he died, and after that, I realised something about myself."

"I'm bored. Take off your clothes," said Miran Shah, but the newcomer ignored him. She must have moved across the room as her voice was suddenly a lot louder.

"Do you know what it was?" she asked.

"That you talk too much?" he suggested.

"That I like hurting people."

Kokochin didn't wait. She scrambled down the ladder, then crawled to the door as fast as she could. An agonised scream reached her ears from somewhere behind and above her position. Slipping out of the storage area, she ran for the front of the building. She'd barely gone a dozen steps when she found the first body. It was one of the Mongol guards. Someone had stabbed him in the side of his neck. Stepping over him, Kokochin ducked past women running in the other direction and went up the stairs.

More screams followed, men and women both, from above her head. Kokochin was going against the stream of bodies, but she knew it wouldn't be long before Mongols flooded the building. By the time she found the right bedroom, it was too late. Miran Shah was already dead.

He'd been stabbed once in the neck and twice in the heart. Kokochin spun around, searching for the perpetrator, but she was gone. The murderer must have found another way out of the building. That's when Kokochin realised what she'd missed. One of the women in the crowd on the stairs was the murderer. She walked right past them.

As Kokochin reached the top of the stairs, two Mongol warriors appeared at the bottom.

"There!" said one of them, pointing towards her. As she looked for another way out, one of the warriors slammed into the wall, a dagger buried in his throat. As the second man turned around, someone collided with him, knocking him backwards. A woman, dressed all in black, had a hand on either side of his throat. Two narrow blades punched down at an angle. The warrior gurgled and immediately dropped to his knees, trying to stem the bleeding. Kokochin thought the Persian woman was familiar, but couldn't place her.

"What are you doing here?" asked the woman. "You should have left days ago."

"Who are you?"

"Jaleh. Now move, before more turn up."

Kokochin hurried down the stairs as Jaleh retrieved her other dagger.

"Out the back," said Kokochin, leading the way as she retraced her steps. There were more bodies scattered about. Mongol warriors and a couple of women. The back door was propped open by one of the guards, who sat in a pool of his own blood.

As they stepped outside, Kokochin heard a commotion at the front of the building. From across the street, four Mongol warriors were running towards them. Jaleh didn't hesitate and charged. The only way out was through them, so Kokochin moved to attack as well.

She ducked a clumsy swing, stepped in close and with a twist, and threw the guard over her hip to the ground. He landed badly on his shoulder and she heard something crack. Screeching in pain, he rolled onto his back, cradling his dislocated arm. Jaleh had already killed one of the warriors and was battling with a second. Kokochin attacked the fourth man, who had been about to stab Jaleh.

He heard Kokochin coming and spun about, his dagger held low. Kokochin let him attack, grabbed his knife-hand with both of hers, and pulled him forward and then around. Dropping the blade, he punched her in the side, and then tried to stomp on her knee. She managed to twist her leg out of the way, but the pain in her kidneys brought tears to her eyes. There was no time for a prolonged fight. They could be discovered at any moment.

When the warrior tried to grab her in a bear hug, she didn't resist. With a cry of triumph, he wrapped his arms around Kokochin and lifted her off the ground. The heels of both hands slammed into either side of his head. Howling in pain, he dropped her to the ground and covered his ears.

"Run!" said Jaleh.

The others were dead, or on the ground, and the commotion behind them was getting louder.

Kokochin sprinted away from the Gilded Lily, following Jaleh through the streets. They ran through the darkness, ducking around corners and up stairs, down alleys and abandoned lanes. As sweat rolled down her face, fresh pain began to build in Kokochin's side. Finally, Jaleh slowed and then stopped at a crossroads. She was breathing hard, and for a while neither of them could speak. As they tried to catch their breath, they listened to the city for sounds of pursuit.

"What have you done?" gasped Kokochin between breaths. "The general was Timur's son."

"I know," said Jaleh. "That was the point. To create chaos."

"The people here will suffer for what you've done. They might burn the city to the ground, and slaughter everyone in it."

Jaleh remained impassive. "It's possible, but necessary."

Kokochin was appalled. "How can you say that?"

"We're not ready. Persia cannot defend itself yet. Every delay that slows Timur's progress is worth it." Jaleh shook her head. "Why didn't you leave the city?"

"I came here to help the people, not leave them to die," said Kokochin. She'd also hoped to make a fresh start, where no one knew who she'd been before. It was a chance to prove to herself she wasn't the same person anymore.

"You should leave, while you still can," said Jaleh. "They'll be looking for you."

Kokochin was under no illusions. If the madam wanted to save her life, never mind her business, she would tell the authorities everything about Kokochin. It wouldn't take them long to find out where she lived. Everything she had built over the last few months would soon be gone. Then, she would be the most wanted woman in the city.

CHAPTER 13
Kaivon

For three days, Kaivon and Esme had been tracking the merchant train carrying the siege engines. Even broken down into their component parts, the weapons would be massive. Therefore, it was a little surprising to see that the twelve covered wagons were not very tall. However, each wagon was pulled by a team of oxen, suggesting they were still heavy.

Ever since Amir-Hossein had told them about the weapons, Kaivon had known it was a trap. Transporting engines over short distances was common. Specific parts might be salvaged from one siege to the next, but the machines were far too big and heavy to move over long distances. The weapons would be rebuilt, under careful supervision from engineers, then dragged a short distance to bombard a city. During his time with Hulagu, Kaivon had seen them used to scare the population and destroy city fortifications.

The questions then became, did Amir-Hossein truly believe what he had told them? Or had someone purposefully filled his head with a fanciful story? And if it wasn't siege weapons, then what was being transported under heavy guard?

The daily progress of the wagons didn't amount to much, unless it was another part of an elaborate charade, but that seemed far-fetched. Kaivon was determined to find out what was being transported. And if it was useful, could they steal it?

Whatever the contents, they appeared to be valuable, as a thousand warriors guarded the wagons day and night. To take on these Mongol warriors would be impossible without a small army of their own. For this mission, a more subtle approach was needed.

At their current pace, the wagons were still a day's travel from Kabul. Someone riding on horseback, at a canter, could cover the same distance in a third of the time. And some truths about an army on the march were common to everyone.

Warriors needed entertainment.

Even here, less than a day from the walls of Kabul, a stream of local people made the journey to the wagons because there was money to be made. Timur's army was rich from conquest, and the warriors were in the middle of nowhere with nothing to do until morning.

Musicians, entertainers, whores, food and drink sellers, as well as traders with trinkets, narcotics, jewellery and even exotic pets, arrived at the camp before dark. As Kaivon expected, most popular with the warriors were the food sellers and the whores.

It wasn't long before the camp resembled something more like a party, with musicians and women making circuits of the fires. Once money had changed hands, individuals disappeared into the dark, away from prying eyes.

Kaivon and Esme had a covered wagon, painted like those around them, which held barrels full of beer, and they were accompanied by six other people. The mission was too critical to rely on young warriors desperate for their first taste of battle. All of those beside Kaivon were either veterans or they had worked for the House of Grace for years. The operation required steady hands, cool heads, and people used to operating under pressure.

As he and the others unloaded barrels of beer, Kaivon noticed that only a portion of the camp was open to visitors. There was a line of sentries who stared with envy at their friends getting drunk. The area behind them contained the wagons, and it was strictly off-limits to everyone. When a warrior tried to head in that direction for a private dalliance with a woman, he was turned around and sent elsewhere. At some point during the night, the sentries would change over, but Kaivon guessed that was hours away. It was going to be a long night.

Kaivon, Esme and four others served the warriors endless mugs of weak beer while the remaining two scouted the camp. There seemed to be an endless stream of men, all of them desperate to part with their money and get drunk. Hours passed in a blur as barrel after barrel was drained. They were going through them so quickly, Kaivon worried they were going to run out before the end of the night. Finally, the tide of drinkers slowed, but it never completely stopped.

He and Esme took a short break while the others carried on serving. The two scouts had only just returned from studying the camp. One of them went to serve drinks while the other met with them in the back of a covered wagon amidst empty barrels. The air reeked of beer, and while Kaivon had almost become immune, Esme wrinkled her nose.

"You were gone a long time," she said.

"They were being extremely careful," said the scout, a rat-faced man called Mehrab. He had worked with the House of Grace for several years, although Esme had been vague about the specifics. Kaivon suspected he was a thief and burglar. On this occasion, he was ideally suited for the job.

"So, what are they transporting?" asked Kaivon. He had theories, and so did Esme.

"Well, it's not weapons," said Mehrab, with a grin.

Kaivon had been sure it was black powder. It was rumoured to have devastating effects on a city's defences, but was also notoriously unstable.

"Then what is it?" said Esme.

Mehrab fished out a gold coin from his pocket, which he held up between two fingers. With a subtle flick, he made it dance across his knuckles. The likeness stamped on the coin was an unfamiliar face, but Kaivon guessed it was Timur, or someone he'd invaded.

"Money. Lots and lots of money." There was a dangerous, greedy glint in his eyes that worried Kaivon.

"Please tell me you didn't steal much," he said, glancing at Esme.

"No, of course not," said Mehrab, just a little too quickly. Esme gripped his wrist and he tried to pull away, but she held on tight. "I only took a few. Just a handful. There are twelve wagons full of gold."

With a sigh, she shoved him away. Hopefully, with so much money, it wouldn't be noticed. It seemed unlikely that the fortune would be tallied until it reached its final destination.

"It must be part of his war chest," said Esme, mirroring his thoughts. "Money he's looted from Delhi and nearby."

"Part of it?" said Mehrab, his mouth dropping open. "I should have taken more."

"Go out there and do something useful," said Esme, shoving a barrel towards the thief.

"Can I keep the gold?" asked Mehrab.

Esme rolled her eyes. "Yes." They couldn't risk him trying to sneak back in to replace it. With a laugh, Mehrab slid out of the wagon, shouldered a barrel and disappeared.

"Timur is readying to invade the Ilkhanate. This year," said Kaivon. He had hoped it would be next year. It seemed as if that had been wishful thinking on his part. While Timur might conquer cities and scourge them for their wealth, it wouldn't be sufficient to fund such a vast and lengthy campaign. He would need support from allies in the Chagatai khanate to continually deliver supplies to his army.

"I cannot believe after all that we've been through, we have to rely on Temujin, and hope that he knows what he's doing," said Esme. Kaivon felt the same, but so far, the new khan had proven effective in consolidating forces across the Ilkhanate. The real test was yet to come, as none of Temujin's forces had gone into battle against Timur.

"For now, our enemy is the same. I trust that, even if I don't trust him," said Kaivon.

"The money will have to pass through Kabul. We need to find a way to steal it before it leaves the city." Esme started playing with a strand of her hair, twisting it into a temporary braid. Kaivon had noticed it was something she did when deep in thought.

"Can your sister's contacts help?"

"Perhaps," said Esme. "Wagons leave the city every day. We may be able to smuggle out some of the money before anyone notices. We won't be able to take all of it."

Once they realised the money was missing, every single wagon would be stopped, and the city would be scoured for the missing gold.

"A job for another day," said Kaivon. "We should keep a close eye on Mehrab. I worry the gold might prove too tempting."

"Me too," said Esme, letting go of her little braid. Almost immediately it began to unravel. They dragged a couple of barrels off the wagon together, then went to serve more beer to drunk warriors.

The following morning, with their pockets heavy with coin and their wagon completely drained of beer, they returned to Kabul. Thankfully, they had been able to keep a close eye on Mehrab, and he'd not attempted to sneak away to steal more gold. Kaivon suspected the only reason Mehrab had behaved, was that Esme had told him they would be stealing all of it once they returned to the city.

Esme dozed on the short journey back, while Kaivon yawned the whole way. After they'd returned the wagon and horses to the stable, they agreed on a time to meet with the others that evening. With both of them yawning, he and Esme went in search of their bed.

After six hours of sleep and a decent meal, Kaivon felt more awake, but his eyes were still sandy. It was early evening when they stopped off at the safe house. He was about to push open the front door when Esme put a hand across his chest. Kaivon started to ask what was wrong, then he saw where she was pointing.

On the door frame at shoulder height was a tiny smudge of blood. The door was also slightly ajar, which he hadn't noticed. As Kaivon's heart began to pound, any remaining tiredness evaporated. Esme drew a dagger while he pulled one from his belt. With her free hand, Esme slowly pushed open the door and he tensed for a fight.

The hallway was empty, but halfway down, he spotted something dark on the floor. It was a small pool of blood. From further inside the building, Kaivon caught a whiff of something unpleasant and familiar. Esme had smelled it too, as she grimaced and shook her head, trying to dispel it. Kaivon tightened the grip on his dagger, then scanned the street for suspicious onlookers. If there was anyone lurking on rooftops or in the alleyways, they were well-hidden. Nevertheless, the hairs on the back of Kaivon's neck rose. It felt as if he was being watched.

Esme glanced over and raised an eyebrow. They both knew it was a trap, but they couldn't just walk away. Kaivon needed to know what had happened, and who was responsible. Only a handful of people knew about their safe house. They had been extremely careful, or so he thought.

Moving slowly, and as quietly as possible, Kaivon followed Esme through the front door and down the hallway. She paused beside an open doorway, knelt down, and checked the pulse of someone lying on the floor. It was Mehrab. His eyes were closed and there was a smear of blood across his forehead. Esme shook her head and stood up.

At the end of the corridor was the main room, where they held their meetings. It was a large space that had previously been used for storage. They'd made it a bit more habitable with a table and chairs, a battered rug, and even a small painting on one wall. Esme stepped into the room and immediately moved to the left, while Kaivon went to the right.

What had once been a pleasant space had been turned into a charnel house. There were bodies, and even individual bits of people, scattered across the room. The floor, walls and even the ceiling had been sprayed with blood. The smell of several open bodies saturated the air, and the ripe stench made Kaivon gag. Propped up in a corner was Amir-Hossein. At first glance, he appeared whole, but Kaivon noticed something was wrong. His head was slightly askew on his body.

Esme knelt beside one of the bodies that was missing its head. Three severed heads had been stacked in a corner. Their lifeless eyes were staring.

"Look at the wound," she said, gesturing at the neck. "It's been cauterised. There's no blood. What kind of a weapon could do such a thing?"

Even with all of his experience of warfare, Kaivon had no answers. A heated piece of metal could seal a wound, but this was something else. Something impossible. Trying to breathe through his mouth, Kaivon approached Amir-Hossein's body in the corner. One of his eyes was still open, and a terrible expression of pain and suffering had been stamped into his features. It was as if he had been frozen at the moment of his death. When Kaivon touched his forehead, Amir-Hossein's head rolled away, revealing another wound sealed with heat. It appeared as if someone had a fondness for decapitating their victims.

"We should leave. The bodies smell fresh," said Esme.

"I was just thinking that," said Kaivon, getting to his feet. "I don't want to meet whoever did this."

As Kaivon turned towards the door, the air in front of him rippled like the surface of a pond. A tall man with blonde hair and blocky features stepped out of the distortion.

"That would be me," said the big man, with a toothy grin. His leather armour and bearing told Kaivon he was a soldier, but he couldn't see any weapons, not even a dagger. The most worrying aspect about the stranger was his eyes. One was dark brown and the other a pale blue that bordered on grey. Given what Kaivon had seen and heard of Behrouz, this soldier had to be one of the other Kozan.

He scanned the room, noted the two of them were alone and then relaxed, leaning against the doorframe. Apparently the Kozan thought the two of them posed no real danger.

"So, you're the troublemakers," he said, totally at ease. They both still held their daggers, and Kaivon had a sword on his waist as well, but the stranger was unconcerned. "Sabotage, assassination, poison. You've been busy."

"How?" said Esme, gesturing at the bodies. "How did you do it?" Kaivon didn't know if Esme was playing for time so they could formulate a plan, or if she was genuinely curious. Either way, he could see that Esme's shoulders were tensed for a fight.

The Kozan held up one hand, turning it this way and that in front of his face. The air around his fingers blurred, and then his whole hand became indistinct.

"Who else do you work with in the city? Who is in charge?" asked the Kozan, turning towards Esme. "Talk, or I'll slice off his arms, one at a time, and then his legs."

The Kozan had no need of a blade to defeat them. His body was a weapon. To Kaivon's surprise, Esme attacked the big man, slashing at him with her dagger. Kaivon had no choice but to step forward and join in. The Kozan's hand became solid again. He caught Esme's wrist, pulling her off the ground with one arm, until her feet were dangling. When Kaivon tried to stab him, the big man simply held up his free hand, with his palm facing outward.

The tip of Kaivon's blade slammed into something hard and crumpled upon impact. The steel shattered into a hundred pieces, as if it had been made of glass. Ignoring the dagger, Esme slipped free of the Kozan's grip, dropped to the floor, and lashed out towards his leg with her foot. She'd been aiming for his kneecap, but he twisted to one side, taking the impact on his thigh. He grunted in pain, and retaliated with a boot. It caught Esme in the chest, sending her spinning away across the room.

Dropping the dagger hilt, Kaivon went for the Kozan's face, clawing at his eyes. The big man was taller and stronger, and someone used to fighting up close. He tilted his head down, to protect his eyes, and held up both arms to protect his head. Kaivon was disturbed to see that the big man was grinning.

Something hard caught Kaivon in the stomach, driving the air from his lungs. As he struggled to breathe, the Kozan's forehead collided with Kaivon's face. Pain blossomed in Kaivon's nose, and a few seconds later he came to, lying on the floor with blood streaming down both cheeks.

Through bleary eyes, he saw Esme trying to wrestle with the Kozan, but for all her skill, he was an immovable object. He constantly intercepted her attacks. It was as if he could predict what she was about to do. It soon became obvious that he was playing with her, like a cat toying with a mouse. All too soon, he tired of the game. Instead, he gripped Esme by the throat and pulled her upright, until her toes were barely touching the ground. Her fingers clawed at his hand, while her face turned red as she fought for breath.

"Leave her alone," gasped Kaivon, struggling to his knees, and then his feet. His nose was broken. It felt as if his ribs were cracked, and he couldn't draw a full breath. Standing upright felt impossible, and all he could do was hunch over.

"Ah, there he is," said the Kozan with a sneer. His fingers tightened on Esme's throat and she began to wheeze. "Is she your woman? Your wife?"

"Let her go." Black spots danced in front of Kaivon's eyes.

"Then talk," said the big man. "Who do you work for?"

"Teague, your time has come," said a new voice.

The big man dropped Esme and spun about, raising both hands towards the newcomer with his fingers splayed. Kaivon watched as a familiar man stepped into the room. It was Behrouz.

Kaivon had not seen the Kozan for months, ever since Behrouz had transported him to the training camp. He had not changed in the interim, but his clothing was that of a local. It seemed too much of a coincidence to be a random encounter. It made Kaivon wonder if he'd seen Behrouz around the city and had not even noticed. How long had the Kozan been watching them and this building?

The big man, Teague, said nothing. He merely stared at Behrouz, and his eyes never wavered. His whole body was tense and utterly focused.

"How long has it been?" asked Behrouz, who by comparison seemed relaxed. He was smiling while walking back and forth across the room. Teague's eyes tracked him, but the rest of him was immobile. "Fifty years? Seventy?"

"Doesn't matter," said Teague. "You're old and weak."

"Old, yes. Weak? I guess we'll see." Behrouz grinned and tilted his head to one side. "We had an agreement. You should not be interfering."

Some of the colour had returned to Esme's face, and she was breathing easier. There were red marks on either side of her neck that would later turn into bruises. Kaivon knew they should not be witnessing this, but there was only one way out, and that was through Behrouz. Kaivon was still winded and in pain. Even if the two of them charged Behrouz together, they wouldn't win.

Teague shrugged. "They meddled too much. Our champion wanted it fixed."

Behrouz glanced at Kaivon for the first time. "You should go," he said, stepping aside.

"Take one step and she dies," said Teague, pointing a finger at Esme.

Behrouz laughed, a harsh sound that bounced off the walls. His genuine mirth caused Teague to back up, his eyes roaming the walls, the floor and even the ceiling.

"I can smell her," said Teague, lifting his head slightly, scenting the air. "Where is she?"

"That's the problem with Chaos," said Behrouz, addressing the big man. "Divide and conquer only works for so long."

"Let's end it," said Teague.

The air pressure in the room changed. It was as if Kaivon had been dropped from a great height. His stomach lurched up into his throat, forcing him to brace an arm against the wall to stay upright. Across the room, he could see Esme was also being affected. She was unsteady on her feet, swaying from side to side.

Behrouz raised both hands with fingers spread towards Teague. Kaivon heard a grinding sound, like the creaking of wood or stone under pressure. The rafters in the ceiling throbbed and jumped. Dust trickled down from above their heads. A second later, his scalp began to prickle and the sense of being watched increased.

"Run," said Behrouz, not taking his eyes off Teague.

Kaivon didn't wait. Esme grabbed his shoulder with one hand, resting part of her weight on him. Holding each other up, they stumbled towards the door. At any second, he expected to feel a rush of warmth from behind as Teague attacked them. When they made it to the doorway, Kaivon sent Esme ahead of him down the hallway. He risked a glance over his shoulder and immediately regretted it.

"Keep going," said Behrouz. It sounded as if his voice was coming from far away instead of just a few paces.

There was something wrong with the air in the building. It flickered and seemed to trickle slowly towards the floor like molasses. Patches blurred and then snapped back into focus.

The effect was disorientating, and Kaivon felt bile rising in the back of his throat.

As he turned to leave, he saw something erupting out of the floor, throwing stone and earth into the room. At the same time, Behrouz surged across the room, hands stretched out like claws. The air in front of him rippled like water while Teague tried to ward off whatever was coming. A split-second later, the ceiling began to collapse into the room.

Kaivon ran for the front door. Behind him it sounded it as if the whole building was collapsing. He scooped up Esme and kept going, while screaming timbers and shattering stone coughed up a wall of sound. Something slammed into Kaivon's back, then both of them were thrown forward into the street. A wave of sound and energy passed over them as they lay face down, huddled together. Smoke, dust and debris surged across them, bouncing off his armour, ripping clothing, tugging at his boots. It seemed to go on forever as the building collapsed, ripped apart by a battle between the Kozan.

Dazed, choking on dust and almost completely deaf, they made it to their knees and then shuffled away down the street. Through a haze of flying grit, Kaivon saw that only a few stray timbers remained upright like jagged teeth. Otherwise, the entire building, and both of its neighbours, had been decimated. It was as if a giant hand had reached down and scooped out the building. All that remained was rubble and death.

CHAPTER 14
Behrouz

Maryam burst out of the floor, Skimming towards Teague. The air crackled with energy as she pushed a cone of corroded time ahead of her. If she managed to brush Teague with her weapon, it would age him a thousand years in a heartbeat. No one could come back from that. Not even their teacher, Melchior.

Despite the odds, Teague was grinning like a maniac. Behrouz knew that for centuries, the former King had been desperate for a battle like this between the Kozan. Down the long years, they had run into each other from time to time. There had been the occasional skirmish, but this fight was different. It would only end when one or more of them were dead. Although he was not in a rush to die, Behrouz found in that possibility a form of peace. Soon, one of them would find out what came next. It was a mystery that none of them had been able to answer.

Teague didn't even use his powers to evade Maryam. Her momentum was unstoppable, but it also meant she couldn't alter the course of her attack. He simply dove to the floor and skidded across the ground, folding up the rug as he went. With a slash of his hand, Teague added momentum to Maryam's attack, which propelled her through the ceiling, into the floor above and then further towards the roof. She punched a hole through stone and wood. Above her head, Behrouz saw a patch of sky.

The building shifted on its foundation. It had been made unstable by Maryam's tunnelling. The floor tilted to one side. While Behrouz struggled to stay on his feet, the walls began to shake themselves apart. Teague came at him then, hands blurred and on fire, hot enough to melt flesh and bone. Seizing the big man by both wrists, Behrouz held him long enough to Skim both of them away.

He didn't focus on where they were going so much as putting some distance between them and the city. And all the while, uncaring of their environment or the damage it would inflict on others, Teague tried to melt his face.

Wrapped in a calming cocoon provided by the Eternal Fire, Behrouz watched all of this dispassionately. When the blur around them changed from streets and buildings to rolling hills and canyons, he stopped Skimming and hurled Teague away.

Behrouz glanced at their surroundings and saw they were in a remote and desolate valley. There were no signs of any life beyond a few scrubby plants and hardy weeds. The rest was broken rocks and dusty scree slopes. There would be no need to hold back anymore. The thought was both exhilarating and terrifying. Never in his life had he used his powers with such reckless abandon.

Howling like a wolf, Teague hurled a boulder the size of a horse at Behrouz. With a flick of his wrists, Behrouz cast a net across it and accelerated time. In the space of two heartbeats, it aged hundreds of years.

Behrouz lowered his eyelids to narrow slits as a cloud of grit and dust blew across his face. It had barely passed by when Teague slammed into him, using his fists. His knuckles caught Behrouz on the forehead, rocking his skull back. Another jab immediately followed, snapping it to the left.

A long time ago, Teague had been a champion pugilist. He'd beaten dozens of men to death with his bare hands. Thinking back to his own youth as a wrestler, and time spent in the *zurkhaneh*, Behrouz ducked another punch, then grabbed the Nord's outstretched arm with both hands. Using his full weight, he twisted Teague's arm in its socket while also shoving him backwards. Teague's ankle collided with Behrouz's outstretched leg, which sent him flying.

Both of them were a little dazed and out of breath. A silent agreement passed between them and they took a moment to recover. There was no sign of Maryam, and Behrouz had no idea if she would turn up. For now, he had to assume it would only be the two of them. He could not rely on any outside help. A different approach was needed.

Behrouz folded the air above his right hand, over and over again, until it formed a long, curved blade of shimmering light. A kaleidoscope of colours was reflected through the impossible blade. A lethal strike would rip Teague's body apart, sending pieces of him across time, scattering his essence beyond repair.

"Good," said the agent of Chaos. A huge blade of air formed in Teague's hand, a two-handed longsword. "This is as it should be."

"Do you have any regrets?" asked Behrouz. Then, seeing Teague's puzzled expression, he added, "Not about me. I meant from your lifetime. Something you wish you'd done, but haven't."

Never one for long speeches, or sharing anything intimate, Teague merely shook his head.

"Nothing?" said Behrouz, pressing him for an answer. He found it hard to believe for someone who had lived for centuries.

Much to his surprise, the big man actually paused and even lowered his blade to think. Finally, he said, "No, because a life, even one as long as ours, has an end. All things must die. To put off what I could have done in the moment, to make an excuse, is to deny life. To deny..." he trailed off, searching for the right word.

"Joy?" said Behrouz.

"As you say," said Teague.

Once, Behrouz had been a prince and Teague a king. Both nations were long gone. There was a time and a place for everything. Perhaps their time had passed.

"Let's end this, brother," said Teague, raising his sword in a salute. Behrouz mirrored the gesture, took a deep breath, then waited for his opponent to attack.

Teague came towards him with a flurry of cuts, testing his defence. Their blades whistled as they sliced through the air, crackling with unspent energy. When they collided, sparks rained down like stray embers from a fire, but these were pieces of time. Moments, that would be lost forever. Fragments from centuries past that had never been preserved with ink. Behrouz wished he'd kept a journal, like his Teacher.

By holding their swords in place with their will, and carving them from reality, it created an echo that had unpleasant side-effects. As Teague came forward again, Behrouz became aware of murky figures at the periphery of his vision. They were vaguely shaped like people, with long spindly arms and legs. He didn't need to see their faces. They would have swirling pits for eyes that hungered for his soul.

Teague fought with precision, using tight cuts and jabs, despite the size of his blade. Against a different opponent, and a sword made of steel, Behrouz would have waited until they tired themselves out, but this was a blademaster with centuries of experience. Behrouz blocked one handed, maintaining distance between them to prevent Teague from using his extended reach.

They surged back and forth across the valley. Their silent audience was eager to consume both of them and bring about an end to their unnaturally long existence.

Behrouz was a fraction too slow with a parry. He tried to step back out of range, but the tip of Teague's blade sliced across the top of his arm, just below his shoulder. At first, there was no pain and no obvious signs of a wound. Then Behrouz started to feel it. A dull ache, like an absence, as if something vital had been cut away from his body. Memories were pared away from him, faces and names of loved ones. He was being unravelled.

A spasm of nausea swept through him, and a cough startled Behrouz. The void in his mind seemed insurmountable. A wound that would, forever, remain open. Somehow, the edges folded together, as if it had never been, and yet he knew there something was askew.

Teague stepped back, giving him a moment to recover. Despite being at a distance from his emotions, Behrouz felt his unease. It was as if someone had fractured the bubble of peace that surrounded him. The Servants surged closer, ravenous, desperate for succour.

Gripping the hilt of his sword with two hands, and with a battle cry of his own, Behrouz went on the offensive. Grunting in surprise, Teague was forced to back away as blow after blow tried to break through his defence. Slicing and cutting, his blade whirling at uncanny speeds, Behrouz felt a smile curl his lips as his blade scored a cut across Teague's ribs.

The big man winced and Behrouz stepped back, knowing exactly what he was feeling. He saw the moment a cloud of confusion passed through the big man's eyes. Pieces of his memory, of his self, had been torn away. Old and new sights and sounds were being mixed together in both of their minds. People who had not lived in the same lifetime, now existed in some of Behrouz's memories.

"I feel unmade," said Teague, rocking slightly on his feet. Old instincts, drilled into the former king and warrior, took over. His sword came up, his eyes narrowed and he stepped forward, ready to engage. Both of them were not what they once were, but each man still had several lifetimes of knowledge to call upon. They had seen countless battles, sparred for thousands of hours, and witnessed the rise and fall of saviours, tyrants and world-breakers. There were but a handful of people in the world who could stand up to them. If they had chosen to work together, and rule, Behrouz could not begin to imagine what the world might resemble today.

When their blades came together, Behrouz knew Teague was equally determined to never suffer such a wound again. Each time they came close to clipping one another, they overcompensated and pulled back out of reach. A scar on the body could be tolerated, but not another of the mind.

Normally, the crawl of the sun across the sky would have told Behrouz the time of day. Here, in this unnamed valley, locked in mortal combat, he lost all sense of time. Part of him forgot the reason, and even the name of the man who stood against him.

He hissed in pain, but then forgot the reason. The rent in his sleeve gave him a clue, but then it was gone. The big man howled like a wolf and stumbled back, clutching his right knee where Behrouz had caught him.

When next they locked blades, shoving and hissing at one another, Behrouz noticed the shadows were longer. The crowd that watched seemed closer, and now he could hear something. Not words or singing, but a sound. It rose and fell, and then the pattern repeated over. A prayer or a mantra, but the purpose of it was beyond his knowledge.

Teague stumbled, his bad knee gave way, and he almost dropped his blade. One fist pressed in the ground, rocks and stone grinding into flesh. His head tipped forward, long hair covering his face.

Behrouz moved to press the advantage, sweeping his blade up. But the big man heard him coming. His head snapped up, and as Behrouz swung down to sever Teague's head from his shoulders, he lunged to one side. It was Teague's desperation that saved him. Instead of cutting into the Kozan's neck, the blade bit into the ground.

"Ughhh," said Behrouz, suddenly winded.

The air had been knocked out of him. He couldn't take a full breath. Looking down, he saw Teague's blade buried in his gut. The mantra was louder. The misshapen people were almost within arm's reach. Memories spilled out of Behrouz. His family, long dead were leached away from him. His wife, children, their descendants, and all of their names were taken.

Instead of staying detached from his emotions, Behrouz released the Eternal Fire. If this was to be his end, Behrouz wanted to feel all of it, good and bad, wonder and agony. From the sad smile on his face, he knew that Teague was also living in the moment.

The world blurred, and Behrouz stared at nothing through unshed tears.

"Stay back!" cried Teague. He held no weapon, but swept his arms back and forth at something, or someone. Behrouz didn't know who or why the big man was doing it. Were they friends? Lovers?

Apart from his name, Behrouz was having difficulty remembering almost anything. As the light spilled from the wound in his body, his mind continued to drain of memories. Like a bucket leaking water from many holes, things fell away so quickly he struggled to feel any emotion as they vanished.

Pain blossomed in his knees and they hit the ground. Rocks ground into his flesh, the palms of his hands, his cheek. Everything became grey, black and white. He heard breathing, someone crying, and a song that was hauntingly familiar. It was something his mother had sung. A lullaby from when he'd been a small boy, afraid of the dark and the lurking monsters. Too soon it faded, his ears were wrapped in wool, but then an older memory resurfaced. He smelled fresh bread and cinnamon.

Staring up at the sky, Behrouz saw an endless blue vista without clouds and a single bird drifting far away on a spiral of warm air. It rose higher and higher, losing shape and focus. Soon it was just a black dot, moving, coasting, and then it too was forgotten, as his being exploded into a million pieces.

CHAPTER 15
The Twelve

Kimya was exhausted. Her job as Trade Minister was consuming more and more of her time. In addition, she had her businesses to run, her work for the House of Grace as One, and she also had to deal with her own network of contacts in Persia and beyond.

Of late, she'd been letting one of her trusted contacts respond to messages from her people. She simply didn't have time to meet with individuals anymore. Only the most important information was passed on by Min, her assistant. The former Empress, Guyuk, was also watching her closely, desperate for the merest hint of treachery. She hungered for anything that she could use to gain favour with Temujin. At this point, Kimya suspected she could commit the most heinous crime and the khan would still not side with his adopted mother. After all, Guyuk had put the bounty on his head and sent people to kill him, including Kokochin. Kimya put the Empress from her mind, for the time being, at least. She would be dealt with soon enough. This morning was all about work for the House.

She read through the messages from Min, sifted truth from rumours, and then sat back to mull it over. Events were moving fast. Attempts at delaying the war with Timur had worked, but only up to a point.

Kaivon, Esme and others had disrupted supplies, poisoned camps of men, stolen money and even killed groups of officers, but it had not stopped the juggernaut. War with Timur was inevitable. It also seemed it would begin in the summer.

The wealth he had accumulated was vast, and his army was hungry for more. The most pressing questions she had were, where would Timur's army strike at the Ilkhanate? And when? Information from the Chagatai khanate was filtering in, but the long distance made it slow to arrive, and their network of contacts in the khanate was small. However, large groups of warriors could not pass through any settlement without being noticed. They required an enormous supply of provisions, and for the locals, it often felt as if they had been descended upon by a swarm of locusts. Timur's warriors stripped towns and villages of all food and wealth, often leaving people starving in their wake. But the war machine needed to be fed, and the people who protested were butchered and left for the crows. Kimya had confirmed several stories of Timur's brutality, creating pyramids of severed heads, filling trees with hanging bodies, and flaying people to death in public squares. But in some places, it had not stopped the notions of rebellion. The last town that revolted had been decimated, but then rebuilt for its strategic position. But that was not before the prisoners were cemented alive within the walls.

As Kimya went over the reports in her mind, she slowly pieced together a pattern. It seemed like a risky approach, and yet Timur was renowned for his strategy on the battlefield. There would be more that she wasn't seeing, which she found enormously frustrating, especially given her resources. She knew Temujin shared in her annoyance, but he had from time to time let slip a few details he'd gathered while journeying alone. Nevertheless, it felt as if both of them were constantly operating with one eye closed.

After glancing at the sky to gauge the time, she tidied up her desk and left her office by the back door. Guyuk had three people following her. It took Kimya a while to lose the woman who had been watching the rear of her building. Kimya took her time and carefully checked for any other spies before making her way to the horse market.

Breeders and merchants from all over were showing off their animals. The market was loud and bustling with armed guards, merchants, dozens of horses in pens, and even families with children who had come to watch the animals. Kimya didn't know a lot about horses, but she passed some huge black beasts from Europe. They were so big that their heads towered over her. Apparently, they were strong enough to carry an armoured knight into battle. She also saw lots of steppe ponies, which were favoured by the Mongols. Bred for warfare, the sturdy beasts could cover huge distances in one day. Doing her best to avoid eye contact with merchants, in case they tried to drag her into a bidding war, Kimya hurried on.

Assuming her role as One again, she waited inside one of the permanent stables for the others to arrive. Only three of the stalls were occupied, but the horses were quiet and comfortable around strangers. As before, several of their number were missing. One knew where all of them were, except for Twelve. Mari had been vague about where she'd been going, but she had said it was urgent and necessary. All One could do was pray, and hope that one day her mentor returned.

When everyone was assembled, it was clear that a few of the women were uncomfortable with the smell of horses.

"What news from the East?" asked One, silencing the other conversations.

Seven cleared her throat and stepped forward. "I wasn't sure, but Five's contacts confirmed it," she said, exchanging a nod with Five. "There's trouble in the Empire of the Great Khan."

"What's happened?" asked Two.

"In an attempt to appease the Chinese people, Kublai Khan wants to move the capital city to Dadu," said Seven. She started to get animated, pacing up and down the stable as she spoke. "Some say it's because of the influence of his wife, Chabi. Whatever the reason, a proclamation was made in court. Kaidu is a respected warlord and a traditionalist. He favours the old ways, but also old beliefs, which has won him great favour."

"He was also noticeably absent at the kurultai when Kublai became the Great Khan," added Five. She picked up a piece of straw from the ground and began to twist it between her fingers. "It seems that he's been bearing a grudge against Kublai for some time. But, he's also been gathering allies over the last few years. Maybe he hoped Ariq would win and solve the problem for him."

"War, then?" said One. "Another civil war?"

"Yes," said Seven, flinching when one of the horses whickered. One had forgotten she had a fear of large animals. She'd been so busy, it had slipped her mind, but to Seven's credit, she had not complained about the location. "Whatever reinforcements Temujin has received from his uncle, they will be the last. However, it also means no more interference or thinly veiled threats, like the one he received from the Venetian."

Marco Polo's visit had been most unexpected. Temujin had kept him in court for two weeks, mostly to prove a point, before releasing the merchant. One had to admit, Marco had a way with words. He could paint beautiful images in the mind with his stories. She could see why Kublai had become so enamoured with him.

The last that One had heard of Marco was that he'd returned to Venice. After being encouraged to stay in the court of the Great Khan for over a decade, One suspected he would never leave Europe again.

"The civil war with Ariq ended sooner than I would have liked," said One. "The more turmoil there is, the better it is for everyone opposed to the Empire. We want this war to continue for years. Let them grind their armies to dust against each other."

"I do not think this one will be quickly resolved," said Five, plaiting her piece of straw. "While change is inevitable, Kublai moves too fast for many Mongols. Freedom of worship is one thing, but traditions are being forgotten or ignored. He's angered many people in Mongolia and his khanate."

From personal experience, One was aware of how much influence the right individual could have in court, and how much access it could give them to the khan. Even if they were an outsider, they could become powerful, and a trusted confidant.

"We need to make sure this civil war stretches on for a long time," said One. Her fear wasn't that Kublai would tire of war. It was woven in every fibre of his being. She was more concerned that Kaidu's forces would be crushed too soon to suit their plans. With the right rumours whispered in the right ears, Kublai's inclusive attitude towards other religions could be used against him. She had even heard stories that he favoured Buddhism and had been spending time discussing doctrine with monks.

There were no chairs in the stables, and Two's fidgeting hinted at pain in her hips. "What are you thinking?" she asked, raising an eyebrow.

"With the absence of Marco Polo, Kublai has lost one of his beloved trinkets," said One. "He collects the strange and unusual. We need to send someone to the court of the Great Khan. A rare and peculiar peacock who can get close to him, then whisper the right thing in his ear."

Running through the list of people in her own network, no one came to mind. One raised an eyebrow at the others, knowing that at least one of them would have such a person in their ranks.

One rubbed her right eyebrow, trying to ease the pain behind it. A headache was starting to form.

"It must be a man," said Ten, before anyone could put forward a name. They all knew about the khan's reputation and his insatiable lust. If they sent a woman, sooner or later, he would attempt to bed her. After that, no matter how interesting her mind or thoughts, he wouldn't value her opinion.

STEPHEN ARYAN   161

They discussed it for a while and came up with a shortlist of individuals. "We should think it over, and next time there's a meeting, we can vote." One's headache was getting worse. They could have voted today, but she didn't want to extend the length of their meeting. The light was starting to hurt her eyes. She needed to lie down in a dark room for a while before dealing with the next thing on her list.

"What about the warriors Kublai sent to support Temujin?" asked Ten, changing the subject.

"They left Tabriz days ago," said One. Part of her job had been arranging supplies for a prolonged journey. "They march to war."

"Where are they going?" asked Two, raising an eyebrow. When the others turned to face her, One noticed some of their gazes were not particularly friendly. They were still uncomfortable that she was working so closely with Temujin. Proximity to the khan had a number of benefits, but it also carried a great deal of risk.

"Temujin wasn't specific, but from all of your reports, I can guess what Timur intends," said One. "I believe he will split his army and strike at the Ilkhanate from two points in the north, and a little further south. Temujin is sending warriors towards Bukhara. I believe they'll meet Timur's forces at the border. Temujin is also sending warriors south from the Golden Horde."

With the removal of Berke, all raids along the northern border of the Ilkhanate had stopped. The alliance with Egypt was over, and the slave trade had ended. Thankfully, the latest crusade was keeping Egypt busy. They were still fighting a brutal war against the Christians for Jerusalem.

There was still some turmoil within the Golden Horde, but Tokhtamysh was proving to be more popular than his predecessor. One was confident he could unite the people, or at least hold them together long enough for his warriors to be useful in the war against Timur.

"And the rest?" said Six. With most of her contacts in the south, her time was completely taken up with the training camps for their young warriors. "What of our warriors?"

"I believe they will face the other half of Timur's forces," said One. "Together with those from vassal states like Georgia. They are veterans, and they have leaders with considerable experience, like King David. Where the battle will take place, I don't know yet. Are our warriors ready?"

Six let out a long sigh. "I'm not the right person to ask," she said, but clearly had an opinion.

"Why would Timur split his forces?" asked Two, mulling it over. "Is one of the strikes a feint to draw away Temujin's army?"

"Perhaps," said One. None of them were experts in warfare, but Two's guess was a good one. "We need to focus all of our efforts on gathering information from beyond our borders. Timing will be critical in this war."

The idea of using their resources to help Temujin was uncomfortable but necessary. He would be dealt with in due course. They discussed other business for a while, and then the meeting came to a natural end.

Everyone hurried away, as a prolonged absence might draw attention, and none of them wanted that. However, Two lingered by the stable door, waiting until all of the others had gone before closing it.

"Is there something on your mind, Shirin?" asked One. Since it was just the two of them there was no need to stick to the usual formality. Shirin leaned against one of the stalls, taking some of the weight off her right leg.

"I was about to ask you the same question," she said. "What are you up to?"

"What do you mean?"

"Don't play games with me, Kimya," said Shirin. "Where is Mari?"

"I don't know," said Kimya. When Shirin raised an eyebrow, she added, "Honestly, she wouldn't tell me."

"But you have suspicions?"

"Yes, and I'm not sure we'll ever see her again," said Kimya. Her headache was persistent. She needed a rest, and Shirin really needed to sit down. Some days, she felt far older than her years, and this was one of them. "The last time we met, she was acting peculiar. She asked me questions about leaving a legacy, and my family. After she'd gone, I found out she'd left instructions with a friend to deal with her affairs. Whatever she's doing, it's dangerous, and she's not sure if she'll survive."

"But there's more to it," said Shirin. "I know you sent Jaleh to Lahore, and now you want to place someone in Kublai's court."

"We've done things like this before," said Kimya, but she was lying to herself. They had always seen killing someone as a last resort, but she'd sent the Widow to kill Timur's general, fully aware of the widespread, damaging repercussions it would bring. Hundreds, potentially thousands of innocents would die as a result. She might not be the one holding the blade, but she had given the order.

"Sometimes, slow and subtle isn't enough. Not anymore. We're doing our best to deal with events in the present, but we also need to prepare for the future. If the worst should happen, and Persia falls to Timur, we need people out there, actively serving our interests. Individuals who can act upon their initiative, and don't need to be told what to do."

"They would be on their own. Totally isolated," said Shirin.

"True, but look at what Kokochin has done," said Kimya. "She built her own network from the local population. There are always people out there who are willing to die for a cause." She knew it was cynical, and manipulative, but it was also necessary.

The challenge was finding suitable individuals who were up to a seemingly impossible task. There were hundreds of people in the House of Grace, but many of them had specialised skills. Many more were useful contacts who supplied information, resources or money, but they lacked the intelligence and determination to act independently. Some of them just lacked the courage. They were happy to serve someone else, especially if it also benefitted them. For more people, they only helped for the promise of extra money.

These contacts also had no idea of who they really served, which protected everyone involved and most importantly, it protected the House. Kimya had been mulling over the idea of independent agents for some time, but it was Mari's sudden departure that had spurred her into action.

"Who else knows?" asked Shirin.

"No one."

"When were you going to tell us?"

"Later," said Kimya with a faint smile. "I just wanted to deal with the current threat before talking about it."

"You should rest. Your squint is getting worse," said Shirin, moving towards the door.

"What will you tell the others?" asked Kimya.

Shirin paused with her back turned. "Nothing, as long as you keep me updated." She pushed open the door and left without waiting for a reply.

After lying in a dark room for two hours, Kimya's headache finally abated. She hadn't really slept and was still tired, but there was a lot to do before she could rest properly. When the urgent summons came to attend the khan, she went in expecting the worst.

Temujin was gripping the arms of his throne so hard that his knuckles had turned white. The usual gaggle of onlookers was absent. Apart from the Kheshig, who were merely ceremonial as Temujin was capable of taking care of himself, the only other individual in the room was Guyuk. The former Empress didn't even try to hide the smug grin that was stretched across her face. It was a strange and worrying sign to see Guyuk so pleased with herself.

"Get on with it," said Temujin. Whatever information Guyuk had, it was clear that she hadn't yet shared it with the khan.

"I know what you've been doing," said Guyuk. She was absolutely confident that whatever she knew was incriminating. "Let's talk of betrayal," she said.

CHAPTER 16
Temujin

Temujin watched his Trade Minister's face with interest as Guyuk rambled on about betrayal and disloyalty. There was barely any change in her expression, but even without additional insight from the Eternal Fire, he could see that Kimya was annoyed.

"My patience is wearing thin," said Temujin, getting tired of Guyuk's gloating.

"Yes, my Khan," said the former Empress, somehow making his title sound like an insult.

"My Khan, before she makes up some ridiculous claims," said Kimya, cutting in. "Are you aware that she's conspiring to release your father and depose you?"

He saw it flash across Guyuk's face before it was buried. The guilt. The fear that she'd been discovered. To her credit, she didn't run screaming from the room, but the Kheshig against the walls suddenly became alert. They did their best to pretend they were deaf and blind, but they heard and saw everything that transpired. Weapons were straightened and they shuffled their feet, ready to charge into a fray.

"That's ridiculous," said Guyuk, after only a small hesitation. "She would say anything to save her own life."

"Silence. Let the Minister speak," said Temujin. It was petty, but he enjoyed denying her the ability to talk.

Guyuk was fuming, but she wisely clamped her mouth shut.

"She attempted to bribe the senior officers sent by your uncle," said the Trade Minister in an eerily calm voice. Temujin noticed her hands were clasped together, and the ridges between her eyebrows were more pronounced. She was enjoying this. To be fair, Temujin was as well. Far too often, he had seen Guyuk make others squirm and suffer.

"They refused to cooperate, and would not release your father. With them heading to war, she looked for an alternative. Lately, Guyuk has been hoarding her wealth. I suspect she's preparing to pay mercenaries to break your father out. It's the mark of a poorly thought-out plan of a desperate woman."

"Where is your proof?" said Guyuk, breaking her brief silence.

"I have witnesses," said Kimya with a shrug, before turning to face Temujin. "But the easiest way to resolve this would be to speak with your father."

Unlike his First Wife, Hulagu was not an accomplished liar. However, Temujin instinctively knew his father would not deny anything, regardless of the consequences. Hulagu truly believed that he was destined to rule. That it was his right, by blood and the favour of whichever god he preferred at that moment, to be on the throne. Hulagu had no doubt that he would leave an indelible mark on history. Arrogance did not begin to sum up the vastness of his father's delusion.

"Then let us all go and speak with him," said Temujin, rising from the throne. Guyuk started to say something, perhaps to put him in his place or tell him it was a stupid idea, but she changed her mind. It remained a difficult adjustment for her, losing all power and authority.

A pair of Kheshig went ahead of them to open doors and clear hallways through the palace. Servants scurried out of the way. Their faces were fearful, in case Temujin's temper proved worse than that of his father. He had no intention of lashing out, but they didn't know that. Many who now served in the palace had been here when he'd taken the throne. It had taken them several days to scrub blood from the floors, walls and ceiling. Their fear served as a constant reminder of how he was perceived by others, and the bloody path it had taken him to get here.

As he descended the stairs to the dungeon, Temujin considered embracing the Eternal Fire and facing his father with serenity. In the end, he decided against it. Its power would keep him calm, and make any barbs thrown at him less painful, but it would also numb him from experiencing other emotions.

Hulagu looked in better health than when Temujin had last seen him. His father's skin had regained some of its natural colour, and he was less haggard. The broken veins on his face from years of heavy drinking had faded, while a simple diet had stripped some of the fat from his body. His eyes, though, they remained the same. Shrewd and calculating.

As Temujin's father glanced at those assembled outside his cell, an amused smile touched the corners of his mouth.

"Don't say a word," said Temujin, waving a hand towards Guyuk. Hulagu glanced briefly at his wife, then refocused his attention on Temujin.

"I'm told that you've been conspiring to escape and overthrow me. That you wish to retake the throne and rule the Ilkhanate again."

Hulagu shrugged. "What of it?" he said. "Did you genuinely expect me to sit here quietly and do nothing?" He shook his head in disappointment, but it had no effect. Temujin no longer needed or wanted his approval.

"I knew you would try something," murmured Temujin, wrapping his fingers around the bars of the cell. "I was more interested in who would help you than when."

"You knew there were traitors in your court?" said Hulagu.

"I knew that a number of rats remained after I took the throne. They smiled along with the rest, but have secretly been plotting behind my back. I needed to be certain who they were before I chose to act."

"Then you're learning what it means to be khan," said Hulagu. It was not the first time he had said something like that. Temujin found the note of approval more than a little disconcerting.

"I have no further use for you," said Temujin, turning towards Guyuk. "You kept a promise to my mother for many years. For that reason alone, I will give you until dawn to leave the city. After that, if you are within its limits, you will be executed."

It took Guyuk a moment to realise he was serious, and then she began to babble. "Leave? Where am I supposed to go? What should I do?"

"I don't care," said Temujin, staring at his father. "Go or die. Those are your only choices."

Temujin watched his father closely, but he saw no anguish as he witnessed the fate of his First Wife. They listened in silence as she fled, her footsteps receding down the corridor and then up the stairs.

"My Khan, with your permission, I will withdraw," said his Trade Minister.

"Stay where you are," said Temujin. It wasn't that he needed an audience, more that he found her presence to be calming. "What did Guyuk mean when she mentioned your betrayal?" he said, fixing the Minister with a hard stare.

Kimya grimaced, but after a long, uncomfortable pause she eventually answered. "I've been using my position as Trade Minister to benefit my businesses."

Of all the potential vices she might have, it was surprising to find she was motivated by greed. He found it quite disappointing. "You've been stealing from me?"

"No. I just made sure that contracts went to friends, and in return, they gave me a gift as thanks."

Hulagu laughed. "I told you, everyone wants something. Now that you know what it is, you can control her."

Over the years, Temujin had seen his father grant favours to many people. Most often, it involved settling old blood debts, or giving them something they desired more than anything in the world. In return, he bought their loyalty, or at least, a passing semblance of it.

"Let me out. I can help you," said Hulagu.

"You will never leave that cell," said Temujin. "You will remain a prisoner for the rest of your life."

Hulagu stood up and approached the bars of his cell. Although Temujin had to crane his neck slightly to meet his father's gaze, he was not intimidated. "You cannot keep me in here forever."

"You have no friends, no allies, and no one is willing to set you free. How will you make this miraculous escape?" asked Temujin, spreading his hands.

"Destiny wills it," said Hulagu with an infuriating smile.

"You are not special, or chosen by god. Heaven, or fate, has not decided that you should rule by some spiritual mandate. The world does not bend around you!"

Hulagu said nothing at first, but his smile remained in place. "We'll see," he said, starting to turn away.

"Don't turn your back on me!" said Temujin, slamming the bars. It felt was as if they were still in court and his father was in charge.

As the smile trickled off Hulagu's face, Temujin saw a hint of the old anger creep in. This was the man he knew. The one who believed he was better than everyone else.

"What did you say?" said Hulagu.

"You will die in there," promised Temujin, "even if I have to kill you myself."

"You can't, because you're weak," said Hulagu. "Seizing the Ilkhanate from me doesn't make you courageous, or strong. The making of a man happens over many years. You have neither the patience nor the will to do what is necessary to rule."

"I should have killed you when I took the throne," said Temujin.

Hulagu stormed up to the bars and stuck his hands through. Gripping Temujin's hands, Hulagu put them on his own throat. "Then do it. Prove to the world that you don't need me. Show everyone that you deserve your place. That you earned it, with blood and sacrifice."

Temujin pulled his hands away, disgusted at his father. "I will not let you manipulate me. There is always a trick with your cunning mind."

"You can't do it," said Hulagu, laughing at Temujin, almost willing him to do it. "Even now, you are bound to me by more than blood."

"Let me guess, if our positions were reversed, you would kill me without any hesitation."

"I would," said Hulagu, revealing some of his simmering rage, "for all that you've done. For murdering my children and usurping my rightful place as ruler. But mostly, because I've always despised you."

"You've made that abundantly clear, for my entire life," said Temujin.

"And now, you are all that's left of my family," said Hulagu, sneering at him. "I will not let that stand. Once you are dead, I will have more children, and this time, if any are weak, I will see them put to death early. It's better that way for everyone."

"You are mad and deluded," said Temujin, pitying his father. Emotions rolled through him. Looking around for a distraction, he realised they were alone. At some point, the jailors and his Trade Minister had withdrawn, perhaps fearing for their lives.

"Maybe I am delusional," conceded Hulagu, moving to stand in front of the bars again. "But you are a fool. You cannot kill me, because in doing so, you would have to become me. Fate didn't choose you for greatness."

"I am a Kozan. There are only seven people in the whole world like me," said Temujin. He attempted to summon the

Eternal Fire, but right now he was incapable of finding any inner calm. "Whereas you are nothing. You are old, spent, and soon you will be forgotten. In a few years' time, no one will even remember you or speak your name."

"You should have died as a baby," said Hulagu.

A heavy silence filled the space, pressing down on everything. Temujin's ears rang until they ached. He should have felt angry or horrified. Instead, a dreadful calm settled over him, washing away all emotions, but this was not the serenity of the Eternal Fire. Temujin felt connected to his body, and yet it was as if he were observing it from outside.

With calm, steady hands, he unlocked the door to his father's cell and stepped inside. There was nowhere for Hulagu to go. The guards in the palace were loyal to Temujin out of fear, but Hulagu didn't even attempt to escape. He merely stared at Temujin, waiting for him to do something.

Putting all of his weight behind it, Temujin drove the dagger into Hulagu's stomach. It slid through his flesh with ease. At first, his father didn't even notice. Part of Temujin thought he'd imagined stabbing him. Everything felt surreal and had a slightly dreamlike quality. It was only when Temujin drove the blade deeper, and the warm tide of blood washed over his hands, that it became real.

Hulagu gripped him by the shoulders, and together they sank to the floor, kneeling opposite one another. Blood pooled around them. Temujin felt it soaking into the material of his clothes, but he couldn't look away from his father's face. More than anything, Hulagu looked surprised. There was no fear or worry in his eyes about what came next. He was simply baffled that this was his end. That it had come at the hands of his most disappointing son.

Hulagu tried to speak, to have the final word, but that couldn't be allowed. Using both hands, Temujin dragged the blade to the left, ripping through his father's innards, disembowelling him. The words on Hulagu's lips were snatched away by pain.

Suffering touched his face, and for a moment, he dared to look down at the damage. Raising a hand, he pressed it against Temujin's cheek, staining it with blood.

His lips began to shape a sound and Temujin shook his head. Whatever it was, he didn't want to hear it, but his father persisted. The will that had driven him in life allowed him to hold on just a little longer. Just long enough to speak.

Hulagu started to topple forward, but Temujin held him upright, his father's head resting on his shoulder. Hulagu's final breaths feathered Temujin's neck.

"Proud," whispered Hulagu.

With a cry of despair, Temujin thrust Hulagu away from him. Suddenly his father had no weight. Hulagu's body fell backwards with ease. His sightless eyes stared at the ceiling, and the cell was filled with the stench of death.

CHAPTER 17
Kokochin

Kokochin ran through the streets of Lahore back to the tea shop. Although no one tried to stop her, plenty of people stared. Every eyewitness would make it that much easier for the authorities to find her.

After flinging open the back door, Kokochin ran up the stairs to her room. Wasting no time, she threw her clothes into a bag, took her two daggers from under the bed, and scooped up any personal belongings she couldn't be without. The teachings of the House of Grace had stayed with her. Nothing had been written down. There were no notes, letters or secret messages to find. There was nothing here to connect her with the murder of Timur's son. With no other clues, she hoped those investigating would assume she'd been operating alone. If not, there was the potential for it to become a lot more dangerous for those in her network. Hopefully, the presence of soldiers would keep everyone away from the tea room, but she needed to be sure.

Every moment she lingered increased the chances of being discovered. Nevertheless, she took a deep breath before carefully checking for anything out of the ordinary. In truth, there wasn't much to see. An unmade bed, some cheap furniture, a writing desk and a broken mirror. Finding nothing amiss, Kokochin went out the back door and didn't bother to lock it. This time, she moved slowly and carefully through the streets, pausing often to hide in doorways, or step into the shadows to avoid being seen. Despite the late hour, there were still people about in the city. It took far longer than she liked, but eventually Kokochin made it to where Olma lived without drawing any unusual attention.

It took a while, but Kokochin's persistent knocking roused the nurse from her bed. The door crept open a hand's breadth, and Olma peered through the narrow gap into the street. When she saw it was Kokochin, she quickly opened the door wide.

"What's happened?" asked Olma, ushering her inside. She gestured for Kokochin to follow her deeper into the house, but instead the princess stayed by the front door.

"They're going to be coming for me. I've had to abandon the tea room and all of my plans."

"What did you do?" said Olma, noticing spots of blood on Kokochin's clothes.

"Not what they said, but it doesn't matter. I need to ask you for a favour, but it could be dangerous," she added, wanting to be upfront.

"Anything," said the nurse, which made Kokochin's heart ache. The longing was still there. Whether it was the sense of danger, or because they were standing close, she could see a hunger in Olma's eyes. Kokochin turned her face away and took a step back before she did something she would later regret.

"You were right. I have a network of contacts in Lahore. They're all people who want something better for their city." The embers of freedom were there in the heart of every person, they just needed a few leaders to fan the flames. "If you don't hear from me in four or five days, you should assume the worst. At that point, I want you to take over."

"Me?" said Olma. "Why me?"

"Because you're clever, and you understand the way people think. Also, you're able to suppress your emotions in a crisis, which makes you calm under pressure. In the coming weeks, there are going to be a lot of scared people. They will need your strength."

"That may be true, but leading a group?" For the first time since they'd met, Olma looked afraid.

"You can do this," said Kokochin. "Besides, everyone in my network believes I report to someone else in the city. They're more likely to accept the change because you're local."

"I don't know," said Olma.

Kokochin sympathised, but every moment that she stayed put the nurse in greater risk.

"One of my friends is called, Nabil. He works for the governor," said Kokochin, pressing on as time was short. "He's naïve. He doesn't understand what I really do." Kokochin had been careful to keep everyone apart in case of an eventuality like this one, but Olma needed to know. "You'll need to convince him that you're in charge, and that it's not safe to visit the shop anymore. He won't just stop because you ask. He's different." She didn't know how to explain it, but Olma understood. She was definitely the right choice.

"I'll talk to him," she promised. Kokochin gave Olma his address, as well as a list of everyone in her network.

"Don't write any of it down, just in case," said Kokochin. "Everyone else will have enough sense to stay away from the shop, except Nabil." The hallway was silent and the air was still. The whole city was sleeping, but soon it would be ringing with noise and awash with light as they hunted for her.

"What are you going to do?" asked Olma.

"I don't know."

"You should run," said Olma, "while you still can."

There was more she wanted to say, but Kokochin knew she had to leave. Even so, she lingered, thankful for being in the company of someone she could trust.

"I wish things were different," said Kokochin, trying to find the words.

"I know," said Olma with a sad smile.

Swallowing the lump in her throat, Kokochin quickly left and didn't look back.

Following the directions from Usman, Kokochin found her way to the carpet shop with the blue sign. As she'd expected, the place was closed for the night and the whole building was wrapped in darkness.

Crossing the road, Kokochin squeezed down an alley and went around the back of the buildings on the opposite side of the street. All of them were quite old and worn. The stone walls were pitted and cracked, which provided her with plenty of hand and footholds. Moving slowly, she crawled up the wall and rolled onto the roof. The shops below her were empty for the night as well, but there was some residual heat coming from one chimney.

In a shadowy corner by the cooling chimney and an adjoining wall, Kokochin lay down. The heat wouldn't be enough to get her through the night, so she huddled beneath several layers of clothing.

Kokochin's temporary bed was hard and uncomfortable, but as the adrenaline from the last few hours drained away, she felt cold and exhausted. Her eyes drooped and her head dipped towards her chest. She fought it at first, worried about being discovered, but unless she fell through the roof, no one would know she was there. Eventually, she gave in and fell into a dreamless sleep.

Kokochin woke up stiff and aching, her neck bent at a strange angle. At some point in the night, she'd curled up into a ball. As she straightened her back, it cracked, making her groan in a mix of pain and relief. The sky was starting to brighten, and she could hear a few people moving about on the street below. She had expected to wake up to the sound of marching feet and a city-wide search.

With no one she could trust, and nowhere that was safe, Kokochin was forced to wait on the roof for hours. Occasionally, she risked a glance at the street, but there was little to see. She heard people moving in the building beneath, but she remained as still as possible. When it was quiet, she gently stretched the muscles of her back and shoulders, working out the kinks. Layla had taught her meditation, so with time to spare, Kokochin revisited her lessons. She slowed her breathing and tried to block out everything around her. Listening only to her heart, she drifted for an unknown amount of time.

A shout from below broke through Kokochin's concentration. The street was bustling with traffic, and all the shops were now open. Kokochin's stomach rumbled, reminding her that it had been a long time since her last meal. The sun had moved across the sky and the heat was rising. After stripping off several layers, she changed into clean clothes. It was tricky, but she managed it in the confined space.

Eventually, later than the other shops, the carpet seller unlocked the front door and went inside. Despite being hungry, Kokochin decided to give him another hour to get settled. After that, she carefully climbed down to the ground. Thankfully, there was no one in the alley behind the shops to witness her descent. Hoping that her luck would hold just a little longer, she crossed the street and entered the carpet shop.

Inside, it was clean, and the air smelled of fresh bread and something floral. The carpets on display were colourful and decorated with fanciful designs of animals, geometric shapes and people. A cursory glance told Kokochin that the quality was exceptional. Each one must have taken months to complete.

The owner came into the shop through a door at the back of the room. He was carrying a tray laden with tea and a plate of dried fruit. Kokochin guessed he was more than sixty years old, as his thinning hair was grey and white and his face was deeply lined. When he saw her, the owner's face split into a big grin. It was almost as if he had been expecting her.

"Welcome, welcome," he said, setting down the tray on a table. "My name is Faran. Would you like some tea?"

"I would, but I don't have time," said Kokochin, stepping closer and lowering her voice. Faran's smile faded, and she saw that he was assessing her. "I'm not here to hurt you. I was sent to find you."

The old man's bushy eyebrows crept up towards his thinning hairline. "Who sent you?"

"He said his name was Usman. Do you know him?" she asked.

"Yes, I know him," said Faran, with a short laugh. "He's my son."

Now that he'd said it, Kokochin could see the resemblance. Usman had been wearing a mask, but he and his father shared the same jawline, and their eyes were similar.

"You look troubled. Sit," he said, gesturing at a chair.

"It's too dangerous. I shouldn't be here." It had been a mistake, but she'd been without options. She didn't want to put Faran at risk. Perhaps if she fled the city, she might be able to stay ahead of the trouble.

"Princess," said the owner, fixing her in place with a shrewd stare. "I know exactly who you are, and why you're here. I've been with the Sons of the White Falcon since the beginning, so I'm well aware of the danger. My son will be here in an hour, to pick up some deliveries. Until then, you can sit in the back room, out of sight."

"Thank you," she said, just as her stomach grumbled loudly.

"And maybe you could have something to eat," said Faran with another toothy grin.

Faran sat on a stool behind the counter with his back to her while she sipped tea and ate breakfast. The bread was fresh and soft. Kokochin gobbled it up, together with some cheese and fruit. The food settled her stomach, but it did nothing to steady her nerves.

A few customers came and went, but none of them were looking for her. With the door slightly ajar, she could hear what was going on, but no one could see her in the back.

The storage room contained several well-built wooden shelves, all of them clearly labelled. Six neatly wrapped parcels were stacked by the table, ready for Usman to deliver. The rest of the room was clean and tidy, which she found encouraging. The House of Grace had remained secret for so long because everyone was careful and organised. Hopefully the Sons of the White Falcon were similar in their approach.

Checking her surroundings, Kokochin saw another door to the rear of the building, and a set of winding stairs that led to a small room. She couldn't see inside, but she guessed there was a window, which would potentially give her another way out. Her mind flashed back to Souri's death and the moment they'd been forced to leave her behind to die. They had barely made it out of the building in time.

It wasn't that Kokochin didn't trust Faran and the others. It was more that she didn't want to test the depths of their loyalty. If the Mongols offered a huge reward, she didn't know of many people who would side with a total stranger.

While Faran was busy with a customer, Kokochin crept upstairs. As she suspected, the room was an office, but there was a window which opened onto the roof. She'd barely made it back to her seat when the old man came in to check on her.

"Usman is here," said Faran. "I usually close the shop for lunch, so it won't be suspicious."

Without his mask, she thought Usman quite an attractive man. He'd not shaven in a few days, and his jaw was shadowed with stubble. As before, his eyes were bright and focused. Usman remained silent until his father had closed the shop and taken a seat at the table.

"You said he was a friend," said Kokochin, tilting her head towards Faran.

Usman shrugged. "I was being careful."

"Do you know what happened last night?" asked Kokochin.

"Bits and pieces," said Usman.

Kokochin told them about the events at the Gilded Lily, but made no mention of the House of Grace or its involvement. She hoped Usman and his father could keep her safe, but she wasn't willing to trust them with all of her secrets yet.

"I was only there to listen, but now everyone thinks I killed the general."

"And the other woman?" asked Usman.

"Gone. I doubt we'll see her again. I thought there would be a city-wide search by now," said Kokochin, fishing for information.

"There is, but they're doing it carefully," said Usman.

Kokochin tensed up, waiting to see how either man reacted or if there was any mention of a reward. Neither of them exchanged silent glances, which she took as a good sign.

"Twenty years ago, if we had killed one of his sons, Genghis Khan would have burnt everything to the ground," said Faran.

"He's right, but Timur is different," said Usman. "Just as ruthless, but he has many wives and sons. He may be upset, but we'll never know. Whatever his plans, this won't distract him from them."

"That's disturbing," said Kokochin.

"For a long time, we've known that he is the real power in the Chagatai khanate," said Faran, tossing some raisins into his mouth. "And we've been studying him. We know a little about how he thinks."

"Do you know what he's planning next?" she asked.

"I can make an educated guess," said Faran, with a smile that showed off his crooked teeth. "Last time, when Genghis Khan invaded from the west, he struck at Multan. From there, he spread his troops north and east. If I was Timur, I would mirror this in reverse before striking at the Ilkhanate from the south."

"We think Lahore is to be a staging area, to gather troops and supplies," said Usman. "Over the last few months, there have been a lot of strangers in the city, but they're not merchants."

Guyuk had revealed little to her of Hulagu's network of spies, but Kokochin had the impression it was fairly primitive. He had relied more heavily on scouts to range ahead and bring back stories. It seemed as if Timur was vastly different and willing to use whatever tool was required.

"There have also been a few peculiar murders," said Faran, chewing thoughtfully. "Not your work, then?"

"No," said Kokochin. "I have been trying to investigate them too. So, the Mongols are hunting for me. I wasn't sure."

"They are. However, not to downplay what happened last night, but right now, you're not a priority," said Usman. "Our contacts report there are thousands of warriors on their way here. The start of the war is near."

"I don't know whether to feel relieved or insulted," said Kokochin.

"If they don't find you in a few days, the search will become more intense," said Usman with a glance at his father. Kokochin didn't know what it meant, but it made her nervous.

"What do you mean?" said Kokochin, glancing at the rear door of the shop. She could knock Usman down and make a run for it. If Faran got in the way, she would go upstairs, block the office door, and go out through the window.

"Timur will order people flogged to death until someone talks. He is someone who expects results," said Usman.

"You need to leave Lahore," said Faran. It took a moment for his words to sink in.

"Leave?" said Kokochin.

"If there are witnesses, that's even better. The search will move elsewhere, and he'll leave the people here alone," said the old man. "I know you want to help, but if you stay, people in the city will suffer."

She'd come to the city to help people, not hurt them, but staying would only make the situation worse. The authorities would continue to hunt for her and she knew that, despite their loyalty, eventually someone would talk. But if she left, the focus of those in charge would return to the war. In her absence, she knew Olma would take over her network, and that she would do a good job. Then they could begin eroding Timur's army from within, just as others had done with Hulagu in the Ilkhanate.

"I was working with a group of local people, patriots," said Kokochin. In her mind, she knew that she had to run. "They might be able to help you."

"Any allies would be welcome," said Usman.

There was a thump within the shop and both men jumped to their feet.

"I definitely locked the front door," said Faran. He reached into the storage shelves and produced a short sword. Usman wasn't armed, so Kokochin passed him one of her daggers. With him in front and Faran a step behind, the three of them rushed into the shop together.

A woman stood in the centre of the shop with her back towards them. There was something familiar about her long black hair that made Kokochin's heart lurch. But she knew it couldn't be her. It wasn't possible.

"What do you want?" said Faran. The woman was watching the street, keeping an eye on people walking by. Everything looked normal outside, but from the hunch of her shoulders, Kokochin could see the woman was tense. "We're closed," said the old man, but the stranger ignored him.

When she eventually turned around, Kokochin's knees threatened to give way. She had to grab the counter to stay upright.

It was Layla.

For a while, they just stared at one another. Kokochin had a hundred questions, but she didn't know where to start.

She noticed subtle differences from the last time they'd been face to face. Layla was dressed in comfortable trousers and a shirt with the sleeves rolled up to the elbow. She had a new scar on her left forearm, probably from a blade, as the mark was perfectly straight and narrow. A headscarf sat on her shoulders to ward off the heat, but there wasn't much dust on her clothes. Also, she wasn't carrying a pack or any weapons.

"I've been keeping an eye on you for a few months," said Layla, by way of explanation. "Who do you think has been protecting you all this time?"

"The murders. That was you?" said Kokochin, still reeling from shock.

"They were spies, sent by Timur. I've done what I can to keep him blind to what's going on in the city."

"Do you know her?" said Usman.

"Yes, we're...friends," said Kokochin. "Why didn't you tell me you were here?" she said, turning back to Layla.

"Not here. Talk in there," said Faran, gesturing at the back room.

"How did you get in?" asked Usman.

"She picked the lock," said Kokochin, heading into the storage room. She sat down at the table as her legs were still unsteady. Layla stepped into the back room, scanned it for ways in and out of the building, then took a seat opposite.

Faran went to reopen the shop and Usman joined him, but not before raising a questioning eyebrow at Kokochin.

"I'll be all right," she said. He nodded and closed the door, giving them some privacy.

"I have to leave Lahore," said Kokochin. Even saying it out loud for the first time was difficult. She wasn't sure why she'd started with that. It wasn't what she really wanted to say. "There was a murder at the Gilded Lily."

"I know," said Layla with a gentle smile. "I've been watching."

"Why?" said Kokochin, forcing back a sob. She cleared her throat, angry at herself for getting upset. "Why didn't you tell me you were here?"

"I came to Lahore on a mission," said Layla. "I volunteered to make the trip," she added. Kokochin thought she looked calm, but then she noticed Layla's left leg was twitching up and down. "I wanted to see how you were. When I heard what you were doing, I decided to stay."

"You didn't answer my question," said Kokochin.

"You were different before. Cold. Ruthless. Willing to do anything." She knew Layla didn't mean to hurt her, and yet being reminded of how she'd been still stung. "I needed to be certain that you'd changed."

Kokochin didn't want to ask but felt that she had no choice. "And if I'd been the same person as before?"

Layla shrugged. "I would have left, and you'd have never known I was here."

Kokochin had forgotten how matter-of-fact Layla could be. They sat in silence for a while, listening to the building. The atmosphere wasn't comfortable, but it was far less hostile than Kokochin had been expecting. She was careful to keep her hands folded and relaxed in her lap. Focusing on her breathing, she tried to keep it even to conceal her nerves.

"I was so angry," said Kokochin, venting her frustration. "I wanted revenge, for all the horrible things they'd done to me, and others. I was angry about Souri, and Ariadne's family, and so many other things. I just wanted to hurt them." She took a few deep breaths until she was in control again. "I'm not the same person anymore."

"I'm glad to hear that," said Layla.

"But now I have to leave and start over somewhere else. I was building a network of my own. A new life." Kokochin stopped talking before she said something embarrassing that she'd regret.

"That's why I'm here," said Layla. "I've been gathering information as well, and I need your help."

"Is this a mission from the House?"

"No. Yes. I mean, it will be."

Kokochin raised an eyebrow as she realised Layla was nervous as well. "Go on."

"I've sent word to the House, but we can't wait for a response. Part of this came from Nabil. He didn't realise what it was when he told me."

"You know Nabil?" said Kokochin. "Never mind. What's the mission?"

"Timur has greater ambition than any of the other khans. He's more dangerous than you can imagine."

"What are you saying?" said Kokochin.

"He's not only planning to invade the Ilkhanate, he's targeting Europe, as well. He's sent letters to Spain, France and England. He also sent a diplomat to Rome."

"Diplomat?" said Kokochin. "Is he trying to make an alliance with the Christians?"

Layla shook her head slowly. "It made no sense to me, either, so I kept digging. Timur is not sending a diplomat. A conqueror has no need of diplomats. It's an Assassin."

"That's not possible," said Kokochin. "Hulagu destroyed the Order."

"He did, but a few escaped to Egypt. The only thing that makes sense is that Timur has made an alliance with the Sultan."

If Europe and the Christian Church were thrown into chaos, then the latest Crusade would fall apart. That would leave the Mamluks unopposed and allow them to claim Jerusalem. That also meant the Ilkhanate would be susceptible to being attacked on two fronts, by Egypt in the west, and Timur in the east.

"I need your help to stop the Assassin from killing the Pope," said Layla.

CHAPTER 18
Kaivon

Kaivon and Esme ran through the streets of Kabul. They were bruised, bloody and battered, but their fear kept them moving. Once they had put some distance between them and the safe house, they ducked into an alley to check their injuries.

Kaivon had a shallow cut on the back of his head that must have come from flying debris. Apart from a few cuts and scrapes, he was otherwise unharmed. Esme had wrenched a shoulder when they'd been knocked over, and she'd scraped the palms of her hands. They'd been enormously lucky to escape without anything serious.

Kaivon had caught only a glimpse of the battle between the Kozan, but even that had been enough to trigger a physical reaction. He was still dizzy, and his throat burned from bile. Esme's eyes were a little unfocused, and from the way she was squinting, he guessed she had a headache.

Leaning on each other for support, they slowly made their way back to their room.

"We need to leave," said Esme, gathering up some of her belongings. "The city isn't safe anymore."

"Maybe we can come back," said Kaivon, but he wasn't sure if that was true. Timur had sent one of the Kozan after them.

187

It didn't get any worse than that. If the hunter had been a normal man, they could've fought back, but there was no way to beat one of the Kozan. They stood apart from humanity.

Even more worrying, Teague had known everything about their efforts to disrupt the invasion of the Ilkhanate. Behrouz had appeared to be working for Hulagu, but had actually been following his own agenda. Kaivon wondered if Teague was doing the same or if he was truly serving Timur and his vision?

"Did you see the woman that burst out of the ground?" said Kaivon, stuffing his clothes into a bag. "I've never seen anything like that before."

"Her name is Maryam," said Esme as she gathered her belongings. "She was the one who told me, and your brother, that you were still alive."

"Do you trust her?" asked Kaivon, scanning the room for anything he might have left behind.

Esme snorted. "No. Not for a moment. She only helped us because, at the time, our goals aligned with hers. I've never met anyone more dangerous."

Esme had told him about her encounter with Maryam in the warehouse. The Kozan had nearly killed her, and his brother, with little effort. If not for one of the Inner Circle, he would have lost everyone he cared about in the world.

"We need some time and space," said Kaivon, thinking aloud. Once they were out of the city, he would feel a little safer. They would have some room to breathe. There was no doubt that the Kozan were powerful, but if Kaivon didn't know where he was going, he found it difficult to believe Teague would know where to find them. After all, the Kozan were not omnipotent.

After haggling with a merchant headed west, they arranged transport out of the city. Kaivon would serve as a guard for the duration, and Esme would ride as a passenger, but she received a reduced price because she was a healer. It wouldn't be a particularly comfortable journey, but it was cheaper than buying their own horses or camels. Also, it gave them the illusion of having strength in numbers. Although, if a Kozan found them, everyone else would serve as a distraction, hopefully giving him and Esme time to make their escape. It was a mercenary thought, and Kaivon hoped it didn't come to that.

An hour later, once they had passed through the city gates without incident, Kaivon relaxed a little. His shoulders were still hunched, and Esme jumped at every loud noise, but by the time the sun had set, they were confident no one was following them. The four wagons stopped off for the night at a caravanserai on the main road. When the gates closed, Kaivon felt as if he could breathe normally. They ate dinner with the rest of the group, then went to bed, exhausted from a long and difficult day.

Kaivon expected to sleep without dreams, but quickly found himself reliving past events. Once again, Kaivon stood beside Bas, the young warrior, doing his best to ignore the boy's shaking. Only this time, they didn't speak, and Kaivon simply put a hand on his shoulder, trying to offer comfort through physical contact.

The dream took him back even further to the attack on Baghdad, when he'd been trapped inside the siege tower. He was surrounded by thick grey smoke, making it difficult to see and almost impossible to breathe. Kaivon's fear rose as he recalled the awful scramble to escape, going down a seemingly endless number of steps before finally stepping outside into fresh air. His lungs ached in remembrance, and he coughed, struggling to draw breath.

Finally, he was back at the safe house in Kabul. Bodies and severed heads littered the ground, but this time, their dead eyes followed his progress. Kaivon wanted to turn back, but he was trapped in the nightmare. Someone, or something, was forcing him to relive this over again. His heart was pounding and his palms were clammy. He tried to speak, to voice his horror, but there was a lump in his throat that wouldn't move. Against his will, Kaivon walked down the hallway and stepped into the room.

Everything was as it had been in real life. The bodies had not moved, and all of them were inanimate. It was only when he turned to speak to Esme that Kaivon realised she wasn't there. The rules of the dream kept changing.

"Where are you?" said a voice. It sounded like his, and yet he was still unable to speak. Kaivon walked into the room to inspect the bodies.

A blurred vision of Teague appeared in the doorway behind him, blocking the way out. His features were distorted and out of proportion, but the threat he posed had not diminished.

"He's still out there," said a woman, "searching for you." Kaivon spun around searching for the speaker, but he was alone. The dream version of Teague had paused in the doorway, frozen in place.

"Where are you? Show yourself," said Kaivon, suddenly able to speak.

"Here," said a voice.

A stranger had appeared across the room. With dark skin and long black hair, she could have been one of his people, but Kaivon knew that she was a Kozan. Esme had spoken about Maryam's peculiar smile, which seemed a little sad to him.

"I'm dreaming," said Kaivon. "Are you really here?"

"I meant what I said. Teague will come for you again," said Maryam, avoiding the question. "The truce that prevented us from interfering has been broken. So I'm here to help you."

"How can you help me?" said Kaivon.

"You can't have travelled far from the city in a day. You could have gone further if you'd flogged your horse to death, but you'd never do that." Maryam looked him up and down, weighing him, somehow. "With a little time, I could find you, which means he can too."

"Then nowhere is safe," said Kaivon.

"Crossing a large distance still takes time, even for my kind," said Maryam. "The further you are from Kabul, the better. My friend, Behrouz, once transported you across Persia. I can do the same for you again."

"I won't go without Esme," he said.

Maryam grinned. "I can take her, too."

When Behrouz had taken him, Kaivon had been partially unconscious, and his body had been unresponsive. A small part of his mind had remained awake, but even now, his memories of what had happened were vague. He'd seen others consumed by light, apparently burnt to ash by Behrouz, and had prepared himself for the end. Finding he was still alive, and hundreds of miles away, had been the biggest surprise of his life.

"Where is Behrouz?" said Kaivon, noting a shift in her demeanour.

"Gone. Dead," said Maryam, fighting back angry tears.

"He was your friend."

"Friend?" scoffed Maryam. "We've walked this Earth together for many lifetimes. Time and time again, we saved the world from disaster. War. Disease. Fire. Famine and flood. Decades of time spent in service to an unknowing and ungrateful people bent on destroying themselves. But somehow, through all of that, he never lost faith in humanity, nor his curiosity. He would marvel at the smallest things. A tiny bird. A brilliantly coloured beetle. A sunrise. You cannot imagine what he meant to me."

"But now he's gone," said Kaivon.

"Yes. Teague destroyed him, and without my help, he will do the same to you. I will not ask you again. Tell me where you are."

"I can't. I don't trust you," he said.

"You shouldn't," said Maryam. "I don't care about you or your fate, but right now my enemies are seeking you. Trust that I want to do everything I can to disrupt their plans. Without my help, Teague will find you and torture you both for days. Before you die, you will spill all of your secrets. Everyone you love will then be at risk."

Maryam's voice was icy. She spoke without emotion, as if it had already happened, as if it was fact.

"Where would you take us?" he asked, playing for time. The dream seemed to be holding, but he had no idea if he was close to waking up.

"You know where you need to go," said Maryam. "The war is almost upon you, and the others. There is much you can do to help."

"Can you help with the war?" asked Kaivon.

Maryam's laugh was bitter. "I've done more than you'll ever know." He was about to ask what she meant, but Maryam waved his question away. "You'll not see me or my kind on the battlefield, but we'll be there, keeping the other Kozan at bay. That's all you need to know. Time is short, Kaivon. It's time to make up your mind."

For the first time since Maryam had appeared in his dream, the strain of what she was doing showed on her face. He took a moment to consider his options while she gritted her teeth against the pain. In some ways, he found her discomfort encouraging. It meant she was not without limits.

Kaivon wanted to discuss the decision with Esme but knew he didn't have time.

"We're at a caravanserai," said Kaivon. "We travelled west with a group of merchants and their wagons."

"Show me," said Maryam. "Picture it in your mind."

The world around him dissolved like smoke in the wind until the pair of them were standing on a featureless landscape. Through the swirling white fog, he caught glimpses of other places, but before Kaivon could look closer, Maryam slapped him. Pain blossomed in his cheek. It felt so real that he put a hand to his face.

"Focus," she hissed. "Where are you?"

Kaivon tried to picture his surroundings. First the room he was sharing with Esme, then the corridor outside, and finally the courtyard at the centre of the roadside inn. Slowly, the white landscape faded until he stood in a version of the waking world, staring down at his own body. Esme lay beside him in bed, oblivious to their conversation.

"Go outside," said Maryam. Her voice had taken on a hazy quality, and her eyes were distant. "Look up at the sky."

Kaivon walked down the hallway and stepped into the abandoned courtyard. It was late at night, but four guards patrolled the wall, keeping an eye out for trouble. The gates would not open until dawn, but sometimes bandits tried to raid caravanserai. They foolishly thought it was easier to attack a stationary object than chasing carts down the road. Torches burned at all four corners, but there were no other lights.

Tilting his head back, Kaivon stared at the vast array of stars. Overhead, the moon was bright and full, bathing him in silver light. It was so low in the sky that he felt as if he could reach out and touch it, which made no sense. Last night, the moon had only been a quarter full.

As soon as Kaivon thought it, the illusion wavered and then broke apart into a thousand pieces.

With a start, he came awake in his bed. Esme was still asleep beside him and everything in the room looked normal. All of it was just as he remembered it. Touching his cheek with one hand, Kaivon found a whisper of remembered pain from where Maryam had struck him.

As Kaivon lay back down to try and sleep, a worrying thought began to plague his mind. Pulling on his trousers and a shirt, he ran down the hallway and then out into the courtyard. The guards and their torches were there, moving back and forth. Dawn was still hours away, and above his head, the night sky was awash with thousands of stars. To his left, the moon was only a quarter full. With a sigh of relief, he went back inside and lay down.

For a moment, Kaivon had worried he'd still been trapped in the dream.

In the morning, Kaivon told Esme everything that had happened.

"I believe you," said Esme, inspecting his cheek, "but I can't see a mark."

"I would have spoken to you about it, but there wasn't time."

"I understand. It's not every day you find a strange woman in your dreams," she said with a wry smile.

"Not usually, no," said Kaivon with a grin, but it soon faded. "I keep wondering, how did she find me? And if she can walk into someone else's dreams, what about the others? Are they always watching us?"

"You said it yourself. She was in pain, so they're not without their limits. Maybe she has an affinity for dream-walking."

"Maybe," said Kaivon, chewing his lip. "I also have a nagging suspicion that if she'd killed me in the dream, I wouldn't have woken up."

Esme crossed the room and wrapped her arms around him, resting her head against Kaivon's chest. They stayed like that for a while, just breathing and listening to each other's heartbeat.

Outside their room, he heard a camel begin to grunt and complain. Despite the early hour, people were already moving about. It wouldn't be long before everyone would be back on the road. Once they'd gathered their belongings, they stepped outside to get some breakfast with the others.

There were lots of people milling about, tending to their animals, loading wagons and finishing their food. Groups of travellers stood around fires, chatting and eating before another long day of travel. The smell of freshly baked bread filled Kaivon's nose. They stood in line beside the oven, waiting for their portion. Huge slabs of bread cooked on stones were slung out of the oven by a skilled baker. Another man picked off any loose pebbles and then stacked up a fresh batch that soon disappeared. With soft white cheese, herbs, dried fruit and mugs of tea, they ate in the shade of a wall, trying to stay cool. The unbroken blue sky overhead told Kaivon it was going to be another hot and unrelenting day.

A commotion by the main gates drew everyone's attention, and a strange hush fell over those gathered in the courtyard. The crowd parted to reveal Maryam striding towards them. She was dressed in trousers and a loose white shirt, but it wasn't her clothing that made everyone stare. They were miles from anywhere, and yet she had suddenly appeared at the gate on foot, with no sign of a horse or camel.

In the waking world, a strange aura hung around Maryam, like an invisible cloak. It felt like the moment before a storm, when the air hummed with unspent energy. The others in the caravanserai didn't know she was a Kozan, but they were visibly unsettled by her presence.

"I remember you," said Maryam, smiling at Esme.

Everyone was watching and waiting to see what happened next. Kaivon could see the tension in the lines of Esme's body. He expected a biting comment, but Esme instead took a deep breath, turned her back on Maryam, and approached the merchant they'd been travelling with.

"We must leave you here," said Esme.

The merchant nodded, hearing the words, but his eyes never strayed from Maryam. "What is she?" he said, biting his bottom lip.

"It's better that you don't know," said Esme.

They gathered their belongings, then followed Maryam out of the front gate. None of the wagons had left for the day, and a crowd gathered to watch what happened next. The Kozan walked a short distance from the caravanserai before stopping. Stretching away in all directions, the landscape was dusty and dry. Rocks, hills and distant mountains. There were a few scrubby plants that hinted at life, but otherwise it was bleak and unrelenting. The heat was already starting to rise, and soon it would be unbearable.

"This will do," said Maryam. "Prepare yourself."

"What happens now?" asked Esme. One hand moved to rest on the dagger at her waist.

Maryam's eyes tracked the movement and her smile became feral. "What I'm about to do is delicate. If you break my concentration, you'll be torn apart by time. Pieces of your body will be scattered across a hundred miles."

"We'll behave," said Kaivon. Esme took her hand away from the blade and nodded.

Maryam moved closer until they were within arm's reach of other. "It might better if you close your eyes. It will be less disorientating."

After his last experience, Kaivon took her advice, but he instinctively knew that Esme would refuse. With his eyes closed, he felt the air around them change. It had more weight and energy. He was suddenly aware of it dancing across exposed skin. Behind the darkness of his eyelids, Kaivon saw shapes moving, and at one point, a distorted face. The urge to open his eyes was overwhelming. Instead, he gritted his teeth and waited for it all to be over.

Pressure built up against Kaivon's ears. Sounds began to elongate, and then he felt the world moving while he stood perfectly still.

Kaivon caught sight of a lone rider in the distance. He saw a bright flash of light, and before he could signal the man, he'd disappeared over the horizon. He had no idea where they were, but the landscape had changed from dry and dusty hills to rolling valleys covered with trees. The arid heat remained, but it was less muggy and not quite as oppressive. Maryam had transported them hundreds of miles away to somewhere in Persia. Her only guidance had been to go west until someone found them.

They had not been walking for long when a dozen riders came charging down the road. The rider must have been a scout roaming ahead of a larger force. The warriors were a peculiar mix, with Mongols sat beside Persians and Georgians, all of them dressed for war.

"General?" said one of the men, a Mongol warrior Kaivon vaguely recognised. "I thought you were dead."

Despite having his identity confirmed, they were disarmed and taken back to camp under heavy guard. There was some light still in the sky, but Kaivon guessed it was already early evening.

The impossible journey with Maryam had taken what he thought was hours, but his body felt battered and worn out, as if he had been awake for days. His eyes were sandy, and his bones throbbed with a peculiar pain. Esme was faring worse, as she had kept her eyes open for some of the trip. She had a haunted look, and she wouldn't speak to him about what she had seen.

When they reached the edge of the vast camp, they were escorted to an empty command tent and told to wait. A short time later, four armed guards came into the tent ahead of King David of Georgia.

"It's good to see you," said David, gripping Kaivon's arms.

"And you," said Kaivon, smiling back at the king. "This is my wife, Esme."

On the walk, they had agreed to the small lie to make things easier and avoid awkward questions. Some of the leaders were deeply religious and this side-stepped the issue.

"Wife?" said David. "Welcome," he said, bowing to Esme.

"Thank you, Majesty."

"Please, call me David," he said. "Kaivon, I am happy to see you, but I must ask, what are you both doing here? And how did you find us?"

"That is a long story, and it involves the Kozan," said Kaivon.

David's smile faded. "These days, when does it not? You look tired from your journey. Let's talk in the morning over breakfast. We can discuss everything then with the others."

"Is he here?" asked Kaivon.

The king shook his head. "From time to time, he appears out of thin air, but we govern ourselves. He mostly leaves us alone."

"That's good," said Kaivon. His worst fear had been that Temujin had taken charge of the army. Despite all of his gifts and experience, the new khan was not a trained warrior and knew nothing of warfare. He also knew nothing of their enemy, of the fear, but also the loyalty he inspired in others.

Timur was undoubtedly a master of strategy, but without a loyal army he was just a man with grand ideas. However, he understood the hearts of men. Timur had gone to great lengths to win the support of important and traditionalist Mongols. He'd been careful not to declare himself a khan in name, but he'd also done everything to show that he was worthy of the title. He'd even married someone descended from Genghis Khan, so that in time, his children could rightfully use the honorific. Defeating him would not be an easy task, and it would place a heavy burden on the shoulders of whoever opposed him.

Kaivon and Esme's weapons were returned, and they were given spacious accommodation for the night. The tent could have housed a dozen people, but Kaivon only had eyes for the bed. As soon as he lay down, he fell asleep. Mercifully, there were no dreams about what he'd glimpsed when travelling with Maryam.

In the morning, they met with all the senior officers, and for a little while, it felt like old times. He'd missed the camaraderie, and the shorthand with which they could talk about strategy without having to explain every detail in full.

Kaivon introduced Esme, and after eating a hearty breakfast, the war council assembled to discuss its plans.

"We have reached an impasse," said King David, sipping his tea. "King Hethum favours a more cautionary approach, while Prince Bohemond and I suggest an aggressive strategy." Some of the other senior officers grumbled in assent, while others clearly favoured the prince's idea.

"My spies tell me Timur is known for his study of warfare and history," said King Hethum. "We have heard what he did at Delhi. No one could have anticipated that. We must be wary and careful."

Kaivon was about to offer his opinion, but then stopped himself out of habit. In the past, speaking out at such a gathering came with enormous risk. When he'd aroused the ire of Hulagu, it sometimes sent him into a rage with unpredictable results.

"We are all equals here," said David, seeing his hesitation. "Speak freely, without fear of reprisal."

"For months, Esme and I have been coordinating precise strikes against Timur, and every time, his response was not what I would have expected. It's not even how I would have reacted," said Kaivon. Most recently, he'd heard about one of Timur's sons being assassinated, but there had been no news of a vicious reprisal. "Caution would be the sensible approach."

"However," said Esme, sitting forward. "He is still a man chasing an impossible dream."

"Meaning what?" said Prince Bohemond.

"He wants to be legitimately recognised as the Great Khan. That makes him reckless in other ways. He is willing to sacrifice anything, and anyone, that stands in the way of that goal. Beating him on the battlefield is one thing, but the fight must continue elsewhere." Esme spoke with such passion, Kaivon was not surprised to see that everyone was hanging on her every word. "He must be derided and disowned, in the courts and the streets. He must be named as a despot and a butcher. He must be loathed in every land he conquers, so that even if we fail, a new rebellion will grow in the hearts of the people. Hulagu and his ilk have invaded and slaughtered tens of thousands, but then they try to appease the people by granting them certain liberties. It makes no difference. We are still ruled by conquerors who have taken away our freedom, our sovereignty and our independence."

"Everything you have said is true," said Prince Bohemond, "but this war council cannot function without strong leadership. This is not Hulagu's army, but there must be one voice that listens and then speaks for us all. One we would all happily follow to the gates of Hell itself." He looked expectantly towards David, but the king shook his head.

"It is not I who must lead this alliance. That role belongs to another," said the king, resting a hand on Kaivon's shoulder.

Kaivon was speechless. He looked around the circle at all of the great men, expecting several to oppose the idea, but all of them gave their approval.

"It is the wise choice," said David. "And it seems as if you have your own War Wife to counsel you as well," he added.

A huge weight settled upon Kaivon's shoulders, and the immensity of it felt crushing. It was difficult to catch his breath, and he was afraid he might faint. But then he saw the confidence and belief in the faces of those surrounding him, and that gave him a glimmer of hope for the future.

It was time to go to war with Timur.

PART TWO
Year of the Water Mouse (1263)

HAVE YOU EVER SEEN

A SEED FALLEN TO EARTH

NOT RISE WITH A NEW LIFE

WHY SHOULD YOU DOUBT THE RISE

OF A SEED NAMED HUMAN

— RUMI

CHAPTER 19
Temujin

Temujin watched his Trade Minister bustle into the throne room, one hand bunching up her dress to allow her to run. Her face was flushed and her dark hair tousled. He thought it suited her, but his placid expression never wavered. Expressing such a thing might be misconstrued as favouritism, and that could get her killed. Bias would also give his enemies something with which to manipulate him. There were more enemies out there than Temujin had realised. In fact, they were all around him.

Safe within the serenity granted by the Eternal Fire, he watched everyone and everything from the perspective of someone slightly removed from reality. The emotions were there, somewhere, but they were distant and buried. At times, Temujin thought they belonged to someone else. Rage was his father's arena. There. He'd barely managed to go an hour without thinking about his father and, inevitably, his final words. Murdering him should have been a relief. It should have eased Temujin's burden, and removed the weight of expectation, but nothing had changed.

"I apologise for being slow to answer your summons, my Khan," she said with a bow, which dragged him back to the present. "I was elsewhere in the city."

Temujin liked his Trade Minister. She was efficient. She didn't offer an opinion unless he asked. She was a little self-serving, but then again, if that was the worst of her vices, what did it really matter? Knowing what she wanted, and what she cared about, made it easier for him to control her. His father had been wrong about a great many things, but he'd been right about how to motivate people.

Temujin thought he should reward the Minster with something. But what should a khan give to someone like her? Land? Title? Money? He thought she would have little use for those, and she had plenty of her own money. It was something for him to consider another day.

"What news?" he asked, noting her eyes widen as she glanced left and right.

Normally, the Kheshig wore leather masks, which protected their faces and made them anonymous. However, after another distant relative had tried to kill him by posing as a bodyguard, Temujin had ordered them to remove their masks, even when they were not in his presence. In fact, Temujin had banned all masks from the city. Anyone caught wearing one, for any reason, be it religious or local custom, was to be put to death. It was for his safety and protection. There was still so much to do, and he needed fewer distractions, not more.

Minister Rouhani tried not to stare, but she also found the Kheshig a little disconcerting. Before, they had been faceless statues that never spoke and barely moved. They were ornaments until the moment they were needed. Most of the time, Temujin had forgotten they were even there, but now it was impossible. It wasn't the breathing or the blinking. He could cope with those things. It was the way that they kept twitching, and although they did their best to keep their expressions neutral, they were affected by what they overheard in court.

In the past, he'd held countless meetings in their presence, and not once had he been concerned about them. Not a single bodyguard had ever shared an opinion. Now, the insight

Temujin gained from his extended senses told him exactly what they were thinking. Every quirked eyebrow or tightening of the jaw was a question or a snort of disapproval, at least that's what he heard in his mind.

Those with faces he found too expressive were sent away. They could guard someone else, but not him. Even now, the two beside the main doors were trying not to stare, but their eyes kept drifting towards him. Both were terrified about what he might do to them. One of them was sweating so badly inside his armour that the stench was permeating throughout the room. It was too much. He couldn't abide the overpowering smell of fear.

With a long gasp, as if coming up for air, Temujin released his grip on the Eternal Fire. Emotions rushed in, but everything else was dulled. His senses became muted. Mercifully, the smell of fear was no longer as prominent in his nose.

An ache in Temujin's stomach reminded him that breakfast had been some time ago. It was already early afternoon and there was still a lot to do. He needed to make another trip to Sarai, to check on Tokhtamysh and the progress of his army. All told, the trip would take at least three days, and one to recover when he got back. It was getting more difficult, not easier. The pain in Temujin's chest was also starting to annoy him.

"My Khan?" said the Minister. Temujin realised she had stopped talking a while ago. The room had been waiting in silence to see how he would respond to her enquiry. He ran through what she had said and leaned forward slightly. It had been something about a delayed food shipment for the army.

"How long?" he asked, pressing his left foot down hard. The stone he'd put inside his boot was sharp enough to cut the skin. He stamped his foot again and it bit into his flesh. Warm blood trickled between his toes.

"Five days. Maybe seven, at the most. It's possible to source more grain from elsewhere, but it will cost significantly more."

"Do we have enough in the treasury?" he asked, tilting his head towards Rashid. His vizier, shadowed by the two most prominent apprentices, stepped forward. He'd never been a particularly robust man, but now Rashid looked old and wizened. Temujin didn't need insight from the Eternal Fire to know that the vizier's health was fading. He'd probably be dead within a year.

"We do, my Khan. The Trade Minister has made a number of beneficial deals." It almost sounded like a compliment, but that couldn't be right. Rashid hated Minister Rouhani. In fact, he seemed to hate everyone. The only person he'd ever seemed to like was the former Empress, but by now, Guyuk was long gone from the city. At least, Temujin assumed she was. He'd have to make sure and get someone to check on that. She was another minor annoyance he could do without.

"Make sure the army has whatever it needs," said Temujin. Right now, it was the most important thing in the world. At least, as far as everyone else knew. Timur was a threat, but he was only a man. One day he would die, but the Kozan were nearly eternal. A hundred years was nothing to them. If they wanted to, they could travel to a remote island, wait a century, and then return to reshape the world. Perhaps the generation that followed would be more cooperative and amenable to their demands. The cycle of manipulation had to end.

"What about that other item I asked for?" said Temujin. "Were you able to find it?"

Rashid's eyes widened in surprise, whereas the Minister just nodded. Temujin only told his vizier what he deemed necessary. However, he had to trust someone. The Minister knew a little more than most, but not everything. She knew what he needed, but not why or how it would be used.

"It will be delivered tomorrow," she promised.

"Good. Let me know the moment it arrives at the palace." Temujin got to his feet and then paused. "Is there anything else?" He remembered summoning the Trade Minister, but he couldn't remember if they'd discussed the reason or not.

The Minister glanced towards Rashid who shook his head. "Nothing that can't wait," she replied.

Any minor issues would be dealt with by them. If something was really important, Temujin knew he would be informed. Besides, he had something important to do.

Temujin sank into the bath, sighing with pleasure as the warm water covered his shoulders. The steam that swirled above the bath smelled of peppermint and something acidic to clear his congestion. Was it lime? It didn't matter. The water eased his tired muscles, and the aroma made the ache in his chest less severe. He'd been having difficulty getting a full breath for a few days.

For a moment, Temujin wondered when he'd decided to take a bath and who had heated the water. It must have been a servant. He'd come here directly from the throne room after his last meeting. It was the only thing that made sense.

In addition to the scented oils, a dozen candles filled the room with a heady smell. They also provided soothing ambient light. The whole atmosphere had such a calming effect that Temujin felt his head dipping towards his chest.

At times like these, he barely recognised his own body. It was so different from what he'd seen for the majority of his life. If not for the gift of the Eternal Fire, he would have died as a warrior in his father's army. Whether peppered by arrows, burnt with pitch, or slaughtered in a skirmish, he knew it would have happened during the siege of Baghdad.

Somewhere in the distance, Temujin heard a bird screeching in the night. The hallways around his rooms were utterly silent. He knew that the servants were afraid of him. They only came into his rooms when he wasn't there or if summoned. Otherwise, they avoided the area completely. This was definitely one of his favourite times of the day. There was no one vying for his attention, and he didn't have to pretend. The stillness and freedom to simply be himself was a relief.

Temujin stood up in the bath, splashing water over the sides. Something was wrong. He was sure it had been early afternoon, and now it was late at night. He was missing hours of time. What had he done in the interim? What was happening to him?

Scrunching his eyes closed, Temujin tried to remember everything he'd done since waking up that morning. He remembered getting out of bed and eating breakfast, but his next memory was dealing with matters of state in the throne room. He could sense other memories from the day, but they were obscured by a sort of fog in his mind. He went back further, trying to work out when it had started.

Pain began to blossom behind his right eye. It felt as if someone was driving a blade into his head. He fumbled for the Eternal Fire, but there was no possibility of being able to meditate. This wasn't natural. Someone was doing this to him.

Cold air touched the bare skin of Temujin's naked body. Slipping on the wet floor, he stumbled into the next room, made a grab for the door, but he somehow missed.

Temujin found he was lying on his bed staring up at the ceiling. He didn't know how he'd got there, or how much time had passed.

That was when he realised there was someone else in the room.

Closing his eyes, Temujin tried to slow his breathing, but the pain in his head had blossomed into something new. The ball of agony was spreading. Clawing tentacles were spreading out, like the arms of some beast.

Pain was a great teacher. In some ways, his father had been right in that saying. It told Temujin that someone was trying to hurt him. He couldn't block it out, but he tried his best to ignore it. He needed to know who was doing this to him.

There. To his left, in the corner of the room. He could hear someone breathing. Rolling over onto his side, Temujin reached under his bed with one arm. His fingers inched across the floor, spider-crawling left and right, but they kept coming up empty. A wave of fresh pain flooded his mind when something sharp cut his fingers. Instead of pulling back, he kept going, dragging the object closer.

Pressure built inside his skull. His right eye bulged and threatened to pop out of his head. There was something inside him that was desperate to get out. A living, squirming entity that was self-aware. All he had to do was shove the blade into his eye and it would all be over.

Blood-slicked fingers tightened on the hilt. His jaw was clenched so tight, his teeth squeaked. With a desperate fling of his arm, Temujin threw the dagger across the room. It missed the intended target, but it must have startled his attacker, as his torture stopped.

With a screech of rage and terror, Temujin charged towards the shadowy corner. It was far too dark to be natural. His arms sank into a dense blackness and disappeared up to the elbows, but Temujin could still feel his hands. His fingers made contact with flesh, and he dug them in tighter, earning a cry of pain.

Something hard collided with the side of Temujin's head and the room spun.

It was the cold stone pressing against his naked body that woke him up. A chill ran down the length of his body, and his teeth began to chatter. Pushing himself up onto his elbows and then his knees, Temujin saw a figure across the room. They were still wrapped in shadows, but he could see that it was a woman. He knew her.

A blistering white light filled the room, inverting all colours, turning night into day.

With a cry of anguish, Temujin covered his face with his hands, waiting for the pain to subside. The heavy silence made his ears ring. Listening carefully to his surroundings, Temujin realised he was alone again.

White spots danced in front of his eyes, obscuring his vision, but slowly they cleared. He pulled on some clothes and carefully moved from room to room, searching for the intruder. There was a dent in the wall from where he'd thrown the dagger, but no blood. The thick darkness was gone, and whoever had been hiding inside it.

His memories from earlier in the day were still fragmented, but now he understood why. Someone had been tampering with his mind. It had been so subtle he hadn't realised what they had been doing. There was no way to know what he had done or said in the missing hours. If he asked anyone, they would begin to worry and think that he'd lost his mind. In a way, they would be right.

Temujin's harsh laughter echoed around the bedroom. It bounced through the empty rooms off hard surfaces, amplifying his utter loneliness. His isolation made his laugh even harder, and once he'd started, he struggled to stop.

"What's so funny?" said a familiar voice.

Teague walked into the room. He was bruised, battered, and there was a nasty gash down one cheek. One of his eyes was a bloody ruin and his shirt had been shredded. A patch of blood was spreading from a wound on his left side, but more worrying was the glowing fissure in his chest. Golden-white light spilled from the wound. Embers of sunlight fell towards the floor, but they disappeared into nothingness before they landed.

The Kozan stumbled towards the bed, then changed direction and fell into a chair. One of his boots was missing, and Temujin noticed the two smallest toes on his right foot were gone.

"I lost them in a war, when I was a boy," said Teague, rubbing the side of his head. More light spilled from his body, pooling on his chest before it faded away like smoke on a breeze.

"What happened?" said Temujin.

"Hmm?" said Teague. His remaining eye was dazed. He didn't seem to know where he was, or why he'd come to see Temujin. "She killed me, even though she's dead." His laughter was bitter, but then grief swept over his face and he began to sob.

"Who?" asked Temujin, sitting down on the edge of the bed. He'd left the dagger across the room. That was a stupid mistake. There were no other weapons in his rooms. Even given his current condition, Temujin wasn't sure he could kill Teague without a blade. He struggled towards a sense of calm, but it was impossible to find. His mind and emotions were jumbled. Adrenaline was still surging through his body at Teague's sudden appearance, and he felt emotionally and physically drained.

"Maryam. She was changing you. Making you into one of them," said Teague, tapping the side of his head. "Balance. Order. They love symmetry. Three and three. That's what they wanted, after I killed Behrouz. But where's the beauty in that?"

"Beauty?" said Temujin, scoffing at the big man. "We spent months together, and not once did I hear you talk in such a way. In fact, you had such disdain for me, we barely spoke at all."

Teague nodded sagely. "Time changes many things. It creates a hard shell. It protects a person, but it also keeps much out. Words. Emotions. Family." The Kozan finally seemed to notice the wound in his chest. "I am being unmade," he said, trailing his fingers through the glowing smoke. Teague's eye widened and became distant. A smile tugged at the corners of his mouth.

"What is that?"

"My memories," said Teague. Temujin could see that part of the Kozan wasn't really in the room. He was watching something again in his mind. Two tears, one clear and one red, ran down his grizzled cheeks. "I remember Erik. It was so long ago, I had almost forgotten him. How could I forget my boy?"

"Did you love him?" asked Temujin.

"Of course," said Teague, as if it was the most obvious thing in the world, but then doubt crept into his face. "I think I did. I must have. Why did he have to die?"

Temujin had no answers to give. "Melchior called you the Nordic King."

"I was a king, once," said Teague. Now that it had started, a stream of red tears continually ran from his injured eye. "I was fair, and my country flourished. Through war, famine and harsh winters, but I did not age like the rest. At first, they said I was touched by the gods. Then they said I was cursed. Eventually, I was driven out. What happened to my family?" Teague stared into the distance, trying to remember their fate, but it seemed as if that memory was already gone.

"Were you coming here to kill me?" asked Temujin. Although the Kozan still intimidated him, Temujin was no longer afraid of the big man.

"Yes," said Teague, showing his teeth. "Your plan could work, and we could not allow that. Chaos must be allowed to flourish."

"Will the others come for me?"

"Eraj will not be able to help himself. He will try to kill you, but not for me, and not for revenge. He will do it because he hates you." Teague shook his shaggy head. "In all my years, I have never met a more wretched soul."

"When will he come?" asked Temujin.

"There is beauty in it," said Teague. Either he hadn't heard the question, or his mind had wandered. "Order can bring safety, but it is a rut that breeds idle minds. It must be uprooted so that freedom of thought can flourish. Chaos does not mean disaster."

It sounded pretty, but Temujin remembered how easily Teague had killed those who stood in his way. In that regard, all of the Kozan were exactly like his father. It didn't matter how many suffered, as long as their objective was achieved.

"How many wars have you started? How many people have you killed? Do you even know?" Temujin was shouting while he stood over Teague, but he didn't remember moving across the room.

"You look like him," said Teague, unfazed by Temujin's outburst. "Your father."

"You knew him?"

"He was ever vengeful, even as a boy," said the Kozan. Some of the colour had drained from his cheeks, but he continued to weep bloody tears. "Someone made fun of him, and everyone laughed. He tried to fight, but the other boy was older and stronger. So he waited. He let the bruises heal and the memory fade in the minds of others. But inside, he was seething, hungry for revenge."

Teague grabbed Temujin by the wrist and dragged him close, until he was kneeling in front of the Kozan. Temujin tried to pull free, but the dying man was incredibly strong. Placing a hand over the glowing wound, Teague plucked at something with his fingers, then pressed it against Temujin's forehead.

Hulagu watched his enemy for days, studying everything about him. What he did, where he went, and what he cared about. Patterns formed in his mind, and with them, a plan of attack. First, he poisoned the boy's friends against him by spreading rumours. Then he tainted the boy's food, so that he was sick for days. When the illness finally passed, he was left weak and dazed.

On a quiet path, away from prying eyes, Hulagu waited with a rock clutched in one hand behind his back. His enemy saw Hulagu and grinned, sure of his strength, in spite of everything. Hulagu's first strike blinded the boy in one eye. His second broke fingers. His third, an ankle.

Temujin fell backwards onto the floor. He was soaked in sweat and his heart was pounding. The memory had been so vivid it took him a while to realise he was back in his rooms in the palace.

He'd seen and heard it all. The unbridled fury on his father's face as he'd beaten his enemy to a bloody pulp. The cracking of bone. The wailing of the boy as he was maimed for life.

"The boy never told anyone who did it. He didn't dare," said Teague. "He understood that your father would kill him. All he needed was an excuse."

"Why did you show me that?" gasped Temujin.

"My time is nearly done, but you still have a role to play in the war. Timur is like your father, in many ways. He has the ambition and a mind for strategy unlike anyone else, but everyone believes there is no heat in him. No rage." Teague's stare was clear and focused. For the time being, he was in the present. "They are wrong."

"He's patient and calculating," said Temujin, thinking about what Teague had shown him.

"Once, Timur conquered a city. Then he asked that every warrior return with two severed heads." Teague gasped a pressed a hand to his chest, trying to stem the flow, but the memories continued to spill out from between his fingers. "He did it because he could, and to send a message. He also did it for every slight he'd ever suffered in his life."

It was petty and arrogant, but ultimately, it was human. Despite all that he had accomplished, Timur was just as flawed as everyone else.

"Timur can still ride, but he will not take to the battlefield. You will not see him trying to carve a bloody path through the enemy. He is not arrogant like your father."

"But he can get angry," said Temujin, "and he can be controlled by it."

"And who knows more about rage than you?" said Teague, trying to stifle a wet cough. When he took his hand away, Temujin saw blood on his fingers.

"Are you afraid of death?" asked Temujin. In comparison to the Kozan, the span of his life and that of every other human would appear incredibly brief. Here, and then gone in the blink of an eye like an insect. Temujin already knew it was a lonely existence, and he was feeling it already, but he wondered if time lessened a person's fears.

Teague's bloody smile had a wolfish quality. "No, boy. Long ago, I used to believe in the old gods. I prayed to them with everyone else. But after a few centuries, I became a god, so what have I to fear?"

Teague let out a long slow breath and his chest stopped moving. The silent trickle of memories pouring from the wound slowed and then stopped. As his eye glazed over, Teague's hand dropped to his side and he died, without spectacle.

Temujin wasn't sure what he'd been expecting. Something grand, perhaps. A final explosion of power to signify the death of someone who had been alive for so long. But in the end, Teague like all of the Kozan, was exactly what he'd suspected for a long time. They were human, just like everyone else.

Teague was no less fearsome in death. He was also still a very large man, and Temujin had no idea what he was going to do with the body. As he got up from the bed, he felt a disturbance in the air, as if something had brushed against his cheek. Fearing the worst, Temujin ran to the corner of the room, picked up his fallen dagger and searched for the source of the breeze.

It was coming from Teague. The shadows in the room started to fade as light poured from every exposed piece of skin. His hands and face glowed until Temujin could see every pore and vein beneath the surface. Golden-white rays moved across the walls, merging with one another as the light intensified. He heard a faint humming in the distance, like the muttering of a distant crowd. Temujin sensed the presence of something alien, and yet familiar. Hairs rose on the back of his arms, and even standing against the wall, he didn't feel safe. The other being was in the room, but their focus was on Teague, whose body continue to glow and then started to vibrate.

Temujin had to close his eyes, but even with his hands pressed against his face, the light was intense. Shapes moved behind his eyelids, and he briefly saw a face. Swirling pits for eyes. No mouth. A slouching beast beneath it.

With a cry he stumbled away, tripped and fell, landing on the cold stone floor.

For a single heartbeat, the world became a featureless white landscape, and then it was gone. Darkness returned, the presence faded, and white stars danced across Temujin's eyelids. Slowly, he opened his eyes and found that he was alone.

Teague's body was gone. Not even a trace of him remained. A Kozan had died, and while the world may not have noticed, something else had, and it had come to claim him.

CHAPTER 20
Kokochin

The long journey to Rome was made arduous by the unforgiving heat of summer. Weeks and weeks of travel along the Silk Road on horseback, riding on creaking carts and sometimes walking on foot. North and west, always west, towards unfamiliar lands that were cooler and greener than Kokochin had anticipated. Finally, they reached Constantinople, and from there boarded a ship that took them across the Mediterranean Sea to Amalfi, a thriving port town. Kokochin was astonished by the number of ships on the docks and the amount of goods that had been imported from the East.

The town, nestled on the coast, was beautiful. Its houses were built into the green hillsides, and a huge cathedral dominated everything else in the town. Distant bells rang in the city, calling Christians to prayer. There had been several pilgrims on the ship, and one of them had told Kokochin about the remains of a famous saint he'd come to visit.

Everywhere she looked, there were lush plants and brightly coloured flowers. The air hummed with a dozen languages, and away from the smell of the busy port, it was clean and crisp. They spent one day in the town, resting after their arduous voyage, before pushing on. After a final ride north, they arrived in the holy city of Rome in early autumn.

In a quiet square, inside a slightly run down tavern, Kokochin and Layla sat drinking wine. It was crisp and a little too sweet for Kokochin's taste, but at least it was cool. Today, the sky was without clouds and the midday sun was sticky and uncomfortable. The tavern owner, a rotund man called Gio, said it was the final gasp of summer and had predicted it would not last.

"I hate this," said Layla, not for the first time.

"I know," said Kokochin, trying not to get annoyed.

For two weeks, they had been trying to speak with their contact in the Church. Several letters had been delivered using specific names and phrases they'd been given, and yet they still hadn't received anything in return. On the journey west, they'd sent letters ahead to the House of Grace in Persia, and in return had received funds and information.

Four, one of the Inner Circle, was focused on Rome, and she had a small group of contacts in the city. The main operative, a local woman named Rosa, had helped them find a safe place to stay and explained how things worked. On the surface, Rosa was just a local merchant's wife, but in reality, she had a dozen people from all walks of life that regularly shared information. Only Rosa knew who she actually worked for, while the rest of the contacts in her network were unaware. They also didn't know about each other, which reminded Kokochin of how she had established her own network.

"It's been two weeks," said Layla, telling Kokochin what she already knew. Frustrated didn't even come close to describing what the two of them were feeling. Apparently, it was not appropriate for someone like Kokochin to simply walk into the Vatican and meet with a senior priest. That meant letters had to be written requesting an audience, starting with someone more junior. Several donations had to be given to the right people to persuade them to pay close attention to their letter, and perhaps prioritise it over others. After two awkward and uncomfortable meetings with junior church officials, with one of Rosa's contacts acting as an intermediary, the only thing they'd established was that their request was being considered.

So, they had to sit and wait. At least during the day, when Kokochin thought it was fair to assume that they were being watched. At night, they had not been idle.

The only good news to come from Rosa's network was that the so-called ambassador from Timur's court had not yet arrived in the city. Kokochin sipped her wine, picked at some olives and cheese and tried, unsuccessfully, not to dwell on the past.

"I can hear you brooding," said Layla, staring out the window. Despite travelling together for months to reach Rome, their friendship was still fragile. There were days when it felt like old times and Kokochin believed that, if nothing else, at least they were still friends. They would laugh and joke with one another, but then a cloud would pass over one of them and a heavy silence would return. Sometimes it lasted for hours. Sometimes only moments, but it was an unavoidable and painful reminder of the past. It was something neither of them could ignore, like a pebble in her shoe. It only took one wrong word, or even a look, and then the pain would return.

A lot of trust needed to be rebuilt before they could move forward. Kokochin wondered if they would ever reach a place where they were more than just friends.

"What if we never get to see the priest?" said Kokochin.

"Then we'll break into the Vatican, sneak into his bedroom, and wake him up," said Layla, favouring her with a rare smile. Kokochin laughed and ate more bread, smeared with butter. The bread was so soft it melted in her mouth.

"Cell," said Kokochin, which soured her moment of pleasure. Thanks to Guyuk, she'd spent time in several cells, but she did not want to think about that, or the former Empress.

"What?" said Layla, turning around to face her.

"I think they call them cells, not bedrooms."

Layla's expression turned bitter. No doubt she was thinking of when she'd also been a prisoner, thanks to Guyuk.

They were saved from any more painful conversation by the arrival of Rosa. Somewhere in her forties, with a curvy figure and raven-dark hair, she oozed confidence and sexuality. Men, and some women, were instantly attracted to her before she even said a word. Even the surly man behind the bar, Gio, perked up as Rosa sat down at their table. Without being asked, he hurried over with more olives and a glass of wine.

"Thank you," said Rosa, reaching for some money, but the man waved her away.

"No, madam. It's my pleasure," said Gio with a toothy smile. He lingered by the table as if to say something else, but instead he just grinned. It was only when Layla cleared her throat that he remembered Rosa wasn't alone. With a bob of his head, Gio withdrew to the far side of the room. Even without looking, Kokochin could feel him staring at Rosa with lust.

"Please tell us you have some good news," said Layla. "This city is a wonder, but I cannot relax long enough to enjoy any of it."

"There is some news," said Rosa, picking her words carefully. "A more senior church official has agreed to speak with you."

Kokochin groaned. "But not the actual priest we need?"

"No," said Rosa.

Layla rolled her eyes and swore loudly, drawing the owner's ire. He bellowed something loudly in his native tongue, to which Rosa responded in kind. She stood up, and her ensuing passionate tirade went on for a while until Gio turned pale and apologetic. He babbled something, his posture became subservient and he disappeared into the back room with his shoulders hunched.

"What did he say about me?" asked Layla, reaching for a blade.

"You don't want to know," said Rosa, settling back in her chair with a smile. It was as if the argument had never happened.

"Where and when are we meeting?" asked Kokochin, not giving Layla a chance to ask for more details about the insult.

"Tomorrow morning. Here's the address," said Rosa, passing her a note.

"We'll be there," promised Kokochin, although right now, she was just hoping they could make it through the day without Layla stabbing the tavern owner.

If not for the large suspicious-looking man standing beside it, Kokochin would never have spotted the entrance to the cellar. Even in the early morning sunlight, it was easy to miss.

She and Layla had scouted the street several times during the night and had found nothing of interest. At first, she thought a section of the stones had merely been lifted one at a time to create the opening. It was only as they approached the entrance that she noticed a narrow metal frame just below the surface of the street. It was worn and tarnished, suggesting it had been there a long time. The city was ancient, and it seemed as if it had many layers and numerous secrets.

The big man guarding the door had a scarred face, sunken knuckles and the poise of a mercenary. He'd watched them carefully from the moment they'd stepped around the corner. Kokochin couldn't see any weapons, but she was certain he had a few blades hidden about his person.

"Please," he said, gesturing towards the black hole in the ground. Kokochin peered past him and saw several worn but deep steps. This was not what they'd been expecting for the meeting. The street was quiet, in a very poor but old part of the city where people knew to mind their own business. It felt like a trap. There was only one obvious way in and out, which was guarded by a large, capable-looking man. Her instincts told her to run.

"I'm here," murmured Layla, briefly touching Kokochin's hand. It was the first time Layla had touched her in months. The physical contact sent a pulse of energy racing up her arm.

Kokochin went first, accepting the mercenary's hand for balance as she stepped down into the darkness. Eleven deep steps brought her into a long, paved room with a low curved ceiling. The floor was covered with cobbled stone, but the ceiling had a dozen evenly spaced arches, like the ribs of some great beast. It felt as if they'd been gobbled up by something enormous and were standing inside its belly.

She'd expected damp and mould, but instead, Kokochin found it was dry and smelled of wood and wine. Two shuttered lanterns provided some light, but the edges of the room were wrapped in thick shadows. However, there was enough light for her to see the large wooden barrels sat on stout racks that lined both sides of the room. Two lines receded into the darkness, long past the illumination from the lanterns. When Kokochin scuffed her foot against the floor, the echo went on for a long time. It gave her a little hope that somewhere out there in the darkness was another way out.

Part of her expected the door above their heads to slam shut, but it remained open. Like a break in the clouds, a small pool of golden light filtered into the space from above.

A short time later, a large man squeezed himself through the narrow gap. He moved cautiously down the steps, clearly as unfamiliar with their surroundings as they were.

Kokochin guessed he was somewhere in his fifties, although the way he moved showed that age had not yet begun to slow him down. His tidy beard was still black, apart from a grey streak on one cheek. He was dressed in plain black trousers and a grey shirt, but there was something familiar about the way he held himself. After spending so much time around Mongol warriors and the Kheshig, she knew this man was a fighter.

"I apologise for the location," said the man, inclining his head, "and for the deception, but it was necessary. A man in my position has many enemies, and some are keen to use any anything untoward to their advantage."

"You are Cardinal Cavicchi," said Layla. She showed no surprise, but it took Kokochin a moment to adjust.

"Yes," said the priest. "I believe you have been trying to speak with me for some time."

"Your Eminence, do you know who we are?" asked Kokochin, curious as to how much he knew, and if her instincts about him were right.

"Your name is familiar to me, but not your face," said the priest, "although I admit, I didn't think you would be so young."

"Your Eminence, do you know who Timur is?" said Layla, getting straight to the point. Her patience had already been worn thin by waiting around for two weeks.

"I know of this man," said Cavicchi. He cracked his knuckles and Kokochin noticed they were scarred and calloused like his bodyguard. They were also the hands of someone who was used to hard physical labour. Nothing about the priest was what she had been expecting.

"Were you a warrior?" asked Kokochin, which made him smile.

"A long time ago," he admitted, leaning against one of the wine racks. "You have keen eyes, Princess."

"We have critical information that the Church should know about," said Layla, steering the conversation back on course. "We were given your name as someone trustworthy. Someone who would actually listen, and then act."

"That depends on what you have to tell me," said Cavicchi, giving nothing away. "Who sent you?" he asked.

The air changed in the cellar. Kokochin had the impression that the answer to his question was critical.

"We don't serve any of the khans, or the Mongol Empire," said Layla, practically spitting out the words. "I serve Persia."

"A rebel and a patriot. And you?" he said, turning to Kokochin. "Who is your master?"

"I have none. I'm simply here to stop something terrible from happening."

The priest folded his arms and took a deep breath. He took a moment to study both of them, his keen eyes moving about Kokochin's face, passing across her clothes. She knew his interest wasn't sexual in nature. He studied Layla just as closely. He was weighing them up. Trying to discern truth from lies and determine their motivation.

"Tell me why you're here, and what it has to do with Timur," he said, after a long and strained silence.

"We believe Timur has made an alliance with the Sultan of Egypt," said Layla. "His desire to rule the world eclipses that of any former khan, even Genghis Khan himself."

"To what end?" asked Cavicchi.

"Timur has called on Egypt's support to crush the Ilkhanate, and in return, the Mamluks will claim Jerusalem."

Cavicchi snorted in derision. "That is not an easy thing to accomplish. If it were, they would have already defeated the Church and its allies."

"That's true. However, Timur has sent an Assassin to kill the Holy Father," said Kokochin.

The Cardinal's posture immediately changed. He stopped leaning against the wine racks, and all good humour drained from his features.

"That's monstrous," said the priest. "Who is it?"

"They're posing as an ambassador," said Kokochin. "The problem is, we don't know who they're representing."

Timur wouldn't be so obvious as to send an Assassin from his own court, or that of the Chagatai khanate. The ambassador could pretend to be there on behalf of the Great Khan, the Ilkhanate or the Golden Horde. They could even be from one of the vassal states within the Mongol Empire, asking the Church to intercede and protect it from its harsh new rulers.

"Does the Pope receive many ambassadors?" asked Layla.

"Yes. There are new faces coming and going all the time," said Cavicchi. He was distracted, cracking his knuckles, and his eyes were distant. "He receives dozens of requests for an audience every day. All of them are carefully vetted. He only has time to deal with a small handful in person."

"The papers will look authentic, but they'll be forgeries," said Kokochin. It was what she would have done. With so much free time on the road to do nothing but sit and think, she'd run through the whole scenario a hundred times in her head. If she was Timur, she would also have sent the ambassador with a number of rare and important gifts. Something significant enough to warrant an audience with the Pope.

"I will need to look into this. It's not my usual area," said Cavicchi with a grimace. "What else can you tell me about the Assassin?"

"Not much," admitted Kokochin. "I assume weapons are not allowed in his presence, and that the Pope always has protection."

"All visitors are thoroughly searched. As for protection, he has some, but not as much as you would think. I will have to see if something can be arranged. As you've seen for yourself, there are many layers between an outsider and the inner sanctums of the Vatican."

"If not a weapon, then they could use something else. Poison, perhaps," said Layla. "A simple handshake, or something slipped into a drink. Then a few hours later, the Holy Father collapses and dies in his bed."

"To make something so potent would not be easy. It would require great skill and rare ingredients," said Kokochin. "We've been trying to make contact with those familiar with Rome's underbelly for some time."

Rosa's network had done their best, but those who lived in the shadows were extremely cautious, especially of newcomers and outsiders. It had proven more difficult to find someone reliable to speak with from the underworld than getting a meeting with a priest.

"I can help you with that," said the cardinal.

"You can?" said Kokochin, which earned a wry smile from Cavicchi.

"We all have a past, good and bad."

"We will need a better way to contact you," said Layla. "Something faster and more direct."

"I agree, but you cannot come to my offices. I would struggle to explain why two foreign women were regularly paying me a visit. We will have to meet somewhere else." Cavicchi pursed his lips, and for a moment Kokochin thought he was going to spit on the ground.

"Why?" asked Kokochin, although she had a good idea about his answer.

"Such a thing would be scandalous. It would suggest inappropriate behaviour."

"Let me speak plainly, Your Eminence," said Kokochin, struggling to hold on to her temper. "I don't understand the complex workings of the Church, and its many layers of bureaucracy, but surely no faction wants the Pope to be murdered?"

She had meant it as a rhetorical question, but Cavicchi chose to answer.

"You would think so, but there are some who are against the new Crusade. They believe we expend too many resources and lives on it. They want to see our energy focused on other areas. Missionary work and the like."

It was not what she had been expecting him to say, which stunned her to silence.

"We cannot help you, or the Pope, if we cannot talk freely with one another," said Layla.

"You need our help," said Kokochin. "There are places we can go and people we can talk to that you can't. We did not come all this way just to deliver a message."

In spite of everything, Cavicchi laughed. "You're right. I see that your reputation is well earned." He gave them directions to a local tavern. "Meet me there in two days' time. By then, I will know more about any ambassadors that are due to arrive."

"And what are we to do in the meantime?" asked Kokochin.

The priest gave them directions to another location. "You should visit The Seventh Bell. From the moment you set foot in the front door, trust no one. Nothing is what it appears to be." Cavicchi's frown deepened, and she sensed his discomfort. "If there's a kindly old drunk in the corner, minding his own business, assume he's a watcher. If there's a one-legged beggar on the street outside, they probably work for someone. Anything you say will be reported to someone, so choose your words carefully. Ask for a meeting with Angelo. He's the owner. That will get you in a room with him."

"Who is he?" asked Layla.

"He's dangerous and powerful. He runs an organised gang in the underworld."

"Should I even ask how you know such a man?" said Kokochin.

Cavicchi shook his head and turned to leave. He was halfway up the steps before he looked back over his shoulder. "Only use my name if he asks. He can find anything, and if he can't, he will know someone who can. He will help you find the poison, and perhaps, the Assassin."

"What if he refuses to help?" said Kokochin.

Cavicchi crackled his knuckles and grinned. "Then you will have to find a way to persuade him."

He left them in the gloom, and a short time later, they followed him back up to the street. The thug helped them up and then sealed the hatch, replacing the heavy stone with a grunt of effort.

Although she tried to keep watch for anyone that was following them, Kokochin was distracted. She let Layla take the lead, guiding them through the winding streets of Rome. She seemed to be choosing their path at random, but Kokochin knew there would be a reason. Layla never did anything without thinking it through ahead of time.

Noon was still hours away. They paused outside a jewellery shop, peering at the objects inside. Layla scrutinised some of the items and sniffed in derision.

"You look worried," she said, glancing over Kokochin's shoulder. "You don't trust the priest?"

"It's not that," said Kokochin, not sure how much she should share. It was beyond anything they'd talked about in months, but she needed to tell someone. "I'm scared about what I might do."

Layla briefly made eye contact, then went back to studying the crowd. "Go on," she said.

"What if we have to pressure this Angelo into working with us? What happens if I get caught up in the moment? I never want to be that person again." Kokochin bit the inside of her cheek to stop herself from saying anything else.

"It won't happen," said Layla.

"How can you be so sure?"

"Because I won't let you," said Layla, gripping her hand. "You're not alone."

Kokochin held on tightly and never wanted Layla to let go.

CHAPTER 21
Kaivon

Kaivon paced back and forth in the tent listening to Esme's latest report from her contacts across the Ilkhanate. She'd already made a comment about him wearing a hole in the rug, but he was too distracted to stop moving.

They were camped several days east of Isfahan, in central Persia. The army's next destination was Nishapur, several days travel north and east. It was late afternoon, and the rest of the army was due to arrive in another couple of hours. The senior officers had gone ahead, and Kaivon would soon be meeting with them to discuss their next move against Timur.

"His ego is astonishing," said Esme, scanning the latest note she'd received. "Timur knows he can't legitimately use the term Khan, but he's doing everything he can to win people over in other ways."

There were many tales and rumours about Timur. All of them claimed he had come from a humble background, as it was a more powerful story, whereas the truth was he'd come from a wealthy family with an estate. Rather than try to hide his injuries, all of the stories about them were centred around a mighty battle where he'd slain fifty men before finally being injured by a cowardly archer. It was slightly less impressive and inspirational to learn that Timur had been wounded by a farmer for trying to steal one of his sheep.

"What's he claiming now?" said Kaivon.

"Well, in addition to being the 'Sword of Islam', bringing righteous fury to unbelievers, he's now saying he was chosen by the Heavens." Esme rolled her eyes and laughed, but it was a sound without mirth. She understood just how dangerous Timur was, and while they thought his claims were ridiculous, there were many who believed. The stories won the hearts of warriors, and that gave him power. Several towns and villages in the east of the Ilkhanate had welcomed Timur as their saviour. The governor had been fair but was not a devout Muslim, so he had been easily cast aside. All who embraced Timur were treated well, and were spared any of his usual savagery. Timur saved the massacres for any who dared oppose him or mock his fervent beliefs. Kaivon wondered if it was just another psychological weapon or if he was a genuine follower of Islam.

"He wants people to believe this war is a holy one, and that he's a tool that's been chosen by God to usher in a new era."

"He hasn't called himself a prophet?"

"No," said Esme, frowning at the note, "but I wonder how long it will be before he does."

Perception mattered a great deal, not only to the people, but also the warriors in the army. Timur styled himself as a humble man who had risen to become a leader, a saviour and now a holy icon. By comparison, the ruler of the Ilkhanate was a peculiar recluse with supposedly demonic powers who disappeared for days at a time on mysterious errands.

Kaivon had heard stories that Temujin was distracted, and there were strange noises and bright lights coming from his rooms at night. Even worse, he'd done nothing to challenge any of the rumours, which didn't endear him to the people. For most, life in the Ilkhanate had not changed from when Hulagu had ruled, as they still enjoyed the same freedoms.

However, for those in the new army, it was a challenging time and they needed strong leaders. The warriors faced a dangerous and unpredictable enemy who led a vast and brutal horde. Each man under Kaivon's command fought because it was the right thing to do according to their own beliefs and principles, but also because of the promise of independence for their respective countries. There were veterans in this army, coming from nations across the new alliance, but there were also a lot of new recruits. He'd done what he could to give many of them a taste of what was to come, but there were days when Kaivon wondered if it was enough.

"Is it ego, or does Timur truly believe any of it?" said Kaivon, stopping in the middle of the rug.

Esme had been sorting through the missives, but she paused and looked up. "Does it matter?" she asked.

Kaivon shrugged. "Maybe not, but it brings together those under his command. Some will be fighting just to get rich or because they love killing and conquest. But others believe the myths he's creating, and as his power grows, so will the number of zealots. As you said, we need to turn the people against him. That's not easy when you compare him with Temujin."

Esme's expression turned grim. "Not everyone is so easily impressed or fooled by Timur's sleight of hand and misdirection. Why don't we ask the people of Herat what they think?"

The city officials in Herat had refused to surrender. They even went so far as to publicly denounce Timur and his ancestral claims of being connected to Genghis Khan. In retribution, Timur had reduced the city to rubble and massacred most of its inhabitants. Those who escaped had spread stories of what he'd done, which had worked in Kaivon's favour.

Timur's mood had become unpredictable after Herat. Some villages and towns that tried to surrender were still destroyed. As a result, many people in the east of the Ilkhanate had turned against Timur. Kaivon assumed that included many who had been undecided, and those who had previously been ready to welcome him as their saviour. The locals suddenly became more accommodating with Kaivon's scouts and spies, sharing information, supplies, and sometimes carrying out small acts of rebellion against Timur. It was difficult to see the benefits of a holy war when someone was about to burn down your home and butcher your family.

"There have been several small uprisings," said Esme. "Some of Timur's scouts have disappeared. Entire villages in his path have been abandoned, and the locals poisoned the water before they left. I've now heard three stories about a rebel group in Lahore causing problems."

It was all good news, and Kaivon knew he should take heart from it, but the looming threat of battle troubled him. There had been a few skirmishes between small groups, and one short battle in a town further east, but it had not been a decisive victory. It had been described in such a manner to inspire others, but the truth was less appealing. They had won due to luck more than skill, despite outnumbering Timur's forces.

"Even after everything we did, I'm still worried that some of the men aren't ready for what's to come," said Kaivon, sharing his fears. "So, as my War Wife, what would you advise?"

Esme snorted. Although they were not married, they had at least discussed it. They had both agreed that if they survived the war, then they would make it official. "Trust in your officers and those closest to you. One of Hulagu's many faults was his arrogance. He believed he was destined for greatness, and that victory was always a foregone conclusion. Until the battle of Ain-Jalut, his forces had never suffered a significant defeat."

"I am listening carefully to the others, but last time I was in charge of an army, I lost everyone," said Kaivon. A few junior officers had survived the Mongol invasion, but he was the last Persian General. "And now, I'm responsible for thousands of lives again."

When Kaivon started to pace, Esme grabbed his hand and held him in place. "You're not alone anymore," she said, wrapping her arms around him. "Did you know King David sometimes leads his men in prayer? They draw strength from him and his faith in god."

"That's not something I can do," said Kaivon. He'd never shown an inkling of following any religion. If he were to suddenly reveal his beliefs, it would be obviously disingenuous.

"I know. Some men believe in god, but others look to individuals for hope. Your history, the mistakes and the victories, inspires many in the army. The Mongols invaded and you survived. You took part in the siege of Baghdad and survived."

"Barely," said Kaivon. His lungs had ached for days, and if not for Esme's help, he would likely have died.

"You were turned to ash by a Kozan, and yet you survived. It wasn't luck," said Esme, putting a finger to his lips, before he could argue the point. "There are many stories swirling in the camps about you. Some are true and others exaggerated, but it doesn't really matter. How you are perceived by others is what matters," she said, echoing what he'd been thinking earlier. "Give the men what they need."

"I will try," he said, tilting her chin up so he could lean down and kiss her mouth. "Thank you."

"You're welcome. Now, as your War Wife," she said, making the term sound like an insult, "I suggest you get some rest. It's going to be a long night. I expect some of the scouts will not return for a few hours."

A frantic guard woke Kaivon late in the night. Apparently, Temujin had appeared out of nowhere and wanted to speak with Kaivon at once. Kaivon sent a messenger to wake up his senior officers, then pulled on some clothes and splashed water on his face. Esme was awake, but Kaivon noticed she wasn't getting dressed.

"Don't you want to be there?" he asked.

"No. He's been spending a lot of time with my sister, and I don't want him to realise who I am." As far as Temujin was aware, his Trade Minister had an extensive network of contacts because of her merchant companies. They travelled the length and breadth of the Silk Road, which put an enormous amount of information at her fingertips. It was safer that he believed that. At the moment, he knew nothing of the House of Grace, and they wanted to keep it that way. As a Kozan, Temujin had a number of overt powers, but they'd also noticed his unnatural insight.

Outside Kaivon's tent, the night was crisp but refreshing. Every deep breath filled his lungs with cold air that made them ache. The temperature helped Kaivon shake off any lingering remnants of sleep, but it did nothing for his tired body. With few stars, and most of the campfires having burnt down to embers, he tripped several times in the dark over hidden obstacles.

When Kaivon finally arrived at the command tent, he was pleased to see that someone had lit several lanterns. He was the first of the senior officers to arrive but knew the others would not be far behind. Inside, Temujin was sat crossed-legged on the ground, his eyes closed in prayer or meditation. As ever, he was dressed in plain clothing that gave no indication as to his rank, or the power at his command as both ruler of the Ilkhanate and a Kozan. With his flowing white cotton shirt, baggy trousers and shaven head, Kaivon still thought that Temujin resembled a monk.

"Sit," said Temujin, slowly opening his eyes. They had never bothered Kaivon before, but now he found them disturbing. Temujin's gaze lacked something that had previously been there. Warmth and compassion for humanity.

Kaivon sat down on some cushions, which Temujin had ignored. He expected the new khan to speak first. Perhaps discuss a few minor issues until the others arrived, but instead he seemed perfectly happy to sit in silence. Temujin closed his eyes and went back to meditating, or perhaps dozing, since it was the middle of the night. Kaivon didn't dare risk closing his eyes in case he fell asleep.

A lot had changed about Temujin. The naïve, bumbling, insecure former prince was gone. There were moments when Kaivon saw glimpses of Temujin's father in his mannerisms or behaviour, but otherwise he was unrecognisable. He didn't know whether it was Temujin's developing powers that had changed him or something else. Their fate was tied together, and as such, Kaivon needed to better understand who he was dealing with.

"We should talk," he said, breaking the silence.

"I'm listening," said Temujin, without opening his eyes. His voice was flat and emotionless.

"One of the most dangerous things about your father was his unpredictability." Temujin sat up and opened his eyes, so Kaivon pressed on. "Because of his bouts of rage, he sometimes gave commands that were doomed from the start. You may have ended it, but his downfall was inevitable."

"When you heard that he was dead, were you pleased?" asked Temujin. He showed no obvious signs of emotion, but Kaivon could hear the heat in his words. Kaivon wondered who Temujin was really angry with. Did a part of him regret murdering Hulagu?

"Not as much as I thought I would be," admitted Kaivon. It was strange. He should have celebrated and toasted Hulagu's death.

"Perhaps you wanted him to live still, so that he could see his dream die," suggested Temujin.

"Perhaps, but I need to know that you're not like your father. That you're not going to make sudden changes to my plan."

"Your plan?" said Temujin, raising an eyebrow. "Are you the khan?"

"I don't want to rule the Ilkhanate, but either I am in command of the army, or I'm not. The others chose me to lead. They need a single voice."

"That's fair."

"Good. Then I would prefer that you and I talk, before you make any significant changes to the plan." Kaivon chose his words with care, as he was uncertain of Temujin's mood. Sometimes he was aloof and distant throughout their meetings, and at other times he was raw and overly emotional.

The other officers entered the tent without announcing themselves. They hesitated on the threshold when they saw who was already inside. David stared at both of them and raised an eyebrow. "Did we miss something?"

"No," said Temujin, with a smile that Kaivon thought was forced. "We were just discussing the General's promotion. Please, sit," he said, gesturing at the floor.

It was too late for food, but Temujin asked for tea, which arrived shortly after. When he personally offered it to those in the tent, only three of the thirteen men accepted a glass. Kaivon knew that most of them hated Temujin, and many were afraid of what he'd become. Paranoia, probably about being poisoned, made several politely refuse. It was highly unusual to be served anything by a khan. If Temujin was attempting to appear humble and ordinary, it didn't work. He only made everyone feel more uncomfortable.

"I have news," said Temujin, once he'd retaken his seat. "Most of the Kozan are gone. Dead," he added, when a few still looked puzzled.

"How?" asked Kaivon.

"It doesn't matter. The important thing is, their interference in the war with Timur will be minimal. The outcome will be determined by you." Temujin's gaze took in every man gathered together in the tent.

"That's good," said David, sharing a strange look with Hethum. "As it should be."

"Do you have any news of Timur?" asked Thoros.

"Or the Golden Horde?" said Kaivon.

His scouts reported that the number of men in Timur's army outnumbered theirs. Without additional warriors from the northern khanate, victory for the Ilkhanate would require a great amount of luck and perfect timing, two things Kaivon could not control. As he'd learned from experience, plans could and often did go wrong. Those unable to adapt in the moment were guaranteed to fail.

Timur was nobody's fool, and he was not someone to be underestimated. Kaivon and the others intended to use all of their combined knowledge to oppose him, but in the battle yet to come, they would not survive on hope.

"We need Tokhtamysh and his men," stressed Kaivon. He knew forces from the Golden Horde had sacked Tashkent, but since then he'd received little information about the army's movement. Over forty years ago, the city had suffered at the hands of Genghis Khan. Most of its population had been killed or enslaved, and it had been part of the Chagatai khanate ever since. It must have come as quite a surprise to the population when they were invaded again by Mongols from the north.

"Tokhtamysh is on his way," promised Temujin. "I will be paying him a visit next, but he already knows what he has to do, and the cost of failure."

A year ago, if Prince Temujin had said such a thing out loud, everyone would have laughed and thought he was making a joke. Such a menacing declaration from Hulagu would have chilled Kaivon to the bone. Temujin's icy stare and emotionless voice was worse than his father's anger. Kaivon thought he was seething with buried rage that was desperate for release.

"What of the stories about Timur's forces in the south of Persia?" asked Temujin. "Are they true?"

"Those turned out to be false," said Kaivon. Information from scouts and contacts in the House of Grace had confirmed what he'd suspected. "I believe it was a ruse created by Timur. He intended to draw more of our forces to the south. He sent a few hundred warriors to cause trouble. They burned villages and murdered people, but they never took any slaves and always kept moving. At first, it made it difficult to get an accurate count. They also proclaimed they were a vanguard for his army, but as their numbers dwindled, they were never replaced. Eventually they split into smaller groups to try and spread panic, but several groups were captured or even killed by locals."

Greed had made Timur's warriors reckless, and it had cost many of them their lives. Drunk on victory, due to Timur's strategies and leadership, the warriors had assumed it would be easy to replicate success without him.

One of Esme's contacts had passed on the information about the ruse. She had not specified how it had been obtained, only that it was reliable and could be trusted. Kaivon suspected several of Timur's warriors had been tortured to death. Given what his army was facing, and what the warriors had done, he didn't feel even an inkling of sympathy for what they had endured.

"Then it will all come down to one battle in the north of Persia," said Temujin.

"At least one, although we expect there will be skirmishes beforehand," said David.

"Where do you think it will happen?" asked Temujin.

A heavy silence filled the tent.

This was what they had been debating every night. When it would take place was equally important as where. Having barely survived the massacre at Derbent under Hulagu's leadership, Kaivon was very aware that they could not be caught unawares.

Berke's forces from the Golden Horde had been lying in wait for several days. His warriors had been well rested, and they had used the terrain to their advantage. Despite making a brave attempt, Hulagu's forces had not stood a chance. They had walked right into a trap.

Many warriors from the Ilkhanate had died in the ambush, and those who survived had been changed by the defeat. Dying with two feet of steel in your belly wasn't a good way to die by any measure, but until Derbent, few had thought it preferable to drowning. Many warriors on horseback had been driven into the river. It had been the weight of their armour, or being crushed beneath their beast, that cost them their life. Kaivon had come very close to being one of them. Sometimes, he still had nightmares about drowning, and woke up clawing at his throat with his lungs on fire.

Temujin's miscoloured eyes moved from face to face around the circle. A few maintained eye contact, but most looked away in fear. They regarded the new khan as necessary, but no one liked him. Esme was right. Inspiration for the men had to come from other places. Temujin was a figurehead, and a useful resource for him and the other officers, nothing more.

"We have many scouts out there gathering information on Timur's army and its movement," said Kaivon. "But they can only move so fast. Can you help with that?"

He didn't understand how it was done, but Kaivon knew that the Kozan could travel great distances in a short amount of time. He'd now experienced it on two occasions, and it was not something he wanted to happen a third.

"Perhaps," mused Temujin. He picked up a sugared almond, kept it in his mouth and slurped his tea around it. Temujin must have been feeling the cold as he cradled his glass in both hands, savouring the steam blowing across his face. "I will do what I can, but you should not rely on me. The remaining Kozan may not interfere with you directly, but I am still a target for their wrath."

"Then what can you do to help us?" asked Prince Thoros. "What have you sacrificed?"

Temujin raised an eyebrow at the impertinence of the questions, but he showed no signs of anger. The old Temujin had died and been reborn as someone far colder and more dangerous.

Ever since Thoros had been abducted and supposedly burned to ash by Behrouz, he'd become reckless. He'd gone through the same process as Kaivon, and now seemed to have a death wish.

Given what Temujin had done to his family, sacrifice was a poor choice of word. There was much Kaivon didn't know about Temujin's dealings, but even a cursory glance at his pale face told Kaivon the new khan was paying a heavy cost. By eliminating his family, Temujin had removed any direct competition, but it had also isolated him. Kaivon wondered if he had any friends, or someone he could rely on. Someone he trusted absolutely, the way he trusted Esme. Looking at the haunted look in Temujin's eyes, Kaivon saw no glimmers of comfort or love.

Thoros seemed to realise that he may have pushed his luck. The flush of anger faded from his cheeks, and he looked to his brother for support. Hethum sighed and placed a hand on his brother's shoulder. Thoros tried to speak but no words emerged. His throat had seized with fear.

"My brother spoke out of turn. Please don't punish him," said the king.

Temujin dismissed it with a wave and turned to Kaivon. "I will visit Tokhtamysh and let him know your exact location, and that of Timur's forces. I will also take care of funding matters back in Tabriz," said Temujin.

Thoros snorted and his brother's grip tightened on his shoulder until he lowered his head in contrition.

Like Kaivon, Hethum was very aware of how much they relied on the capital for money, equipment, armour, weapons, and most importantly, food. It was critical that trade continued to flow across the Ilkhanate. Without it, the army would become like locusts, consuming every scrap of food in each town and city they passed through. Without trade, they would leave only starving locals in their wake. Any victory against Timur would be hollow if half of Persia was left impoverished and unable to feed itself.

"I will also pay a visit to Samarkand," said Temujin.

"Why there?" asked one of the junior officers.

"Wasn't Timur born somewhere near there?" said Kaivon, remembering something he'd been told by Esme. Her contacts had been gathering all sorts of information about their enemy, including personal details.

"While Buqa-Temur played at being ruler of the Chagatai khanate, Timur was ruling from Samarkand. He made it his home, and it was from there he grew in power," said Temujin. "There is much in the city that he cares about."

"Even if he could get there in time, he will not rush home to try and save it," said David, rolling his glass between his hands. He had not risked taking a sip. He'd accepted the tea when it had been offered to show that he wasn't afraid, but David was scared. They all were.

"That's true, but that's not the point," said Temujin with a smile that Kaivon found incredibly troubling. "No one has caused Timur significant hurt in a long time, especially on a personal level. Trying to attack him physically would be impossible. He is guarded at all hours and is surrounded by thousands of warriors. Before the battle, we need him to be distracted, angry. He should be worried about his home, and his family."

A horrible sinking feeling started to spread from Kaivon's stomach. He was suddenly reminded of what Temujin had done to his siblings. In one day, he had killed every single one of them, effectively ending his father's bloodline. Looking at the faces of those around him, Kaivon could see the question was on all of their lips, but none dared ask it.

"He has a unique mind," said Temujin, breaking the uncomfortable silence that had settled over everyone. "Brutal and unrelenting, but he is human, and fallible. He has made mistakes, and he will make more of them. His lies and hypocrisy must be exposed. The people he has conquered, even those he has treated kindly, must come to resent him.

They must continue to rise up and reject him as their ruler. He is not a prophet, or a khan, or a holy Sword of Islam. He is a tyrant and a brutal warmonger. He loves death, nothing more."

It seemed as if making speeches ran in the blood after all. For a frightening moment, Kaivon had thought he was listening to Hulagu instead of his son.

"When?" said Kaivon. It was a cowardly question. Asking when it would happen, and not how far Temujin was willing to go. But there was no rebuke on the faces of those that surrounded him. They all understood because they felt the same about the unpredictable tiger in their midst.

Temujin grinned, as if he knew what Kaivon was thinking. "Soon. By the time you meet him on the battlefield, I will have broken his spirit."

The Kozan stood up to leave and everyone followed, but they did it out of fear rather than respect. Kaivon saw only pale and worried faces around him. Even Thoros was troubled, his eyes distant and focused on something elsewhere.

Of course, Temujin had noticed his impact on everyone. He gave Kaivon a wry smile and then stepped out of the tent. Like a gang of frightened children huddling together for safety, they gathered at the entrance to watch Temujin leave. He walked a dozen steps away from them and then disappeared, walking into thin air. It was as if he had stepped from one room into another and closed the door behind him.

A few of the officers beside Kaivon made the sign of the cross on their chest to ward off evil. He didn't think Temujin's powers were demonic in nature, but they were disturbing.

David held up his glass of tea and poured it out onto the ground. "He is not human. Not anymore."

"Perhaps," said Kaivon. It was late, he was tired, and he didn't have the energy for a lengthy debate.

"If we survive this," said the king, "do you really think Temujin will honour what he's promised?"

Kaivon had considered it many times and he didn't have an answer. Right now, it was a problem for another day. He had to focus on the larger and immediate threat, which was Timur, who loomed in his mind.

"One enemy at a time," he said, which pleased the king.

CHAPTER 22
Temujin

Despite the size of the Golden Horde's army, it still took Temujin a while to find it. Starting at the ruins of Tashkent, he Skimmed south and west, combing the land for any sign that a large force had passed through. Eventually, he found the army's vanguard, perhaps a thousand men that were miles ahead of the main body of the army.

Sacking Tashkent would have fired up Tokhtamysh's men, and from what he could see, they had been hungry for more murder and destruction. Their canny leader may even have promised them more of both. It was bluster and noise, but it was effective.

Berke had never been one for making speeches. Instead, he'd led groups of men in prayer, asking his god to protect them while they carried out His glorious work. It had inspired a few, converted some to his religion, and made others into zealots. Some of the warriors had seen themselves as righteous and justified in their actions, no matter how cruel. It was for a good cause, and therefore, it could be excused.

Temujin noted it had taken little for the same men to embrace the darkness within.

From a distance, he watched them revel in bloodshed, feeding their savage urges as they destroyed the village. It posed no threat, and the vanguard could simply have gone around. Instead, the order had been given to burn every building, slaughter every animal and kill every man and boy. The women were murdered or used and then led away in chains to be sold as slaves. From his elevated position at the top of the valley, Temujin heard coarse laughter and screams of the dying.

Eventually, it was done. With no one left to torment and nothing else to burn, the warriors decided to move on. Some made jokes about their victims, while others traded items they'd stolen from the dead. Black plumes of smoke, rich with the aromas of charred wood and roasting flesh, drifted through the air. Bodies had been haphazardly stacked and set alight, but the fire would not erase what the warriors had inflicted upon the innocent.

Temujin walked a short distance to the road and then waited, knowing that the vanguard would eventually reach his position. He used the time to wash his hands and face with water from a canteen. One nostril was clogged with blood, and when he rinsed his mouth out, he noticed the water was pink. He had been pushing himself too hard for too long, but now was not the time to slow down.

Tokhtamysh had not taken part in the attack, but he had surely given the order to whoever was in charge of the vanguard. When the first of the scouts pulled up alongside Temujin's position, they rode on before he had a chance to speak. The man probably thought that he was a monk on pilgrimage. He saw no threat from a single man without any weapons, or even a horse.

The next scout was more cautious. He drew his sword and approached slowly. The moment he saw Temujin's eyes he slid from his horse and fell to his knees.

"Please forgive me, great Khan," he begged, pressing his forehead to the dusty ground. The scout's horse was skittish, and it almost stepped on its owner's head. With his eyes averted, the warrior didn't notice.

"Rise," said Temujin, getting up from where he had been kneeling at the roadside. "Where is Tokhtamysh?"

"With the rest of the army. Please," said the man, offering the reins of his horse. "Take my beast, Lord Khan."

Temujin was surprised by the man's fealty, but also pleased that Tokhtamysh had told them about him. With the Eternal Fire filling his being, he could smell the scout's fear and hear the frantic beating of his heart. Tokhtamysh must have advised what Temujin might do if they didn't show the appropriate level of respect. To command such fear without having to lift a hand was thrilling.

He graciously accepted the scout's horse and slowly rode it back down the road. Temujin came across three more scouts who were also obsequious to the point of being submissive. A few miles down the road, he saw the vanguard coming towards him at a leisurely pace.

"Oho, what do we have here?" said one of the officers at the front. He was big and bearded, his armour splattered with dried blood. There was more of it matted into his dark hair, but he hadn't noticed or just didn't care. He probably wore it as a badge of honour. "Are you lost, boy?"

They were drunk on bloodlust and victory. One or two had noticed Temujin's eyes, but they didn't react like the scouts. He heard whispers and nicknames no one had dared speak to his face in a long time. Several men laughed, and the others joined in until a chorus of it rang in Temujin's ears.

One of the warriors at the front had keen eyes, because he'd noticed the horse. "Where did you get that?"

But his words were lost in the next wave of laughter at Temujin's expense. The officer made crude gestures, which the others imitated. In turn, it made them recall what they'd done to their unwilling victims, all of it with humour. He could smell the blood on them, but several warriors were actually drunk in the saddle. A group of six passed skins around, and the air was full of an acrid, bitter smell.

Temujin slid from his horse and moved without considering what he was doing. His emotions were distant, locked away behind a wall in his mind, which made it simpler and easier. The first man slid from his saddle. He was in two parts, but still grinning, totally unaware that he was already dead. His legs had been severed from the rest of his body. The next warrior flinched as his arm came off, but he could do no more than that. Temujin was moving so fast, the pain had not even registered. He wove between them, making it into a dance. He left the horses alone, being careful around them, but many had large wide eyes. They were as scared as their riders, but also frozen in place by the slow crawl of time.

When Temujin stopped Skimming and returned to the side of the road, only a few seconds had passed. Temujin wondered if the warriors' victims had screamed as they did now. Begging for their mothers, praying to their god, howling like savage animals. Some crawled towards their severed limbs, unable to comprehend why they were no longer attached. One man, sitting in a pool of his own blood, just sobbed and waited for death which was not long in coming.

Despite being well trained for war, several of the horses ran, stepping on the dying and the dead. One or two had pieces of men still bound to the saddle, and they ran the furthest, desperate to escape the bleeding thing clinging to their back.

Ten men lay dead. Now that they were in so many pieces, Temujin thought it looked like a lot more. With blood up to the elbows on both arms, and his fingers dripping gore onto the road, Temujin knew what they saw when they looked at him. He was the monster, not them.

"I will wait here for Tokhtamysh," he declared, sitting down in the middle of the road.

The other riders in the vanguard dismounted, their progress utterly arrested. Dozens were kneeling. Half a dozen warriors were riding away, heading north, running for their lives. Some were riding back down the road towards the rest of the army, seeking reinforcements. It was funny, as there were several hundred of them and only one of him. The rest milled around, uncertain of what they should do. Several offered him gifts of gold, jewellery, food and drink, spices, scented oils and whatever other trinkets they had in their saddles.

With time to spare, Temujin was provided with water, which he used to wash off all of the fresh blood. His robe was utterly ruined. The sleeves had turned brown, and the front was splattered with more blood. Breeches, shirts, flowing scarves, gloves and even boots were laid out on the ground in front of him. More and more were piled up until he raised a hand and the tide of items slowed and then stopped.

Uncaring if they saw him naked, Temujin changed into fresh clothing in the middle of the road. He selected a coarse white shirt and dark trousers that were too long, which he rolled up. He ate sparingly from the food that they'd provided, and then sat in meditative silence. Witnessing the death of their friends had scared them, and now his stillness unnerved them even further. They avoided eye contact or walking into his line of sight. They gave him a wide berth and fell silent whenever they were forced to stray close to where he knelt. The rest spoke in whispers, pretending not to care, but Temujin could feel the jab of their furtive stares, like ants crawling across his skin.

For over an hour, Temujin remained motionless, while all around him the surviving warriors set up a temporary camp. Fires were lit, mostly for comfort rather than warmth, as the day was already hot. More sat around drinking, cleaning their armour, weapons, and even scraping blood from their faces.

Eventually, a dozen horsemen appeared on the horizon, and riding at the front of the group was Tokhtamysh. Before approaching Temujin, the khan of the Golden Horde spoke with several of his men. They crowded around his horse, casting furtive glances towards Temujin as if he were a bully who had been teasing them. Tokhtamysh listened intently, asked a few questions and then came closer to inspect the carnage. He

didn't avoid the gore like the others. The khan stepped into
the pool created from the blood of his men without hesitation.
He even moved the remains of one warrior with his toe, then
stared at Temujin with reproach.

Temujin thought life on the road suited Tokhtamysh. He was
more grizzled and windswept, and his dark skin was tanned
from days in the sun. He'd lost some weight, and there were
dark shadows under his eyes. There was also a slight stoop to
his shoulders from the weight of leadership. Nevertheless, he
seemed to be bearing up well, which gave Temujin confidence
that he had chosen the right man.

A dozen warriors cleared some space and began to assemble
a large pavilion. It was erected in record time, and once it was
finished, no one dared go inside or even get too close. Only
then did Tokhtamysh approach Temujin, moving to stand in
front of him. The khan's expression was still neutral, and he
showed neither deference in front of his men nor any hint of
fear. Temujin's intuition told him it was there, but Tokhtamysh
hid it better than most.

"Join me," he said, gesturing towards the tent. Again, he'd
chosen his words with great care, while showing no signs that
Temujin was his superior. Temujin let it pass for now, following
the khan into the tent. Tokhtamysh gave his men a reassuring
smile and then lowered the flap, giving them a small amount
of privacy from those waiting outside.

"Why?" hissed Tokhtamysh. He moved closer and kept his
voice low to avoid being overheard. "Why did you kill those
men?"

"Did you give the order for them to burn the village and
slaughter everyone?"

"Village? Who cares about a pissant village?" said Tokhtamysh
with a laugh, dismissing everything Temujin had witnessed.
"Shock and awe. That's what you told me. Draw Timur's focus
away from the Ilkhanate. Distract and worry him. That's exactly
what we've been doing. It's why we sacked Tashkent."

"Some of your men were drunk."

"So what?" said Tokhtamysh.

Temujin's hold on the Eternal Fire evaporated and he surged forward, gripping Tokhtamysh by the throat. The khan started to fight back, but then he remembered himself. Instead of trying to tear Temujin's hand away, he just prised the fingers back so that he could breathe more easily.

"What did you think was going to happen?" he wheezed.

Temujin shoved him away with a snarl. He wasn't naïve, but in his mind, the murder of innocents with no purpose was different. "Your men didn't show me the proper respect, so I disciplined them."

"Respect?" said Tokhtamysh. "How were they to know who you are?"

"Most of your scouts knew, and they acted accordingly." Temujin glared at the northern khan. "You, on the other hand, have not. Outside, you even talked to me as if we were equals."

Tokhtamysh took a deep breath before speaking. "If you want me to bow and grovel, then I will. But not out there in front of my men," he said, gesturing at the world beyond the tent. "They need to see that I am in charge. They need to believe that I rule the Golden Horde. I cannot be seen as a subordinate to you. If you undermine my position, I will lose all authority. The khanate will descend into chaos and infighting. Again!"

Temujin knew that what he was saying made sense. However, echoes of how he'd been treated by Tokhtamysh's men still rolled through his mind, reminding him of childhood taunts. The warriors had made jokes at his expense. He was almost certain that it had happened. Then again, Maryam had been altering his mind. What if he'd imagined the whole thing? What if they'd just asked for his name, and the rest had been a hallucination?

"Do you want me to kneel?" said Tokhtamysh, rubbing his throat. The red marks from Temujin's fingers were already fading. For a moment, he thought about apologising but changed his mind.

Temujin waved the question away and sat down on the ground, surprised and annoyed at his own behaviour. How they had treated him shouldn't have mattered, and yet even within the meditative cocoon of the Eternal Fire, anger had reached him. He hadn't thought that was possible. Had he been suppressing his emotions for too long? Or was it because of something else?

"I have news from the Ilkhanate," he said, changing the subject. Not wanting to shout, he beckoned Tokhtamysh closer, and he sat down opposite. Temujin gave him detailed information about the army's position, their numbers and its movement across Persia. By the time he'd finished talking, Tokhtamysh's scowl had deepened.

"Unless I know where the battle will take place, there is no way for me to know if we can get there in time." He licked his lips and looked around for something to drink, but the tent was empty. "We're making good time on the road, but if I push the men too hard, they will arrive exhausted. Then our numbers against Timur won't matter."

"I'll do what I can to bring you more precise information on his location," said Temujin. It would mean another difficult and challenging trip using his powers as a Kozan. More time spent away from Tabriz and his responsibilities as khan, although those he had put in charge seemed to cope in his absence. If he disappeared, would they notice? Would anyone even care?

"I must go to Samarkand," he said, getting up suddenly. It was better to keep moving. To focus on the next task, rather than wallow in such melancholy and small thoughts. "Expect me, when you see me." It was vague and unhelpful, but Tokhtamysh nodded as if everything he'd said made perfect sense.

Outside, everything was as it had been before, only now the men looked towards Tokhtamysh for guidance.

Remembering what the khan had said, Temujin turned and made a point of giving him a short bow, barely inclining his head. It was a nod between equals. A warrior's grip would have been better, embracing each other with hands on forearms, but everyone knew that Temujin was not one of them.

"Thank your scout for the loan of his horse," he said. For some reason, Temujin thought it was important to mention. Tokhtamysh clearly had no idea what he was talking about, but nodded. His eyes strayed towards something and Temujin followed his gaze.

The pieces of the dead men had been gathered up and taken away, but the blood spatters remained. Glancing at his hands, Temujin noticed there was still some blood beneath his fingernails.

Wasting no more time, he summoned the Eternal Fire and sank into the blissful calm it provided. All of his fears evaporated. The only thing that mattered was destroying Timur.

Skimming away, Temujin headed east, pausing often to navigate through an unfamiliar landscape. If he'd learned anything about the stars, it would have been much simpler, but he'd never been to an observatory. Eventually, he arrived about a mile outside the ancient city of Samarkand.

As a city on the Silk Road, it was incredibly busy with travellers. Dozens of wagons waited in a line at the gates with guards checking their paperwork before letting them in.

It was now late into summer, and the arid heat was intense and dry. Fresh sweat burst from Temujin's pores, and he noticed almost everyone had covered their head with colourful scarves or chequered headdresses. In addition to the merchants awaiting entry at the nearest gate, there were countless people leading camels, as well as individuals and groups on foot. If he had been dressed in his usual robes, Temujin could have posed as a monk. A short distance ahead of him in the queue was a group of six men who looked similar to him, all of them with shaven heads and matching grey robes.

Although there were undoubtedly markets within the city, makeshift stalls had been set up outside, where merchants traded some of their wares. A small selection of goods sat on sheets beneath awnings on wooden poles to protect items from the worst of the sun's heat. Men and woman roamed about, talking, bartering in loud voices. All of it sounded good-natured to Temujin's ear, which he found familiar and comforting.

He was used to seeing a wide variety of goods in the markets of Tabriz, but here there were many more Persian goods available. Carpets and colourful pottery, beautiful paintings and delicate jewellery. Vast sacks of rice, a rainbow array of spices, colourful bolts of cloth, and a huge selection of dyes.

Merchants were shadowed by armed guards, but the mercenaries kept their distance from the discussions, even when it became heated. He watched a pair of merchants talking loudly at one another, their faces just inches apart. Both men gesticulated broadly with their arms to emphasise their point. To an outsider, it would appear as if they were on the verge of violence, but when the bartering concluded the two men embraced and kissed each other on the cheek.

Although he could have simply Skimmed into the city or announced himself to gain immediate entry, Temujin was content to wait in line. It gave him an opportunity to observe how much of the city had been rebuilt since it had been conquered by his great-grandfather. He idly wondered if every accomplishment by every tyrant would forever be compared to that of Genghis Khan. Would a time come when someone else would replace him? For all that he had done, and all that he still had to do, Temujin hoped he was not remembered in the same fashion.

Rising above the tallest buildings in the city were the walls and colourful domes of mosques and mausoleums, schools of learning and medicine, and three observatories. Oddly, he spotted a large church, with a huge white cross at the top of its pointed steeple. There was more work being done as well. Even in the intense heat, men were constructing enormous new structures that were half-finished. Timur had been busy. He must have invested a lot of time and money into the prosperity of the city.

It was a shame that Temujin had to tear it all down.

Less than an hour later, he passed through the gates, tagging onto the end of another group of travellers. Since he carried no weapons and didn't look dangerous, they simply waved him in.

It was a beautiful city that had been prospering of late. He saw faces from all parts of the world and heard more than a dozen unfamiliar languages. He passed by an open-air forum where a group of poets were performing. Their flowing words sounded like music to his ears. In the next street, three architects were standing in front of a huge area that had been cleared. The foundation of a new building had been completed, and they were arguing over the next stage.

In all the time he was there, no one gave Temujin a second glance. No one recognised him, and no one cared who he was. It was isolating and yet also refreshing. Part of him was tempted to simply disappear. Start a new life in some remote corner of the Empire, or maybe somewhere else further west.

Many years ago, there had been a visitor to his father's court from England. He'd spoken with such passion about it being a green and lush place, and it had sounded so appealing. That was until Rashid, his father's vizier, had told him the truth. It was a small island where it never stopped raining. Why else would it be so green?

The memory should have made him smile, but it never reached Temujin's face. Wrapped in the calm of the Eternal Fire, he felt nothing. Summoning fire in the palms of both hands, he walked into the first mosque on the street. At first, no one noticed, but once he'd set fire to the rugs and curtains, people began to panic. Temujin waited in the middle of the room while everyone ran for their lives, surging past him on both sides. When he was confident the building was empty, he carried on, melting stone pillars with fire and crumbling others to dust by accelerating the passage of time.

He'd seen the other Kozan do it before, but they'd never shown him how it was done. With time to spare, he'd practised, binding the energy into a tight cone which he compressed and folded over and over. His third experiment was a little too successful, as one of the principle beams holding up the roof started to collapse.

Before he was crushed to death by tonnes of falling stone, Temujin Skimmed out of the front door. He stopped three streets away and a heartbeat later heard the mosque coming apart behind him. While everyone was focused on that tragedy, he moved elsewhere, choosing his targets with care. Even though he knew Timur had invested in the library, Temujin avoided it. Unlike his father, he would not destroy all of that knowledge, and after what had happened with Reyhan, he already felt guilty. So he walked past the grand façade and didn't set foot inside.

Whenever possible, he waited for people to evacuate before he tore down the structures. After the fifth building had collapsed, word began to spread like wildfire across the city. He only had to step inside the front door before people started to scream in panic. Perhaps it was his eyes that alerted them to his identity. At one point, a brave group of six or seven men rushed at him with knives. Temujin took the blade from the hand of one man, then used it to kill the others before stabbing the owner through the throat. After those bodies were discovered, he encountered no more resistance. He also moved from site to site more quickly, waiting less time before starting to tear them apart. It was likely they were empty, but after a while, he just stopped checking. He'd given them plenty of warning.

Most of the time, he brought the buildings down with ease, but with a couple of stubborn structures, he was forced to set them on fire. Plumes of black smoke and geysers of dust marked his progress through the city. It took what felt like hours, and by the end of it, Temujin was gasping for air. His clothing was soaking wet and his sides ached with a dull pain. When his vision swam, he entered a tavern to get a drink.

The owner didn't even wait. He simply ran screaming out of the back door, followed by all of his customers. Looking at himself in a mirror, Temujin didn't blame them. He was covered in dust and blood, with smears of soot across his clothing. Sitting down at one of the recently vacated tables, he helped himself to someone's food, gobbling up rice and some kind of bean stew. The tea was a little sweet for his taste, but as there was no one to make him a fresh pot, he drank in silence. When he'd cleared the plate, he moved to another table and scooped up a bowl of black olives.

While Temujin stood in the doorway, idly chewing an olive, he watched several groups of people running past. All of them were so distressed, they didn't even look in his direction. He'd moved in a zig-zag pattern across the city, but had not touched any of the buildings in this area. He'd hoped for a little peace and quiet before another long and difficult journey back to Tabriz. Apparently, that wasn't going to happen. More refugees from the chaos began to pour into the area. Temujin spat the last of the olive stones into the street, went back inside and closed the front door.

Upstairs, he found a small apartment and a storage room. He blocked the bedroom door and lay down to rest for a few hours. The howling of the injured filtered in through the window, so he closed it and pulled down the blind.

When he lay down again, Temujin expected it would take him a long time to fall asleep. But he was more exhausted than he'd realised, as when he next opened his eyes, it was already morning. He must have slept for over twelve hours. Bright sunlight was slipping into the room through a crack in the blind. Mercifully, it was silent outside on the street, and the endless crying had stopped.

The blood, soot and filth from the previous day had stained the bed. His clothes were grimy and stiff. Wrinkling his nose, Temujin realised the awful smell in the room was him. With no fresh clothes, he had no choice but to suffer in silence. As soon as he got back to the palace in Tabriz, he was going to take a very long, hot bath.

Inside a Rigour, it took Temujin two of what passed for days to reach Tabriz. He'd walked for a whole day, stopped at a roadside caravanserai and slept for almost a full day before moving on. Speaking to a Kheshig at the gates of the palace, this one beardless but with a long drooping moustache, Temujin found out he'd been gone from the city for six days.

It was hard to understand. Time was different now. Is this how it was for all Kozan? Did entire decades pass before them in a blink of an eye? Was the present no longer solid, but something fluid and malleable? If everyone around him died quickly, wouldn't that also mean the death of loneliness? Surely there wasn't enough time for him to become attached.

By the time he reached the door to his rooms, Temujin had no answers, only more questions. He was filthy, exhausted down to the marrow of his bones, and he stank. A dozen servants were already fluttering around inside his rooms, filling the huge tiled bath with water and scented oils, laying out fresh clothes. Four servants brought in plate after plate of food, most of which he dismissed.

While the servants worked, he stripped off his clothes and sat in a towel at the end of the bed, picking at some grapes. Finally, the bath was full and they all filtered out in a line, leaving him alone. The silence in the rooms was so deep it hummed in his ears. Temujin scrubbed his skin clean, then soaked in the bath until it was cold.

Just as he was about to get out, the door to his rooms were flung open. A dozen men, armed with crossbows and daggers, burst in. No two were alike, in terms of armour or clothing, but all of them looked to be veteran warriors or mercenaries. They worked as a team, covering their rear while six others pointed bows at him in the bath. Walking at the centre of the group was a tall, familiar figure. Her haughty expression was just as he remembered it. As ever, she was impeccably dressed in a stylish silk dress. Much to Temujin's surprise, she had a slim blade in one hand and a pair of daggers on her belt.

"Did you really think I would run?" asked Guyuk.

CHAPTER 23
Kokochin

After their meeting with Cardinal Cavicchi, Kokochin and Layla spent most of the morning observing The Seventh Bell. They approached the tavern with extreme caution and initially stayed at least a street away at all times.

The tavern was in a slightly run down neighbourhood, where the people had some money but everything was in need of repair. The stonework on buildings was chipped or cracked. The features that must have once made it beautiful were either worn smooth by age or they had simply broken off. There were several frescos, but they were battered and scarred. The identities of the people in the paintings had been obscured by age or defacement.

The slightly ostentatious buildings were not a style that Kokochin recognised, but she assumed it was old and quite outdated by the current standard. When it had first been built, this must have been a rich and flourishing area, but those people had moved on a long time ago, taking a lot of their money with them.

The cost of everything was reasonable, and all of the shops only sold necessities that people actually needed. The clothing was functional, and no one wore any silk or anything ostentatious. Butchers, bakers, spice merchants and an apothecary sat alongside two taverns with worn facades and battered signs with peeling paint. Nearby, a constant ring of a smithy hammer fought for attention with church bells. Wherever they went in the city, Kokochin always heard them.

The people on the street were not aggressive, but there were furtive glances cast at anyone who looked as if they didn't belong. The only exception seemed to be priests and church officials in dour clothing or robes. Most people made room for them, but some strangers probably at odds with the church glared, which made the clergy walk faster.

All of this made it impossible for the two of them to go unnoticed. The moment they walked down the street, people would stare, even if they were just bystanders. There was a mix of people in the city from all parts of the world, but most did not come to this street unless they had a very good reason. Kokochin assumed several people that stood in plain sight worked for Angelo. As the Cardinal had told them, it was safer to assume that everything the crime lord's people observed was reported back to him.

"The merchant with the red felt cap," said Layla, gesturing towards the chubby man from their high vantage point. Getting up to the roof without being noticed had been difficult, but it gave them an excellent view of the street. "He never glances at the tavern. Not once. It's like he refuses to look at it."

"Guilt? Or perhaps it's fear?" suggested Kokochin. "Maybe something happened there he didn't like. A fight. A gambling debt."

Layla snorted. "If it turns out he does work for Angelo, he's not very good at his job."

After being a member of the House of Grace for many years, she had strong views about those in other clandestine organisations.

"I think the baker's wife is someone to watch," said Kokochin. The shop was constantly busy, with a stream of people coming and going with baked goods. The smells were certainly enticing. The baker and two members of staff worked inside, but his wife was always on the move on the street, walking up and down the queue. She seemed to know everyone, or at least be familiar with them. It was possible she was just a gossip, but Kokochin guessed she was also gathering information while watching the street.

The people walking through the front door of The Seventh Bell were a mix of workers, travellers and locals in search of a drink. However, every now and then, someone who clearly didn't belong entered with some reluctance. They would take a deep breath before opening the front door, or they would double check the sign three times while furtively glancing at the street. Most of them returned to the street unharmed, but one or two emerged via the back door bruised, shaken and sometimes bloody. One man was carried away by two others, the both of them laughing and joking as if drunk, but the man in the middle didn't join in. No doubt his body would be found in an alley that night.

They ate lunch at a different tavern a few streets away. Layla looked relaxed, but Kokochin's stomach was clenched so tight she could barely keep anything down.

"Are you done?" said Layla, gesturing at Kokochin's plate. She'd mostly pushed the fish around and only taken a few small mouthfuls.

"Yes."

"Are you ready?"

Kokochin shrugged. "Let's find out."

A few people gave them curious glances, but no one stared in an obvious fashion. Even so, Kokochin knew they were under scrutiny. There was a familiar prickle running across the back of her scalp.

She had a narrow blade in her left boot and a second concealed inside her clothing. Layla was also similarly armed, but Kokochin doubted they would be allowed to carry any weapons if Angelo even agreed to see them. Without hesitating, she pushed open the front door of The Seventh Bell and entered the tavern.

Much like its exterior, the main room was worn, scarred and had seen better days. Despite sunlight filtering in through windows at the front, it still had quite a gloomy and oppressive atmosphere. All of the wooden tables were old and scratched, and no two chairs were alike. Some customers sat on stools, some on high backed chairs, and others on padded seats that didn't belong in such frugal surroundings. The floor was covered with stone, but it had been poorly laid, creating an uneven surface peppered with trip hazards. The bar at the back of the room was the only thing that looked as if it had been well made. The wooden surface glowed, and the smooth, soft lines were oddly feminine. A beefy barman with a suspicious glare stood behind it, polishing the bar with a cloth.

Customers kept their eyes on their drinks, and if they spoke, it was in low voices, but only to those at their own table. There was no healthy murmur of overlapping conversations, just whispered snatches that suddenly trailed off. There were two doors leading to other parts of the building and a small empty stage in one corner. Perhaps musicians or entertainers performed at night, but Kokochin wondered what kind of a person would put on a show in such a grotty tavern.

As they made their way across the room towards the bar, Kokochin knew that everyone in the room was watching them from their eye corners. One or two heads turned in their direction, but no one said anything or tried to stop them.

The barman was tall with broad shoulders. Once, he might have been muscle for hire, but from his greying moustache and thinning hair, Kokochin guessed he'd given up that life.

"Help you with something?" he said in a surprisingly soft voice.

"We were told to come here," said Kokochin, gesturing briefly at Layla who was staring down anyone who looked in her direction.

The barman pursed his lips. "What do you need?"

"We'd like to speak to Angelo."

Conversations in the room continued as before, but Kokochin had the impression that behind her back, more people had suddenly taken an interest in her.

"Are you sure you're in the right place?" said the barman, trying to give her a way out. He must have seen countless people approach in this manner. For an ordinary person to seek out Angelo's help, that meant they were either desperate or in serious trouble.

"I'm sure," she said.

"Wait here," said the barman. He disappeared through a door in the back and remerged a short time later. "It might be a while. How about a drink while you wait?"

Kokochin glanced at the bottles behind him. "Is any of it decent?"

"Not really."

"Do you have anything that won't rot my insides?" she asked.

With a smile he reached under the bar and produced a half open bottle of white wine. He poured two glasses and then recorked it.

"None for me," said Layla, sitting down on a high stool. She faced towards the bar, but kept an eye on the room behind them in the mirror behind the bottles.

"For you," said Kokochin, sliding a glass towards the barman, together with a few coins.

"To your good health," he said, raising the glass in a salute.

Much to Kokochin's surprise, it wasn't bad. Light, crisp and dry. She didn't want to even think about what everyone else was doing.

One at a time, several people in the room were called up to the bar. All of them were despondent with scared or furtive expressions. People at the end of their rope with nowhere else to turn. They went through the back door and a short time later, all of them emerged pale and shaken, but otherwise physically unharmed. Only one man came out with a bloody nose, a rag pressed against his face. Some of them stayed after to drink, to drown their sorrows, but he raced out the front door.

"He's ready," said the barman, rapping the wood in front of Kokochin with his knuckles. He gestured at the door behind him, but didn't leave his post behind the bar.

Without being asked, Layla went first and Kokochin followed. A short, bare corridor with cracked wooden panelling led to a large room at the rear of the building. At the door to Angelo's office, they were checked for weapons by a large man with a battered face. He found Kokochin's blade in her boot, but not the one inside her clothing. When he was satisfied, the thug opened the door and gestured for them to go inside.

The room was in the same condition as the rest of the tavern, with two doors leading elsewhere in the building. However, the office itself was as neat as a money lender's. She had the impression that everything had been placed in exactly the right location. One wall was lined with a neat stack of books from floor to ceiling. Two wooden chairs sat equally spaced from each other and the desk in the exact centre of a worn rug. A thick ledger sat in the middle of the desk, and beside it several long pens made from reeds or bone.

Given everything that she'd been told and had seen, Angelo was not the intimidating figure she had imagined. He was a small man with a slight build, balding on top and with a wispy beard clinging to the tip of his pointed chin. His head was dipped towards the page, and as they got comfortable on the hard seats, he finished scribbling something in his neat handwriting. The thug closed the door and took up his position behind them, leaning against the far wall.

When he'd finished writing, Angelo blotted the page, cleaned the pen and then returned it to its place on the desk. Only then did he look up at them for the first time.

"So, tell me your troubles," he said. His voice, like the rest of him was soft and gentle. But all of it, like the entire building, was a disguise for the real man.

"We're not here to borrow money," said Kokochin.

"Then you've come to the wrong place," said Angelo, gesturing at the thug. "Luca will see you out."

"We know who you really are," said Kokochin, even as Luca rested a hand on her shoulder and another on Layla's. "We're here to talk business."

"Business?" said Angelo, raising an eyebrow. Luca's hand tightened, but he didn't try to move them out of the room. "I'm just a humble tavern owner who occasionally lends money to people in need."

"You're far more than that," said Kokochin with a snort.

"Oh, really?" said Angelo, cocking an eyebrow. "And what is that?"

"You're the most feared man in this neighbourhood. I've seen people on the street that were so afraid, they won't even look at the tavern."

"Luca can be a bit hands-on at times," said Angelo with a toothy grin. He was good at playing humble, but Kokochin wasn't fooled. "Sometimes people aren't happy with the deals I offer, or they're late repaying their loan, and that's not acceptable."

"No, it's not that," said Kokochin, piecing it together from what she'd seen. "I knew you were a gang leader, and I thought a money lender on the side, but there's more."

The little man leaned back in his chair and held up one hand. Luca released Kokochin's shoulder and stepped back out of sight behind them. "Then, who am I?" said Angelo.

"You're someone to whom money means nothing. You have a use for it. You control others with it, but personally, you don't care about it. Otherwise, you wouldn't be sitting in a run-down tavern with an uneven floor and cheap furniture. You could afford to make this into a palace, but you won't."

"And why is that?" he asked.

"Well, apart from the obvious of it sticking out like a sore thumb in this neighbourhood, you don't want others prying into your business. People in power might think you're getting big ideas beyond your station." She didn't know if Angelo was devout or not, but in this city, it was obvious that the Church's power was absolute. "You want people to assume you're barely scraping by, so that you can carry on your real business without interference. And since money doesn't interest you, I'm willing to bet you trade in favours." Kokochin shook her head and laughed. "I thought you had a few people working for you as spies in the street, but it's bigger than that. In fact, I wouldn't be surprised if you own a few of the businesses on the street, or at least a healthy stake."

Angelo nodded thoughtfully. "In fact, I own most of the neighbourhood. Some pay me protection money to keep them safe. Some, a portion of all their profit. Others trade in information. Rumours. Secrets."

She'd learned a great deal from Guyuk and the House of Grace, but here was another approach. Angelo's mix of fear and intimidation meant everyone knew exactly who they worked for and the repercussions if they refused to comply. She expected several would already be lining up outside to tell him about the two foreign women they'd seen.

"We need your help finding something in the city. We're willing to pay handsomely," said Kokochin.

"There are shops just outside. I suggest you try one of those," said Angelo.

"This isn't something you can buy on the street."

Kokochin could see that Angelo was curious. One corner of his mouth quirked upwards in amusement, but he still dismissed them with a wave.

"This has been interesting, but it's time for you to go. I have other appointments." "Let's not make a scene," said Luca.

Kokochin stayed in her chair facing Angelo as Layla surged to her feet. Behind her, she heard a surprised grunt, the quick exchange of a few blows and then something heavy landed on the rug in front of her. Layla pressed her foot onto the back of Luca's neck, pinning him to the floor.

Angelo giggled and applauded, giving Kokochin the impression that he'd enjoyed it. "Wonderful. So, what are you looking for?"

"Do you know of the Assassins?"

"Yes," said Angelo slowly, a frown creasing his brow. "I thought they were all dead."

"No. One or more of them is here in Rome, and we believe they're going to use poison against their intended target."

Luca grunted and tried to get up, but Layla kept him there, using her bodyweight. She also twisted his left arm to a painful angle. Angelo seemed happy to leave Luca there, so Kokochin didn't call Layla off.

"Poison," he mused.

"I think it will be something fast-acting and rare."

"Certain venomous animals come in and out of the city," mused Angelo, rubbing his little beard. "They can be milked for various toxins, but those have to be ingested."

"Where would someone in the city go to acquire something like that?" asked Kokochin. "More importantly than the poison, we need to know who has been asking. Like us, they would be a newcomer to the city. We need to find them." Kokochin was reluctant to give him too much information in case it prematurely narrowed his search.

"There are couple of people," said Angelo. His eyes were distant, but he came back to the present when Luca growled. "Be quiet, Luca, you're distracting me. You've only yourself to blame, being overpowered by a woman, of all things."

The thug fell silent again, but Kokochin could see that he was stewing. She tapped Layla on the shoulder, and she let the big man up. While the two of them faced off, she focused on the man behind the desk.

"So, can you help us?" asked Kokochin.

"I can," said Angelo, with an oily smile, "but what do I get?"

"Would it matter if I told you the target was someone important in the city?" said Kokochin in return.

Angelo shrugged. "No. It doesn't affect me. So, what are you offering?"

Cavicchi had said to only use his name if it was necessary, and it seemed as if she had run out of options.

"A favour."

"You're new to the city. I can practically smell the sea on you," said the little man. "You have no power or connections. So, whose favour am I getting?"

"Cardinal Cavicchi," said Kokochin.

"That barbarian sent you," said Angelo with a chuckle. "It must be important."

The cardinal's position didn't impress Angelo, but from the corner of her eye, Kokochin saw Luca make the sign of the cross on his chest. "Then the target is someone in the Church."

It was Kokochin's turn to shrug. "You said it didn't matter. So, do we have a deal?"

Angelo wanted to know who it was, but she didn't think he would ask. He'd have to trade something for it in return, and she doubted he ever made a deal that wasn't in his favour.

"Boss, you must help them," said Luca, who was clearly more devout than his employer. "I mean, I would like you to help them," he added, when Angelo's expression turned grave.

"We have a deal," said Angelo, holding out his hand, which Kokochin shook across the desk. "I'll get you the names of any buyers. After that, you're on your own."

"Don't worry, we'll take care of them," said Layla, getting to her feet.

"I have no doubt," said Angelo, staring up at her with a grin. "Thank you for the little show. I don't suppose you'd like to come another time and fight someone for me? Just for sport, not to the death." He was practically drooling at the notion.

Layla snorted and headed for the door.

"We'll be in touch," said Kokochin.

"I'm looking forward to it," said Angelo as they headed down the hallway.

The barman ignored them on the way out, but on the street, Kokochin noticed at least four people watching them. All of them were unsettled and possibly afraid, which meant they were in debt to Angelo. She expected at least one or more of them to follow them once they left the neighbourhood.

Perhaps naively, she'd thought it would be different here, but in some ways, it was exactly the same as Tabriz. At least in Persia, Kokochin had known who her enemies were. Here, the Assassin could be anyone, and that made it even more dangerous.

CHAPTER 24
Kaivon

The scout's horse was spent. Its sides were already heaving, but he mercilessly drove it on towards Kaivon. Even before the man slid off his horse and ran forward, Kaivon knew what he was going to say.

"It worked," said Kaivon. "Timur has taken the bait."

King David and the other senior officers grinned, but Kaivon couldn't summon a smile. Not yet. Not until it was over.

"He's here," said the scout as he stumbled forward. "He's here," he said again.

"How many men?" asked Kaivon.

"Five, maybe six thousand. All on foot."

"Get some rest. Someone will tend to your horse," said Kaivon, dismissing the scout.

For weeks, Kaivon and Timur had been spying on each other to ascertain troop numbers. Kaivon's people had caught six spies in his camp, and he'd lost three of his own to the warlord. The heads of his scouts had been delivered to him, their mouths stuffed with horse dung. Kaivon worried that there were other spies from Timur who had come and gone unnoticed from his camp. If so, there was nothing to be done about it now. At it stood, they both had a good idea of the size and composition of each other's army.

All that remained was a definitive battle to determine the victor of this war.

"This will be a glorious day," said General Subedei. He was a keen warrior with a good eye, but Kaivon thought the general prone to celebrating too early.

This was the eleventh skirmish they'd had with Timur's forces, and it was set to be the largest. By comparison, the previous ten had been small affairs. Fifty men here, two hundred there. On a quiet mountain, two groups of scouts had run into each other, and it had swiftly devolved into a scramble to see who could kill each other the quickest. On two occasions, Timur had set traps, essentially throwing away the lives of his men just to see how Kaivon would react. To see if Kaivon would grant mercy to an outnumbered group of enemy warriors, or kill them down to the last man. It was a test of not only Kaivon's approach to war and his thinking, but also his morality. He suspected Timur was also trying to determine if there was a line Kaivon would not cross.

Today was different.

This time, Kaivon had set the trap, but unlike Timur, he had no intention of throwing away the lives of his warriors. His forces were already outnumbered by those of the Chagatai khanate. It was one of the reasons Timur could be so cavalier with his own men. He had plenty to spare. Kaivon had committed ten thousand men to this battle, and he intended to win, but not at any cost.

He was also still waiting for reinforcements from the Golden Horde, but there was no guarantee that they would arrive. Scouts and messengers sent to Tokhtamysh had not returned. Temujin had promised that the newly appointed khan of the north was on his way, but Kaivon had his doubts.

"Are we certain his scouts saw our forces?" asked Prince Thoros.

"They did," said Kaivon. He'd been careful to place his men out in the open.

"But he only sent five or six thousand warriors?" said Subedei. "Why?"

"That is the question," said Kaivon.

From his vantage point, Kaivon watched as his men retreated, slowly at first, and then in full rout. They were only wearing light armour, and their retreat was covered by archers on a narrow rocky shelf. Only one or two of his men went down, caught by a stray enemy arrow, but the rest made it safely to the entrance to the valley. The channel was wide enough for ten men standing shoulder to shoulder, making it the perfect choke point for a large force. The cliffs on either side were too steep to climb. Only an idiot would throw away his men like that, and Timur was no one's fool. Kaivon understood that it would be a dangerous mistake to underestimate him.

Kaivon's men ran through the channel in small groups of no more than four. It took longer this way, but it was necessary. The archers kept Timur's men busy and distracted. The last of his men filtered through the channel and down the half-mile passage to the safety of the valley. Beside him there was a collective sigh of relief. The most dangerous stage of the trap was over. They'd bloodied Timur's forces, cutting into them with savage glee before pulling back. After seeing their friends cut down, Timur's men had not stood idly by and waited for orders. It didn't matter how much they feared their leader. They wanted revenge and were out for blood, except now they suddenly hesitated, just out of range.

"Come on," said Subedei, willing the enemy to rush forward. "What are they waiting for?"

"Orders," said King David, sharing a look with Kaivon.

Fear was one thing. Discipline was another. Many tribes and groups of warriors from different nations had been folded into Timur's army. However, it seemed as if all of them had learned the importance of following orders, or perhaps the repercussions of breaking them. The self-styled Sword of Islam had not accumulated such a large army by being reckless, no matter what he'd done in previous skirmishes. Nevertheless, the enemy was angry and flustered at being caught unaware. Kaivon's raiders had attacked before first light when many were still asleep and others just breaking their fast.

The enemy ranks parted, and senior officers made their way to the front. Kaivon saw the glimmer of spyglasses as they surveyed his archers on the cliffs. A hundred of Kaivon's archers were balanced on a rocky shelf above the entrance to the valley. Their position was accessed via a series of narrow paths, probably made by goats. There was no cover and little space for any more men. However, they held the high ground, and anyone trying to enter the valley would be an easy target.

There was no obvious way to go around and attack Kaivon's forces from the rear. Channels and gullies fed into the valley, but it would take Timur's men days to explore them, days which they didn't have. The only sensible course of action was to attack with caution and rely on strategy.

More enemy troops began to gather. Soon they were facing a vast horde, and still the enemy didn't attack. Subedei was muttering under his breath, willing the enemy to make a mistake. The general and David stood on either side of Kaivon, reflecting both of his moods, one careful and calm, the other agitated and reckless.

"Come on," said Subedei.

It was almost as if Timur's men heard him, as they marched forward, rank upon rank, slow at first and then at a run. Even with shields held above their heads, several fell with arrows in their flesh. Ten, twenty, perhaps a hundred men went down before the first row of warriors reached the safety of the channel. There they spread out, ten men abreast but still moving fast, as behind them more warriors were being picked off. The noise of so many men moving quickly with armour and weapons rattling filled the air. The thrum of a hundred bows added to the cacophony, as well as the screams of the injured.

More than half of Timur's forces had moved out of the archers' range before the first one made it to the end of the channel. There must have been almost three thousand men crushed into the space, and yet the trap had not yet sprung.

"It hasn't worked," said Subedei, all hope gone from him in one breath.

"Patience," said Kaivon, feigning confidence, although a small part of him wondered if the general was right.

They never heard it, the first crack, but Kaivon saw the results. A hundred of Timur's men suddenly vanished from sight, falling away as if they had dropped to the ground as part of some game. A heartbeat later, the next section of the floor collapsed under the combined weight of so many men.

That was when the screaming reached Kaivon's ears. Piece by piece, the ground beneath Timur's forces gave way. The timbers Kaivon's men had used were strong, but even they could not fully support hundreds of men. Using a spyglass, Kaivon peered down at the enemy. Even before the valley came into focus, he knew what the lens would show him.

Hundreds of men impaled on wooden stakes. The trench had been painstakingly dug, taking weeks. It was not deep enough for the fall to kill anyone, but the spikes took care of that. Men slipped and tumbled, desperately grabbed onto friends for aid, only to pull them in as well. The weapons and armour weighed everyone down. The press of so many bodies pushed those at the bottom further onto the pikes.

Many of Timur's warriors were dead or dying, and the rest would have to clamber over a carpet of corpses to reach Kaivon's forces. Many had been killed in an instant, but there were many others injured or trapped beneath the dying and the dead who would suffer for days.

"Give the order," said Kaivon. A flaming arrow flew high into the sky above before it slowly arched down. Beyond the mouth of the valley, Kaivon heard what sounded like a rumble of thunder.

Hundreds of mounted warriors poured over the hill from behind the enemy, leaving them nowhere to run. His cavalry rode hard, sweeping into the ranks of the enemy warriors, who tried to take up a defensive position, but they were too badly shaken. As the old adage said, they were trapped between a rock and a hard place with nowhere to go.

Desperate and with nothing to lose, Timur's men charged. It was brave and heroic, but against a mounted force that outnumbered them, it would only end one way.

The countless moans and screams of the dying in the trench tugged at Kaivon's ears, which he tried to ignore. To smother any lingering pity, he reminded himself that given a chance, any one of those now suffering below would slit his throat.

"May God have mercy on their souls," said David.

Their combined cries would have reached the ears of their allies, but they had no sympathy to spare as they were being mowed down. Kaivon's archers continued with their deadly rain, picking off individuals. One or two still alive in the stakes tried to crawl to safety, but they were spotted and dealt with. It was inevitable that Kaivon's forces would suffer some losses, as a cornered man with nothing to lose fought that much harder, but the number would be small. Half Timur's men were dying or dead, and the rest were being slaughtered. The victory belonged to Kaivon.

Timur had won countless battles against experienced warriors, as well as those who were leading for the first time. In the midst of combat, his mind was agile, and he was used to coming up with solutions to tackle the unexpected. The outcome of this battle had been pre-determined before his first man had stepped into the valley. It had required weeks of careful preparation, choosing the right terrain and the right valley, and countless hours of digging.

Kaivon didn't think Timur would mourn the men under his command. He would regret the loss because it had weakened his army, but he did not care for the individual. It would also teach Timur that his enemy had foresight, patience, and the ability to execute complex plans. At best, it would make him worry and second guess every encounter between the two armies in the future.

An hour later, it was all over. The last of Timur's men were dead or dying. With nowhere to run, none of them had chosen to surrender. It wouldn't have mattered. Today, Kaivon had not intended to take any prisoners.

"Victory is ours," said Subedei, clapping Kaivon on his shoulder. "God is good," he said, smiling as if he'd never shown any doubt. A cry went up from the mouths of his men. A ragged cheer that swelled in volume until it became a wall of noise celebrating victory.

"Celebrate with the men," said David, drawing his sword and raising it above his head. "We are alive and they are not. If nothing else, celebrate that."

Taking the king's sage advice, Kaivon drew his blade and added his voice to the throng. Thousands of men screamed in one voice, in defiance of death.

Esme grunted with effort as she loosened the straps on Kaivon's armour. There had been no chance of him fighting today, but he would have felt foolish and naked without it. It was a mask, just as much as the confident expression he wore whenever he was around the men. It didn't matter if Kaivon was worried, he never let it show. His armour always made him feel safe, but lately it was not his own well-being that he worried about.

"Timur will not fall for such a trick again," said Kaivon as she pulled off one of his boots.

"No, but neither will he creep forward one step at a time. His ego and the persona he has created will not allow it. His men will expect him to exude confidence. If the situation was reversed, what would you do to save face?"

Kaivon considered it. "Send out more scouts. A lot more, and pretend as if nothing had changed."

"Then I would expect the same from him. Now, he's aware that you're not an idiot, and not someone he should underestimate."

"True," said Kaivon, "but I think it will be difficult to surprise him again."

"Then it will come down to strategy on the day, and the ability to adapt when the situation changes." Esme passed him a mug of tea, which he blew on to cool the liquid.

"We've found a location," said Kaivon, holding the tea close to his face so he could inhale the aroma. It smelled of cinnamon, lemon and ginger.

"For the final battle?"

Kaivon nodded. "I've discussed it with the others, and we think it gives us the most advantages, at least initially, in terms of the terrain. After that, as you say, plans can and will fall apart."

"But?" said Esme, sensing his reluctance.

"Temujin told us to expect support from the Golden Horde, but the others believe we are on our own." As Kaivon had expected, Subedei believed they would receive reinforcements, but everyone else had less faith. "My men don't trust Temujin, or any of the Mongols from the north. Even though Berke khan is gone and no longer in charge, it wasn't that long ago the same warriors were raiding in the north. Burning towns and villages within the Ilkhanate."

Esme sipped her tea and sat back, leaning on the cushions. Their yurt was luxurious and comfortable, with thick rugs on the floor and plenty of blankets to keep them warm at night. But after so many years of being of warrior, Kaivon was getting tired of sleeping on the ground.

"Can we win without their support?" said Esme.

It was the most important and difficult question to answer. It was what Kaivon had been discussing with the others for days. They had brought together all of their warriors from within Persia and its vassal states, pooled all of their knowledge of warcraft, and had run through countless scenarios together. And yet, they still didn't have a definitive answer.

For the last week, Kaivon had been wrangling with the question in his sleep. Every morning, he'd woken up feeling more tired than when he closed his eyes.

"I honestly don't know," he admitted, taking a gulp of tea. It was sweet and spicy, the ginger burning the back of his throat. "It's a huge gamble."

"As leader, the others are waiting for you to make a choice." Esme gripped his hand tight. "I can't imagine the pressure, but just remember you're not alone."

"They've given me their advice and made suggestions, but ultimately the decision has to be mine."

A long time ago, Kaivon had been a general in the Persian army. He'd been responsible for the lives of thousands under his command. After receiving the most up-to-date information on the invaders, he'd made a decision that, at the time, he thought was right. In the end, it had been the wrong choice. The Mongols had been too strong. Kaivon's forces had been defeated, thousands had died, and the enemy had been living in Persia ever since.

"Last time, I made the wrong choice," said Kaivon.

"You're only saying that now because of everything that happened after," said Esme. "There was no way for you to know what was to come. Tell me, if you could go back, and the only information you had was the same, would you make a different decision?"

Kaivon mulled it over as he drank his tea. The heat from it seeped into his stomach and warmed his throat. He chewed a date, savouring the taste of home, trying to take his mind back to the time Esme had mentioned.

"I would have given the same order to fight," he eventually said. "They had to be stopped. If we'd run, more Persian warriors would have survived, at least initially, but the Mongols would have hunted them down. The rebellion grew, in part, because of the sacrifice that others made on their behalf. The warriors gave their lives for a cause, and for their nation."

Rage played a part, but the desire to be free of their seemingly benign Mongol invaders was what beat in the heart of every rebel Kaivon had ever met. Each individual wanted to scour the enemy from Persian soil. To hurt them so badly that any Mongols who survived would remember what it had cost them in blood.

"Given what could happen during the battle, and given the worst possibility, where the Golden Horde doesn't show up at all, can we win?" Esme sat forward, hungry for an answer, reminding him again that it was not only the men who had been fighting all this time. The House of Grace had been working to improve the lives of everyone in Persia, long before he'd started a rebellion against the Mongols.

"We can. We must," said Kaivon, finding that there was no other answer. Once again, they could not delay. They could hope and wish for more allies or more time. However, right now there was an opportunity to best Timur, and Kaivon didn't know if it would come again.

"Then we fight," said Esme. "Down to the last man and woman, on the battlefield and at home in the streets. And if the worst should happen and we lose, those who come after will remember our sacrifice."

"They will know that we did everything we could in this moment," said Kaivon.

Whatever happened in the battle to come, Kaivon was glad that he wasn't facing it alone.

CHAPTER 25
Temujin

Temujin stared at Guyuk and the armed men from the comfort of his bath. The dirty water had grown cold and the skin on his fingers was starting to wrinkle. Three mercenaries checked the room for anyone else while the rest kept their bows pointed at him.

"I gave you a chance to live," said Temujin, leaning back and spreading his arms wide. The three men returned and the leader shook their head. Satisfied that they wouldn't be disturbed, two stepped outside while the rest watched him carefully from across the room for any sudden moves.

"Live?" scoffed Guyuk. "What, like some kind of peasant? What did you expect me to do? Work on a farm?"

"To be honest, I didn't give it much thought. You're just not that important," he said with a shrug. "I was feeling sentimental, and I did you a favour."

Guyuk sneered at him. "Not that important? I am the only reason your father conquered so many nations. Without my support, he couldn't have gone to war. For years, I kept the Ilkhanate running while he was away."

"For which I am grateful, but I don't need or want you. I have other servants to take care of that now."

Guyuk's jaw fell open, but she quickly recovered. The former

Empress showed considerable restraint, far more than Temujin had expected. Instead of giving the order to kill him, she just stared, taking a moment to gather her thoughts.

While she was distracted, he focused on his breathing, forcing away all emotions and sinking down into a quiet meditative space in his mind. As he embraced the Eternal Fire, the edges of the world blurred, and even sounds changed. Temujin felt slightly nauseous and swallowed the bitter taste of bile. Nothing like this had ever happened before. He put it down to pushing himself too hard and not getting enough rest.

Guyuk started talking then in a low, threatening voice. Promises of the colourful horrors she would inflict upon him if he failed to do exactly what she said.

With insight from the Eternal Fire, he stared with fresh eyes at Guyuk and the mercenaries. All of the men were taking their lead from her, but only one of them was not afraid. They must have heard the stories about his powers and what he could do to them. One or two tales might be dismissed as inflated rumours, but there were too many for them to ignore completely. Only one of them was arrogant enough to think it was nothing more than smoke and mirrors. Despite what had probably been a huge fee, none of them wanted to be here.

In spite of everything that had happened, Guyuk wasn't afraid, which was admirable, but stupid.

"Are you even listening?" she said, when he failed to reply. "Do you understand what will happen if you don't cooperate?"

Temujin stood up suddenly, not embarrassed by his nakedness. One of the mercenaries panicked and fired, but his shot went wide, shattering some tiles on the bath. Guyuk wasn't impressed and merely raised an eyebrow.

"I'm not doing anything without getting dressed," he said. Without waiting for permission, Temujin walked to his bedroom and pulled on some fresh clothes. He did his best to ignore them and pretend they weren't there. The warriors shuffled along at a distance, keeping their weapons trained on him while Guyuk lurked a few steps behind.

"You will take me to the dungeon, but let me be clear," said Guyuk, moving forward when he was dressed. "If you try anything, these men will hurt you. You won't die, not for a long time, but you will suffer. Once we are down there, you will release your father into my care." Her eyes were burning with a desperate need he struggled to recognise. Temujin wasn't sure if it was love that had driven her to such extreme lengths, or something else. Fear of being alone, perhaps.

"You've been blinded by your hunger," he said, taking a deep breath. He floated in a void without emotion, but if he'd been able to feel something, Temujin liked to think it would be pity. Even for her. For the space of two heartbeats, his bubble of calm wavered but then returned to normal. He desperately needed more sleep.

"What are you talking about?" she said.

"My father is dead. I killed him."

Much to his surprise, Guyuk just chuckled. "No, you didn't. I was there, moments after you were born. I cared for you and protected you, when no one else would. Deep down, I know who you are."

"You knew who I was, not who I am," said Temujin, calmly meeting her gaze.

"You have changed," admitted Guyuk, "but not as much as you think. Your destiny remains the same. You will die an unremarkable death, and soon after, you will be forgotten by history."

"I have a limitless well of power at my fingertips," said Temujin holding up one hand. The mercenaries tensed, expecting some trick, but he didn't summon the Fire. "I've never been more in control of every aspect of my life. Destiny?

That's just a word used by dreamers and arrogant fools who lack the willpower to take control. My father thought he was destined for greatness, and now he's dead."

"Stop," said Guyuk, but he ignored her.

"You know what he was like," said Temujin. "Even when he was locked in a cell, his arrogance was unmatched. He absolutely believed that you would save him, but you couldn't. And when I stabbed him, he looked so surprised."

"Stop talking," hissed Guyuk.

"He was so surprised. He couldn't understand what was happening. It had just never occurred to him."

"Kill him!" snarled Guyuk, gesturing at the mercenaries.

Ten crossbows fired at once, all of them aimed at Temujin's chest and head.

Skimming across the room, he drew both daggers from Guyuk's belt and then moved down the line, gutting the men, one by one. By the time Temujin was finished, his sleeves were drenched in blood, his fingers slick on the hilts. The screams and wailing summoned the other two, who burst through the door to his room. They were just in time for Temujin to stick a blade in each man's throat.

Choking and gagging on the daggers, they dropped to their knees trying to stop the bleeding, fighting for air. While they were distracted, he took a short sword from one of the dead men, since he wouldn't need it anymore.

Guyuk stared in horror at the dead and dying men littering the floor, their eyes pleading or glazed over. The room stank of blood and filth from where he'd disembowelled at least one mercenary.

As Temujin stalked towards her, soaked in the blood of a dozen men, Guyuk saw him for the first time. Not the shy, naïve boy, or even the young man without any sense of purpose or direction. She saw him as he was now, the rarest and most dangerous kind of person in the world.

"You're a monster," she said, eyes wide with terror.

A dozen responses rose up in his mind, but in the end, Temujin said nothing. Whatever he said, she'd have a biting, witty or sarcastic reply ready. Just to have the final word, as if it mattered, or would make a difference.

Temujin had repaid his debt to her, and she'd rejected the chance of a new life. It had been a moment of weakness. There would be no more second chances. If any failed to serve him, then they had to die.

With a whipping motion of his hand, Temujin's blade bit through Guyuk's neck. Her severed head bounced across the floor, coming to rest amidst the tangle of bodies littering his bedroom.

Temujin heard the rattle of armour as four Kheshig came running down the corridor, far too late.

"Deal with it," he said calmly. He then picked another set of rooms at random. The air was a little stale, but it would do for now. It was only when he released his grip on the Eternal Fire that Temujin realised one of the mercenaries had cut him. There was a shallow wound on his arm, but he didn't remember it even happening. He stripped out of his ruined clothes, washed his skin clean again, and then climbed into bed.

Raw emotions flooded Temujin's mind as he replayed what had just happened, but he was so tired that in spite of everything, he fell asleep in moments.

Without being told, Temujin instinctively knew that it was a dream.

At first, waking up in the palace seemed normal, but he quickly realised he was still asleep. As Temujin moved down the hallways, everything felt slightly remote, almost as if he was watching himself.

When he left the palace, Temujin found he was shadowed by two Kheshig in masks, but it wasn't that detail which had tipped him off. Dismissing them with a wave, he proceeded alone. There was nothing to be afraid of in a dream.

Out in the city, something about the people was wrong. On the surface, they looked ordinary. They moved around as normal, talking, browsing, eating and drinking, but whenever Temujin looked at their faces, there was something wrong with them. Every person had lifeless painted eyes, like those of a child's doll.

The city, and everyone in it, was a charade that had been created for Temujin's benefit. It had been conjured by someone's mind, but with so many aspects slightly askew, Temujin knew this wasn't his dream.

He had a strong instinct to keep moving, as if someone was guiding him forward, gently pressing a hand against his back. Fighting the urge, he wandered aimlessly through the streets, turning down roads at random, stepping into shops to browse items that didn't interest him.

The pressure became more intense, and without being aware, he headed east across the city. Whispers in his ear made the hairs on his forearms prickle with fear. Fighting to stay calm, Temujin sought the quiet space in his mind that came with meditation, but nothing happened. He could hear his breathing, but when he put a hand against his chest, there was no heartbeat. This dream version of himself was flawed and incomplete. However, Temujin somehow understood on a primal level that if he died in the dream, his body would die in the waking world.

With each passing moment, he had less control over this version of his own body. When Temujin tried to lean backwards or walk in another direction, he was yanked forward, feet skidding across the ground. Rather than keep fighting, he started walking under his own power. Even though it was only a dream, Temujin was afraid of tripping and being dragged face first to whatever destination the dreamer had in mind. So he walked and walked, for what felt like at least an hour, a prisoner in his own skin. The loss of all control and the sense of being puppeted by someone else was horrifying.

Eventually, Temujin's unfaithful feet brought him back to Katarina's house. At the threshold, he was finally released and allowed to move under his own power again. Part of him wanted to turn and run, but it felt childish given how much effort it must have taken to bring him here. Besides, the dreamer could probably just hook him and reel him back in if he tried to fight.

The courtyard and fountain were just as he remembered. The creeping vines and flowers around the edges were in bloom, creating a small, hidden garden in the city. In the dream, there was no cat wandering around, which made Temujin realise what else had been missing. There were no animals. Not once had he seen a cart being pulled by a horse or camel. He'd not heard a single bird or seen any stray dogs running through the streets. As he sat down on one of the benches around the edge, Temujin expected to hear the hum of insects, but the silence was absolute. The atmosphere had previously soothed and relaxed him, but today he couldn't have been more on edge.

"We need to talk," said a familiar voice.

"You!" said Temujin, staring at Eraj with surprise. The Cynic was just as he remembered, dressed in a loose-fitting shirt that showed off his hairy chest and a pair of black trousers and matching boots. All of it was inexpensive, worn and lived in, just like the man. Even in a dream, his long hair was wild and untamed.

"I have nothing to say to you," said Temujin, getting to his feet. In desperation, he tried to reach for the Eternal Fire, but nothing happened. There was nothing to which he could surrender.

"Calm down, boy," said the grizzled Kozan.

"You can keep me here as long as you want. I will not change my mind."

"Are you sure?" said Eraj with a grin, drawing a dagger. "What do you think happens to your body if I cut you here?"

"Leave him alone," said Katarina, stepping out of the house. The first time he'd met her, Temujin had been awed by her presence. He'd felt a kinship with her that he didn't share with the other Kozan, but it wasn't sexual in nature. Anyone could see that she was an attractive woman. It was something he still struggled to put into words, but he'd felt it. Temujin had trusted her absolutely, and then she'd betrayed him. "Go back in the house. Please," she said, placing a hand on Eraj's shoulder.

The Kozan sneered, but he eventually left.

"Why did you bring me here?" asked Temujin.

"Would you have come if I had asked?" said Katarina, getting comfortable as she took a seat. Temujin sighed and sat down at the far end of the bench, keeping some distance between them. Katarina leaned back against the bench, tucking her bare feet under her, completely at ease. A vein throbbed in her forehead and her jaw was slightly clenched from the strain of keeping him in the dream.

"Did you know I used to have a husband?" said Katarina.

"No," said Temujin, unsure of where she was going, "but given how long you've been alive, I'm surprised it was only one."

"That's fair. After he died, it took me decades to get used to his absence. People say ridiculous things like, 'time heals all wounds' or 'you'll get over it', but the truth is, you don't. You never do." Katarina fiddled with the hem of her dress, playing with a loose thread.

"Then what happens?" he asked.

"You just get used to carrying the pain. It's like having a large stone resting on your back. Some days, I can forget it's there." Her voice was tinged with loss, regret and even a little anger. "Other days, the wrong word can trigger a memory, and then it all comes flooding back. The love we had, but then what came after. The absence. The suffering I endured after he'd died, and later, the days when I needed him more than anything, but he wasn't there anymore."

For a time, she fell silent, staring at the water in the fountain. The surface was flat and motionless, like a sheet of mottled grey glass. In the dream, there were no fish.

"And you never married anyone else?" he asked, breaking the silence.

Katarina shook her head. "In time, I met other men, I had relationships, but I never let them progress to talk of marriage, or children. Most days, I hate my father, but I also admire him. He has endured more pain and suffering than any other person in the world. In spite of everything, he still gets up in the morning. I don't know how he does it. It genuinely baffles me."

"Why tell me any of this?" said Temujin.

"I want to spare you the same agony," said Katarina, looking him in the eyes. "Teague was family. Even Eraj, who annoys me more than I can say, is family. I would do anything for them. There are no words to express how I feel about them, because they haven't been invented. No human has ever lived long enough to come up with a term to match."

"I see," he said glancing towards the house, but he found the upper window was empty.

"What are you looking for?" asked Katarina.

"Eraj. I expected to see him perched in the window again with a crossbow."

"I know you weren't responsible for Teague's death," said Katarina. "If you were, we wouldn't be having this conversation. I don't want you dead."

"Then what agony of mine are you trying to prevent?" he asked.

"The pain of being alone." Part of Temujin wanted to mock her, and yet he could not. Her life experience was not something he could understand or just dismiss because he didn't like being summoned in a dream. "Temujin, you could live for centuries, but very quickly everyone you know and care about will be dead. The scale of that isolation is incomprehensible compared to anything you've endured in your life."

"In spite of everything that's happened, you want me to join you." Temujin was so surprised by the absurdity, he started laughing. "This isn't about saving any future pain. It's about you and your endless war."

"You tried to stay out of the conflict between our kind, but it cannot continue. You must choose a side."

"Why? Why now?" he asked, straining for the Fire, but once more he came up with nothing. It felt as if a piece of him had been cut away. There wasn't even an echo of the power.

"Your plans are interfering with ours. We cannot take the risk that your forces might win in the war between the humans."

In spite of being dragged here against his will, Temujin grinned. "You're afraid."

"Of you? Don't be ridiculous."

"No, not me. Maryam and Behrouz are dead. Your father is now alone, and yet you're still terrified of him."

"His family are gone. His real family," said Katarina, with a hint of bitterness. "You have no idea how powerful he really is. There is nothing more dangerous than someone who has nothing to lose."

"What will he do?" asked Temujin.

"I don't know, and that's what scares me," she admitted.

Tilting his head backwards, Temujin stared at the sky, but he found its unnatural stillness very disconcerting. There was no breeze, and the clouds were frozen in place. The waking city was awash with overlapping smells, good and bad, but here, all of them were absent. He couldn't smell the flowers or any of the plants in the garden. On his walk across the city, there hadn't been anything either.

A cold prickle of intuition ran down Temujin's spine.

"Where is your cat?" he asked, playing for time.

"Elsewhere. Why?" said Katarina, suddenly suspicious.

Despite not being in any discomfort, Temujin stood, stretching out his back as if stiff. "I was just curious."

"I need an answer," said Katarina.

"I haven't changed my mind," said Temujin, staring down at her. "I will not join you, but I will not side with your father either."

"That's a shame," said Katarina, moving towards the door. "I'm sorry it has to be this way," she said before going inside. Temujin sat down on the edge of the fountain and ran his hands across the surface of the water. It felt like the mottled hide of some beast. One of the stones around the edge was slightly loose, so he shuffled over to avoid knocking it in.

A moment later, Eraj emerged from the house. A nasty grin stretched across his face. "She might not want you dead, but I do." The Kozan drew a dagger from his belt and held it up to the light.

Temujin's heart pounded. He should have been sweating, but his clothes were dry. "Poison?"

"Of course," said Eraj.

"Nothing I say will make any difference, will it?"

Eraj stalked closer. "No, boy. This is long overdue. I never liked you."

"I know. I felt the same."

"No tears or pleading for your life?" said Eraj with surprise.

Temujin shrugged and stood up, keeping his hands behind his back. He even lifted his chin, exposing his throat. "What's the point?"

As Eraj started to answer, Temujin hit him on the side of his face. The stone from the fountain smashed into the Kozan's head, snapping it to one side. Eraj tumbled sideways, tripped and fell, but then he disappeared before reaching the ground.

Closing his eyes, Temujin forced himself out of the dream and back into the real world.

He woke up and found he was in the same location, standing beside the fountain outside Katarina's house. In Temujin's left hand, he was still clutching the loose rock. Eraj was on the ground, blood pouring from his mouth. Using both hands, Temujin brought the rock down on one of Eraj's knees.

The Kozan screamed and curled up into a tight ball, cursing and crying as he rocked back and forth. Temujin moved to the far side of the courtyard and sat down on the bench, waiting to see what would happen next. In one hand he held a bloody rock, and in the other, Eraj's blade.

Slowly, the Kozan managed to control the pain long enough to sit upright. Eraj was still hissing through his teeth, both legs stretched out in front of him.

"Idiot boy," said Eraj through gritted teeth. "Don't you think I can reverse this?"

Eraj closed his eyes and held both hands just above his knee. The skin on his face was already deathly pale, and as Temujin watched, it turned grey. The Kozan's eyes widened in alarm, and he started to choke and splutter. Far too late, he finally understood.

After a frantic search of his body, Eraj found the small cut on his forearm. The skin around the wound was already red and inflamed.

"I was always curious what the spider venom would do," said Temujin. "You said it would stop my heart in seconds."

Eraj started clawing at his throat with both hands, desperately trying to breathe. His eyes bulged and he gasped for air as the toxins flooded his blood. Next, he lost control of his muscles. His mouth fell open, tongue lolling like a dog, arms splayed out on either side. Temujin wondered if Eraj was still trying to find some inner calm and surrender to the Eternal Fire. His body slid to one side, drool trickling from one corner of his mouth. The veins stood out on his face and neck. The paralysis seemed complete, as Eraj sank lower against the wall, folding in on himself, chin dipping towards his chest. The only way to tell that he was still alive was the slight rise and fall of his chest.

One of Eraj's eyes glared at Temujin, full of hate. If he'd been able to speak, there would have been a string of abuse, but Eraj was powerless and dying. Right before the end, before the distant wailing of the Servants began, he remained defiant and unafraid. Temujin waited until the light had gone out of his eyes before he went into the house. He dropped the stone but kept the dagger with him, just in case.

In every room there were artefacts and relics from Katarina's travels across the world. He couldn't identify the origin or even the age of many, but he was certain each was unique and would be worth a fortune. The amount of wealth contained in Katarina's small house was staggering. It was carelessly piled up in places, as if worthless.

Temujin wasn't naïve enough to imagine this was her only home, just the one she'd shown him. In one of the bedrooms, he found an unmade bed and more of Eraj's belongings, but there was no sign of the owner. Either Katarina had never been here in person, or she'd fled in fear, which seemed unlikely, given what she'd said about family.

By the time Temujin returned to the courtyard, there was no sign of Eraj's body. Now there were only three Kozan still alive in the world. It was time to end the war, once and for all.

CHAPTER 26
Kokochin

The day after Kokochin's meeting with Angelo the crime boss, she received a note from one of Rosa's people. They returned to the quiet street where, once again, a large man was guarding the entrance to the subterranean winery. As he offered Kokochin a hand to step down into the darkness, she paused and turned to him.

"What's your name?"

"Matteo, my lady," said the big man, surprised that she'd bothered to ask.

"Thank you, Matteo," she said, accepting his support as she went under the street. Layla and Matteo just exchanged a look, and then she followed Kokochin without any assistance.

Cardinal Cavicchi stomped down the stairs a short time later. He was flustered and agitated.

"I take it the news isn't good," said Kokochin.

He paced back and forth, cracking his knuckles, the sound echoing off the bare stone walls. "No. I have spoken, discreetly, with several people about the Assassins, and despite impressing upon them the severity of the situation, the Holy Father's schedule will not be changing."

"Which means what?" asked Layla.

"He has several meetings with ambassadors and dignitaries from the east in two days' time. The story I'm being told is that His Holiness refuses to live in fear." The cardinal ran a hand through his hair, which was slightly unkempt. He still gave Kokochin the impression of being a soldier more than a priest. Someone more comfortable with action than sitting quietly in prayer.

"But you think it's something else?" said Kokochin.

Cavicchi sighed and looked to the ceiling, and perhaps beyond to the heavens. He took a deep breath, and a peculiar stillness came over him, washing away some of his distress.

"I doubt he has been informed at all. As I said, when last we met, there are factions in the Church. There are serpents within the Vatican."

"Is there nothing you can do?" said Kokochin, surprised at his tone of defeat.

"There is always hope," he said with a grin. "I have a list of six names and descriptions for you. One of them must be your Assassin. In addition, there have been a number of rumours floating around about spies and agents from the barbarian courts in the east."

"Rumours which you started," guessed Kokochin.

Cavicchi shrugged. "Of course. That allowed me to persuade some of the other cardinals that increased protection around the Holy Father would be a good idea. I'm making an arrangement with some Swiss mercenaries."

"They won't stop an Assassin," said Layla, frowning at the priest. "If one of them gets in the room with him, it will be too late. They don't care about getting out alive afterwards."

"Then you need to find and stop them before they get inside the Vatican," he replied. "What did Angelo say?"

"He will help us," said Kokochin, skirting around what it would cost, "but only up to a point."

Cavicchi snorted. "He's a self-serving little sadist. I'd expect nothing less."

"But can he be trusted?" said Layla, staring at the priest. "We don't have time to waste if he lies to us."

"No, his reputation and his pride wouldn't allow it. He doesn't enjoy those sorts of games." The cardinal sounded confident, which came as a relief. Given how thrilled Angelo had been during the fight in his office, Kokochin didn't want to know what kind of games he did enjoy.

"I will do what I can," said Cavicchi, "but I fear this will come down to you."

"Why do you say that?" asked Kokochin.

"Because time is short. With a few weeks, I might have been able to steer some people away from such meetings. However, His Holiness is adamant that our enemies," he said, gesturing at the two of them, "can be brought into the light. He believes it is the Church's duty to save your souls, which is why he's willing to meet with such people."

Layla snorted while Kokochin and the priest shared a smile. The irony was not lost on any of them.

"Here," said the cardinal, handing Kokochin two slips of paper. "The first is a list of names for Angelo. The second is an address. If you discover something urgent and need to reach me, go to that house. Matteo will be there," said Cavicchi, then offered his hand, which was a surprise.

"Thank you," said Kokochin, gripping his fingers.

"And if you'll permit it," said the cardinal, "I'll pray for you both."

"It can't hurt," said Layla, shaking Cavicchi's arm in the warrior style, gripping his forearm. He raised an eyebrow but said nothing.

"Is there anything else you need?"

"Just good luck," said Kokochin, studying the list of names.

"I'll pray for that, too," he said with a wink.

* * *

Angelo and his network of contacts in the city proved to be as reliable as Kokochin had hoped. He'd not only given them three locations where someone could acquire unusual poisons, but also three names. The names didn't match those Cavicchi had given them, but the descriptions were similar.

All three men were new arrivals in the city from somewhere in the east, and all of them had some connections to the Mongol Empire. Even better, all three had been asking questions and making contact with figures in the city's underworld. One of them had to be the Assassin. It was too much of a coincidence, and far too risky, to assume otherwise. The difficulty now was determining which of them were just criminals, and which one was trying to kill the pope.

Angelo had agreed to follow two of the men while Kokochin and Layla trailed the third. She had left clear instructions with the crime boss that under no circumstances were his people to interfere with the strangers' business. They were to remain out of sight and just observe from a discreet distance. Their only purpose was to gather information on where the potential Assassin went and who they saw. Nothing more. If the Assassin realised they were being followed, it was possible they would change their plan. At the moment, Kokochin knew exactly when and where the Assassin would be in two days.

"He's moving again," said Layla, whispering in her ear. Kokochin felt the hair on the back of her neck prickle as Layla's breath warmed her skin. She nodded, not trusting herself to speak, and followed Layla around the corner.

The man they were shadowing, Majid, was young, charismatic and verbose. He wore expensive clothes, carried no weapons and seemed at ease in any situation. As far as everyone knew, Majid was the second son of a warlord who had prospered thanks to the guidance of his son. Instead of attacking travellers on the road, the warlord had started protecting them. After that, Majid had created several businesses, transporting goods along the Silk Road. Now, he ran the merchant companies while his father stayed at home in a palace, getting fat. None of which explained why he was talking to criminals across Rome, or why he'd been given an audience with the pope.

"Maybe it's smuggling," said Layla.

"Perhaps," said Kokochin, pausing on the corner with Layla. Majid had stopped at the far end of the street to talk with a beggar. The one-eyed man was dressed in rags and had only one leg. The other ended at the knee and was wrapped in a filthy bandage. The two men had a short conversation, and then some money subtly changed hands.

There weren't many items that couldn't be bought and sold in the Mongol Empire. It seemed a long way for Majid to come if it was for business. It would have to be for something he couldn't acquire elsewhere. If he wasn't an ambassador, then perhaps he represented a significant business that was of great importance to the Church. Operating in a strange city where she didn't know how anything worked made Kokochin feel as if she was constantly wandering around with one eye closed. There was a lot going on in her peripheral vision that she was missing.

Majid strolled through the city as if he didn't have any concerns. It was almost as if he felt untouchable. They trailed him through some of the most colourful neighbourhoods, but not once was he set upon by anyone. Either he was an Assassin who had no fear, or he was under someone's protection.

Layla kept Majid just in sight at all times. It prevented him realising anyone was following him, but on two occasions they briefly lost him and had to backtrack. After nearly an hour, and a long and strangled route across the city, he arrived at a battered old building. From the end of the street, they watched Majid knock on the door, and after exchanging a few words, he was let inside.

"Roof?" said Kokochin, glancing at the adjoining buildings. They were bunched up against each other, the sloping roofs almost overlapping. The whole street was falling apart, and the stonework on every building was crumbling. Cracks and deep gouges marred the front of many, like battle scars.

"Roof," said Layla, pulling out her gloves. A back door would be easier, but there was no way to know if it was locked and guarded. Also, given the lengths that Majid had gone to get here, they were not willing to take any chances. They needed to stay out of sight.

Glancing at the sky, Kokochin was surprised to see that it was already early evening. They'd been following him for most of the afternoon. It explained why her stomach was rumbling and shadows were pooling in dark corners. In a quiet spot, they slipped off their dresses and shoes. The black garments underneath were not quite the same as those Kokochin had trained in back in Tabriz, but they came close enough.

In a narrow alley between the buildings, Kokochin found the space was so tight she could spider-walk up the walls. Bracing her arms and legs against each building, the pair of them scaled the walls to the roof, then crawled across it until they found a narrow gap. Voices drifted up from inside, which was well-lit, giving them a good view of what was happening.

"It's all there," said Majid, sounding aggrieved. The confidence he'd shown on the street had evaporated. He was unable to stop fidgeting. Whatever he was involved with was not his usual business, and the people were dangerous enough to make him nervous.

Majid was standing in the centre of the room opposite four men. Three of them, clearly there as muscle, stood behind a fourth smaller man who was unarmed. He was also the only one with a chair. The slight, balding man at the front was carefully counting coins out onto a table between him and Majid. He didn't stop until he was done, and then he looked up.

"We're good," said the accountant to the men behind him. One of them moved out of sight, disappearing into another part of the building. "It's just business," he said to Majid, who was still offended.

The thug returned carrying a large cloth bag which he put down on the table. Majid carefully opened the bag and took out a small packet of leaves.

Layla grunted in recognition. "Drugs. He's a smuggler," she whispered. "He's not an Assassin."

"A new shipment will be ready, every three months," said the accountant. "They'll be inside icons like this one," he said, showing Majid a clay idol of the baby Jesus and his mother.

They moved away from the roof and carefully made their way back down to the street. Once they were wearing their own clothing, they hurried through the streets towards The Seventh Bell. If Majid wasn't the Assassin, that meant it had to be one of the two men that Angelo's people were watching.

As soon as they set foot inside the tavern, Kokochin knew that something was wrong. On their first visit, the atmosphere had been gloomy and depressing. Tonight, it was hostile. Several people had weapons on display, and more than a dozen people stared at them when they opened the door. One group of four men stood up as they closed the door behind them.

"Leave them be," said a voice from the back of the room. A bruised and battered Luca waved at them to follow him behind the bar. The previously friendly barman ignored them. His focus remained on the front door, and as they walked passed him, Kokochin noticed he had a loaded crossbow under the bar.

A familiar and unpleasant odour assaulted her nose when they set foot inside Angelo's office. Layla had smelled it too, as she drew a dagger from inside her clothing.

The office was tidy and organised as usual, but Angelo was not behind his desk. A pallet had been set up on the floor and he was kneeling down beside a young man. He had a blood-soaked bandage wrapped around his torso and another on his head. Kokochin couldn't make out the words, but Angelo was murmuring something to the dying man. From the amount of blood and the colour of his skin, he didn't have long.

"What happened?" said Layla.

Luca didn't even raise an eyebrow at her naked blade. He was in pain and distracted. "It was a bloodbath," was all he said.

"You got too close," said Kokochin. The office smelled of fresh blood, and there was a whiff of something more unpleasant. Her worst fear had come true.

The dying man gave a huge, desperate gasp. Tears streamed from his eyes and he started muttering something that sounded like a prayer. He lurched forward, gagged and then fell back on the bed. A thick stream of blood ran from one corner of his mouth, and he exhaled one long, final breath. Luca murmured a prayer, made the sign of the cross on his chest and kissed a crucifix hanging around his neck. Angelo bowed his head over the dead man and then tried to close his eyes, but they remained firmly open. Instead, he pulled a blanket over the body, which quickly began to turn red.

"My people were watching this ambassador of yours. This Simin," said Angelo, in a quiet voice. His eyes were dry, but Kokochin could see that he was grieving. He stared at nothing, the muscles in his jaw twitched with barely contained rage, and his shoulders were hunched. "They trailed him for hours. Simin seemed meek and easily cowed. They went against my orders and abducted him. Four of them held him while a fifth man asked questions. I only found out after a couple of hours when one of them came to tell me." Angelo trailed off and glanced at the dead man behind him.

Luca picked up the story. "By the time we got there, it was too late. All four of our men were dead, or dying," he said, waving a hand at the corpse.

There was something more that they weren't being told. In his line of business, it couldn't be the first time Angelo had lost one of his men. Also, given what Kokochin knew about him, she couldn't see him being particularly sentimental.

"Who was he?" she asked.

"My nephew," said Angelo. "My sister's boy."

"Then what happened to you?" said Layla, gesturing at Luca's face.

"It was the other ambassador," said the bodyguard. "I got too close, and he panicked and ran. I went after him and he caught me by surprise."

"You were reckless," snarled Angelo. "He could have killed you, too."

Kokochin didn't know if he was upset because Luca had failed to follow orders, or if Angelo genuinely cared.

"So, which is the Assassin?" said Kokochin.

"It has to be Simin. He slipped his bonds and gutted four of my men like it was nothing," said Angelo. "Before he died, the boy said the man changed."

Layla raised an eyebrow. "Changed how?"

"When they caught him, Simin was like a lamb, but then he transformed and became a wolf."

"So, the other ambassador was what? Just good with his fists?" said Kokochin.

"He was not a no one," said Luca, bristling at the implication that he'd been bested by an ordinary man. "He knew how to fight."

"So, are you saying both men are Assassins?" said Kokochin.

Angelo and Luca exchanged a look, but neither had an answer.

At this point, whether it was one or both, Kokochin knew it didn't really matter. Both men knew someone was following

them. If she was in their position, Kokochin would abandon
the mission. However, an Assassin never broke a contract, and
the timing of events was critical. They would not be able to
get another face-to-face meeting with the pope for months,
perhaps longer. What they could do until their meeting was
remake their identity, change their name, clothes and where
they were staying. Avoid anything that was familiar, making it
almost impossible for anyone to find them in Rome. The one
thing that would not change was when they would be allowed
inside the Vatican.

"Do you want revenge for your nephew?" said Kokochin.

"Whoever this man is, whatever his purpose, he must die,"
said Angelo, his whole body shaking with rage. "His blood will
soak the stones."

"Amen," said Luca.

"Then you have to get us into the Vatican," said Kokochin.

Angelo stared at her for a moment, and then he began to
laugh. "You are insane. It cannot be done."

"What of the Necropolis beneath the city?" said Kokochin.

In the two weeks while they waited for a response from
Cardinal Cavicchi, they had been gathering information on the
city. Since before the time of the Romans, many pagans and
Christians had been buried beneath the city. Rosa's network of
contacts had grown up with stories and heard many rumours,
but none of them had ever found a way inside.

"What do you know of the underground city?" said Angelo,
dodging the question.

Kokochin shrugged. "Just the rumours. Tombs full of
priceless relics and treasure. Hordes of gold and gems. A whole
church, completely intact, buried deep underground. Don't
pretend you haven't had people looking for a way in."

"Desecration," hissed Luca. "We cannot disturb the dead,"
he said, but everyone else ignored him.

"I may have hired a few historians over the years," admitted
the crime boss.

"You mean treasure hunters," said Layla.

"Call them whatever you want. They found a way in. However, there wasn't much that was of real value," said Angelo.

Kokochin laughed, which given what had just happened, surprised everyone and felt callous and out of place. "You mean they got too scared before they went too far. Jumping at ghost stories and shadows."

"Do you think I care about money? Or relics?" hissed Angelo, clenching his fists. "I want blood. I want to carve my name into his flesh."

"Then help me get inside and you will have your revenge."

Angelo moved to the far side of his office, standing above the body of his nephew. He stared down at the blanket, his expression hidden from view.

"Do you know who they're trying to kill?" said Kokochin, now speaking to both men in the room. "The target is the Pope."

"Mother of God," said Luca. "We must help," he said, forgetting his earlier reticence.

"I love you like a brother, Luca, but do not use that word with me." Angelo sounded more weary than angry. "Never tell me what I must do."

"Even if he does not help, I will go with you," said the big man. "My life is yours."

Layla gripped him by the shoulder and Luca nodded grimly. Any animosity that had existed between them was gone.

Angelo's shoulders moved up and down, and then his whole body shook. Kokochin wasn't sure if he was laughing or crying until he turned around. His smile was grim, and it looked out of place.

"And people think I'm monstrous," said Angelo, glaring at Kokochin from across the room. "To use my grief and rage against me, just to get what you want."

Kokochin folded her arms and stood her ground. "I'm trying to save a life and prevent a war. But you don't care about the repercussions, do you?" Her emotions were so raw, she struggled not to shout. "So don't stand there pretending you're an innocent with a noble heart. We both have blood on our hands."

"True, but at least I don't pretend otherwise," said Angelo.

"Time is short," said Layla, stepping between them, ending the staring match. "Will you help us, or do we need to go elsewhere?"

A strained silence filled the room. She could see that Luca wanted to speak, but he wisely chose to keep his mouth shut. Kokochin thought he'd already tested the limits of Angelo's patience. The crime boss sighed and walked over to his desk before dropping into his seat. He closed his eyes, and at first, Kokochin thought he'd gone to sleep. Somewhere, she heard a dog barking, and in the distance, there was a faint murmur of voices from the tavern. She was about to say something when Layla shook her head, putting a finger to her lips. So they stood in silence and waited for Angelo to make a decision.

Finally, he opened his eyes and sat forward, placing the palms of his blood-spattered hands flat on the desk. "I will help you," said Angelo. "The Assassin will die."

CHAPTER 27
Kaivon

Kaivon stared at the army spread out before him, trying to take it all in. A sea of warriors on foot and thousands more on horseback. He knew some had hoped for a brighter day to raise everyone's spirits, but instead the sky was grey, clogged with endless clouds. There was also a constant shower of light rain.

"An ominous day," grumbled General Subedei.

"A good day for a battle," countered King David. "Too much heat would sap the men and the horses. This is better."

"True," said King Hethum. "Although, if the rain gets worse, mud will become a problem." Beside the king, his brother Thoros grunted but said nothing. His eyes were scanning the men. Kaivon didn't know what he was searching for amongst the sea of bodies. Perhaps he had friends down there.

"God has blessed us with cool weather," said Prince Bohemond.

A few of the others murmured prayers, but not David. Today, his expression remained grim, like Kaivon's. He was focused on what was to come. Prayers for the dead or thanks to God for victory would come later.

The others continued to talk, but Kaivon said nothing. His mind was turning their plans over and over, running through various scenarios and counter-moves. The battle would flex and change, and when that happened, they needed to be ready to adapt. It was where Timur excelled, and they had to be ready.

Everyone around him knew what needed to be done. If Kaivon should fall or become separated from the others, there was a reliable chain of command to make sure that his orders were carried out. David was his unofficial second, and his knowledge of warfare was as good as Kaivon's, if not better. If it came to it, he would manage well.

Today there were no nations, factions, tribes or religious groups amongst the warriors. There was only their army and the enemy. Every single man had been made to understand that the only way they would get through this day was by relying on the man standing beside them. Today, that man was a brother. Someone for whom one would lay down their life, without question or second thought. It was the only way to win this fight, especially when they were outnumbered.

"A rebellion?" someone said, but Kaivon wasn't really listening.

"Sons of the white who?" said another officer. Any disruption to Timur's hold on the Chagatai khanate was something to celebrate another day. First, they had to survive today.

It had been a long time since Kaivon had been this far east in Persia. He didn't recognise any of the landmarks, and had no friends or relatives in the area. The land was hilly and green, as they were far in the north. In the distance was a vast forest, and to the south of their position, the ragged peak of some mountains.

He'd not spent any time thinking about it before, but the air here smelled different. There was a hint of something familiar, but he couldn't name it. Kaivon recognised that a part of him was trying to memorise every aspect of this day, not only because it could be his last, but because regardless of the outcome, it would be a momentous day in history. Idly, he wondered how he would be remembered in the history books. Would they even mention him? Or would he simply be another nameless leader that was cut down by Timur?

"I can hear you brooding," said Esme, moving to stand beside Kaivon. The others made room, welcoming her presence. Subedei was the only one who frowned. The Mongol general had seen Hulagu's War Wife countless times, and he even understood that she had counselled him on matters of war, but Subedei wasn't comfortable with women on the battlefield. If he knew all that the House of Grace had done, he might have been more welcoming.

In the distance, Kaivon caught sight of something moving. Using a spyglass, he confirmed what his scouts were racing towards him to report. Timur's army had arrived.

"Ready the men," he said. Kaivon's words stopped all conversations. "He's here."

For a while, Umar just blinked, surprised to find that he was still alive.

When the Persian cavalry had smashed into his unit, sending men flying in all directions, he'd thought he would die. Dazed and confused, he lay there staring up at the sky. A group of horses thundered past on his left. They didn't stop, so Umar ignored them and kept staring at the sky. He'd hoped for a break in the clouds, but there was none.

Before he tried moving, Umar tested his body. He could wiggle his fingers and toes, so that was good, although there was something heavy across his legs.

With a grunt, Umar sat up and wiped the rain from his face. There were bodies everywhere. He had been lying in the pile of them. One or two men groaned, but no one was trying to stand up. Most of the men were intact, but their bodies were crushed and bent. Heads were smashed in and chests collapsed. One or two were missing a leg or an arm. Four were without heads. The expression on the faces he could see was a mix of terror, surprise and horror. Only one man looked peaceful in death, as if he was sleeping. The rest had suffered. And the blood. It was everywhere. It had poured out of so many bodies. Umar's boots were red and sticky with it.

For once, Umar was glad not to have a sense of smell. There was no sign of his sword, but there were plenty of other weapons that no one else was using. He tucked a dagger into his boot and picked up a long, curved blade with a fox head on the pommel. Umar considered looting some of the bodies, but unless he survived, the money would be useless. Besides, it would only slow him down.

Not far away, the battle was still raging. On his left, a huge living wall of cavalry swept across the plain. At this distance, Umar didn't know if they were allies or the enemy. At the front of the wedge, riding a grand horse, was a large man with a sword. When the cavalry ploughed into the infantry, the initial sound was horrendous. Metal screeched, there was a rumble like thunder, and then the screaming began. Men and horses wailed in agony. The sounds merged into something grotesque and then it was gone, swallowed by the noise of battle.

Umar could track the progress of the big man on the horse by the great spurts of blood and flying limbs. More infantry rushed in to support their friends, overlapping their shields, trying to create a solid wall to stop the charge. Umar expected to see the big man emerge on the other side, riding into the open, but there was no sign of him. The fighting devolved into a thousand smaller fights.

"Are you injured?" said a voice. A vaguely familiar man was staring at Umar. Behind him were a hundred more warriors, all of them armed with spears.

"I don't know," said Umar, checking himself. His hands were covered in blood, and he didn't know if it was his or not.

"Come on!" said an officer, running up behind them.

The spearmen moved away, running towards the melee. Umar wanted to go in the opposite direction, but he understood what would happen if he deserted. Others had tried and been caught. They'd been tied to four horses and torn apart.

With a sigh, Umar trotted after the spearmen.

The moment before Rustam's horse had collided with Timur's forces, he'd spotted a lone warrior wandering around amongst the dead. A second later, he smashed into the front rank. His sword came down on the right, severing a man's arm, then on the left, splitting open a head. His armoured horse kept its head down as it charged forward. Its speed and weight scattered warriors stupid enough to get in the way. Some were crushed underfoot. One man raised his sword, intending to strike Rustam's mount, but he disappeared with a squeak as another horse ran him down.

Rustam was at the tip of the spear, but the others were just behind him on either side. Momentum kept them all moving forward and they rode deep into enemy ranks. Then the press of bodies became too much and they slowed to a walk. Someone grabbed his leg and Rustam lashed out, stabbing down. The hand fell away, but another angry face took its place, and another. His shoulder was aching. For some reason, his toes were tingling and his left foot was numb, but it kept twitching. He started laughing because it was ridiculous, but once he started he couldn't stop.

All around him men were staring, as if he were mad. A large, blood-soaked man on a horse, hacking apart the enemy. Some turned and ran, eyes wide with terror. Another wet himself, dropped his sword and begged for his life. Someone else cut him down, opening his throat. Rustam tried rubbing his thigh, but instead, his left leg jerked and he kicked a man in the face, breaking his nose. He hadn't even felt it. There was definitely something wrong with his leg. Was he dying? Had someone wounded him and he didn't even realise? Maybe walking would be a good idea.

The enemy began to rally. Six brave men armed with spears grouped together and started to charge. Rustam was going to die. He knew it, but he still couldn't stop laughing. He didn't want to watch, so he threw back his head, cackling and now crying at the sky, tears of frustration and sadness mixing together. He had been named after a hero, and now he would die in the mud with the rest. Unnerved by something, perhaps by his laughter, his horse kicked out. Rustam toppled backwards and landed face down in the mud.

That silenced him, forced him to close his mouth. He spat, swore, then clambered to his feet. Somehow, he was still gripping his sword, but there was mud in his eyes. Trying to wipe it off only smeared more of it across his face. Something heavy collided with his hip. Half-blind, he reached out with both hands and found a patch of cloth. After scrubbing his face clean, he realised it was someone's cloak. The man was dead on his mount, missing his head. The horse was frozen with terror. Speaking nonsense in a calm voice, Rustam approached the beast, as his own had wandered off. Moving slowly, he slid the dead man from the saddle, gently held the reins and climbed into his place.

The spearman who had been about to kill him was gone. Dead or scared off by Rustam's behaviour. The battle had devolved into a thousand smaller fights. It was utter chaos, but high above everyone on a hill, Rustam saw the generals. At this distance, they were nothing more than specks, but then one pointed to his right and he knew that it was Kaivon. Following his hand, Rustam saw hundreds of archers raising their bows towards the sky.

He stabbed a man on his right, then leaned down and yanked the shield from the dying man's hand before he fell.

"Shields!" shouted Rustam, nudging his new horse forward. At first, it refused to move, but after he swatted it on the rear, it ran, desperate to get away from the chaos. Turning his horse, Rustam charged directly towards the enemy archers.

Other warriors on horseback followed his lead. At first, it was only a few, but as he picked up speed, more joined in behind him. Infantry started to panic, turning to get away from the churning hooves that were bearing down on them.

The sky turned dark, but it had nothing to do with the weather.

"Shields!" cried Rustam, knowing it was pointless, knowing it wouldn't make a difference.

The first wave of arrows fell. Men and horses screamed, but he kept riding. Two arrows pierced his shield, one skimmed his horse's flank and it whinnied but kept moving. Another went through Rustam's forearm, nearly punching into his cheek. He stared at the point, grateful it had missed his eye.

Glancing over his shoulder, Rustam saw that a number of the men behind him were gone. Horses rolled about on the ground, legs kicking. Others lay dying or dead on their sides. Men were trapped beneath, or crushed to death, or pierced with multiple shafts. It was a bloodbath, but enough riders remained only a few steps behind him. Their faces were grim and angry, hungry for revenge.

A second wave of arrows fell, but he and the others were too close. In the distance, he heard screams, but they wouldn't stop him. The archers would not get a chance to fire a third wave.

Facing forward, Rustam picked out one individual, a weasel-faced archer with a black moustache. Whatever happened, that man had to die.

Horror gripped Barlas as the rampaging horseman charged towards them. At the front was a blood-spattered giant. Barlas couldn't be sure, but for some reason he thought the big Persian was looking directly at him. As if he'd personally done something to the man.

"Give them another volley!" bellowed the officer, a dim-witted man they all called Carrot.

"It's too late for that!" said Barlas. "We need to pick our targets."

The big man was getting close. He was definitely staring at Barlas. That was when Barlas noticed three arrows sticking out of the Persian, two in his shield and one in his arm. There was no way to be absolutely sure they weren't his arrows.

On either side of him, men started picking off individual targets. The sound of the horses was getting louder and louder. Barlas nocked an arrow and took a deep breath to try and calm his nerves. When that failed, he drew, took aim at the big man, and released.

He'd done it a thousand times. More. He didn't wait, knocked another arrow and let it fly. Again. And a fourth arrow, just in case. The first went long, catching a man behind in the thigh. The second missed. The third bounced off the horse's armoured head. Finally, the fourth hit the big Persian in the shoulder.

Barlas didn't have time to celebrate as the pair kept coming, riding straight for him. The man was wobbling in the saddle, but the horse hadn't slowed down. It was nearly on top of him. All around Barlas, men were screaming, dropping their weapons and running for their life. He wanted to do the same, but his legs wouldn't work. He felt something warm trickling down his leg. The big man's smile was knowing. He understood.

Barlas nocked another arrow, took aim and fired. He had no idea if it hit anyone as the horse was already looming over him. Dropping his bow, he reached for his dagger. His fingers had just closed around the hilt when something heavy rammed his shoulder.

The world turned upside down. The sky was down and then it was up again. He landed in a heap and heard something crack. Cold liquid soaked into his clothes and a fierce smell filled his nostrils. Blood trickled into his eyes, but when he tried to wipe them, his arms wouldn't move. The smell was getting worse. It was all around. Barlas was struggling to breathe, but he didn't know if it was the smell or the heavy weight on his chest. Turning his head to the left, he saw the big Persian crawling across a sea of bodies towards him. One of his legs was missing, just gone at the knee. His eyes were mad, white showed all around, and he was holding a dagger between his teeth. Barlas was sure it was his. The man was relentless. Nothing would make him give up.

When Barlas tried to get away, nothing happened. One of his arms flapped a bit, but he couldn't feel anything below the middle of his chest. It was all still intact, but he couldn't feel it. Oddly, there was no pain.

Harsh, rasping breathing grew louder and louder. A hand tugged him to the left, but Barlas was powerless to make it stop. The Persian warrior filled the sky, his face battered and bloody. The dagger was now clutched in one hand and he was shouting something. Barlas saw the blade come down, but he couldn't feel it, so he just shook his head. Swallowing was a problem and he couldn't take a full breath in order to speak. The dagger came down again and again, but it didn't make any difference.

The Persian was raging while he expended all of his energy, stabbing and stabbing. Barlas would have laughed if he'd been able to make a sound. Instead he just smiled. That made it worse. The blade came down towards his face, but it missed, slicing off the top of his ear instead. That hurt, but the pain was distant and he didn't think it really mattered.

In the distance, Barlas heard a faint noise that quickly became unbearably loud. Men and horses were dying, but it wasn't that. It was the sound of the fire itself. There was a whoosh and then a loud roaring. Flames danced in front of his face. The Persian warrior screamed, his hair suddenly alight, and then the world turned black as smoke filled Barlas's vision.

* * *

Subedei cheered as the small catapults launched clay pots of pitch over the battlefield. Kaivon knew they didn't have time to celebrate. Their left flank was crumbling. While the forward momentum of Timur's cavalry had been disrupted, it wouldn't take long for them to regroup. He didn't have enough men to overwhelm the enemy, which forced him to rely on cunning.

Several times now, Timur's forces had attempted to outflank them, and Kaivon's forces had been forced to withdraw, giving up ground. But this had been inevitable and Kaivon had planned for it.

A hundred flaming arrows followed the clay pots, arching high into the air before they came thundering back down again. Kaivon knew some of his own men were still down there, but he couldn't wait. Every warrior was precious, but he couldn't risk the war for a few.

Shock and awe. More than anything, it was what they needed now to disrupt the enemy. It would give his men time to withdraw and regroup at the next fall-back point.

Portions of the ground had been soaked for days. Markers had been left to highlight these areas, but once the plain was covered with a sea of bodies, it became difficult to pinpoint their exact location. More fiery arrows fell, and finally one landed in the right spot. There was a loud whooshing sound and then a wall of flame erupted from the damp ground. The rain had stopped hours ago. Thankfully there hadn't been enough to cause a serious problem.

Kaivon had seen hundreds of men die in some of the most hideous and unpleasant ways imaginable. This was one of the worst. Wreathed in flames, warriors ran back and forth like headless chickens, desperately searching for something to smother the fire. But there was no water and no relief for their torment. Mercifully, most of them didn't last very long. They dropped to the ground, suffocating to death or dying from shock, littering the battlefield with numerous twitching pyres.

The charge from the enemy slowed, faltered, and then broke apart before turning into a full rout. Officers were shouting orders trying to restore some discipline, but they were completely ignored. Weapons and shields were dropped, bows forgotten, and countless brave warriors ran to save their lives. The smell of charred flesh reached Kaivon's nose, sickly sweet and unpleasantly familiar. Patches of black smoke dotted the battlefield as the dead continued to burn. It wasn't long before the gloomy sky overhead was made worse with a thick layer of grey cloud.

"Give the order to fall back," said Kaivon.

"But we've got them on the run," said Subedei. "We should press our advantage."

"We don't have the men," said David. "I pray their spirits are broken enough that they don't attack again today."

Looking at the sky, Kaivon couldn't see the sun, so he had no idea of the time of day. The fighting could have been raging for several hours or less than one. It was difficult to know.

"It started about three hours ago," said Hethum, answering Kaivon's unspoken question.

That made it early afternoon. Normally, Kaivon's stomach would have been rumbling by now, but the sights and smells of the battlefield had taken away his appetite. Sunset was not for at least a few hours, time enough for Timur to pull his forces together and attack again.

"Any word?" he asked, not taking his eyes from the battlefield.

The signal to pull back was given and passed down the line. Riders were sent and then officers started bellowing orders at the men.

"Nothing," said Thoros. "I don't think they're coming."

Kaivon had previously believed that without reinforcements from the Golden Horde, it was possible for them to win. After what he'd witnessed today, he was less sure. Timur didn't always respond in a predictable way. His strategy was not chaotic, but rather than fall back, he'd risked losing five hundred men to Kaivon's archers. When Kaivon's cavalry had swept in from the west, cutting into Timur's flank, he'd responded with hundreds of spearmen. His own cavalry had been held in reserve. They'd barely taken to the battlefield at all. That worried Kaivon a great deal.

Kaivon had already lost about a fifth of his men, and the rest were tired and bloodied. Esme was working with the other healers, but she'd stopped by once to say that many of the injured would not recover.

At some point today, almost all of his warriors had taken to the battlefield. Only a small number had been held in reserve. If Timur regrouped and sent out his cavalry, Kaivon worried that his men would be unable to stop them. From experience, he understood exactly how tired they would be feeling after today's fighting.

Timur's forces withdrew. The gulf between the two armies grew until all that remained between them was a litter of the dead and the dying. Plumes of black smoke still drifted skyward from a few blackened bodies. Dying horses kicked and screamed. Men groaned and bled into the cold ground, dying in pain, while both sides just watched and waited. Leaving them to suffer was unforgivable, but sadly, it was necessary. If the fighting was truly over for today, then attempts would be made to save them. Most would not make it, as time was critical.

Kaivon stared at the ranks of Timur's army trying to guess what he would do next. His imagined Timur's officers were giving him their opinions, while he made calculations and judged the mood of his men. The distance was too great to know, but Kaivon wondered if Timur was searching for him, hoping to catch a glimpse.

"Is it over?" asked Thoros.

"I don't know," said Kaivon, shaking his head. "We need it far more than his men."

"He's known for being ruthless," said David, a note of warning in his voice. He was right. Now was not the time to relax. Brazen assumptions and hoping for the best, especially against such a fierce enemy, would lead to defeat.

"Gather arrows, pitch, whatever else we have," said Kaivon. "Tell the cavalry to stand ready to charge."

"How many?" asked Hethum, gesturing for several runners to approach.

"All of them," said Kaivon, turning to face his officers. "We need everyone. Nothing can help in reserve."

It was important that they saw his eyes. That they understood what he was saying. This was it. If Timur attacked again, everyone would be expected to fight. Even them. It was why all of them were armed for battle and there were horses standing by. Kaivon was not about to charge against the enemy in the front rank like Hulagu had done in the past, but if the tide of battle turned against them, they would not stand idle.

There would be no chance for them to withdraw, regroup and fight another day. Timur could not allow it. If Kaivon knew anything about his enemy, it was this. The army from the Ilkhanate had to be defeated, here and now. This was the decisive battle that would shape everything that came after.

Prince Bohemond had been quiet up until now. Suddenly, he pointed over Kaivon's shoulder, eyes wide with fear. Even before he turned around, Kaivon knew what the prince had seen.

A lone warrior walked a short distance ahead of the rest of the army, well past the front rank of warriors. At this distance, it was difficult to make out his features, but Kaivon could see that he had red hair. He also walked with a pronounced limp. Those around the warrior made space. All eyes were trained on the warrior as he drew his sword and then pointed it across the battlefield.

"Is that him?" said Thoros, squinting at the man.

Kaivon didn't need the spyglass. He knew it was Timur. The warlord was sending all of them a clear message. It wasn't over.

CHAPTER 28
Kaivon

A wave of conflicting emotions passed through Bas as Kaivon drew his sword.

Pride, love, admiration and despair.

It wasn't a good sign that the general was getting into the fight. It meant that the battle was lost. No help was coming, and they were completely on their own. Their reserves were already fighting, and now their leaders were stepping forward to fill gaps in their ranks. They didn't have to, but every senior officer in the army had inspired their warriors through personal sacrifice and hardship.

Arrayed beside Kaivon were kings, princes and generals, all former vassals and slaves of Hulagu. They were legendary warriors, holy and righteous men, whose mere presence inspired others to greatness. Bas felt stronger just for seeing them draw their weapons, and he was not the only one.

A wave rippled through the army as their leaders came forward. Despite the dire circumstances, men cheered and called out their names. Bas thought the army had been on the verge of defeat, but something began to change. Maybe this wasn't the end after all. Bas could see it in the faces of the men around him. A glimmer of hope.

He had never felt more proud to stand beside the great

Persian man. Kaivon had survived one Mongol invasion, fought back against them from the inside, and now here he was, leading another army against them.

Unofficially, Bas and a few of the others who had been on missions with Kaivon had taken on the role of his personal bodyguards. A dozen young men hovered nearby, mixed into the ranks of others, but they only had one purpose. To keep the general alive. They could not protect him from every fight, but no one would be allowed to sneak an attack from his flanks. It was the least they could do.

Bas had learned the hard way. There was no honour in war. Every rule, as part of a warrior's training, would be broken. The only rule that mattered was survival at any cost. The winners would then decide upon the story of how they won, with glorious deeds, bravery and respect for the enemy. And if everyone else was dead, who could say otherwise?

A gangly man with a chunk missing from one ear nodded at Bas. He returned it, slow and with meaning. Most of the other warriors around them were oblivious. They had their own lives to worry about. Bas owed the general. He would have died a dozen times over if not for Kaivon. It was the same for countless others.

All eyes were now on Kaivon as he strode through the ranks of men who parted as he approached. It was as if they could sense his presence. Bas and the others trailed after in his wake, going unnoticed and almost unseen. After today, win or lose, they would make sure that historians remembered Kaivon and wrote about his momentous deeds.

Thoros knew all hope was lost. They should have run, but after all that he'd been through, he would have refused the order. Never again. Never again would he bow down or kneel to another man. Timur would have to take his head before he surrendered. He would punch and kick and bite until the moment his heart stopped.

His noble brother, Hethum, was a true king. He had been destined to rule, but his power had been usurped by the Mongols, his nation made into a vassal state. While Thoros thought Kaivon to be arrogant, and did not agree with all of his choices, today they were of one mind.

Victory or death. Normally, Thoros would have mocked anyone who made such a ridiculous proclamation, but not anymore. When the black sorcerer had taken him away, in many ways the old Thoros had died. The experience had taught him much. He couldn't care less for social niceties or what others thought of him. Unlike his brother, he was not a man of faith. Now, he knew there was no afterlife, no Heaven, no reward for good deeds. There was only the now, so he intended to live it to the full. In every moment and with every breath.

Warriors hailed his brother, their Christian king, as he approached and though weary, they all stood taller in his presence. The battle had already been long, but even now, they wanted to impress their king. Thoros wished he could inspire such passion. Instead, he would earn it, through his deeds.

"Never again," muttered Thoros, bringing his sword down on a warrior's shoulder. It went through the man's armour and cracked the bone. With his mouth open in a silent scream, the Mongol fell away, but was quickly replaced by another. Sweeping his blade from left to right, Thoros disembowelled the next man. He took the right hand from a third and tripped a fourth with his shield. With a quick motion, he thrust the tip of his blade into the man's gaping mouth. Teeth fountained up into the air as he yanked his sword free, but the warrior was already dead.

As their numbers had dwindled, any semblance of winning through strategy had faded. It had devolved into one giant, heaving mass of bodies. Groups surged this way and that, pushed each other, drowning some in the mud, pressed down by the weight of those above. It was a horrific way to die, but Thoros had seen worse fates. A thousand small fights erupted, with pairs, dozens and sometimes fifty men on either side. In some quarters, the Persian army was winning, but it wouldn't make a difference to the overall outcome. They were outnumbered, and eventually, they would lose.

Timur had not sent in his cavalry yet, but he would. Thoros thought he was waiting until the Persian army was bruised, bloody and worn out. Maybe he'd waited until the battle tilted briefly in Kaivon's favour. Until the Persian army felt as if there was a small chance that they might win. Then Timur's cavalry would surge in, mercilessly crushing all hope, decimating everything in their path. It would crush their spirits, and what came after would be a slaughter.

"No!" shouted Thoros, smashing his shield into a man's face. The Mongol tripped and fell back. Someone stabbed him with a spear, denying Thoros a chance to finish him off. A new wave of energy surged along his tired limbs, fuelled by rage, which he channelled into his sword arm. Howling like a mad man, Thoros hurled himself at the enemy, startling everyone with his ferocity. Other voices joined in, added their defiance to his, furious for their own reasons.

Hack and stomp. Slice and kick, over and over again, until his face was covered with blood, his shoulders screamed and his lungs burned. Thoros stabbed another man in the face, stepped over his body and found no one waiting behind. The fighting raged elsewhere, but in front of him, there was a pocket of empty space.

With hands on knees, he vomited and spat bile on the ground. He hadn't eaten in hours, and there was nothing in his stomach to cough up. Standing upright, he tried to catch his breath, waiting for the inevitable to happen. Someone would notice him and move to attack.

A mile away to the east, a group of warriors on horseback were watching the fight unfold. It had to be Timur. Thoros had wanted to see him dead before this was over, but he had no horse and not enough men to attack the warlord.

In the distance, he heard a faint rumble that quickly grew louder. It seemed as if Timur had no patience. He wanted to finish the battle as soon as possible. Scanning the horizon, Thoros tried to locate Timur's mounted warriors. To the north, he saw a massive churning wall of horses and men. It was sweeping down towards the battle like a tidal wave, coming to crush anyone that stood its path. Others had spotted it now, and Thoros saw them try to run, but there was nowhere to go. On his right, to the east, he caught sight of more warriors on horseback. It was even worse than he thought. Timur had held back thousands of warriors. He intended to crush the Persian army from both sides. The men around him had noticed, and panic started to creep in.

"Steady," said Thoros, but it wasn't enough. He wasn't one prone to speeches. That was his brother, but he felt that he had to say something. "Make no mistake. This is the end for us all, but I will not die with a spear in my back. I won't be cut down by some Mongol dog as I run." At random, Thoros pointed at one of the warriors riding towards him from the south. "Before this day is over, and my blood is cold, I will kill that man. I will do this, so that when the new rebellion comes, there is one less bastard to fight. Choose your target, make a difference, and stand with me."

At first, no one moved. Thoros gritted his teeth, angry at the warriors around him. He couldn't really blame them. None of them were ready to die. None of them had shared in his experiences.

Facing the enemy, he took a final moment to savour the feeling of the wind against his skin and the air in his lungs. Thoros remembered the day he'd fallen in love, the heartache that followed, the passion and the tears. Good and bad. Days of feasting and joy. Days of mourning and torment. The death of his mother. The birth of his niece. All of it filled his mind. Countless memories he'd not dwelled on or thought to cherish. Today, every single one of them mattered, because after today, those thoughts would no longer exist in this world.

A bald warrior stepped forward on Thoros's left. He grimaced, pointed at one of the approaching Mongols and hefted his shield. On his right, a tall man with a shock of red hair did the same, choosing his final victim. Up and down the line men chose their mark, tightened up their ranks, and waited for the inevitable.

The rumbling to the north became louder, but Thoros did his best to ignore it. There were thousands of men standing in the way to slow them down. Eventually, they would ride over him, but right now, the only enemies that mattered were those in front. All he had to do today was kill one man. That was it.

The ground shook beneath his feet. The roar of battle filled his ears. There was a resounding crunch, and a shockwave of sound rolled through both armies as they collided. The ring of steel became deafening, mixing with the shouts and bellowing of men at war. Curses and cries for mercy blended into one chaotic blast until it was all just meaningless noise.

The features of the riders became clearer. Thoros's final victim had a gash across his left brow and a red eye painted on his shield. The bald warrior beside him spat, rolled his neck and braced himself. Those with less experience copied the veteran, not knowing that it would make little difference. Many of them would die against an armed enemy on horseback. It would all come down to luck. Thoros was determined to survive the initial charge, so he lowered his head and braced for impact.

The horses' churning legs filled his vision. Thoros felt the thump on either side as shields overlapped with his to create a temporary wall. He tried to shout, to scare the beast, to worry its rider, but a lump of fear clogged his throat.

Something heavy smashed into his shield, numbed his arm. A blow to his shoulder spun him around and he tripped, landing face down in the mud. Fear of drowning made him flop over onto one side. His left arm was still useless, flapping about, but Thoros braced himself with the right and sat up. The wave of horses had passed over them, and he was somehow still alive.

"Help," begged the bald man, but Thoros could see it was already too late. Blood was leaking from his ears, and the wound in his head was grave. He gasped a few more times and then he was still.

As he stumbled to his feet, Thoros saw a few others doing the same. Each was amazed to find that he was still alive. Many were dead, or so badly injured that death was only heartbeats away. His own sword was gone, but Thoros found another and then started to trot forward. Pain jumped up and down his left arm as it slowly came back to life. His right leg was bleeding and his skull ached, but he wasn't done. That one man still had to die, and at least one more for his bald friend.

The charge had stopped, and now the Mongols were laying into men on either side. Finding an abandoned spear, Thoros picked it up and charged at the enemy from behind. He'd been aiming for the man's back, but the horse turned at the last second. The spear went into the man's side, punching through his ribs. With a scream of alarm, the horse reared, tipping its rider to the ground. All around him, Persian warriors rallied, pulling Mongols from their horses, stabbing and hacking until almost everyone was on the ground.

It didn't make sense. The enemy seemed outnumbered. The Persians were still winning. Right now, it didn't matter. Thoros still had a job to do. He stabbed one man with his sword, and when the blade became wedged, he picked up a fallen mace and shield.

His breathing was ragged. His eyes were watering, and trying to stand upright felt impossible. With shoulders on fire, Thoros brought the mace down on another man. Four dead. Now he just had to make it five. Then he could rest. Then it would be enough.

The man in front of Thoros was enormous. He was like something out of mythology, towering over everyone with legs like tree trunks. A warrior tried a clumsy attack, which the giant casually parried. With a roar, he split the man in half from shoulder to groin. Thoros charged at him from behind, but the giant heard him coming and spun about. A roaring sound filled Thoros's ears. The world shook. This was his final moment. The end he had fought so hard to avoid was finally here. He'd already had one close brush with death, but now she had come to collect that which was long overdue.

Time slowed, and Thoros watched in horror as the giant's arm went up and up. He raised the shield to block the coming impact, but a part of him knew it wouldn't make any difference. The giant would break his arm and shoulder, stamp on his head, and leave him to drown in the mud.

The giant's eyes widened with glee, his arm at its apex, but then he paused. Surprise washed across his face, and a second later, a sheet of blood. The top of the giant's head flew off and he toppled over dead.

Wave after wave of warriors on horseback flashed in front of Thoros. They ploughed into the enemy, hacking them down, driving them back. It took a while for Thoros to realise he was still alive. At first, he couldn't understand why. There were no warriors being held in reserve, and yet those engaging with the enemy were fresh-faced and eager for a fight. None of them were haggard or spattered with mud, blood and shit from hours of battle.

"We're saved," said someone on his left. "The Golden Horde has arrived!"

Despite the arrival of the Golden Horde, the battle raged for another hour.

Kaivon had hoped that their appearance would result in a swift and decisive victory. He expected that once it became clear Timur's forces couldn't win, he would surrender. However, since the beginning of Timur's campaign, few warriors under his command had experienced the bitter taste of defeat. There had been minor setbacks and a few skirmishes lost, but since the start of his campaign, Timur had never lost a major battle.

This absolute faith in their leader was what kept his men fighting for longer than they should. Not for a moment did they expect to lose. Even when Tokhtamysh's forces ploughed into them, cutting deep into their ranks. Even when Kaivon's forces rallied and, with both armies working together, began to squeeze Timur's warriors from either side.

Timur must have known what was happening, but for whatever reason, pride, arrogance or an inability to admit defeat, he never gave the order to surrender. Small groups threw down their weapons. However, it was not widespread, and in the heat of the battle, they were cut down without mercy. Kaivon tried to stop those nearest him from committing slaughter, but after everything they'd endured, few men would listen.

Piece by piece, Timur's army collapsed. Already weary after a long fight, warriors crumbled when suddenly faced with energetic opponents. Whole units turned and ran. Some were ridden down and others died with arrows in their back. Kaivon expected a few would get away, but not enough that they would be a problem.

A short distance away to Kaivon's left, a group of Mongol warriors tried to run at him. As before, many times during the battle, other men stepped forward to obstruct the enemy. Kaivon recognised some of the warriors, but there was a mix of veterans and young faces. None of them looked to Kaivon for orders, but all protected him at any cost. Twice already, young warriors had stepped in the way of a weapon that was meant for him. Sadly, both had died, but neither one had cried or begged at the end. Oddly, they seemed to be at peace. Kaivon suspected Esme's hand in keeping him safe, but he couldn't prove it.

"We have him," said King David. Although his face was bloody and spattered with mud, and his armour damaged in a few places, he seemed in good spirits. "It's not my blood," he said, wiping his armour.

"Then, it's over?" said Bohemond. He was limping and had a nasty gash on one cheek. If it scarred, then perhaps he would no longer be called The Fair. "Praise God," he murmured.

"Everyone must see him," said Kaivon. Some of Timur's men would keep fighting. They needed to see that he was in captivity. They needed to understand that the battle, and the war, was truly over. "Take him up there," said Kaivon, pointing to a nearby rise. The elevated position would give him a good view of the battlefield.

Kaivon and the other senior officers made their way to the ridge. He was pleased to see that all of them had survived, although most had at least one minor wound. It took a while, but eventually Timur was dragged before them by three men. Someone had placed a bag over his head and tied Timur's hands behind his back.

This was the first time that Kaivon had seen Timur in person. His impression had been of a man with intellect that towered above others. On reflection, Kaivon wondered if his image of the warlord had been coloured by the time he'd spent with Hulagu and his siblings. All of them had been physically large men, with suitably big appetites and reputations.

Kaivon gestured for Timur's bonds to be cut and the bag removed. When they were finally face to face, Kaivon found that he was disappointed. Although tall, Timur was skinny, with a narrow face and rather ordinary features. Two fingers were missing on his right hand and his right leg was unusually bent. It was only when their eyes met that Kaivon caught a glimmer of the self-titled Sword of Islam. The man whose vision rivalled that of Genghis Khan, and whose rise to power had been swift and brutal.

Most of the others stared at him with horror and revulsion. They hated what he had done, but it was clear that some of them admired and feared him.

"General, he cannot be allowed to live," said Tokhtamysh, moving to stand beside the others. This was something that Kaivon had discussed with Esme. On the nights when they had dared to dream that the war ended in victory, they had made plans for what came next. That which had previously seemed so far away was suddenly here.

"This is not over." Even in defeat, Timur was defiant. He sneered at them, as if they were beneath him, and that this was only a momentary inconvenience. Kaivon remembered Hulagu exhibiting the same level of arrogance, even in his cell.

Kaivon struck Timur across the face, mostly because he could, but also to see how the other man reacted. As blood welled from his split lip, Timur reeled back, possibly to spit blood or hurl curses at them. Using a closed fist, Kaivon hammered it into the warlord's face again, breaking his nose. Timur's weakened right leg gave way and he fell to the ground. He remained genuinely surprised that this was his fate.

As Kaivon's foot pressed down on Timur's throat, he made sure the others were watching.

"Look closely at him. He is just a man, greedy and arrogant, with an inflated ego. He is no different from Hulagu and others like him. Tyrants who believe they are great men, destined to rule, but they are only flesh and blood. There is nothing divine about them." Kaivon spoke calmly, but the rage bubbling underneath was difficult to control. More than anything, he wanted to drive down his heel and end Timur's life. When the warlord's face went from red to purple, it was a struggle to ease back, but he did, allowing Timur some air.

"He is not someone to be admired. If he was given a chance, he would slaughter every single one of you and burn your nations to the ground." Kaivon thought it was better for them to hate Timur than fear or even admire him. In truth, he was not worthy of their thoughts at all, but even dead men cast long shadows in the mind. He knew some of his senior officers still feared Hulagu. He did not want the same for Timur.

Before Timur had a chance to speak again, Kaivon grabbed him by the collar and hoisted him upright. The rocky ledge they stood upon was twenty feet above the valley floor. Kaivon marched Timur to the edge until his toes were dangling off the side. He instinctively tried to move backwards, but Kaivon held him in place, precariously balanced on the edge.

Any remaining fighting on the battlefield slowed and then stopped. Any remaining Mongol warriors wondering about the fate of their leader now had a clear answer. Tokhtamysh was pushing for decisive action against Timur, while others were suggesting a delay in his execution so that they could squeeze him for information. Kaivon was only half listening. In truth, he was watching the warriors below. They also had created extensive mythology around the man that now dangled over the precipice.

Timur had achieved his position by manipulating religious beliefs, claiming titles and status by marrying the right people, then extorting his new family for favours and wealth. He had slaughtered entire cities and desecrated countless people to establish an aura of fear in the minds of his enemies. All of it was a shadow play. A puppet show for different groups in order to manipulate them to his own ends.

"Do you even believe anything you said?" muttered Kaivon, shaking Timur. His feet scrambled on the edge and the warlord nearly fell, but Kaivon kept him upright. Perhaps somewhere in the dark recesses of Timur's mind, beneath all of the games, he had a vision of the future. Not for a single moment did Kaivon imagine Timur's dream was one that involved bringing peace to the world.

The eyes of every warrior rested on Kaivon. He could feel them like a tangible weight. Previously, he would have hated such attention, but today it was necessary. Not that they remember him, or his name, only what happened.

Timur's eyes bulged in surprise as the sword burst from the centre of his chest. With grim determination Kaivon pressed his blade deeper into Timur's back, forcing more steel through his enemy's torso. Letting go of the warlord's clothes, Kaivon held him upright with the sword. The blade had snagged on Timur's ribcage, and now he danced like a puppet with cut strings, choking and gagging on his own blood. His feet jerked, and one hand feebly pawed at the sword, trying to dislodge it.

Despite his intentions to prolong the moment, to make sure that every single warrior saw Timur die on this day, the weight of his slumping body was too much. Kaivon let go of his sword and everyone watched as Timur's body tumbled down the rocky slope, bounced a few times and then came to rest on the ground below. The blade remained in his chest, blood pooled beneath his body and his eyes remained open.

There would be no more talk of destiny or dreams of conquering the world and creating one all-encompassing nation. Some dreams were actually nightmares, and Kaivon thought it right that talk of such things should die along with those who had birthed them.

CHAPTER 29
Temujin

The city of Tabriz looked no different from the top of the spire of the Christian Church. Temujin had been hoping for something. A fresh perspective on the streets and the people below. A revelation that would open something in his mind, but nothing was forthcoming. Of late, whenever Temujin managed to embrace the Eternal Fire, the serenity and the insight it normally brought him was fleeting. Holding on to the Fire, and the gifts it provided, remained a constant challenge. It had been like this for some time, but he couldn't pinpoint when it had begun. Temujin didn't know if it was because he'd been relying on it too often to suppress powerful emotions surging within, or because Maryam had tampered with his mind. Either way, it remained a struggle, which did not bode well for what lay ahead.

The narrow walkway around the spire was not designed for spectators to enjoy the view. In truth, it was little more than two wooden boards with a short guardrail around all four sides. It was only there so that whoever climbed the narrow stairs had space to work on the bell. A thick, knotted rope descended to the ground below where a nervous priest waited. As Khan, they could not refuse his request to climb the tower, but his presence inside the church made everyone anxious. Temujin didn't need his powers to realise that. It was obvious from the hand-wringing, obsequious bowing and strained smiles everyone offered him. They had done the same to his father.

Temujin laughed. His thoughts always seemed to come back to him. Hulagu was dead and buried, but still he remained a large and almost constant presence. Temujin wondered if this was one of the reasons Katarina hated her father so much. Whatever he was feeling, it would surely pale in comparison to her situation. She had been living in the shadow of her father for centuries, and even worse, he was still alive.

As if she'd heard his thoughts, Temujin felt a disturbance in the air. A moment later, Katarina Skimmed into view. She glanced at their surroundings, searching for guards or perhaps archers on rooftops, in case this was a trap. Finding nothing untoward, she visibly relaxed.

"Why are you here?" asked Temujin, his gaze lingering on a mosque that was under construction. It was far larger than any of those that currently existed in the city.

For a long time, Katarina said nothing, but Temujin was content to wait for an answer. Part of him liked to imagine that she'd waited this long before coming to see him because she'd had been mourning the loss of her true family, Eraj and Teague. However, given what Teague had said about the Cynic at the end, and her constant agitation in his presence, he doubted it was that. The truth was probably something far simpler.

In a hundred years, everyone currently alive in the world would be dead. Their children and other descendants would have taken their place, living in their homes, carrying out their roles. The only exceptions to this would be him, and Melchior.

Katarina was lonely, and she needed him.

As a Kozan, they were no longer human, but there were some aspects of humanity that could never be fully erased. The need for companionship being one.

Temujin now understood why it was pointless to make friends with anyone that was not one of them. For the span of a human's lifetime, their companionship and love would ease the isolation, but the pain of losing them would be severe. To endure that countless times would not only be torture, seemingly without end, but he thought it would drive a person mad.

"Have you ever lived apart from humanity?" he asked, breaking the silence that hung between them. He'd intended to wait for her to speak first, but he was genuinely curious about the answer.

"For a time, when I was a girl," said Katarina, watching a bird drift by overhead. "When he's not out in the world, my father lives in such a fashion. Although, he is still surrounded by servants. He hasn't done anything for himself in centuries."

"You didn't enjoy it?" said Temujin, trying to steer Katarina away from another angry spiral that involved Melchior.

"For many years, I didn't know it wasn't normal. I thought everyone lived as we did. There was much my father kept from me." For Katarina's anger to remain so prominent after all this time, Temujin idly wondered what those things might be.

"And now, only three of our kind remain," he said. To the west of the city, he spied dark grey clouds that promised a powerful storm.

"Yes, which is why I have come to beg an alliance with you." Katarina sounded sincere, which came as a surprise. It must have cost her greatly to make such a request, but given all that she'd done, Temujin had no sympathy.

"No trickery this time? Drawing me into a dream, or some kind of trance between waking and sleep?" he snarled, angry at what she and Eraj had done.

"No," said Katarina holding up her hands towards him, exposing her wrists. "No tricks, no games, no threats or promises. Although I am tired of the endless war, I never thought it would come to this. I didn't believe that everyone would be dead, except for you and I, and my father," she added bitterly.

"If we were to form an alliance," he said, making it clear from his tone of voice that it was only one possibility, "what would you want to do going forward?"

"To rest and be free."

Temujin raised an eyebrow, knowing there was more. "And then?"

Katarina shrugged, frowning at the oncoming storm. "We found you. In time, there will be others."

A cold prickle ran down Temujin's spine. "Others. What do you mean?"

"It could take twenty or a hundred years, but eventually, somewhere in the world, another Kozan will be born. If we can find the child before something unpleasant happens, or before they die of old age, we can recruit them. We can create a new order."

"Only this time, you would be unopposed by those who support Order." Temujin spoke in a neutral tone, but Katarina was no fool.

"I know you do not believe in the path of Chaos. So it would be up to you and I to choose when, and if, we should interfere with the natural flow of human events," said Katarina. "It would be different this time," she promised.

With a sigh, Temujin leaned on the fragile wooden rail that circled the bell tower. Upon the streets below, people went about their day as normal, completely oblivious of what the two beings above were discussing and how it would impact humanity's future. The Kozan had undoubtedly played a significant role in all major events up to this point in history. It made Temujin wonder how different the world would have been if the Kozan had not interfered.

"Even if I were to agree, and I'm not saying I do," he said carefully, "there is still one rather large obstacle standing in the way."

Katarina grimaced. "I've been giving that some thought. I believe, if I appeal to him as a father, and request a meeting in private, I can lure him into a trap."

"Use his love for you as a weapon?" said Temujin.

"Exactly!" she said, delighted that he understood.

Temujin didn't even think about it. He just shoved Katarina over the railing.

With a startled yelp she fell, but halfway towards the ground, she disappeared into thin air. Her latest revelation had stirred deep emotions inside him, but Temujin managed to smother them long enough to find a moment of serenity. As the calm of the Eternal Fire filled his being, he Skimmed west, away from the city.

The world turned into a blur, but he kept moving, putting some distance between him and Tabriz. In the city, there would be too many places for Katarina to hide. This had to be done in the open. Seven miles to the west, Temujin stopped. He had landed in the heart of a lush green valley, on the edge of a forest. A storm was raging, and heavy wind whipped the trees about, their branches casting rain into his face. After a few seconds, he was soaked through, but he ignored it as best he could.

Keeping his breathing slow and even, Temujin waited.

It didn't take Katarina long to find him. She appeared out of thin air, and as expected, she was furious. How she managed to hold on to the Eternal Fire was a mystery. If there was a skin of calm over the rage she was displaying, it had to be thin and tenuous.

"Even your father has lines he will not cross," said Temujin, focusing on maintaining his calm demeanour. "But you are without any limits. That doesn't make you powerful or special or ruthless. It means you are weak, and less than nothing."

"You are a child," hissed Katarina, stalking towards him. "You have no concept of what it means to be a Kozan. You think my father is a good man? You cannot imagine the things he has done over the centuries."

The wind whipped her hair about, blowing it into her face. Using both hands, she quickly gathered up the loose strands, tying them together with a leather bracelet from her wrist. Every movement was jerky and stiff. Her whole body was seething with anger that was barely held in check.

"If you had seen the mountains of bodies, you would want him dead as well."

"Perhaps," said Temujin. "But that is not the reason you walked away from him. Lie to me all you want, but do not lie to yourself."

Katarina's grip on the Eternal Fire evaporated as she laughed. It was a bitter sound, devoid of any real mirth. "You would attempt to lecture me about my father? What about yours?"

Temujin ignored her question, not wanting to get dragged into an argument. "Of all the gifts the Eternal Fire grants us, not once have you spoken about the insight it gives us into other people."

Katarina crept closer, but her voice remained loud to combat the sound of the storm. "What are you talking about?"

"I may not have lived for as many years as you, but I see a great deal," he said. "And I know the real reason that you turned your back on your father."

Even without a grip on her power, Katarina was terrifying. Here was a woman who had lived through countless centuries. The knowledge she must have accumulated in so many lifetimes was what troubled him the most. If she had dedicated a small portion of her time to fighting with weapons or martial arts, she would know of a hundred ways to kill him.

With uncanny speed, Katarina lunged at him. Temujin instinctively raised his arms, but she only gripped him by the shoulders. Using both hands, digging her fingers into his skin, she held him in place.

"You don't understand anything," she snarled.

"I know that humans are not meant to live for centuries," said Temujin, trying not to wince. The pain was remote, as if it belonged to someone else, but with every passing second it hurt a little more. If this continued for too long, it would be difficult for Temujin to maintain his focus. It almost didn't matter what he said, only that she stayed emotional and off-balance. Some of what he'd said must have been close to the mark, as Katarina still wasn't thinking clearly.

"When did it happen? How old were you before you realised you'd stopped growing?" he asked.

"I will kill you," promised Katarina, lashing out with a fist. Temujin moved, but her knuckles still caught him in the side of the head. One of his ears began to ring, transforming the wailing of the storm into a chorus of spectral voices. With both arms Temujin shoved her away from him, breaking her grip. Katarina stumbled back but didn't fall to the ground. Her face was churning with a tangle of emotions. Her hands bunched up into fists and her shoulders were hunched. This pain was old and deep. Drawing it to the surface was tearing her apart.

"Even now, you remain a version of that child who was angry at her father," he said. "I doubt if you ever truly believed in Chaos. I think you only did it to spite him."

Temujin didn't even feel the ripple of energy. Melchior simply appeared, walking out of the trees to their left.

"What are you doing?" shouted Melchior, his voice carrying over the wind. He addressed them both, but most of his attention was on Katarina.

"Do not project your own issues upon me," said Katarina, jabbing a finger towards Temujin. Her voice was icy and cool, which was a bad sign. He needed her to stay angry.

"Then tell him of your plan," said Temujin, gesturing at Melchior. "Tell him how you intended to lure him in, so that we might murder him together?"

Seething rage emanated from every line of Katarina's body. Her face was flushed and her hands began to shake. If he hadn't been struggling to remain emotionally detached, Temujin would have grinned.

The storm moved closer, bringing with it fiercer winds, but none of them attempted to travel elsewhere. This meeting between father and daughter was long overdue, and bad weather was not going to stop it.

"All my life, I have cherished only two people," said Melchior, moving towards Katarina. Temujin edged closer so that he could hear their conversation. They stood in a loose triangle within arm's reach of one another, and yet, in so many ways, the three of them could not have been further apart. "Your mother and you."

"You would say anything," snarled Katarina. In that moment, standing opposite her father, she had never seemed more child-like. In Temujin's mind, it was as if Melchior had grown to the point of towering over her from a great height.

Melchior continued to beseech his daughter in an attempt to make her understand his choices while Katarina squirmed. Temujin was only half listening. Moving slowly and carefully, using minute hand gestures in the hope of going unnoticed, he pulled together a Rigour.

"What are you doing?" said Melchior, turning to face Temujin.

Melchior was a second too slow to act. The egg-shaped bubble snapped into place, enveloping them all. Beyond the confines of the Rigour, the world had turned into a hazy blur, and all sounds were transformed. The howling wind became the mournful cry of some horrific beast. The hammering rain became the repetitive thump of many feet on the ground, as if an army was on the march.

"Stop this, Temujin," said Katarina. "Before it kills you."

The strain of holding the Rigour in place was worse than anything he'd experienced before. It had never been easy, but today it was different. Deep inside Temujin's chest, there was a dull ache like a strained muscle, but this was centred around his heart. Sweat coated his skin, Temujin's breathing was ragged and he stumbled to one knee. In spite of this, he continued to feed energy into the net. Even though he hadn't attempted to move the Rigour, Temujin sensed it beginning to fray around the edges.

"Let go!" warned Melchior. He grabbed Temujin by the shoulders, perhaps intending to shake him. Before he could act, something else caught his attention. Melchior's fingers loosed and his head whipped around.

In the dark, beyond the confines of the Rigour, something was stirring beneath the trees. A roughly man-shaped creature shambled into view. It should have been a blur, like everything else outside the bubble, but Temujin could see it clearly. The face without a mouth. The swirling red pits for eyes. On their right, another figure appeared out of the gloom. It was like the first, only taller, and its hands were too large for its narrow body. A loud huffing sound announced the arrival of a third Servant of Time, only this one was riding one of the monstrous beasts. Like vultures drawn to the carcass of a dead animal, more and more Servants swarmed around them.

"What have you done?" said Melchior. If he achieved inner calm, it would be possible for Melchior to use his powers, but not while they were within Temujin's Rigour. If Melchior attempted to rip his way out, the repercussions would be far-reaching and likely deadly for everyone.

"Temujin," said Katarina, trying to appear calm. "Just let go. The pain will stop and they will be gone."

The dull ache was getting worse. It felt as if it was spreading, stretching down towards his hips and up to his throat. Six points of pain drilled their way into the crown of Temujin's skull. His ribs creaked with every breath and he felt dizzy and off-balance.

Energy flowed around the net he'd created, shielding them from the terrors that now lurked nearby. Still down on one knee, Temujin raised his head, staring at the monstrous faces outside the Rigour. He could not fathom what had created such a being or even begin to understand them, and yet he now relied on their anger.

Whether it was because the three remaining Kozan were in one location, or because there were so many Servants together, Temujin thought he could hear them speaking. At first their words were muffled, but soon the repeated message penetrated the pain gripping his body.

"Temujin," said Katarina. Her voice was so strained he looked to where she was pointing. One of the Servants had its hands pressed against the edges of the Rigour. Its spindly arms were corded with tight muscle, but he immediately felt the strain when it tried to force its way inside. Something must have clubbed Temujin on the side of the head, as he found he was suddenly lying on his back. But when he looked around, both Melchior and Katarina were facing outward, their eyes on the swarm of Servants.

The blackness on the edges of his vision became more pronounced. One section of the Rigour started to come apart. The fraying was getting worse, only this time, he did nothing to try and repair it. The churning chorus of voices in his head became louder. The Servants became more animated, and now several of them were trying to break the Rigour, as if cracking open an egg. Only one of them was standing perfectly still. With its head cocked to one side, it seemed to be listening to something far away, and yet Temujin instinctively knew it was watching him.

"Mercy," whispered Katarina, but Temujin didn't know to whom she was praying.

It was only when the patient Servant reached inside the Rigour, gripping Katarina by the upper arm, that Temujin realised it had been properly breached. Howling in terror, she tried to pull away, but its vice-like grip would not be broken. The skin on Katarina's arm began to turn grey, and thin green tendrils spread out beneath the surface of her flesh.

The fissure in the Rigour was only wide enough for one Servant, and despite the frantic clawing of the others, they couldn't fight their way inside. Temujin continued to trickle energy into the remaining points on the web, but he didn't try to repair the hole. Using her full weight, Katarina leaned backwards, trying to force the Servant to let go, but it wouldn't relent. Its upper body was inside the Rigour, but its hips and legs remained outside. With a surge of uncanny strength, it dragged Katarina towards it. As her feet skidded across the muddy ground, she wailed in despair.

Melchior rushed to his daughter's aid, but there was little he could do except add his weight to hers. A dreadful tug of war began, with Melchior pulling on one arm and the Servant of Time on the other. Katarina screamed in pain at being pulled in two directions, but also from the continual spread of the poison. It moved down her forearm, turning the skin into a marbled grey as it went, and also crept up towards her neck. Any visible veins turned black, and Temujin could only imagine what it was doing beneath the surface.

Scrambling like a pack of starving wild dogs, the Servants continued to pound on the Rigour while more tore at the hole, desperate to get inside and feast.

As the poison enveloped her throat, Katarina's agony became a silent struggle, but her eyes still bulged with pain and fear. Temujin could see that Melchior was talking, but the blood rushing Temujin's ears was so loud that he couldn't hear the words. The swelling ache in his chest had reached a level he'd not experienced before. A thousand needles seemed to pierce his skin simultaneously. Temujin felt something trickling from his nose and his ears. This agony could not last. It was the end for all of them.

Two Servants added their weight to the one that was gripping Katarina. Melchior didn't stand a chance against their combined efforts. With a final heave, they tore Katarina from Melchior's grip. The three Servants tumbled backwards into a heap, but Katarina was now outside the Rigour beside them.

The horde descended upon her. Most of what they did was obscured from sight, but Temujin saw her flailing limbs as they tore at her flesh. The Servants dipped their hands through her skin as if it were water, but instead of blood, they emerged wreathed in the golden light of memory and time. Thrashing about, Katarina tried to free herself, but they had pinned her to the ground. There was no escape.

But not all of the Servants were feasting upon her. Two others were now pawing at the gap in the Rigour. Temujin didn't have the energy or concentration to repair the fraying points of energy. The moment before it collapsed, one of the other Servants managed to step inside. It swiped a hand at Melchior, merely grazing his side, but it was enough to make the Kozan cry out as if he'd been stabbed.

Temujin's focus shattered. The Rigour came apart, and mercifully, the Servants and whatever remained of Katarina disappeared from view. Until that moment, Temujin thought he knew pain, but without a shield of serenity, he suffered the full weight of his injuries. His jaw stretched wide in a silent scream. His eyes scrunched shut and every part of his body felt as if it was being consumed by fire. It raced down his nerves, tore the flesh from his bones and drove steel needles deep into his brain. Carried away on a wave of torment, Temujin lost all awareness of the world around him. He didn't care about his fate, or that of Melchior or Katarina. He only wanted the pain to stop.

Eventually, after an unknown period of time, the torture ebbed and slowed. The simple process of breathing became the only thing that mattered. Tremors washed over him, making his limbs thrash as if he was inflicted with palsy. A stream of tears ran from his eyes, but they eventually dried long enough for him to see his surroundings.

At some point, the eye of the storm had passed. All that remained was a gentle wind, which tugged at Temujin's blood-stained robe. There was nothing to show what had happened aside from a few footprints in the mud left by him and the others. There were no markings in the world to show any evidence of the Servants of Time, and nothing remained of Katarina. Not a scrap of clothing or a drop of blood. She was dead.

Temujin expected to see Melchior, waiting for him to regain consciousness, but there was no sign of the Kozan. Even so, Temujin knew that he wasn't dead, and that this was not the last time he would see the first Magi.

CHAPTER 30
Kokochin

As Kokochin descended another narrow flight of stairs, going deeper underground, she began to understand why the entrance to the Necropolis had been so difficult to locate.

There was a vast labyrinth of tunnels and grottos beneath Vatican City. However, due to landslides, earthquakes and erosion, many promising tunnels had collapsed. Finding the right one was what had taken criminals years of exploration and patience.

Angelo had led their party to a narrow house whose tenant owed him a favour. They wisely stayed out of sight, but Kokochin heard the scrape of feet coming from upstairs. It was safer that way. Whatever the owner didn't see could not be dragged out of them if they were questioned by city authorities.

The crime boss walked ahead of Layla, Luca, Kokochin and a twitchy man named Sesto. He had the bearing of a thief and endlessly searched his surroundings, as if looking for a way out. Kokochin also thought that it was a reaction to being uncomfortable with tight spaces. However, he was the one who had found the path into the Vatican. Sesto's greed, or perhaps his debt to Angelo, must have been significant for it to overcome his concerns about being underground.

"There's no air down here," whispered Sesto, gulping loudly.

"We're only about fifteen feet beneath the city," said Angelo, "Now, be silent. Someone might hear."

The tunnel was narrow enough that Kokochin's shoulders brushed the walls on either side. It was crudely fashioned from slabs of ancient stone whose age she couldn't begin to determine. Numerous repairs had recently been made, for which she was grateful, given how many other tunnels had collapsed. Wooden frames had been used to shore up the roof where it was sagging, and metal poles braced the walls where they tilted inwards. On occasion, they had to duck under or even crawl around support beams before they could stand up again. It was slow, dusty and awkward for everyone, particularly Luca who was broader than everyone else. But he bore it stoically and never once complained, unlike Sesto who grumbled continuously.

Angelo carried a lantern at the front of the group, and at the rear Luca held another. The group existed in a warm pool of light, but on either side, there was nothing. Just black space. Occasionally, Kokochin saw a glimmer of light through a crack in a wall or even the ceiling. Whispers of voices and snatches of conversations drifted in, reminding her how close they were to other people.

The tunnel sloped downwards, but far gentler than she had expected. There were several openings on either side, but Angelo didn't hesitate in choosing a path. Eventually, after perhaps an hour of walking, they reached another crude set of stairs that spiralled down into the dark. There was so little room that even Kokochin had to lower her head or risk scraping her scalp. The air had steadily grown warmer as they descended until all of them were sweating. As they paused to catch their breath, she realised the sounds from the city had faded. Kokochin had been so focused on placing her feet, she hadn't noticed when it had happened. The silence was unbroken and deafening.

At the bottom of the stairs was a small crossroads. All four tunnels appeared identical, but even this far underground, there was an accumulation of dust and debris. Footsteps in the dirt showed two of the tunnels had been explored while one had barely been touched.

While the others took a moment to drink some water, Sesto paced back and forth.

"How long will it take to get there?" said Layla.

"Maybe an hour. Could be more," said Sesto, which wasn't very helpful.

It was difficult to judge the passage of time, but Kokochin thought they had been walking for a couple of hours. That meant it was still before midnight. They had to get into the Vatican itself before dawn, then find a safe place to hide until the Pope's meeting with the Mongol ambassador. If she didn't think about it for too long, it didn't sound too difficult.

"One thing at a time," said Layla, brushing the back of Kokochin's hand.

Kokochin forced a few deep breaths and tried not to hunch her shoulders.

"This is as far as I go. I have business elsewhere," said Angelo, giving them a tight smile. "The rest is up to you."

"Very well," said Kokochin. "Thank you, for everything." She should have said more, about using his grief to get what she wanted, but the words caught in her throat.

Angelo pulled Luca to one side, but there was no real privacy, so she overheard every word.

"Are you sure you want to go with them?" asked the crime boss.

"Yes. I must do this," said Luca.

Angelo's sigh echoed down the empty tunnels. "As you wish. May God watch over you," he said, briefly gripping the big man's arm. "Look after them, Sesto, and remember your debt to me is not yet paid."

The thief bobbed his head and offered an oily smile. Kokochin believed he would do as he was told for selfish reasons, not because he cared about the Pope or their well-being. Angelo's reach was significant, and Sesto knew that if he abandoned them in the labyrinth, he wouldn't live for very long. Taking his lantern with him, Angelo turned down a different tunnel and disappeared into the dark.

Opening his pack, Sesto took out a shuttered lantern, which he lit with care. It created a pool of light in front of him but nowhere else, making it the perfect tool of a thief.

"There will be things you see in the darkness," he said, pointing down one of the gloomy tunnels. "They will be statues and doorways, shadows that look like faces. The wind will find a way inside as well, so do not trust your ears. Focus on the light."

"We're ready," said Layla, shouldering her pack.

Sesto set off at a brisk pace. Kokochin wondered how many times he'd come down here. Perhaps spending so much time alone in the dark was what had made him so twitchy. Perhaps he wasn't always looking for a way out, but for things he'd glimpsed in the dark.

At first, the tunnels were plain and identical, with bare stone walls and no decoration. All of them were crudely fashioned with a gently sloping arch at the top. Kokochin saw numerous chisel marks from where they'd been carved out of the rock. She was alarmed to see cracks running through some of the walls, but they didn't linger, so her fear of them collapsing faded.

A short time later, the tunnels began to change. They passed through a low doorway with no door attached. The top of the frame bore a huge slab of grey rock, and the walls were made from uniform stone bricks. Beyond the doorway was a chamber with an arched roof fifteen feet high. Different sections had been painted ochre, yellow, and blue, although age and damage had erased some areas. The walls were covered with a range of different sized alcoves, all of them bearing plaques with writing she couldn't decipher. Some of the alcoves held pottery jugs, others urns, wide ceramic bowls and what resembled drinking vessels. On the floor was a partially intact mosaic with a repeating pattern of flowers and birds. She had expected a gloomy and cramped tomb, but Kokochin was pleasantly surprised by the size and the colours.

There were two other ways out of the chamber, and Sesto turned right, leading them between raised biers that were cracked and broken. The lids of several had been moved aside, and inside Kokochin glimpsed bones and a few scraps of cloth.

"Graverobbers scraped this place clean," said Sesto.

Kokochin thought he wasn't peeved because of what had been done, but that he'd not found the treasure first.

"Monstrous," said Luca.

A low doorway took them into another chamber, smaller than the first but no less packed with effigies to the dead. Paintings of birds, trees and other small animals decorated the walls. Pillars outlined more alcoves, some barely wide enough to reach inside, while others were as tall as doorways.

Watching their feet for trip-hazards, they crept through room after room. It would be the work of several lifetimes to catalogue all of the dead that had been interred. Finally, they came to a small chamber that led to a narrow corridor, but on either side, and even on another tier above Kokochin's head, she saw more alcoves. It came as a surprise when Sesto led them to what appeared to be a dead-end and a solid brick wall. On their left was a six-foot bier adorned with a carved stone plaque that detailed the occupant.

"What's this?" said Layla, reaching for a dagger, but Kokochin put a restraining hand on her arm. Sesto was busy scratching at the wall and hadn't noticed the threat to his life.

"It's down here," he muttered. "Luca, can you help?"

The big man passed over his lantern and then knelt down beside Sesto. Working together, they gripped the side of the pedestal and heaved backwards. It gradually slid to one side, revealing a small opening to another chamber. Someone had patiently chiselled away the stones to create a crawlspace. Sesto took his lantern and shuffled through first on elbows and knees. Light blossomed on the opening as he redirected the beam from the lantern. Kokochin followed him and found herself in a narrow chamber that held only one grave. Sesto helped her up, but he put a finger to his lips before turning to assist the others. The underground room was small, but the level of detail far exceeded anything she'd previously seen. There was a marble statue of a man against one wall, upon which was a grand painting. It showed a vast crowd of people, all of them focused on a figure dressed in white in the distance. The bearded man stood above the rest with his arms raised, as if blessing them or speaking with passion.

When the others had squeezed through, Sesto gathered everyone together. In a huddle, with the light pointed at the floor, he spoke in a low voice.

"These are the tombs of holy men," he whispered. "Priests, martyrs and saints. There are no guards until we reach the gate, but sounds carry a great distance. Place your feet with care."

Kokochin thought the tombs were newer than those they'd passed through, and each one was richly decorated to celebrate one occupant, from the materials used to the amount of detail on the walls and even the ceiling.

A single corridor, with rooms on either side, curved slowly upwards. She didn't notice at first, but at some point, the shadows peeled back a little. Pools of absolute black became grey, and she could see a little more easily. Light from outside was filtering in from up ahead, but it was still early in the morning. Dawn was approaching, but hopefully it was still a few hours away.

A final set of stairs led to a massive iron gate with a sturdy lock. Sesto took out a set of metal tools, which he used to probe the lock. Beyond the gate, the path continued upwards and then curved out of sight. If someone came around the corner, they would be in serious trouble. A cold prickle ran down Kokochin's spine.

"What's taking so long?" said Layla. All of them were feeling the pressure. They had already come so far, and yet the level of danger was only going to increase from this point forward. The lock dropped with a loud thunk, which echoed off the stone walls. Sesto gripped the gate, and with slow, careful movements to avoid it squeaking, he eased it open.

Layla went first, dashing ahead to the corner to keep watch. She peered around and then waved for the others to join her. Kokochin and Luca followed, but when she looked for Sesto, she found he had remained behind.

"What are you doing?" she asked as he closed the gate with him on the other side. With a final twist of his tools, the lock dropped back into place. Luca lunged at him through the bars but Sesto stepped back out of reach.

"Angelo will kill you for this," promised the big man.

"No, he will not. My job was to get you in," said Sesto, dry washing his hands. "This is as far as I go. I wish you good luck."

Luca tried to force the lock, but it wouldn't move. "Leave it," said Kokochin. "If we survive, we wouldn't be going back through the catacombs. Angelo will deal with him."

"We're better off without him," said Layla, coming to join them. "Around the corner is another set of stairs. Hopefully there isn't another gate, but I heard someone moving about."

At the top of the stairs was an empty corridor, which they ignored. They could hear people at the far end and didn't want to run into someone this early. Instead they took the stairs up towards the surface. Judging by the smells, they were passing through what had to be a level full of prisoners, as the stench of unwashed bodies was horrific. The next level had only a series of heavy black iron doors, but Kokochin heard whimpering coming from behind more than one. Someone else was repeating a litany, promising to confess if only the pain would stop.

On the next level up, they found a guard dozing at his post. Kokochin didn't recognise his uniform, but Luca seemed familiar with it. Layla went first, snuck up behind the guard and clamped a hand over his nose and mouth. At the same time, she got him in a chokehold with both forearms. He thrashed about, but the fight quickly went out of him. Kokochin could see she was being careful not to kill him. After all, he was only doing his job, and they couldn't suspect everyone of working with the Assassin.

"We should hide him somewhere," said Layla once the guard was unconscious.

"Wait," said Luca, checking his shoe size against the guard. "If I lead you both, it will be slightly less suspicious," he said, starting to undress.

They stashed the semi-naked man in a storage room after binding his hands and gagging him with a piece of cloth. With a bit of effort, he would be able to break free, but it would take him a few hours.

The guard's uniform was tight across Luca's shoulders and chest, but he still managed to look the part. With Luca marching boldly at the front, and the others trailing behind with downcast eyes, it was a thin veneer that would quickly unravel under scrutiny. However, it was better than nothing, and time was short. Moving quietly and ducking into rooms when they heard anyone approaching, they avoided contact with other people.

Finally, they reached the ground level. There weren't many guards, but there were plenty of servants. The kitchen wasn't far away, as Kokochin could hear the rattle of pans and there was an array of tantalising smells. Peering at the sky through an open door, she guessed it was still an hour until dawn.

"We need to find somewhere to hide," she said. It was only going to get busier, and moving around would become almost impossible. If discovered, they would be thrown into a cell before being given a chance to explain, and then all of this would have been for nothing.

Luca was studying the surrounding buildings through the doorway, trying to orientate himself. "We need to get in there," he said, pointing at a building just across from them.

Walking right behind Luca meant he functioned as a shield for anyone approaching from the opposite direction. Kokochin kept her head down, letting her hair obscure her features. She sensed people moving around, passing in and out of other buildings, but she never turned her head to investigate. Approaching the next building, there was no guard at the door, and Luca went inside as if he belonged and did this every day.

They managed to make it down two corridors before Luca hissed and jerked one hand behind him as a warning. While she and Layla ducked into the nearest room, Luca strode ahead, calling out to someone. Kokochin found herself in a storage room, piled high with bed linen, cushions and brightly coloured blankets. Leaving the door slightly ajar, she listened to Luca conversing. Layla held a dagger in readiness, but Kokochin hoped it wouldn't come to that. Luca said something and another man laughed. She couldn't follow what they were saying, but the tone of the conversation seemed gentle. Still chuckling, she heard Luca approaching, moving down the corridor towards them.

"My friend gave me some directions. Quickly, get changed. I will stand guard."

With Luca in the corridor outside, they changed into the elaborate finery they'd been carrying in their packs. The silk gown was the kind of thing Kokochin had worn for years, but now it felt slightly odd. She applied her make-up first, before attempting to put some on Layla.

"Don't bother," she said. "We don't have time. Besides, no one will be looking at me."

When she re-emerged into the corridor, Kokochin made sure to stand upright and lift her chin, even going so far as to imitate Guyuk's haughty expression. Layla trailed behind in a plain dress as her maidservant.

Luca led them up several flights of stairs before they emerged onto a richly appointed corridor. The tiled floor gleamed with polish, and the arched ceiling was covered with a majestic fresco. Lining the walls were paintings from across the world of a variety of styles, no doubt gifts bequeathed to the Church. The air smelled of incense, and at regular intervals along the corridor she passed a different kind of guard. Their uniforms were brightly coloured and almost comical, but there was nothing funny about their piercing gazes or gleaming pikes. Ignoring the flutter in her chest, Kokochin followed Luca, doing her best to pretend that the guards, and everyone else, were beneath her.

Luca had a more terse conversation with the guard, but eventually he relented and let them proceed.

"This way, Lady," said Luca, gesturing for Kokochin to follow. As she walked past the guard, Kokochin fought the urge to stare at him. Her disguise, posing as a foreign ambassador seeking an audience, would only get them so far. Luca had to speak with two more guards before they finally reached a vast hall full of chairs. Since it was early in the morning, they were the first ones to arrive, but the room was capable of hosting a hundred people or more.

"This is where those waiting for an audience will gather," said Luca. "The Assassin will come here."

"We need to determine who it is before they leave this room," said Layla.

"You need to get to safety," said Kokochin, gripping Luca's hand.

"No. I cannot leave now."

"If you stay and are discovered, they will come for us." They both knew that within the next few hours, security would become tighter and there would be more guards on duty. At that point, it would be a lot more difficult for him to blend in with the rest. She knew that Luca didn't want to jeopardise the plan, but he felt it was his duty to stay and protect the Pope.

"Please, Luca," she said, but still he hesitated in leaving.

"If needed, we will give our lives for his," said Layla. It was the right thing to say, and Luca squeezed Kokochin's hand before letting go.

"I will pray for you," he said, smiling at them both before going out the door.

"And now, we wait," said Layla, looking around the empty room.

A few hours later, the room was packed with people, all of them waiting for an audience with the Holy Father. Despite arriving hours early, none of the servants or guards paid them much attention because they were in the right place. The guards came and went at regular intervals, delivering petitioners, foreign nobles, ambassadors and merchants to the room. An army of servants turned up regularly to drop off food and drink to keep everyone refreshed while they waited.

Like Kokochin, a few of the more unique individuals had servants with them, but they had also been limited to one individual. Much to Kokochin's surprise, Layla played the role of maid with ease, even going so far as to make conversation with the others of her station. While Layla gathered gossip amongst the staff, Kokochin circulated the room in her role as foreign ambassador. In other circumstances, she doubted if some of those gathered would deign to speak with her, but because they were all trapped together for hours, the usual protocols were more relaxed.

There were fifty-seven men and thirty-eight women in the room. The only details she knew about the Assassin, or potentially two Assassins, was that both of them were men. Of the fifty-seven men, she was able to discount all but eight due to their age, infirmity, or their demeanour. She clearly remembered what Angelo had told them about one of the Assassin's transforming from a lamb into a wolf, but even with that in mind, she trusted her instincts. Layla agreed with her assessment, and with information she'd gathered from other servants, she helped Kokochin narrow down the list to four individuals.

The first was a slender merchant called Hasim, who was dressed in some of the most flamboyant clothing she'd ever seen. The peacock feathers in his hat clashed with the red pantaloons, yellow shirt and green jacket. Staring at his clothes for too long gave her a headache. His black hair was oiled, and the ends of his moustache curled around his cheeks.

"He's worried about something," said Kokochin. "He smiles all the time, but he's always watching the room," she added, averting her gaze so he didn't notice them watching.

Layla leaned closer, pouring her some tea. "All of it could be an elaborate disguise. Dress as a fool and people will expect little of him."

"What about Emre?" said Kokochin, without turning her head. Across the room was a man dressed in ordinary clothes, but she knew he was a warrior. He kept adjusting his belt and then righting it again. It was something she had seen countless soldiers repeat in order to adjust the weight and balance of a sword resting on their hip. Without his armour and weapons, dressed in finery that didn't quite fit right, he was a curiosity more than a threat. But underneath the anxious smile, there was a stillness to him that worried her.

"He could just be a soldier that's found God," said Layla. "Look at Cavicchi."

It was one possibility, but she needed to know more.

The third possibility was a bumbling noble called Oguz, who had tripped over chairs, a table leg, his own feet and had broken a glass and two plates. He did his best not to draw attention to himself, but his antics meant that a lot of people were watching him at all times. If it was a performance, Kokochin thought it remarkable, but it could also be serving as a distraction from his real purpose, or that of his partner.

"What if there are two Assassins?" said Kokochin, accepting the tea from Layla. "But the second is merely a distraction."

Layla nodded thoughtfully, tilting her head towards the fourth candidate. "Sometimes it's the quiet ones," she said. The haughty man, Yusef, sat apart from everyone and was doing his best to pretend none of them existed. He regularly held a cloth to his nose as if revolted by the smell of other people in the room.

Those waiting had been told by an officious priest that it would be at least a couple of hours before the Pope would be meeting with anyone. With plenty of time to spare, many people in the room were socialising with one another. Kokochin crossed the room to greet Hasim, who rose from his chair as she approached.

"Madam, you honour me," he said, unsure of her title.

"I had to come and speak with you. Your clothing is remarkable," she said, pretending to be entranced by his garish outfit. All the while, Kokochin was watching his features for any signs of deception. A short distance away, Layla was standing at an angle studying his face, but also his posture, while she eavesdropped on their conversation.

As Hasim burbled on about the tailor and the cost of all his finery, she noticed he kept pulling at the collar of his shirt, clearly nervous about something.

"So, why have you come?" she asked, getting straight to the point.

"Oh, it's to do with the family business," he said, rather vaguely.

"And what business is that?" she asked, feigning interest. "I'm looking to invest in new areas."

Hasim's eyes widened and he swallowed hard. He was afraid, but she didn't think he was an Assassin. He had no guile and seemed ill-prepared for awkward and difficult conversations. "That's very kind, but I'm hoping the Church will do the exact opposite. I'm trying to secure rights to what they recently acquired."

Kokochin didn't think anyone was paying them much attention, but she still leaned closer and lowered her voice. "They took land from you? By force?"

"Acquired," said Hasim, licking his lips. He glanced around the room, nervous of anyone overhearing their conversation and it reaching the wrong ears. He wasn't so dim after all. It sounded like it was going to be a delicate negotiation. "I'm sure an accommodation can be made so that it comes back to my family."

"Then I wish you good luck," she said, moving away. Glancing across the room, Kokochin was reassured when Layla shook her head. It wasn't him.

Kokochin hadn't realised she was so on edge until her skin started to itch. It took her a little while before an opportunity arose for her to speak with Emre, the former soldier. When several other women approached Emre, equally intrigued by his peculiarities, and no doubt his good looks, Kokochin merged with the crowd of admirers. Emre was immediately on edge, and as the six women surrounded him, he looked mortally afraid. She thought he'd rather face a dozen enemies than a group of amorous women with designs on his future.

"No, I'm not married," he was saying with a weak smile.

One of the women purred and stepped closer. "A big, strong man like you. Why ever not?"

"I've just not had time to find the right woman. I've been too busy."

"Too busy with what?" someone asked, a step ahead of Kokochin. She did her best to look at the warrior with genuine interest while also trying to gauge how he reacted under pressure. She was also curious to see if he was drawn to a particular woman in the crowd. He was flustered, but in such circumstances it wouldn't be difficult to fake.

"I was a warrior," said Emre, with a hint of pride.

"For your khan, or your god?" asked Kokochin, drawing his focus. He briefly made eye contact and then looked away, as if embarrassed. Had there been a glimmer of recognition, or had she imagined it?

"No, not for God," he said, and she noticed a subtle change in his posture. He stopped fidgeting. A serenity came across Emre's features, and his hand stopped reaching for a phantom sword. His mind and focus had turned inwards towards something else.

Although he was probably flattered by the attention, it was clear Emre had no interest in any of the women. Kokochin thought it was being drawn to a higher power that overshadowed all earthly desires. "But that is something I hope to rectify."

"You want to become a priest?" said one of the women, horrified at the idea.

"I wish to serve God," said Emre.

"How awful," said the woman, losing interest. Most of the others trailed away, leaving Kokochin and one other. Only then did she notice the scuffed knuckles and scrapes on his hands. They were recent injuries and signs of a fight.

"What happened?" asked Kokochin, gesturing at his hands. It was possible they were from a scuffle several days ago with Luca.

"A misunderstanding," said Emre, calmly meeting her gaze. There was something behind his eyes that unsettled her. A familiarity, as if he knew who she was, if not why she was here. The other woman, bored by their conversation, left the pair of them alone and went in search of another distraction. Kokochin remained fixed on the spot, searching his face.

"Who did you fight?" she asked, readying herself in case he attacked her.

Emre shrugged. "Just a local thief. He thought I would be an easy person to rob."

"Did you kill him?" said Kokochin.

"No, of course not," said Emre, sounding genuinely shocked. "I just taught him a lesson. A few bumps and bruises, but he will live."

"But, as a warrior, you have killed."

"That's different."

"How so?" asked Kokochin.

"That was war. Besides, I'm not the same person anymore."

Kokochin still wasn't convinced by his newly pious attitude. She sensed he was lying about something. She needed a genuine and raw reaction. "What changed? Did you nearly die? See the face of God?"

To her surprise, Emre didn't get angry. In fact, he looked at Kokochin with something like pity. "I regret many of the things I've done in my life. But I am not ashamed of finding God. He came to me, not when I was near death, or even in the midst of battle, but when I was still and at peace. I only wish I had come to this realisation sooner."

"So that you can serve God, as penance?" she said, annoyed at how he was looking at her.

Emre didn't rise to her ire. Instead, he favoured Kokochin with a calm smile. "I hope that the Holy Father can help with whatever has made you so angry, but I know that I am not the cause."

His smug attitude was starting to grate, but before she could reply, Layla appeared at her elbow. "Milady, someone would like to meet you," she said, quickly steering Kokochin away.

"I don't like him," said Kokochin when they were across the room.

"It doesn't matter. It's not him. Whatever he said is irrelevant. Let it go. Time is growing short." Layla gestured towards the door where a pair of men in smart uniforms were being led away. The audiences had begun.

Trying to smother her ire, Kokochin approached Yusef, who still sat alone. All previous attempts at conversation had been rebuffed with sharp comments or merely a prolonged silence until the other person became bored and moved away.

With a huff, Kokochin sat down in the chair next to him. From her eye corner, she saw Yusef glance at her once and then back at the room. The rest of those gathered continue to mingle, vying for attention, influence and ultimately power.

"They remind me of ants," said Kokochin.

To her surprise, Yusef laughed. "I was thinking the same thing, Princess."

Raising an eyebrow, she looked over at him. "You know who I am?"

"Of course."

"I don't remember you," said Kokochin, studying his profile. As hard as she tried, she couldn't place him.

"We haven't met, but I've heard of you. Last of your tribe. Married off to one of the khans, like a prize breeding sow. I heard you'd gone rogue and tried to kill him."

"You're well informed, although not all of that is true."

"Which part?" said Yusef.

"Someone else murdered him, although if the opportunity had come up…" she trailed off, leaving the rest unsaid. Yusef said nothing in reply and his expression didn't change. It was so difficult to read him. She couldn't tell if he was glad or angered that Hulagu was dead. She had no idea who he served or why he was even here. She decided to try another tack.

"You're not here for money, power or influence. I don't think it's redemption, or a new beginning either," said Kokochin, gesturing at Emre. "So what is it?"

"Perhaps I'm here for spiritual reasons," said Yusef, showing her the first glimpse of a sense of humour.

"No, it's something else," she replied. If he was the Assassin, it was a strange choice to stand out from the crowd and not blend in. But at this point, Kokochin was running out of viable suspects, so she hadn't discounted him. Across the room, Layla was talking to another servant. Following her gaze, she saw Layla was staring at Oguz, the clumsy noble.

"They're all here, asking for something," said Yusef, dismissing the entire room with a casual wave of his hand.

"But you are not?" said Kokochin, finding it a strange thing to say.

"No. I come to send a clear message to the world."

Kokochin didn't know what he was talking about. If Yusef was the Assassin, then perhaps he intended to show that no one was beyond their reach and that everyone was vulnerable. That safety was nothing more than an illusion. It was a bleak thought, but given the widespread destruction of the Assassins, she thought it possible.

Turning in her seat to face Yusef, she openly studied him. There was definitely something off about him. He wasn't a Mongol, and yet his expensive clothes were like those from home. His accent was hard to trace, and yet she thought his attitude wasn't fake, which suggested noble or royal lineage of some kind. He was an oddity. The kind of person one of the khans would collect and make a prisoner in all but name, like the merchant, Marco Polo. He was an enigma and made no sense to her.

"I came here seeking only one thing," said Kokochin, deciding to take a huge risk.

"Sanctuary?" asked Yusef.

Kokochin snorted. "No. The Church would not grant that to someone like me. I'm here to prevent a murder, and in doing so, hopefully prevent another war." Yusef didn't reply, but it was clear that he was still listening. "I'm here to stop you from killing the Pope."

Yusef was quiet for so long, Kokochin didn't think he would reply. Eventually, he took a deep breath and turned to face her. "And why would I do that?"

"Because you're an Assassin, one of only a handful that are left."

"You have quite the imagination, Princess."

Kokochin watched the room as she spoke, wondering how much time remained. "I know that Hulagu drove the last of your kind from Persia. That he tore down the last fortress at Alamut." Yusef's jaw tightened, but still he didn't speak. "I also know that he killed your great leader. While he knelt in the mud, Hulagu beheaded him. For my husband, it was personal, but I genuinely don't know if you hate all Mongols. Maybe this is about money, or some kind of blood debt for you."

"You understand little," hissed Yusef.

"Perhaps," said Kokochin, "but it doesn't really matter anymore. All I have to do is stop you. All I have to do is shout for a guard, and then it's all over."

Something hard punched Kokochin in the side, beneath her ribs.

"You won't be shouting for anyone," said Yusef, dragging his blade free.

It was a short, fat dagger, half the length of his hand. When he drew back to stab her again, she gripped his wrist, but some of the strength was already ebbing out of her body. She tried to scream, but she couldn't draw a full breath and no sound emerged.

At the sight of them struggling, a few people were curious, but no one did anything to stop them. Kokochin pressed one hand to the wound in her side, then covered Yusef's eyes with her bloody fingers. He recoiled, spitting and crying out in surprise while trying to clear his eyes. At the sight of fresh blood, people in the room began to scream.

Yusef punched her in the face with his free hand while trying to stab her again with the other. Stars danced in front of Kokochin's eyes as she felt the blade bite into her a second time. After bringing her head forward sharply, her forehead collided with his face. The blow was ill-timed, catching Yusef above one eye, making him howl and reel back.

As they wrestled for the blade, she was aware of another scuffle, but couldn't turn her head to see what was happening. Kokochin had lost time. Somehow, she was now lying on the floor, Yusef was above her with both hands on the blade, trying to drive it onto her face. He was bigger and heavier. The struggle would be brief if she couldn't dislodge him, but he had a wide stance, his knees on either side of her body. The blade inched down, hovering above her eye, the point catching on her lashes.

When her knee collided with his crotch, it took a few seconds for the pain to register. Yusef began to wheeze, his eyes watered and the pressure on her wrists eased. A sharp punch to his shoulder made him drop the dagger, his fingers numb and useless. A second blow to his throat made him stumble back, struggling to breathe.

As darkness crept in around the edges of Kokochin's vision, she heard footsteps running towards her. People were screaming and praying. A man was crying, which she found odd, and someone else was cursing her name between each breath. Turning her head was difficult, but Yusef was lying not far away, curled up in a ball, rocking back and forth in pain.

Rough hands seized Kokochin, dragging her across the floor away from Yusef. Kokochin caught a brief glimpse of guards in uniform with grim expressions, then the darkness swallowed her whole.

CHAPTER 31
Melchior

It was all gone. Everything Melchior had been tangled up with for centuries. The other Kozan. Katarina. The endless war.

He released the Rigour, returned to normal time and stumbled. The pain in his side was so agonising it shattered his concentration and grip on the Eternal Fire.

No one had ever hurt him so badly before. It was humbling. It reminded Melchior that although he was different from everyone else, he used to be human. He didn't like it.

Hunched over with hands resting on his knees, Melchior took a moment to try and catch his breath. Every deep inhalation tugged at the injury on his side. It flexed and then eased, like stitches on a wound, but instead of pulling the flesh, this poison was in his soul. With hands resting on hips, he slowly limped up the winding path towards home.

He should have felt relief. It was over. He was free. To go wherever he wanted. To be anyone. He could change his name, his clothes, even shave his beard and head if he wanted. In the past, no one could have stopped him, but he'd been bound by duty and responsibility. To maintaining the balance between the two factions of Kozan. To ensuring that world events were not altered too dramatically from their natural course by the agents of Chaos.

The freedom was exhilarating, and yet it also terrified him. Could he live without structure? Without any kind of ambition or goal to work towards? Could he simply become an explorer of mysteries?

In time, Temujin had the potential to cause problems, but he lacked the skill. However, there was no one around to teach him how to use his powers. Melchior wasn't worried. If Temujin lived through the next century, then perhaps he would become a concern. But with all the turbulence in the current climate, Melchior doubted the boy would live ten years. Temujin would probably be killed by an enemy or blow himself up while experimenting with his powers.

The huge grey slabs, worn smooth by the passage of Melchior's feet over the centuries, were as familiar as old friends. He was neither peculiar enough nor disconnected enough from reality, to name the lifeless rocks. Nevertheless, it was nice to see them. It meant he was almost home. However, for once, the winding path and seven hundred and seventy seven steps up to his villa posed a significant challenge. Melchior could have called on someone from the village to help him, but that would not do. Grunting with effort, he began the ascent alone, pausing often along the way to rest.

Showing any kind of weakness might start rumours that their eternal Lord and Master was vulnerable, and therefore human. It might encourage the idea of rebellion in the minds of some. He really didn't want to cull the population and start over again with new villagers. He'd not had to do that in over five hundred years. It was such a waste, and it took forever to train new people.

Eventually, most of the villagers came to accept their way of life, and they even grew to enjoy it. He didn't make any great demands, and only visited the valley for short periods of time. For the rest of the year, they were free to do whatever they wanted. The only rule was that they couldn't leave the valley, otherwise he'd kill them and their entire family.

The sturdy gate always stood open, and merchants came and went, even staying a night or two at the tavern, but no one ever hitched a ride out on a wagon. Strangers never stayed long either. They found life in the valley too slow and boring. "Dull," several had called it, because nothing ever changed and nothing exciting happened. It was perfect.

Once, long ago, the distant ancestors of Melchior's servants had made human sacrifices to him. Bending bodies backwards over altars. Carving still-beating hearts out from chests. Rivers of hot blood had trickled down the stones, running through channels to be collected in sacred bowls. Later, they'd sent him naïve virgins as tribute. All to appease him. To beg protection from demons, the sky gods that brought thunder, or for a good harvest. The old beliefs were gone, and many superstitions had been replaced with monotheistic religions. Abstract, eternal gods that lived in the sky. Distant and vague entities that followers could neither see nor hear. At times, it baffled Melchior that they would seek out a new deity when in many ways, the people in the valley served a living god on Earth. This was why people were endlessly fascinating.

Halfway up the steps, Melchior paused to peer down at the lush greenery below. Centuries ago, sections of the slopes had been fashioned into terraces. The valley, with its particular climate, produced a great amount of food, plenty for everyone and some for trade. There was no hunger, no crime, no war and no natural disasters. It was perfect. Quiet. Peaceful.

At this height, the people working on the tiered fields were as small as his hand. Men and women worked side by side, some with children strapped to their backs. When Melchior reached the top, they would appear more like nameless ants. It was easier to think of them in the same manner as insects. That way he didn't have to learn their names, make friends and become emotionally attached. After all this time, the most fragile part of him, the most human, was still his heart.

Despite the air becoming cooler as he climbed, Melchior was sweating profusely. The strain caused by his fresh injury was intense. By the time he reached the top, he was exhausted. It was a wound that would never heal. He would have to manage it, just like Katarina had done for centuries.

No.

He wasn't ready to think about her, not just yet. About how she had died, torn apart by the Servants of Time, begging him for help right up until the end. Regardless of the manner, no parent should see their child die in front of them. No parent should live long enough.

Turning back to the present, Melchior focused on getting his breathing back under control. His right side throbbed, the ache straining his lungs. The pain had not diminished since it had happened.

"Lord?" said a familiar voice. Gavvi emerged from the villa, a concerned expression on his round face. He was short and stocky, like his ancestor, and the many other Gavvi's before him. All of them acted as head of household, and Melchior's personal aid when he was at home.

"I was just admiring the view," said Melchior, forcing a smile. "Is it harvest time already?"

He'd been away from home for several months. Perhaps it was a couple of years. It was difficult to keep track, but Melchior was positive this Gavvi was the same as last time.

"You look tired, Lord. Would you like me to have a bath prepared? Perhaps a nice meal?"

"That sounds wonderful," said Melchior, walking upright as if he wasn't in any pain.

The villa was a long and wide, in the shape of a horseshoe with no upper floor, only an elegant terracotta-coloured roof. With pale grey tiles on the floor and neutral decoration throughout, it could have belonged to some extravagant noble that used it as a summer home. The building did have a certain air of neglect, but Melchior suspected the feeling was mostly in his mind. Since his brush with the Servants of Time, he'd noticed an increase in dwelling on the past, and introspection. There was a hole in his mind. They'd taken something from him, and his memories were trying to bridge the gap, rearranging themselves around the absence.

There was no damp and not a speck of dust. Gavvi and his staff always kept the place spotless. Melchior bypassed his office and completely ignored the steps that led down to the vault. It was the one place in the house that was off-limits to the servants. It was where he kept his most important, dangerous and personal items. Even if they could have opened the door at the bottom of the steps, they would have been baffled to discover a solid wall of stone. The only way to gain entrance was to Skim through ten feet of solid granite.

Water, heated elsewhere in the villa, was piped into the tiled sunken bath. It was large enough to host ten people, but it had been a long time since Melchior had indulged in an orgy, especially in water.

When the bath was full, Gavvi held up a basket containing a selection of aromatic oils. Melchior selected one, and a small amount was added to the steaming water. It filled the air with a citrus aroma that burned the back of his nostrils. Gavvi and the other servants withdrew, leaving him to undress alone.

After soaking in the water until he felt more relaxed, Melchior sat on the edge of the bath to study his wound. The skin over his ribs was red, angry and inflamed. At the point of impact was what resembled a purple bruise, but green tendrils snaked out in all directions like poisoned veins. Gently probing the skin with his fingertips, Melchior was glad to discover his ribs weren't broken or cracked. He wasn't sure how or if they would have healed after such a peculiar injury.

From his vast wardrobe, Melchior selected a loose-fitting grey shirt and soft cotton trousers. He'd barely sat down in the sun room when Gavvi approached with a pot of tea and a plate of sugared almonds.

"No baklava?" said Melchior, gobbling up three almonds.

"No, Lord, but the cook can prepare some, if you want."

"No, no. These are fine," he said eating two more sweets. The almonds were full of flavour, and seemed to explode in his mouth. "Is the cook new?" asked Melchior, suddenly unsure of how long he'd been away. The wound to his body was one thing, but the potential damage to his mind was terrifying. How much had he lost? Staring at his manservant, Melchior was less certain he was the same one as last time. Had Gavvi always had a notch in his right ear?

Melchior busied himself inspecting the tea, noting that the jasmine flowers had only just begun to unfurl.

"Fairly new," said Gavvi. Then he said something else, but Melchior wasn't listening. He popped another almond into his mouth and crunched it between his teeth.

"Good, good," said Melchior, when Gavvi had finished talking. "I'll have dinner at the usual time."

"Any preference, my Lord?"

"Whatever is in season," he said, mostly because he wasn't sure what season it was in this part of the world.

His manservant withdrew, leaving Melchior alone to meditate. Normally, surrendering to the Eternal Fire was like slipping on a pair of comfortable old shoes. He barely thought about it. It simply happened. For the first time in many years, he had to concentrate, focusing on his breath and the stillness in the air. Finally it came, suffusing his being, filling him with vast potential and insight.

The pain in his body faded to a dull niggle, faint enough for him to ignore for now.

Using techniques he'd learned over hundreds of years, Melchior turned his senses within. He traced the lines of energy in his body, searching the boundaries of his mind for what had changed.

There. It was like someone had ripped a healthy tooth from his mouth, leaving behind a ragged, bleeding gum. But this wound was in his mind. A spasm of pain ran through his body and Melchior came back to the present. The Fire was gone and his senses were dulled again. The pain had become significantly worse. It was spreading out from his abdomen, passing through his body in waves.

How had Katarina contained the poison? Her wound had not been too dissimilar. She'd managed to localise the damage to her flesh and her mind. Melchior sipped the tea, found it was brewed to his liking and filled the cup. Sitting still for long periods of time was normally comfortable, but today his joints were aching. Walking back and forth around the room with a cup of tea in one hand, he considered the problem.

There were certain medicines that would slow or cleanse the blood, but this was not a toxin in the traditional sense. He would have to stem the flow using his powers, hem in the damage and, if possible, reverse it. Another wave of pain made him grunt. He'd become so lost in thought, he'd stopped moving. Melchior refilled his cup and kept walking around, working through the problem in his mind.

He completely lost track of time and was brought back to the present by Gavvi loudly clearing his throat. From his slightly concerned expression, Melchior guessed his manservant had been there for some time.

"Dinner is ready, my Lord," he announced.

Gavvi led him to the dining room where a modest feast had been laid out. The room was small and cosy, with three framed paintings of mountains, streams and a murky forest in autumn. The artist had been dead for centuries, his name and work forgotten by time. The walnut dining table was large enough to accommodate four people, but tonight he was eating alone.

Melchior dined on river salmon that was so tender, it almost fell apart on his fork. The herb glaze was unusual, but it was rich and tasty, leaving a sticky coating on his tongue.

The vegetables tasted so fresh, he thought they must have been harvested earlier in the day. The wine was dry and crisp, perfectly complimenting the meal. The new cook was definitely an improvement over the previous one.

When he'd finished eating, Gavvi returned to clear away his plate. "Wonderful. Truly. I would like to meet the new cook and thank them personally."

"I'm not sure that's a good idea," said the manservant, which made Melchior raise an eyebrow.

He didn't molest or exploit his servants, but he expected obedience at all times. Perhaps this was a new Gavvi. Someone he'd not met before who didn't understand the rules. "Bring them out. Immediately," said Melchior, his tone brooking no argument.

Gavvi bowed his head and withdrew from the room with the empty plates. Melchior topped up his wine and shifted on his chair, trying to get comfortable. If anything, the pain in his side felt worse. The skin was unbearably warm, and now there was a peculiar tingling sensation in his extremities. Melchior stifled a yawn and found he was starting to doze off. It had been a difficult journey to get here. It must have taxed his reserves more than he realised, as his head dipped towards his chest.

Melchior came awake with a start, wincing in pain at the stiffness in his neck. He was still at the dining table, but through the window he could see the sky was purple and black. He must have been asleep for at least a couple of hours. The tingling in his hands and feet was worse, and a stronger spasm of pain washed through his body.

Someone had been in the room while he slept, as several lanterns had been lit. Much to his surprise, he wasn't alone. An unfamiliar woman sat in a corner of the room, deep in the shadows.

"What's happened?" he said. Wiping his forehead, Melchior was surprised to feel it damp. When the woman failed to answer, he tried to stand and found his legs wouldn't bear his weight. One leg folded under him, and Melchior collapsed onto the floor. He yelped in surprise when his cheek slapped against the cool tiles and for a second he lost consciousness.

When he woke the second time, he was sitting upright with his back against the wall. The silent woman was on the far side of the room, face concealed in the shadows. Melchior took a moment to assess his injuries. The wound in his side was throbbing, but more agonising was what felt like a pit of fire emanating from his stomach. He couldn't feel his feet, and when he tried to move his toes, they failed to respond. Taking a deep breath was incredibly difficult, and he heard a damp rattle coming from one lung.

"What have you done?" he asked.

The woman finally moved, crossing the room to step into the light cast by the lanterns. She was old, with dark skin and had a blue scarf wrapped around her head. She slipped it off, revealing short iron-grey hair, and as she tucked the scarf around her throat, he saw a faded scar.

"I'm the new cook," she said in a gravelly voice. Her face was strained from talking, and both hands twitched at her sides. "I've poisoned you."

"Poison?" he said, trying to laugh, but all that emerged was a faint wheeze. "Do you know who I am? What I can do?"

All he had to do was embrace the Eternal Fire and turn his powers inwards. He might not be able to heal the injury from the Servants of Time, but he could reverse the flow of a toxin in his blood. But when Melchior tried to calm his mind, he found it didn't work. Random thoughts kept imposing. Memories from his childhood. Images of Katarina as a young girl. The day a boy had broken her heart. The day she betrayed him and had walked away. The day she was born. The day he married his first wife. His three hundredth birthday.

One after another, they piled on, racing through his head. Forward and then back. An endless stream of memories. His life spanned centuries and his brain bounced around in time. Staring down at his hands, he marvelled at the whirls and patterns on his skin. Why had he never noticed them before? Intricate loops and lines. Were they unique or were everyone's the same?

"What have you done?" he gasped. His heart was racing and the room was far too hot. He couldn't breathe properly.

"You have nine different poisons in your body," said the woman. "Also three accelerants."

"Gavvi," he croaked, but it barely came out as a whisper.

"We're alone," said the woman. "I sent everyone away. They're in their homes, in the valley."

"Who are you?"

"My name is Mari. Or it was, a long time ago," she said with a faint smile. "Well, a long time ago for me. You were the first? The first Kozan?"

"I am," he said, trying to concentrate. The walls of the room were moving. The colours from the painting were running. Greens and browns, streaming out of the frame, trickling down the walls. When he blinked, the painting was back to normal.

"All things must come to an end," said Mari. "Your death is long overdue."

"Who are you to decide?" said Melchior.

"Who are you to decide the fate of humanity?" she rasped. Mari helped herself to the wine, sipping it slowly. "How many centuries have you walked across the Earth? Do you even remember?"

"I earned the right. I was given a gift," said Melchior. "One I did not squander, or use for selfish reasons. I used my power so that people like you had the freedom to choose. It was the others that wanted to pervert the natural course of events."

"People like me?" said Mari, easing her voice with more wine. "Do you mean humans?"

"Of course."

Mari chuckled, a dry wretched sound. "Such hubris, and yet a mighty being such as yourself has been brought low by a mere human."

"I will not be prattled at by the likes of you," said Melchior, snorting with derision. "I have saved countless lives down the centuries. Without my intervention, entire nations would have been wiped off the map."

"You speak of the natural order," said Mari, hissing through her teeth, "and yet your continued existence defies it. You do not belong."

For a time, a heavy silence settled on the room, broken only by the laboured sounds of Melchior's breathing. The numb sensation had risen to reach his hips. It was as if his body now ended at his stomach. Somewhere in the distance, someone was moaning. A low, keening sound that made the hair on the back of his neck prickle with alarm. It was a primitive reaction of his body. It reminded Melchior of when he'd been a boy, hearing wolves howl in the forest at night.

"Do you know many months it took me to find this place?" said Mari, gesturing at his home. "You live like a king, but at some point, most rulers allow their servants to retire when they get old. Here, they are slaves who can never leave. It took some persuading, but eventually they told me what you'd done. You've kept entire families in a prison, for generation after generation, going back centuries."

"You are not fit to judge my actions," said Melchior. He stifled a sob as another wave of pain wracked his body. It felt as if his nerves were burning. The muscles in his neck were so taut, he was afraid that if he moved it would shatter like glass. The howling sound was getting louder. "Can you hear that?" he asked.

Mari shook her head. "I am your judge and executioner," she said, ignoring his question. "Soon, your kind will be gone. Forever."

Melchior wanted to argue, but a part of him knew that she was right. Temujin would not last, and once he was dead it would be the end. In time, another Kozan would be born, but without a teacher, they would die or be murdered. As the first Kozan, he had stumbled through his first hundred years, shunned, cast out and demonised, moving from place to place until finally he'd discovered this remote valley. Then, he'd been free to test his powers and gradually master his skill.

"Who are you?" said Melchior. He didn't really care about the answer. It was more that the drugs in his body were tricking his senses, creating phantom sounds and emotions. One moment he was wracked with such despair he wanted to scream, and the next he felt such euphoria his eyes welled up. Memories swirled inside his head in an endless cycle, all of them vying for attention. Thousands and thousands called out, like screaming voices in a crowd with no limit.

"A patriot," said Mari, taking another swig of wine, "but like you, my time has come to an end. Something new must take my place. The world cannot stand still."

"It never stops changing," said Melchior. "Progress is inevitable."

"After all that you've seen, tell me there's hope for humanity."

Melchior sighed then reached for the wine with one hand. His fingers barely twitched, but Mari understood. She placed the glass to his lips, trickling some wine into his mouth. He'd never tasted anything so delicious.

"There were times when I despaired," he admitted, thinking of past centuries. "When the world was coming apart. Famine, disease and always war. Endlessly, war comes again and again. Nations fall and new empires rise, sweeping across the continents. Today, it is the Mongols. Tomorrow, it will be someone else. But always, they fail. The world will never truly be united under one flag. Even if such a thing were to happen, it would not last."

"Why?" asked Mari, taking back the wine.

"Because you are all so different. Diversity is humanity's greatest strength and weakness. It's why, after all this time, I still find people so interesting."

A tight band squeezed Melchior's chest. He tried to cough, but lacked the lung capacity and only managed to wheeze. The pain was subsiding as more parts of his body became numb and immobile, signalling that his end was near. The distant voices were much closer now, and he imagined there were words mixed with the noise. Impossibly, he couldn't understand the language, which told him it was an hallucination. There was no language or dialogue he could not recognise, let alone speak. The alien whispers were hypnotic.

"There is hope for the future, but it's a tenuous, fragile thing, like a butterfly," he murmured, barely able to move his jaw. "Someone must keep watch and nurture it."

"Someone is," said Mari. "My group, and others, but we do not place ourselves above everyone else. You can rest now."

Melchior found that thought reassuring, but he could no longer speak. At the periphery of his vision, he saw them creeping closer. The swirling pits. The faces without mouths, and yet, he could hear them speaking in his mind. His eyes widened in horror, and somehow his terror rose to a new height.

In a rush, they swarmed over Melchior, hands sinking through his clothes, into his flesh, into his being. From deep within, they tore him apart. Light spilled out of his body and Mari fell back, shielding her face, suddenly blind. More and more hands grabbed him. Ten, twenty. A dozen Servants were crouched over him, pawing at his body as if they were starving and he was a banquet. There was a loud huffing in his ears like some vast, slouching beast was breathing down his neck. The whispering voices merged into one vast howling cacophony. Mercifully, the poison had numbed his body, so he could not feel what they were doing. But the memories. They erupted out of him in all directions, as if they had severed every artery in his body at once.

Whole decades disappeared in the slow blink of his eyes. Centuries of memory were erased, wafting away, fading into light and then nothing. Soon, he struggled to remember his own name, and finally, even that was gone. He blinked his eyes once, twice, and then nothing.

CHAPTER 32
Temujin

It was over.

Temujin sat alone in his throne room. He'd dismissed all of the Kheshig, as well as his advisors and ministers. The empty room rang with silence. It rebounded off the walls over and over until even the slightest sound hurt his ears. The scuff of a shoe. The rustle of fabric against his skin. Everything was too loud. It clawed at his senses.

He'd won.

From somewhere deep inside, a giggle bubbled up. First, he snickered, then it erupted from his mouth. The laughter slapped off the stone walls, then came back towards him, twice as loud. He sounded ridiculous. He sounded slightly mad. The Kheshig standing outside the doors probably thought he was insane, laughing to himself in an empty room.

With considerable effort, Temujin stifled his mirth, holding his jaw shut, pinching his lips. Slowly, the laughter faded, but it left behind a smile that stretched across his face.

His ridiculous and risky plans had succeeded. None of it had happened as expected, but nevertheless, his enemies were dead and he was still alive.

Timur was gone and his army was broken. The Chagatai khanate was in revolt and coming apart at the seams. Conquered nations within its borders were rising up, demanding their freedom from Mongol occupation and rule. A few provinces even wanted their own independence, with governors trying to secede from their former countries. It was as if someone had poked an ant nest, and now they were all boiling out and running in a hundred directions.

Temujin wasn't naïve. There would be blood. Groups of warriors would turn to raiding, robbing merchants and unwary travellers on the road. Some would band together under the leadership of a charismatic figurehead, but he doubted they would amount to much. They might claim a little bit of territory here and there, but no more than that. For the foreseeable future, there would be a constant churn of minor conflicts, a few murders and perhaps some pillaging. But those responsible would be caught and punished. Order would reassert itself.

In time, someone would succeed in uniting a few nations as they attempted to create a new empire. But it wouldn't happen just yet, and not at all if he stopped them. All of the other Kozan were dead. Katarina had been torn apart by the Servants of Time, and her father, Melchior, had been gravely wounded. Temujin had seen the monsters sink their hands into Melchior's flesh and rip something away. The intense pain on his face had been overshadowed by shock. It was as if the Kozan could not believe that it was happening to him of all people. It was unlike anything Temujin had ever seen. If Melchior was still alive, he would have resurfaced by now, angling for an alliance like Katarina or seeking revenge for her murder. A small part of Temujin thought the first Kozan might still be alive, but he silenced the doubting voice. No. He was the last. That meant there was no one in the entire world that was his equal. No one could oppose him.

His uncle was still tangled up in a civil war with Kaidu, and Tokhtamysh had withdrawn to the Golden Horde. As it was, the Mongol Empire was no more. In time, Tokhtamysh might attempt to expand his borders, but if he tried to invade the Ilkhanate, Temujin would demonstrate his powers in the northern khan's court. Something vulgar and brutal. It needed to be unforgettable. Something that would scare Tokhtamysh and any others who might think about invading the Ilkhanate in the future. In a hundred years or so, Temujin would be forced to do it again, reminding any who sat on the northern throne that he was still powerful and dangerous.

Melchior, and the other Kozan on his side of the endless war, had been right about one thing. Interfering in the natural flow of events was never a good idea. Even a slight change could create ripples that went on and on, like dropping a stone into a still pond. It was impossible to calculate the repercussions through time.

Like empires, wars came and went, but one thing remained. Trade. It was the true lifeblood of the world, not conflict. If Guyuk, and the various jobs Temujin had endured over the years had taught him anything, it was the importance of trade. Above all else, the Silk Road had to be preserved. Regardless of who sat on any given throne or if there was a Mongol Empire or not, the flow of goods had to be protected.

It was the best way for him to sustain the Ilkhanate for centuries to come.

The biggest mistake made by the Kozan was to keep themselves apart from humanity. To step out of the shadows, tinker with events, and then fade away until they were needed again. Temujin intended to live among the humans, and even pretend to be one of them. The other Kozan had said they were not human, and in his arrogance he'd scorned them. However, Temujin understood now that he was not human. At least, not anymore. He wasn't a god, either. He wasn't deluded. There would be no temples, statues or priests. No holy books or relics, or pilgrimages to his home. But he would be the Eternal Khan. Temujin was confident he could be a fair ruler, he just needed to stay in touch with his emotions, and therefore, a semblance of his fading humanity.

The thought of his father no longer upset Temujin as it once had. Not even the day when he'd murdered Hulagu in the cells below the palace. It made sense now. He understood that, in some ways, it had been inevitable. It was the only way Temujin could eclipse his father. If Hulagu had lived, he would forever have been in his shadow. Now, everyone understood who Temujin was and exactly what he was capable of doing. Nothing would stand in his way. Not his father, his siblings, and not his enemies.

A loud knocking at the door disturbed Temujin's thoughts, bringing him back to the present. It was time for the first of today's meetings. It was important to set the right tone for a new era of the Ilkhanate, and that required a calm façade.

Temujin tried to relax and find his way to the Eternal Fire, but it continued to elude him. It had been like this for over a week. For some reason, his mind would not settle as it once had. Normally, it only happened when he was stressed or distracted. He'd even tried meditation, but after two hours, the Fire had remained a vague and abstract concept. Perhaps he'd been pushing himself too hard over the last few months. He had experienced nosebleeds and unusual pains. Starting from today, Temujin made a promise to take better care of himself. Plenty of sleep. Good food and exercise outdoors. Perhaps he would take walks through the city. It was important for the people to see their leader.

The knocking came again, louder this time. He would just have to stay in control of his emotions the old-fashioned way, with willpower. But it was a shame that he would have to rely on the limited insight provided by his senses.

"Enter," he said. Temujin started to fuss with the cuffs of his robe and then forced himself to stop. He adopted a placid expression and willed his body to stillness.

His ten most senior military officers cautiously entered the throne room. At first, they huddled together in a clump, like a gaggle of frightened geese. Once the Kheshig had closed the doors behind them, and they saw that no one else was present, a few relaxed. General Kaivon stood at the front of the group. Beside him were the kings of Georgia, Cilician Armenia, his brother Prince Thoros, and Prince Bohemond of Antioch. All of the men were warriors to the core. Even now, they were dressed in their battered and scratched armour, with swords and daggers on their hips. They were always ready. Always waiting for the next battle, the next war.

The three Christian officers appeared calm and oddly at peace, while Kaivon was visibly anxious. It made sense. Temujin had made promises to them about what would happen if they were to win the war. His meeting with King David in Tbilisi felt as if it had taken place over a decade ago.

"We came as you requested, Lord Khan," said Kaivon.

"Lord?" said Temujin, noting the peculiar phrasing. "Not, 'my Khan'? Are you no longer my faithful servant?"

A few of the others grumbled, but Kaivon silenced them with a cutting motion of his hand. Temujin had the notion that their half of the conversation had been rehearsed.

"The war against Timur is over, Lord Khan," said Kaivon. "I would ask that I be released from all of my oaths. I have fulfilled my obligation to you."

"It's true. This war is over," said Temujin, musing on the notion, "but what about the next one? Who will lead my army against a new enemy that rises against us?"

The others were starting to get agitated, but not Kaivon. He had gone still and cool, thriving under the pressure. It was what made him such a good leader. While others floundered, he rose to the challenge.

"Your father–"

"Was a fool," said Temujin, cutting him off. "Did you know that when I was a boy, he tried to teach me about life, war, women and leadership? Most of his lessons didn't stick, because I was different from all of my siblings. I used to think that I was the problem. That I was a mistake."

"Your father is dead," said King David. "You are now the Khan. I had hoped you would be better than him. Honourable. Different."

"I am different," said Temujin, warming to the subject. "His final lesson was one that he didn't even realise he'd taught me. My father was greedy. He was so determined to fulfil the pointless dream of his grandfather, that it left him with an eternal hunger. No matter how many cities he conquered or how many nations he absorbed into the Ilkhanate, it was never enough. Nothing would satisfy him. Even if he had ruled over the whole of the known world, my father would have been restless. Endlessly searching for new lands overseas, where no Mongols had ever walked before, just so that he could conquer them."

"What does this have to do with us? Or you?" said Prince Thoros, losing his temper.

"It matters because I'm not interested in growing the Ilkhanate." Temujin gripped the arms of his throne and sat forward. His emotions were bubbling up and he fought to control them. "All that it encompasses at the present is more than enough. I will rule it as Khan, and you will maintain the peace and safeguard my borders."

A strained silence filled the room as the warriors absorbed his proclamation.

"You made promises," said King David. "You said that ours would become free and independent nations again."

"I did, but I'm changing the deal," said Temujin. "There are still wolves out there, and I cannot keep them at bay with stern words. I have powers," he said, lifting up one hand, in pretence of summoning the Eternal Fire. It was enough to send a ripple through the men. Several took one step backwards towards the door. "But I am not without my limits. No, you will all remain in service to me and the Ilkhanate."

Temujin had chosen his words with care. To make it an announcement, and a forgone conclusion, so that they understood he was not asking for an opinion. It would happen this way. The shock on every face was apparent. Several wanted to argue, but they were obviously worried about what he or the Kheshig might do to them if they refused.

To try and soften the blow, Temujin smiled and came down from the throne to stand among them. He looked them in the eye and pretended that he was just the same as them.

"I know what you're thinking," he said, focusing on Kaivon, who was still the leader. "That I lied and broke my promise. I did, but you should know that this wasn't premeditated. I fully intended to give all of you independence, but over the last week, I've been thinking a lot about the future."

"The future?" said Kaivon, speaking over the grumbles and whispers behind him.

"Someone will come, because they always do. Someone that wants to conquer everything. And then, what would be your choice?" asked Temujin glancing at the warriors. "By themselves, none of your countries are strong enough to repel a large force. You would have to form new alliances and negotiate, and make promises to one another. All of that politicking takes time, just to get you back to where we are now. Together, as one nation, we are stronger. You know that it's true."

A few wanted to deny it and call him a liar, but even the reckless Prince Thoros was silent.

"And you would rule over everyone," said King Hethum.

"Yes," said Temujin. "But all of you would remain as my senior military advisors."

"And what happens should you die without an heir?" said the king. "It would be chaos. There would be another civil war."

"You're right," said Temujin with a laugh that startled everyone.

"Why are you smiling?" asked Kaivon.

"You all seem to forget. I'm not just a khan. I'm also a Kozan. The last one, in fact."

"They're all gone?" said King David, glancing at the others around him. A few made the sign of the cross on their chest. "Dead?"

"Yes. Which means no one can oppose me. Don't you see?" said Temujin.

"Forgive us, Lord Khan," said Kaivon.

"In every form, my powers manipulate time. I am its master. There would be no civil war, no fight for the throne, because I would be an Eternal Khan. I would never die," said Temujin.

It was so simple, and yet the warriors were utterly speechless. He understood it was an overwhelming concept, so Temujin generously gave them some time.

General Subedei made a peculiar whooping noise and then signed something against his chest with one hand. It took Temujin a moment to realise it was an old gesture to ward off evil.

"It is the devil's work," someone muttered.

"Forever?" gasped Kaivon.

"Yes," said Temujin, thinking of Melchior and how old he had been at the end. What would the world look like in five hundred or a thousand years? What had the first Kozan seen in his time? It made him wonder if Melchior had kept any kind of journal or record of his life. Such information would be priceless. That also meant it would not be easy to find. It was a puzzle for another day.

"While other nations struggle, the Ilkhanate will thrive," said Temujin, painting the future for all of them. He turned around and held up his arms, drawing them into his vision. "We will remain strong and mobile. Strengthen our borders and cities, but stay on good terms with our neighbours. They may need our aid, and we need them for trade. Can you imagine what we'll become in five hundred years?"

Temujin stumbled forward, thrown off balance by something. He managed not to fall over, but when he straightened up, pain shot through his back. Hissing like a cat, he spun around to face the warriors.

Kaivon held a dagger in one hand, its blade red with fresh blood. That was when the source of the pain finally registered. Putting a hand to his lower back, Temujin was surprised when it came away red.

"What?" he managed to say.

"God forgive me," said King David, stepping forward with his own dagger. Temujin threw up an arm, but the king's dagger went into his shoulder. Another blade pierced his torso under the ribs. A third in his arm. A fourth in his back, scraping against his shoulder blade. A fifth and then a sixth. Someone was weeping. Someone praying, another cursing him, another begging forgiveness.

The blows continued to rain down, but he couldn't feel them anymore. And then they simply stopped. Temujin was on the floor, staring up at the ceiling of the throne room. Something warm was seeping into his clothes, but his skin felt incredibly cold. He tried to summon the Eternal Fire to chase away the chill, but nothing happened.

His stomach was churning, his throat filling up with liquid, which he spat. Fresh blood dribbled from the corners of his mouth, and faces appeared above, staring down. He thought they were familiar. Did they serve his father? Someone was whispering something. A prayer for his eternal soul. Temujin tried to laugh, but he couldn't speak or make a sound.

Someone was gurgling and spluttering. It sounded as if they were drowning. It should have mattered, should have been important. Temujin was so tired, he just didn't care anymore. The room was getting dark, and he was cold. Maybe if he just slept for a little while, things would be better in the morning. He just needed to rest.

CHAPTER 33
Kaivon

Despite the early hour, the palace stables in Tabriz were quiet. Kaivon knew there were a few stable hands lurking about, but for the most part, the servants were unsure of what to do. They also didn't know who they now served. They were like everyone else in the city, waiting to be told who was in charge now that the latest khan was dead.

The news that Persia was free from Mongol rule was still new. It would take some time for it to spread, and even longer for many to believe that it to be true. Day to day, little seemed to have changed in Tabriz, except that there wasn't a maniac sat on a throne. The Kheshig were gone, as were Mongol patrols in the streets, but otherwise the city operated as before. Merchants came and went, but most people were on edge, holding their breath and waiting to see what happened next.

There were meetings, forums and gatherings where endless hours were taken up by debate. Regional governors were vying to remain in control of their territory, while others wanted a more central arrangement. It was work for someone else. Kaivon had neither the stomach nor the desire for such affairs of state.

Over the years as a warrior, Kaivon had killed a lot of men. The faces of some still haunted him. They mostly came to him in nightmares, their faces and bodies still ragged with the wounds from their death. Sometimes, he caught glimpses of them standing in the deepest shadows on a sunny day. But it was only ever a trick of the light and of his guilt. Others, he could barely remember. They had been in his way on the battlefield. The only thing between him and life. At such times, there was no diplomacy, discussion or debate. All notions of civility, kindness and care were squashed beneath the desperate scramble to stay alive.

It had been five days since they'd killed Temujin, and not once had his conscience been pricked with regret. It didn't matter that they had done it together. Each of them driving a dagger into his flesh. That didn't lessen his role in what had happened. Whether or not the others had joined in, Kaivon had stabbed Temujin with the intention of killing him.

Despite Temujin's powers, and the likelihood that all of them risked being turned into ash, it had worked. Some of the others were questioning the reason for their success, but it didn't matter to Kaivon. The past was done and could not be changed. The present was all that mattered. Building something today to make the future better than what had come before.

Killing Temujin had been necessary, but more than that, it had felt right. However, these last few nights, that was also what had been keeping Kaivon awake. What had he become?

"Are you sure you won't change your mind?" said David, approaching from behind.

If what they had done was troubling the king, it didn't show on his face. In fact, Kaivon had never seen him looking so well rested. Before, there had been a shadow hanging over him. A threat of violence against his country if he did not comply, first with Hulagu and then Temujin. Now David had gained a new vitality, and although he was not an old man, he appeared younger.

"No, my path lies elsewhere," said Kaivon, clasping the king's hand. "Although, I thank you for the invitation."

"You are always welcome in Georgia," said David with a warm smile. "Have you decided where you will go?"

"No, we're still discussing it," said Kaivon. "I think not knowing is what I find so appealing. Up until now, my entire life has been regimented. The notion of no fixed destination is both terrifying and exhilarating."

David's expression turned serious. "I know that what we did has been on your mind, but you should not dwell on it."

"As a man of faith, does it not worry you?"

"A little," admitted the king. He gestured for Kaivon to follow him into the stables. A young lad saw them coming and quickly ran off to saddle the king's mount.

"On my day of judgment, if there is a price for my actions, then I will pay it in full," said David. "But until that time, I will live free of guilt because he was a monster. Just like his father."

When Kaivon had set out to murder Hulagu, he could not have anticipated the road he would travel or the people he would meet along the way. Now, as they prepared to say goodbye, potentially for the last time, Kaivon realised how much he would miss David. The king was a calm, reliable and solid presence, never wavering in his faith or dedication to his country. Everything he had done was to protect and serve his people. To shelter them from the wrath of Hulagu and invasion by the Mongol horde.

The king was as human as everyone else, and had his faults, but pride was not one of them. Others would have demanded to command the army against Timur, or they would have felt slighted and bitter at not being chosen, but not him. It was as if he understood his place in the world. Kaivon envied him.

The boy reappeared leading the king's horse. Together, they walked in silence out of the stables to the far end of the yard.

"Go with God," said David, clasping him on the shoulder.

"Travel safe," said Kaivon. It was not an idle remark. The Mongols no longer ruled in Persia, but they had not disappeared overnight. Already there were rumours of Mongol warriors that had fled when Temujin had been killed, who had turned to robbing travellers on the road.

Kaivon watched the king ride out of the gate and down the street. He stayed until the king had moved out of sight before going back inside. He found Esme in their rooms, packing up the last of their belongings.

"Did you tell him?" she asked.

Kaivon shook his head. "It's better that he doesn't know where we're going, or about the House of Grace."

"Are you sure you want to do this?" she asked, crossing the room to stand in front of him. He instinctively reached for her, enveloping her in his arms. The two of them fit together perfectly. The top of her head tucking just under his chin.

"I haven't changed my mind," he said. While dread had kept Kaivon awake, he'd not been idle during the long hours of the night. He'd spent them thinking about what he wanted to do next.

David would have many issues to deal with at home. In some ways, he had been a king only in name, spending most of his time in the company of Hulagu. They had been servants and prisoners in all but name. The sacrifices David had made to protect his people would matter little to some of them. To truly become their ruler, and create an independent nation that was free to pursue its own destiny, would not be an easy path. And if David had asked, Kaivon would have gone with him, but it would be the work of many years.

"It won't be the same as before," Esme warned him. "The way we operate is slow and subtle. It's how the House has remained secret for so long. Murder is the last course of action."

"I have had my fill of bloodshed," said Kaivon. "I've been a warrior all my life. It's time to try something different."

If the House of Grace had taught him anything, it was that they needed people out there, watching and listening. Waiting for the next invader, or even the next war, was not enough. Spies had their uses, but they were not active participants, they merely dug for information.

In Kaivon's absence, others would train Persian warriors to serve in the army, for when conflict inevitably became necessary. Being proactive, diffusing situations before they could spread, or at least making an attempt, was vital and important work. Kaivon knew that they would not always be successful, and he might die in the trying, but he preferred it to the idea of merely waiting. It was not work he would be doing for reward or recognition, but if they could prevent even one major disaster, it would be worthwhile.

"Are you ready to meet her?" said Esme.

"I'm a little nervous," said Kaivon, reaching for a sword he wasn't wearing. It was something else he would have to get used to. It was going to be a difficult transition, but at least he wouldn't be doing it alone.

In the back room of a quiet tea house, Kaivon sat down for lunch with Esme and her sister, Kimya. He could immediately see a strong family resemblance, but Kimya had a sharpness to her features that was absent from Esme's face. She was lean, and given all that she had endured, he knew she was tough as iron, but when she smiled, it reached her eyes.

"Finally. This feels long overdue," said Kimya, gripping her sister's hand.

"There were times when I didn't think we'd get here," said Esme.

"Hopefully, the dark times are over and the Mongol Empire will crumble." Kimya fell silent as two young women came into the room bearing trays of food. There was a large bowl of salad, warm flat bread, soft cheese, yoghurt and a jug of doogh. Next, they brought a huge plate of saffron rice with barberries, bowls of stew and a platter of chicken kebab. There was enough food for at least six people.

All of them tucked in with relish, as if they had not eaten in days. Kaivon cleared his plate and then refilled it. Over the meal, they talked of simple and pleasant things. Mostly the sisters told him stories from their childhood. It had been a much happier time, before the weight of responsibility and then the invasion. The two sisters laughed at their shared memories, of triumphs and embarrassments that even now, many years later, still made them uncomfortable.

"You should have seen the boy," said Kimya. "A kind soul, but he could barely see past his nose. It was so big, and that's coming from me," she cackled, gesturing at her own face.

"It wasn't that bad!" said Esme, but Kaivon could see a smile tugging at the corners of her mouth. The serving girls returned and cleared away the plates before replacing them with fruit, and a huge pot of tea.

"I haven't eaten that well in a long time," said Kaivon, patting his strained stomach.

"Good food, good company," said Kimya, pushing her empty plate away.

Once the tea had steeped, Kaivon poured for everyone before sitting back, using the glass to warm his hands.

"What is the latest news from the east?" he asked, now that the pleasantries were over.

"The civil war between Kublai Khan and his cousin, Kaidu, is still raging," said Kimya. "The death of Hulagu, and then Timur seizing the Chagatai khanate for himself, has weakened Kublai's authority. Now, with the destruction of the Ilkhanate, he is only the leader of one territory. Others who previously opposed him are now siding with Kaidu."

"Has there been any word from Tokhtamysh?" asked Esme, turning towards him.

"Not since the battle with Timur ended," said Kaivon. The timely arrival of his army from the Golden Horde had changed the course of the war. Whether it had been out of a sense of obligation, fear of Temujin, or self-interest, Kaivon still didn't know. If Timur had won, he would have inevitably turned his gaze north, as well as west. Whatever the reason, Tokhtamysh had done as he had promised and no more.

Afterwards, he had not stayed to talk. Despite the victory, his army had been brutalised and many were dead. They had retreated north, and the latest from scouts was that his army was returning to Sarai.

"What do you think Tokhtamysh will do now?" said Kimya, thinking along similar lines to him.

"I suspect he will wait and see which way the wind is blowing," said Kaivon. "If Kublai is victorious, he will bend the knee and pledge allegiance to the Empire. If not, I can't say what he will do."

"There are many within the Golden Horde that want freedom and independence," said Esme. "Before, it would have seemed like a dream, but now they understand that it's possible."

"There will be many factions," said Kimya, sipping her tea. "Regardless of its current state, there will be many loyalists in the north who will want to continue serving the Mongol Empire."

"Tokhtamysh will be under a lot of pressure. I assume your plan is to send people north," said Kaivon. If the House sowed seeds of discord while also igniting patriotism in the minds of locals, then it was possible that what had happened in the other khanates would happen in the Golden Horde.

"I already have," said Kimya with a smile that was a little unsettling.

Without a Mongol ruler, or any strong leadership to take over, the Chagatai and the Ilkhanate would soon begin to break apart. It would be chaotic and messy for years to come. Nations would have to come to terms with governing and defending themselves. There would be years of rebuilding, internal struggle and perhaps civil wars until something new was put in place.

"Think of them as growing pains," said Kimya. "Even the bloodshed that is bound to follow."

It would be the same for the territories consumed by the Chagatai khanate, with strife and turmoil.

"Kublai is not done yet," said Kaivon, thinking beyond his worries for Persia. "I would not discount him. He defeated his brother, so he could yet prevail against Kaidu, and if he does, he still has a powerful army."

"Are you sure you want to do this?" said Kimya, echoing what Esme had asked him. Esme gripped her sister's hand, and the joy they'd shared over the meal trickled away. In its wake, the room felt cold and forlorn, as if it had not been used in a long time.

"We must do all that we can to disrupt what remains of the Empire from within," said Esme. Tears stood out in her eyes and her smile was tinged with sadness.

"I know," conceded Kimya, "but does it have to be you?"

Esme stood and hugged her sister tightly, while both of them shed tears. Kaivon had gone through a similar conversation with his brother, and it had been equally painful. This was not goodbye forever, at least in theory. Once they reached the heart of what remained of the Mongol Empire, it would, potentially, take them months to get established. They needed to create a new and convincing life. Blend in with those around them, and find a way to get close to the court of Kublai Khan via a network of recruits. They needed to make sure the civil war continued, to further destabilise any plans of Mongol conquest.

"I am sorry," said Esme, once the worst of the emotional storm had passed. "We will be careful and patient, but it will take some time."

"Will I ever see you again?" asked Kimya.

There was a slim chance that, one day, they would return to Persia and be reunited. At times like these, when the future was so uncertain and dangerous, making promises was unwise. There would be so many things beyond their control.

At his lowest moment during the Mongol invasion, when Kaivon realised he was the last surviving general, hope had been like a fading shadow on the wall. It was there for a moment, and then gone in the blink of an eye. Against all the odds, they had prevailed.

"One day, we will come home," said Kaivon. "I promise."

He stepped out, leaving the sisters to say their farewells without him getting in the way. By now, news of victory against Timur would have reached the ears of most, but compared to yesterday, it was hard to discern any difference. On the streets of Tabriz, life was continuing as before. Merchants were coming and going, transporting their wares along the Silk Road and beyond. In the city, shopkeepers were haggling with customers. Further down the street, he spied a group of old men arguing at length about something, determined to put the world to rights. A mother and her two children passed by him, the boy fighting some imaginary beast with an invisible sword, the girl sucking on her thumb. All of it was so ordinary and wonderful.

They had not seen the gruesome conflict that had ended the war. The torn open bodies. The swarming flies and carrion birds circling overhead, waiting to feast. In one day, thousands of men had been turned into nothing but cold meat. The noise of the battle, the screams and barely human sounds would haunt him for a long time.

Kaivon was glad that children like these had not witnessed the whole truth. In time, they would learn what had happened, but it would be presented as cold facts. Words spoken, perhaps with passion, recounting the brave deeds of Persian warriors. Perhaps if people were exposed to the brutal truth at an early age, they would be less inclined to think of war as some tantalising thing they might wish to experience for themselves.

A dangerous melancholy was settling over him again. This was another reason Kaivon could not be a warrior anymore. Every man had a breaking point. In his mind, he imagined himself as an empty glass that, over the years, had slowly been filled with the blood spilled at every battle he'd experienced. Now, the glass was overflowing.

Turning his mind away from such dark thoughts, Kaivon looked again at the people around him. Here and there, he could see remaining signs of the Mongols' occupation. The House of Grace was dealing with those behind the scenes. Anyone in a position of power connected to the Empire had been removed or had gone missing. Those with any sense had fled. Those without were found dead in the gutters. Now, local people were back in charge of every layer of bureaucracy, government and trade.

Although Mongols no longer walked the streets, Kaivon could see a lingering fear in people's eyes and posture. It was there whenever they saw anyone openly carrying a weapon. When a cart had collided with another going in the opposite direction, several people overreacted. Most had laughed or pointed at the unfortunate merchant who was trying to deal with his stubborn horse. The beast was so startled that it refused to move forward or back. But some people looked genuinely frightened, as if they expected harsh justice to follow, or perhaps some violence from heavy-handed Mongols. It was going to take a long time for everyone to accept their independence and freedom.

When Esme rejoined him on the street, her eyes were red from crying, but she looked determined.

"I've been thinking," said Kaivon as they headed back towards the palace. "There's much we could learn from Hulagu and the Mongol Empire."

Esme stopped suddenly. "I never thought I would hear you utter those words."

"Neither did I, but they are true."

"Tell me," said Esme, looping her arm through his before they resumed walking. Her whole body was stiff with tension. Kaivon was equally nervous and excited about what lay ahead.

"Whenever Hulagu conquered a nation, he learned as much as possible from that culture about warfare. Most of his engineers were from China or Persia. If we are to grow stronger, we should do the same."

Kaivon led them on a winding path so that they would have time to speak at length. Mostly, it was an excuse to take a long look around the city that had been his home for the last few years.

"Although not quite in those terms, I've said something similar to my sister," said Esme, pausing at a spice merchant's table. She perused his offerings and tested the quality of a few items before ultimately rejecting everything. "It's all old and stale," she complained. The merchant tried to tempt her with fresher stock he'd been holding back, but she ignored his pleas and moved on.

"The House of Grace has networks of contacts in several nations, but I think we could be doing more. Not just creating new groups in more cities, but being more proactive, as well."

"Slow and subtle. That's what you've told me, many times," said Kaivon.

"True, but look at the Kozan. They existed for hundreds of years in secret. Operating from the shadows, steering the future of humanity, and no one even knew their names or faces. Turning patriots into reliable agents is not easy. It's slow and delicate work, but there are faster ways to motivate people. We usually have people working for the House, often without knowing. We should be doing more of that. They don't always need to be believers in the cause in order to serve our purpose." Esme sighed and shook her head. "I've told Kimya all of this and more. Now it is up to her and the others. I'm no longer a member of the Inner Circle, so they will decide the future of the House without me."

"So we will go into the east, and become new people," said Kaivon, pausing at the entrance to a park. They strolled inside and stood together in the shade of a tree.

"Are you scared?" asked Esme.

Kaivon knew there was no point in lying. She always knew when he wasn't being truthful. "A little, but as long as we're together, I can face anything."

"This city feels like home. I've not experienced that in a long time," said Esme, glancing around the park. "One day, I hope that both of us can return home and live in peace."

After that, there was nothing else to say. They gathered their belongings and left the city. Kaivon hoped that one day, they would be able to return home to Persia, and when they did, it would be thriving, fairer to women, prosperous and free.

CHAPTER 34
The Twelve

It felt strange to be meeting in the open, during the day, but One knew this was just the first of many necessary changes. The House of Grace had to evolve.

One was sitting beside a window on the first floor of the restaurant. It gave her a spectacular view of the market, only two streets away. It was a thriving hub of activity, where a seemingly endless stream of people flooded the stalls. Dozens of merchants were having enthusiastic and animated conversations with customers, their voices all mingling into one chaotic din. The air was full of rich smells from colourful fruit, fresh fish, spices, and meat sizzling on skewers.

As ever, the rest of the Inner Circle arrived one at a time, never in pairs, and their timing was evenly spaced out. She recognised individuals weaving through the crowd below with care, checking for anyone that might be following them. Being cautious was second nature for all of them.

When the last had arrived, everyone looked around the table with interest, making a note of who was absent. Their numbers were severely diminished.

"Where is everyone?" said Ten.

"A few weeks ago, Twelve left on a vitally important and

dangerous mission. She wouldn't tell me all the details," said One, "but even if she's successful, I don't think she will return."

"Well, no one has done more for Persia than Twelve," said Two. "She deserves her retirement, and whatever peace she can find in her remaining years."

"Amen," said Four.

"What about Nine?" someone asked.

One still had trouble thinking of Esme as Nine. "She's gone east, with her husband, Kaivon. They will watch, learn and interfere in whatever remains of the diminishing Mongol Empire. They will do all they can to disrupt the Great Khan."

"That is bold," said Six. "I wish them good luck."

"Three is gone. She left a note outlining her intentions, but I believe it's a doomed mission. I don't think she wants to live anymore. Ever since her husband died, she has not been the same." A few of the women bowed their head. None of them knew she was The Widow, but they mourned her nonetheless. One hoped Jaleh found some peace in death.

"Where is Seven?"

"Dead," said One. Seven had been the loudest and, as it turned out, the most unpredictable member of the Inner Circle. "I don't know why, but she attacked a group of Mongol warriors on the street. Witnesses said she had been screaming something, but no one knew what triggered the outburst."

"When was this?" asked Ten.

"Two days ago. She was heavily outnumbered, but she killed three Mongols before she was cut down." Coming at a time when they were expelling the Mongols from across Persia, One thought it had been a pointless death. She would make sure Seven's family would never starve, but One would keep digging for the truth. She had to believe there was a reason.

"Why would Seven do that?" said Ten, staring at the floor in shock.

"I suspect it has something to do with her eldest daughter," said Two, "but I only have suspicions."

"We will talk later," said One.

"So, why are we here today?" asked Eleven.

"How many years have we met in secret?" said One. "Things are different now. I thought we should all enjoy one last meal together before we decide what happens next with the House."

A short time later, the owner and his staff came up the stairs laden with plates of food. There was a mountain of saffron rice, lamb stew, salad and fresh greens, smoked fish, and plate after plate of kebab. Several bottles of expensive wine were set on the table as well. Sometimes it paid to be the owner of several businesses that transported goods along the Silk Road.

Decisions about the future were put on hold for an hour while they ate their fill and made small talk. For the first time amongst these women, One spoke of her family and businesses. She shared stories about her daughters, which made her proud, and anecdotes about her son. In return, she heard about the triumphs and tragedies of other families. The hardships and the wonderful celebrations that were often taken for granted until years had passed. Then, those golden moments would be looked back on with warmth and nostalgia.

Eventually, when all of them had eaten their fill, a different kind of silence filled the room. There was still a bit of lingering tension in the room, but it had become muted by their conversations. None of them were strangers, but each woman had hidden a part of herself from all of the others for years. Some of the barriers between them had been removed, and for the first time, One felt as if the others were friends, not just allies.

"The Mongol Empire is in chaos," said One, effectively ending all conversations. Smiles faded but did not completely vanish. They all understood that this was a different meeting from those they'd experienced before. "The Ilkhanate is gone, Kublai is still at war with his cousin, and the Chagatai khanate finds itself without a leader. The latest Crusade rages on, and now that Timur is gone, Egypt finds itself without an ally."

"Wonderful news," said Five, raising her glass. Her eyes were a little glazed, and she wasn't the only one.

"You're going to say there's more work to be done," said Two with a grin, to soften the blow.

"I am, but even so, some things need to change. There will always be an Inner Circle, and there will also be a House of Grace to protect Persia, but it's not enough. Slow and subtle has kept us safe, but we could be doing more." One was thinking about the conversations she had with her sister, and those with Two. She'd promised not to make any big decisions by herself. Now was the right time.

"In what way?" asked Six.

"We have sent out individuals before to spy and report back. And we sent a curiosity to Kublai's court to interfere, but we need to send out more like him. Rare and special individuals, with the will and the intelligence, to bring about change. To subtly interfere in events for our benefit. More importantly, we want them to try and prevent disasters before they happen." Some of this was what Esme had said to her, but it also had been on One's mind for some time.

"We need to be more proactive," said Two, nodding in agreement.

"They would be completely alone," said Ten, mulling it over. "It would be a heavy burden for anyone to bear."

"What you are suggesting goes far beyond anything we've done before," said Eleven.

"This is why I wanted to talk about it with all of you," said One, looking at all of the women around the table. "We cannot ask another to do this if we are not willing to make a similar sacrifice."

One was reminded of the first time she had met Kokochin. She made accusations, that the House had been unwilling to save her and Layla. The rule was that the House had to be protected. That its continued existence was more important than any individual, even a member of family. But ever since that day, there had been a knot of anxiety in One's stomach. The main reason each of them had been chosen for the Inner Circle was their abilities. They were all rare and unusual individuals, and while age might prevent some of them from taking on certain roles, there was much they could be doing.

"I will go to Rome," said Four. Her network was based there, but she had not visited the city in a few years. "The Church is difficult for people to navigate. It has strange tides and unseen currents that most cannot recognise. I can do more for the House if I am there in person."

One had not expected anyone to volunteer so quickly. It must have been on Four's mind for some time as well. "Are you sure?"

"It's where I need to be," said Four.

"I have never been to Paris," said Eight. "I have heard so much about the city, and the court of King Louis. I would like to see it at least once before I die."

Her focus had been in France for the longest time. At such a great distance, communication was slow and often unreliable. The contacts they had in France did little except send the occasional letter, by which time the news was out of date. Most of the time, they sent news the opposite direction, from Persia to France. If Eight could find a way to become an active participant in the king's court, it would be extremely beneficial. One did not need to mention the danger involved, they were all more than aware.

"My days of playing the young innocent girl are long gone," said Two with a wicked smile. "I have become fat and lazy."

"You're hardly lazy," said One. She knew all about the investigations Two had been doing that she didn't talk about. A number of disreputable individuals in the city had come to unfortunate ends, much to the sadness of no one and the relief of many.

"Well, just fat, then," said Two, with another grin. "Even so, there is more I could be doing."

"I will go north, to Sarai," said Five. "Now that he is free of Temujin's interference, Tokhtamysh will not just idly sit around for the rest of his life. I am certain he has ambitions and will seek to learn from the errors of others, like his brother."

"I am sure there are some who regret the death of Berke," said One. The previous khan had been divisive, but there would still be some who secretly supported him.

"He needs to be watched, and steered, if possible," said Five.

"So, are you all going to leave?" said Eleven. In the wake of their victory, her anger had faded somewhat, but One thought it still there, like glowing embers. It would not take much to reignite.

"Not all, but you and I are going to recruit more to the Inner Circle," said One.

"I would like that," said Eleven. For once, she had nothing to be angry about and actually managed a smile. One thought it looked odd and out of place on her face.

"We have driven out the Mongols, and I am enormously proud of you all. What we have accomplished, together, will echo through the halls of history for a long time." One smiled at the other women, thankful for getting to know all of them. "One day, another callous regime will take the place of the Mongols. And when that happens, the fight for the heart of Persia will begin again. But I know that the House of Grace will still be here, to fight alongside all of our brothers and sisters."

She had not meant to, but One's words changed the mood around the table. All of what she had said was true, and it would come to pass, but not today.

"To the House of Grace!" said Two, raising her glass.

For the rest of the day, the women talked, drank, laughed and even sang a little, until late into the afternoon. When the sky started to turn black, One realised she was more than a little drunk. Her sides ached from laughing, and her stomach was groaning from eating too much food. But she was surrounded by friends, and for now, she was content.

CHAPTER 35
Kokochin

As far as cells went, Kokochin thought it was one of the nicest she'd ever been in. Sunlight moved across her skin, chasing away the chill. The bed beneath her was made of fresh straw. There was a discreet hole in the corner of the cell, but also a pitcher of water and two wooden cups. She had been covered in a blanket that was surprisingly clean and warm. She couldn't hear any vermin or feel any lice crawling against her skin. The only thing dispelling the thought that it was a dream was the bars and locked door.

Tilting her head to one side, she was relieved to see Layla asleep on the other bed. The ache around her heart faded and she breathed more easily. For a while, Kokochin did nothing, just lay there, feeling the scratchy material beneath her fingers.

Part of her was surprised to find that she was still alive. Someone had cleaned and bandaged her wounds. When she breathed too deeply, the stitches holding her skin together were pulled tight, and an echo of remembered pain ran through her body.

"You've been asleep for a long time," said Layla. She'd turned over in bed and was facing towards Kokochin. Her clothes were different and slightly ill-fitting, but at least they were clean. Seeing her in a dress had been nice, but she looked more comfortable in a pair of trousers and a shirt.

"How long?"

"Three days."

Kokochin tried to sit but couldn't manage it without hissing in pain. Instead she just rolled over to face Layla.

"Where are we?"

Layla pursed her lips. "Somewhere close to the Vatican. Once they were sure you'd live, they moved us here on the second day. We're the only prisoners."

Through the bars of their cell, Kokochin could see others, but there was nothing else to hear. No crying or moaning. No prayers or whispered conversations. The whole cell block also lacked the smells common with incarceration.

"We're a better class of prisoner," said Layla with a wry smile. "Political prisoners."

"The Pope?"

"Alive," said Layla. "The Assassin, Yusef, is dead."

"What about Oguz?"

"He wasn't a threat to anyone. I thought you were dying," said Layla. There was a catch in her throat. Kokochin instinctively reached out towards her. Thankfully, the cell wasn't very large, and they could touch across the empty space. Layla's hand was warm, and the skin of her fingers was soft.

"So, what happens next?" asked Kokochin.

"That's a worry for tomorrow," said Layla. "Don't borrow trouble. There's enough to deal with today."

"When did you become so wise?" said Kokochin, shifting on the straw pallet.

"I had an excellent teacher," said Layla.

Kokochin raised an eyebrow. "Oh, is it anyone I know?"

"No, you've not met her," said Layla, struggling to supress a grin.

Further conversation was interrupted by the rattle of a lock. Kokochin reluctantly let go of Layla's hand and eventually managed to sit up in bed.

At the far end of the corridor, a heavy metal door opened and a familiar figure strode towards them. Today, Cardinal Cavicchi was dressed as a priest. His black cassock extended almost to the floor, and a silver cross rested against his chest. Kokochin still thought his clothes looked a little out of place. In her mind, he was more soldier than priest.

Several armed guards lurked at the far end of the corridor, but they did not enter the cell block. At Cavicchi's gesture they closed the door, giving them some privacy to speak without being overheard, but they didn't lock it.

"I'm glad to see that you're awake," said Cavicchi. "There was some concern that you wouldn't make it."

"I'm glad to still be here," said Kokochin.

"First, for what it is worth, I want to give you my personal thanks," said Cavicchi, leaning against the bars of their cell. "I realise that both of you have sacrificed much. I know you do not love him as I do, but I thank you for saving the Holy Father's life."

Much to Kokochin's surprise, the priest bowed deeply at the waist, pressing one hand against his heart. Such an outward sign of respect was unusual and unexpected. Cavicchi was full of surprises.

"Thank you," said Kokochin, resting her back against the wall. Sitting up without support was still difficult, and the pain from her wounds was becoming more apparent.

"What is the position of the Church?"

Cavicchi frowned, casting a glance over his shoulder. Even though the guards would be hard pressed to hear what was being said, he lowered his voice. "There are some that will use the attack as an excuse. To condone all Mongols as barbarian heathens in need of saving."

"How ironic," said Layla, "that the Pope's life was saved by a pair of barbarians."

Cavicchi's grimace deepened. "You have been labelled as agents of the Great Khan. Most of those who witnessed the attack are gentle folk, and many were traumatised by the event. Others have been, persuaded, to remember it a different way."

"That doesn't make sense," said Kokochin.

"The official story is that you were there to assist the Assassin." Cavicchi shook his head in dismay. "I know the truth, as do many others, but this is politics. The Church cannot publicly thank or even name you. There is too much as stake. There are factions within the Church…" Cavicchi trailed off and gripped the bars of their cell. Kokochin watched the knuckles on both of his hands turn white from the pressure. A thick vein began to throb in his forehead.

"Have you ever considered that the life of a priest is not for you?" said Kokochin.

Cavicchi's laugh echoed off the bare stone walls. At the peculiar sound, one of the guards stuck his head around the door. The cardinal waved him away, and the guard pulled the door closed again.

"Over the years, it has crossed my mind," said Cavicchi, letting go of the bars. "However, I can do more good as a priest than as a soldier. Here, my voice is heard, and I have power to affect real change."

"So, what does that mean for us?" said Layla.

"The story is that all of the Assassins were executed. The Great Khan is the great evil, and those who do not believe in our Lord Jesus must be destroyed." Cavicchi spoke calmly and without any religious passion.

"So, another lie, then," said Kokochin. She knew they would not have bothered tending to her wounds if the plan was to kill her and Layla.

"Yes. A lie."

"Isn't lying a sin?" said Layla, earning a wry smile from the cardinal.

"It is, but this is politics. The truth rarely goes hand in hand with it." Cavicchi shrugged. "Being faithful to God is difficult. I would be worried if it were always easy."

"What of Persia?" said Layla. "What is the latest news?"

Cavicchi filled them in on what he knew. The defeat of Timur, the death of Temujin and the continued crumbling of the Mongol Empire.

"Then, Persia is free?" said Layla.

"It will be soon," said the priest.

"So, what happens to us?" asked Kokochin.

"Well, this attack on the Pope will be used by some to demonstrate the importance of the latest Crusade. Others will argue that bringing the message of the Lord to heathens is more important. That we should be saving souls, not killing them. But you need not worry about any of that. You're free to leave."

It took a while for his words to sink in.

"Free?" said Kokochin. She wasn't really sure what that word meant to her anymore.

Cavicchi produced a key from a pocket, which he used to unlock the cell door. He swung it open, gesturing for them to step out into the corridor beside him. "The Holy Father wanted me to pass along his personal thanks. However, even he is not without limits. So, once you're beyond the borders of Rome, he has asked that you do not return."

"We can agree to that," said Kokochin, stepping out of the cell with support from Layla.

"Good. Then I wish you good luck, and if you'll allow it," said Cavicchi, "I'll say a prayer for your safe journey home."

"Thank you," said Kokochin. On impulse, she embraced him, hugging him tight. Cavicchi initially tensed up, but then he relaxed and hugged her back. He exchanged a hearty handshake with Layla before walking ahead of them down the corridor.

The guards saw them coming and cleared the way. Outside in a courtyard, Kokochin found two horses and enough food and supplies for at least a week on the road. They both wrapped scarves about their heads and faces to ward off the sun, but also conceal their identities. Once they were outside the city, they would be less conspicuous.

As they rode through the streets of Rome, Kokochin turned in her saddle to face Layla. "So, where are we going?"

"I have no idea," said Layla. Despite the circumstances, she remained alert, watching for anyone taking an interest in them. Some things would never change. "He said 'safe journey home', but I don't know where home is anymore."

"You don't want to go back to Tabriz?"

"No, I think I'd rather start afresh, somewhere else in Persia." Layla nodded to herself, as if confirming something. "In time, I'm sure the House of Grace will find us. Then there will be work for us both, but right now, I'd like a little peace."

"Then should we just see where the road takes us?" suggested Kokochin.

"As long as we're together, I don't really care where we go," said Layla, with a rare smile.

"I feel exactly the same," said Kokochin.

MAIN CHARACTERS

Hulagu Khan – ruler of the Ilkhanate, brother of Kublai, Möngke and Ariq

Kokochin – The Blue Princess, from the Mongol tribe of the

Bayaut and newest wife of Hulagu Khan

Kaivon – Persian General and former southern rebel

Temujin – Hulagu's youngest son, a disappointment to his father

THE ILKHANATE AND ALLIES

Guyuk – First Wife of Hulagu Khan and Empress of the Ilkhanate

Doquz – Second Wife of Hulagu Khan, also known as the War Wife

Rashid – Vizier of the Ilkhanate, a powerful and very shrewd man

Abaqa – eldest son of Hulagu Khan and heir to the Ilkhanate

Jumghur – second eldest son of Hulagu Khan, a violent and impatient man

Subedei – A reliable and rather unimaginative Mongol General

King David of Georgia – has historic grievances against all Muslims

Prince Bohemond of Antioch – A Christian, also known as the Fair, he surrendered to Mongol rule when caught between the Mongols and Mamluks

King Hethum of Cilician Armenia – A Christian, surrendered to Mongol rule before they were conquered

Prince Thoros of Cilician Armenia

Karveh – Kaivon's brother and a Persian rebel

Layla – a jeweller who lives in Tabriz

Ariana – a healer in Tabriz

Shirin – owner of a tea shop in Tabriz

THE KOZAN

Katarina – The Eternal

Eraj – The Cynic

Teague – The Nordic King

Melchior – The Magus

Maryam

Behrouz – an unholy man

THE CHAGATAI KHANATE

Buqa-Temur – Ruler of the Chagatai Khanate, the south eastern Khanate

THE GOLDEN HORDE

Berke Khan – Ruler of the Golden Horde, the north western Khanate, cousin of Hulagu Khan

Gurban – Vizier to Berke Khan, a clever man loyal to his Khan

Yotaqan – a prince of the Golden Horde and the youngest son of Berke Khan

Ahmad – a prince of the Golden Horde and son of Berke Khan

Tinibeg – a prince of the Golden Horde and son of Berke Khan

OTHER PROMINENT CHARACTERS

Kublai – Grandson of Genghis Khan and brother of Möngke – Grandson of Genghis Khan, fifth Great Khan of the Empire

Ariq – Grandson of Genghis Khan and brother of Möngke, Hulagu and Kublai

We are Angry Robot, your favourite
independent, genre-fluid publisher,
bringing you the very best in
sci-fi, fantasy, horror and
everything in between!

Check out our website at
www.angryrobotbooks.com
to see our entire catalogue.

Follow us on social media:
Twitter @angryrobotbooks
Instagram @angryrobotbooks
TikTok @angryrobotbooks

Sign up to our mailing list now: